A Match for Melissa

Kathryn Kirkwood

Zebra Books
Kensington Publishing Corp.

http://www.zebrabooks.com

ZEBRA BOOKS are published by

Kensington Publishing Corp.
850 Third Avenue
New York, NY 10022

Zebra and the Z logo Reg. U.S. Pat. & TM Off.

First Printing: July, 1998
10 9 8 7 6 5 4 3 2 1

Printed in the United States of America

For John Scognamiglio, Duke of Kensington

(With many thanks to Lady Lyn)

One

Melissa Harrington shifted uneasily in one of the expensive new chairs that formed a group under the tall narrow windows of Harrington Manor's Morning Room. There were three such chairs, upholstered in rose-colored velvet, with a matching sofa placed in opposition and affording a view of the manor's formal flower garden. Melissa had chosen her seat deliberately, selecting the chair in the center. Her choice placed her back to the pleasant aspect of multi-colored flowers in splendid bloom, but she had an unobstructed view of the doorway and the hall beyond.

The Ormolu clock on the mantelpiece chimed the hour and Melissa sighed as she counted eleven silvery peals. The clock was another recent acquisition. The hand-painted roses that decorated its face matched the color of the new draperies exactly. The furnishings of Harrington Manor's Morning Room were quite lovely. Melissa's stepmother had chosen them and Jane, Lady Harrington, had impeccable taste. But Melissa suspected that the cost of the recent refurbishment to a once-comfortable and presentable room had been excessively dear and totally unnecessary.

As Melissa watched the dainty hands of the clock create an ever-lengthening arc, she frowned. The summons from her stepmother had come a full hour ago. She had no doubt that her two stepsisters had received the same summons and that they would appear in short order. Much was at stake for their collective fate was to be decided this morning.

The new chairs were lovely, but exceedingly uncomfortable. Melissa rose to her feet and paced across the rose and blue patterned Aubusson carpet to the bevel-edged mirror that hung in pride of place over the mantel. The mirror was imported and had been procured at great expense. It was made of the finest Italian glass and had been etched with a border of trailing roses around its circumference. Melissa agreed that it was indeed lovely, but she feared her stepmother had paid far too much for the glass.

The mirror was too high to be of much use, but by standing on tiptoe, Melissa could manage to view her face. Although some shorter tendrils of curly hair had escaped, the majority of her glossy, midnight-black tresses were still neatly confined to the twist she had fashioned at the nape of her neck.

Her manner of dress was appropriate, Melissa was certain. She had donned the very best her clothes press had to offer for this all-important family gathering. It was an afternoon dress that had been fashioned for her three years past, only a sennight before her father's death. The baron had insisted that it was time his daughter cease wearing the cast-off clothing of her elder stepsisters, Regina and Dorothea, and had ordered that Melissa be presented with a gown that was suited to her exclusively. It was to be the first of many such gowns that would herald Melissa's Season in London.

Melissa smiled at the fond memory. Jane had objected, claiming it was not seemly for Melissa to come out until Regina and Dorothea had experienced their First Seasons, but her father had put his foot down firmly and refused to be budged. He had decided that all three girls should be launched simultaneously and no argument that Jane had presented had swayed him from his stand. In the end Jane had agreed, albeit reluctantly, and arrangements had been set in motion to introduce Melissa, Regina, and Dorothea to the glittering world of the *ton*.

Melissa smoothed her hand across the soft muslin of her

dress. The sea-green color matched her eyes perfectly and the vivid hue set off her flawless white skin. The tightly-fitted bodice accented feminine curves that had been merely a budding promise when her gown had been fashioned, but Melissa's own nimble fingers had let out the seams and altered the lovely frock to her mature figure.

Melissa's glorious First Season had never come to pass. The sea-green gown had not yet been delivered when tragedy had struck. Melissa's father had died quite suddenly in a carriage accident, and the baron's family had all gone into the appropriate mourning. Propriety had demanded that their plans for the Season be canceled, and Melissa had been so stricken with grief over the death of her father, she'd given no more than a fleeting thought to the parties, routs, and Venetian Breakfasts she had missed. She had assumed that there would be another Season, another time to dance and be gay, when the family had recovered from its devastating loss.

But when the following Season had come, there had been other, more pressing concerns. The primary of these had been financial. The baron's title and his holdings had passed to his male heir, a distant cousin Melissa had barely known. This Melissa had expected. But her father had settled Harrington Manor and its surrounding lands to Lady Harrington for her lifetime. It was clear he'd assumed that his second wife would care for Melissa until she married, but this was not the way the wind blew. The lands provided ample revenues, but the Widow Harrington's expenses had been extraordinary. There had been new gowns for Jane, Regina, and Dorothea, new furnishings for the manor, and the expense of frequent and lavish entertaining. Though she had no real proof, Melissa suspected that her father's merry widow was squandering the money that had been intended for Melissa's support.

Melissa sat down in her chair once more. There was nothing to be done, no action she could take to set things in a more equitable favor. By the terms of her husband's will, Jane was in control of the purse strings. If Melissa objected, or had the audacity to request an accounting, it would serve no purpose other than to incur her stepmother's disfavor.

The hands of the clock had reached the quarter hour. Melissa sighed once again and remembered the past year, when Regina and Dorothea had enjoyed the pleasures of their First Season. There hadn't been enough money for Melissa to have a Season as well, but Jane had explained that since Regina and Dorothea were older than Melissa was, they should receive first preference.

Though she had been bitterly disappointed, Melissa had agreed with her stepmother. Gina and Doro had been twenty-one and twenty respectively, and the longer their Seasons were delayed, the more their chances for securing successful matches would dwindle. Jane had solemnly promised that the following Season, *this* Season, would be Melissa's debut, and Melissa had dutifully stayed behind, at Harrington Manor, while her stepmother and stepsisters had journeyed to London.

Footsteps approached and Melissa turned towards the door. Regina and Dorothea had arrived, but they had stopped at the doorway, so engrossed in their discussion that they failed to notice that Melissa was already seated in the Morning Room.

Regina, Melissa's elder stepsister, was dressed in a dark brown dress with a high, rounded neckline, an unadorned bodice, and long sleeves. Her gown was cut in severe lines that did nothing to compliment her sparse figure and the drab color made her appear pale and wan. This was the dress that Regina donned when she was about to embark on one of her many charitable errands and Melissa surmised that her stepsister had been preparing to leave for the rectory when the summons from Jane had come.

Melissa gave a rueful smile as she gazed at her elder stepsister. While it was appropriate that one wear a subdued, serviceable gown when visiting the infirm, or delivering baskets of food to the more unfortunate members of their small rural community, she ardently wished that Regina would choose attire of a more flattering nature. With her stepsister's nut-brown hair arranged in a tight cap of feathery curls, her diminutive stature, and her quick, efficient movements, Regina looked like nothing so much as a small brown wren.

Regina's younger sister, Dorothea, was a study in contrast. Dorothea had golden blond hair dressed in an elaborate style, with hundreds of tiny curls and bows that framed a face that was much too round. Dorothea's figure was also ample, and she possessed an unfortunate tendency towards corpulence. To add to this disadvantage, Dorothea had a marked preference for ruffles and flounces that only served to make her appear larger.

On this particular morning, Dorothea was dressed in a bright pink gown of a hue so intense, Melissa found herself wincing at the sight. Dorothea's complexion was healthy by nature, and the intense color of her gown gave one the impression that she had stayed in the sun, unprotected by a parasol, for far too long.

Melissa studied the pair for another moment and then she smiled. Dorothea's gown would look lovely on Regina. It would serve to bring out the color in Regina's pale cheeks and give her sparse figure the rounded curves that society preferred. Dorothea would also be well served by Regina's gown. The dark color would set off her complexion to advantage and the severe lines would disguise her ample figure.

Though Melissa had no intention of eavesdropping, her stepsisters' conversation had escalated in volume until it was now clearly audible. Melissa tried not to listen, but such a feat was quite impossible as she could hear every word that passed their lips.

"But you must have a second Season, Gina!" Dorothea's voice was trembling with anxiety. "Mama wants both of us to marry well. She has told us so, over and over. And there are no wealthy and titled gentlemen anywhere in these parts!"

Regina nodded in agreement, her soft brown curls bouncing gently. "I am sensible of that fact, Doro. But marrying me off to a wealthy, titled gentleman is Mama's intention, not mine."

"You must be bamming me, Gina." Dorothea's eyes searched

her sister's face. "Surely you want to marry well and please Mama!"

"That is a matter for Providence to decide. If such an event does not come to pass, I shall be quite content to live out my life right here at Harrington Manor."

"And remain a . . . a spinster?" Dorothea's expression was even more anxious.

"Perhaps, dear sister. It would not be the worst fate that I could envision. With no family encumbrances, I should be free to continue my chosen vocation."

"Good works?" Dorothea paled as her sister nodded. "Oh, Gina! There's time enough for works of charity when you're old and grey."

Regina laughed and took Dorothea's hand. "Perhaps that is true in your case, Doro, but you and I are very different. You are so full of life, so ready to seek excitement from every encounter. You take pleasure in meeting new people and are not the least bit shy. I am of a quiet and more reflective nature. I shrink from the very social encounters you crave and wish only to keep my own counsel."

"But . . . but that is not true, Gina!" Dorothea looked ready to burst into tears. "Think of the fun we both experienced last Season, all the balls, and the routs, and the assemblies. You must not be disappointed that no gentleman declared for you, for I did not receive an offer either!"

Regina smiled. "I am not disappointed, Doro, for I did not expect to take. I found I had very little liking for the gentlemen I met in London."

"It will be better this Season, Gina." Dorothea did her best to convince her sister. "This year we will know what we're about. Mama has promised to buy us new gowns in the latest styles, and we'll receive invitations to the finest parties. Titled gentlemen will ask us to stand up with them, and they'll come to pay calls on us in droves. We'll take this year, Gina. I'm certain of it!"

"I am certain that *you* will take, sister." Regina smiled at Dorothea kindly.

"And so will you! You must not give up hope, Gina. There will be new gentlemen to meet this Season and I am convinced that you shall find one who will take your fancy. Surely you don't wish to forgo this grand opportunity!"

Regina nodded. "But I *do* wish to forgo it, Doro. The pleasures of London cannot entice me in the slightest when my true calling is here, with the church."

"I truly do not understand, Gina! Only last Season, you were enthralled with the prospect of meeting eligible gentlemen of the first stare. What has happened since then to so drastically change your outlook?"

Regina smiled kindly. "Perhaps I have seen the folly of my ways. I have come to realize that there is more to my existence than new gowns, and lavish parties, and making an exemplary match. I wish to devote my life to helping others who are less fortunate than I am."

"It is the new parson's influence. He said those very words this past Sunday!" Dorothea seemed certain that she had discovered the cause of her sister's uncharacteristic rebellion. "But you have taken them too much to heart, dear Gina. The Reverend Mr. Watson was merely seeking donations, not asking you to give your life over to the church!"

Regina smiled. "I know that, sister. But his words struck a chord within me. My place is here, giving what aid I can to the needy. It is not in London, seeking a match."

"Hush, Gina!" Dorothea's expression was panic-stricken. "If Mama were to hear you speak this way, she would accuse you of having windmills in your head. She would forbid you to see Mr. Watson again and insist that your first duty is to her."

Regina gave an amused chuckle. "I am in little danger of forgetting that, Doro. And if, by chance, I happened to do so, Mama would be certain to remind me. Come let us take our places in the Morning Room. You know how overset Mama becomes when we are late."

The two girls entered the Morning Room and sat down on the sofa. Regina nodded a greeting to Melissa and then continued their conversation. "You know how important the church is to me, Doro. I truly feel I'd be remiss in leaving now, so soon after I've started my first reading class."

"But you *have* to come to London for the Season!" Dorothea was truly in a panic as she turned to Melissa. "You must help me, Lissa! Gina is refusing to go to London and Mama will surely take her to task for her obstinacy!"

Melissa studied her elder stepsister. Regina was a quiet person, but she had a strong will and she seemed adamant about not wishing to have another Season. "Is this true, Gina? Have you reached that decision?"

"I have, and Mama will simply have to bow to my wishes. I had my Season and I did not take. A second Season would be a waste of her purse and my efforts."

Melissa wasn't sure what to say. She knew that Regina had not enjoyed the social whirl in London. Several months ago, while they were having a comfortable coze in Regina's bedchamber, she'd confessed to Melissa that she'd found most of the members of the *ton* to be shallow and only interested in the pleasures of the moment.

"Lissa?" Regina broke the long silence. "You do not think that I'm in the wrong, do you?"

Melissa quickly shook her head. "No, Gina. I am sensible of your feelings and I applaud you for speaking them, but . . . I am not certain that your mother will have the same understanding."

"That is *truly* understating the case!" Regina gave a rueful laugh. "Mama will fly into the boughs, you may be certain of that! Perhaps we should fetch her vial of aromatic vinegar before I make my wishes known to her."

Regina and Melissa shared a smile, but Dorothea was too distressed to appreciate their humor. "I know that Mama will somehow contrive to blame me in all this. Must you tell her now, Gina?"

"I am sorry, Doro, but I am obliged to inform her without delay so that she may revise her plans. You must take heart, sister. It is my decision and I shall gladly shoulder the blame."

The fates conspired to prevent any reply that Dorothea might have made. At that exact moment, they heard footsteps approaching and a moment later, Jane Harrington swept into the room.

Lady Harrington was a poised beauty, well past the first blush of youth. No expense had been spared on her appearance and on this occasion she was wearing a pale yellow gown, the color of early morning sunlight, that served to set off her deep auburn hair to advantage. A necklace of rubies adorned her slim neck and for all appearances, she was the pattern card of a Lady of Quality.

"You have news, Mama?" Dorothea was the first to speak.

"I do, although I should prefer it to be of a better nature." Jane arranged her skirts carefully as she took the chair that Melissa had vacated. "Sit down, girls. We must discuss our situation."

Melissa joined her two stepsisters on the sofa. She could not fail to notice that Jane was avoiding her eyes, and her suspicions began to grow. Would she have her promised Season this year? Or had her stepmother filled her with false hopes?

"The revenues from the estate are not so generous as I had expected." Jane's voice was firm. "We have enough for the necessities, never fear, but our other expenses shall have to be cut to the bone."

Dorothea looked ready to burst into tears. "But, Mama . . . we shall be allowed our Seasons, shan't we?"

"Yes." Jane dipped her head in a nod. "That, dear Dorothea, *is* a necessity. You shall have your Season, but you must promise to take full advantage."

Dorothea gave a deep sigh of relief. "Thank you, Mama. I promise I shall. And Regina? She is to have her Season as well?"

"Of course." Jane turned her attention to Regina. "I was not pleased with your performance during the past Season, Regina. The members of the *ton* do not regard shyness as a virtue. You must be gay and vivacious if you wish to attract a gentleman of the first rank."

Regina frowned as she regarded her mother. She opened her mouth to speak, but Dorothea created a timely interruption.

"Regina will be vivacious, Mama. I shall see to it. And she shall find her match this year, a perfect match!"

Jane nodded in satisfaction and then she turned her attentions to Melissa. "I fear that your Season will have to be delayed another year, Melissa. Our purse is not so deep as to fund a Season for three young ladies."

Melissa averted her eyes. Her disappointment was so keen, she feared her stepmother could read it without a word passing her lips. As she gazed around the room to avoid looking at her stepmother, Melissa's eyes rested briefly on the new draperies, the gilt clock on the mantelpiece, the imported Italian mirror, and the Oriental vase her stepmother had acquired at such great expense. Had Jane not seen fit to refurbish the entire manor, there would have been enough funds for her!

"Melissa shall have her Season." Regina faced her mother squarely. "Since I am not planning to go to London, you may use my portion of the funds for her."

Jane was shocked into silence for a moment, but when she recovered, her voice was sharp. "What nonsense is this, Regina? Of course you are going to London. I demand it!"

"No, Mama." Regina's firm voice reflected her resolve. "I have decided not to marry and a second Season should be wasted on me. I intend to devote my life to the church and perform charitable works."

Jane stared at her elder daughter in utter disbelief and then she gave a most unladylike snort. "Fustian! You shall do as I say, Regina. You *will* go to London, you *will* have a Season, and you *will* make a suitable match. We are closing Harrington Manor for the duration and no one will be permitted to stay behind."

"Then Melissa is to go with us, even though she is not to have a Season?" Dorothea was clearly confused.

"That is correct." Jane nodded. "Melissa's presence is most necessary to the success of our Season. We have no funds with which to engage an abigail and Melissa shall assume that duty."

Melissa did her utmost to contain the anger that threatened to consume her. Regina, who staunchly maintained she did *not* want a Season, was to have one foisted upon her. And Melissa, who *did* want a Season, was to be denied once again. To make matters even more unpalatable, her stepmother intended for Melissa to act as their servant!

Regina spoke up in her soft, firm voice. "I beg you to reconsider, Mama. Such a plan is not just. Lissa is not a servant and it is unfair of us to treat her as such."

"Melissa has offered no objection." Jane favored her stepdaughter with a speaking glance that brooked no dissent. "That is correct, Melissa, is it not?"

For one brief moment, Melissa thought about giving voice to her rebellion, but better sense prevailed. What purpose could possibly be served other than to vent her spleen? She dropped her eyes to the carpet and nodded her acquiescence mutely. At least she would be carried to London and not left behind, as she'd been last Season.

"There! You see?" Jane turned to Regina. "Think of the advantage this plan will provide for Melissa. Though she will not be formally presented this Season, she shall have the opportunity to mingle with the best of London society. Perhaps your dear stepsister will even form a *tendre* for one of your rejected suitors."

Melissa kept her lips pressed firmly together to stifle her urge to laugh derisively. Jane was desperate to find suitable matches for Regina and Dorothea. If she saw fit to reject any gentleman, he would be the most miserable of husbands, indeed!

"We shall depart at daybreak tomorrow." Jane rose gracefully to her feet. "Come, girls. There is much to do in preparation. We must begin straight away."

"Yes, Mama." Dorothea's eyes began to glow with excitement as she rose from her place on the sofa. "Regina and I shall select the gowns we wish to take."

Jane nodded her approval and swept toward the door, but she turned for one last word with Melissa. "Go up to the attics and collect the holland covers for the furniture. When you've put them in place, you may begin the packing. Everything must be in readiness before we sleep tonight."

Dorothea followed in her mother's wake, but Regina placed her hand on Melissa's arm to detain her. When her mother and sister had left the room, Regina spoke up, in a voice that trembled with emotion. "I hope you're not overly disappointed in me, Lissa. I'm truly sorry I failed to convince Mama to give you my Season."

"Your mother is a very difficult woman to convince." Melissa favored her stepsister with a forgiving smile. "You tried your utmost, Gina, and that does signify."

"But I know how much you wanted to be presented this Season! I should have argued longer."

"To what purpose? Your mother's mind was firmly set. Any further disagreement from your quarter would only have served to anger her."

"Perhaps you're right." Regina nodded thoughtfully. "Mama is easily angered, and when she is overset, it causes distress for all who are . . . oh, Lissa!"

Melissa gasped as her stepsister sank back down on the sofa. Regina's complexion had paled and her hands were trembling. "What is it, Gina?"

"I gave my promise to Mr. Watson!" As Regina uttered his name, color flooded over her pale complexion. "I assured him that I would accompany him when he visits the sick, and now I shall be unable to do so. I do so hate to break a promise, Lissa! He will think badly of me, I know."

Melissa reached out to pat Regina's hand. "I am certain he will not. Breaking this promise is in no way your choice. You must go to him and explain."

"But what if he should suppose that I desire this Season?" There was anguish in the depths of Regina's brown eyes. "I should hate for him to believe that I am as frivolous as the other young ladies who court favor with the *ton*."

"He could not think that, Gina. The reverend is aware of your commitment to good deeds and I am certain he would not suspect you of being in the least bit frivolous. It is simply not in your nature."

Regina thought about this for a moment and then she nodded. "It is possible that you are right."

"Of course I am. Do not forget that the reverend is well acquainted with your mother. When you tell him that she has ordered you to London, he will appreciate your dilemma."

"Perhaps." Regina nodded and then she began to smile. "Now that I consider it, I am certain that you are correct. The Reverend Mr. Watson is the most understanding of men. I dare say he will commiserate with me when he learns of my circumstances."

Melissa drew a deep breath of relief. Regina's hands had ceased their trembling and she looked much more composed. "Perhaps you had best tell him straight away so that he can find someone to help him in your stead. If your mother inquires as to your whereabouts, I will tell her that you have left on an errand and will return shortly."

"Thank you, Lissa." Regina rose to her feet and fairly flew to the door. "If I hurry, perhaps Mama will not even take notice of my absence."

There was a thoughtful expression on Melissa's face as she watched her stepsister rush out of the room. The color had been high in Regina's pale cheeks when she'd spoken of Mr. Watson. And though Regina had insisted that she wished to forgo her Season to continue her charity work, Melissa wondered if her stepsister was doing it up much too brown. Could it be that Regina's heart was already engaged? Perhaps by the young man of the cloth who had so recently come into their midst?

Melissa sighed, hoping this was not the case. Even if the

Reverend Mr. Watson should come to offer for Regina, Jane would never approve the match. The resulting quarrel would leave her stepsister with naught but a broken heart, and dear Regina deserved a much better fate than that!

Two

The house Jane had rented in Belgrave Square was nothing if not impressive. As Melissa carried her modest carpetbag up the brick steps and stepped inside, her eyes widened at the opulence she saw displayed before her. The entrance hall was paneled in the richest of mahogany and the floor was laid with an intricate pattern made up of colorful marble tiles. Gold-framed paintings of lords and ladies who Melissa assumed were the owner's ancestors graced the walls, and tall porcelain urns, at least four feet in height, held lovely arrangements of dried flowers. Two chairs, covered in blue and white striped satin, flanked a small round table that was inset with a design of delicate gold filigree. A silver salver, overflowing with cards and invitations, sat on its highly polished surface and Melissa moved closer to examine the contents. If sheer quantity was an accurate indication, the current Season was off to a successful beginning for her stepsisters.

Dorothea, who had emerged from the coach carrying the box of sweets she had insisted they bring in the event they required sustenance on their journey, was the next to enter the house. The moment she spied the contents of the silver salver, she gave an excited exclamation. Then she rushed back to her mother, who was just coming through the door, and gestured toward the array of envelopes. "Look, Mama! Invitations have already begun to arrive!"

"Yes, indeed." Jane smiled with evident satisfaction as she

picked up several of the envelopes to examine them. "There are even more than there were last Season. We are being very well received by the *ton* this year."

Melissa nodded pleasantly, and successfully managed to curb her tongue. It wasn't Jane and her stepsisters who were being well received. The members of the *ton* were merely paying their respects to the widow and family of a man they'd loved and respected, Melissa's father.

Jane glanced at Regina, who had been the last to enter, and she frowned as she saw that her eldest daughter was attempting to carry her own portmanteau. "There's no reason to exhaust yourself, Regina. Melissa will see that our baggage is carried inside."

"But the trunks are much too heavy for Melissa!" Regina defended her stepsister. "Surely you don't expect her to—"

Jane held up her hand to silence Regina's objections. "The postilions will carry in our belongings. Melissa will merely supervise their placement."

"I'll help her." There was a determined expression on Regina's face.

"That is not wise for you." Jane gave her daughter a disapproving glance. "I fear you must be quite exhausted as your complexion is a most unbecoming shade of white. If you do not spend the afternoon resting, you will be a sorry addition to Lady Farthington's dinner party this evening."

Melissa took one glance at her stepsister and rushed to help her to a chair. "Don't make a cake of yourself, Gina. You must sit down and gather your strength."

"Here, Gina." Dorothea rushed forward with her box of sweets. "You must take one of these to restore you. Chocolate is said to have curative powers."

Melissa surmised that the last thing Regina wished for was something to eat, but she took a sweet from the box to please her sister. "Thank you, Doro, but I am perfectly well."

"How can that be true?" Dorothea frowned. "There's not a drop of color in your cheeks and you appear as pale as a corpse."

Regina gave an embarrassed laugh. "You have all forgot that I am prone to succumb to motion illness. I shall recover nicely now that we have reached our destination and my feet are once again upon firm ground."

"Of course!" Dorothea clapped her hands. "You are right, Gina. Your affliction had entirely slipped my mind in the excitement of the moment. It is no wonder that you seldom wish to venture far from home."

Jane did not look convinced as she studied her eldest daughter. "Are you certain, Regina?"

"Yes, Mama." Regina nodded. "I promise that I shall recover long before this evening. And I shall act lively so that my dinner partner will not suspect that he's dining with one who's already stuck her spoon in the wall."

Melissa and Dorothea burst into peals of delighted laughter and even Jane had to smile. But she sobered as she turned to Melissa.

"If Regina has not fully recovered by the time we are to leave, a touch of the rouge pot may serve. Which gown shall you press for her, Melissa?"

Melissa mentally reviewed the gowns she had helped Regina pack. The colors her elder stepsister had chosen were all drab and dowdy, more suitable to a widow just emerging from mourning than to a young lady who was to attend a lively dinner party. "Perhaps I could alter Dorothea's pink gown for Regina. I should think it would suit her very well."

"The pink will lend her complexion more color." Jane gave a nod of approval. "Yes, I should think it would do very nicely. And for Dorothea?"

Melissa sighed. Dorothea owned only one gown without flounces, furbelows, or ruffles. It was most unfortunate that her stepsister disliked it so. "I believe the white would be most appropriate."

"But it makes me look like a child!" Dorothea voiced an immediate objection. "I wish to wear the red sarcenet with the blue underskirt."

"That gown is much too elaborate for this evening's dinner party." Jane dismissed Dorothea's choice with a wave of her hand. "Melissa is right. You shall wear the white."

Tears rushed to Dorothea's eyes. "But the color will not set off either my hair or my complexion to advantage. Please, Mama . . . I should rather *die* than wear the white!"

"Do not put yourself in a taking, Doro." Melissa spoke up quickly to calm her stepsister. "I shall embellish your gown to suit your complexion and the color of your hair."

Dorothea turned to look at Melissa hopefully. "How will you accomplish this, Lissa?"

"I shall dress the neck with a wide green ribbon and sew another around the hem. With a sash of the same deep green hue, it should be perfect for you."

Dorothea gave a tentative smile. "Green is one of my favorite colors. But I should not like to be out of fashion."

"I am certain you will not be." Melissa hastened to reassure her. "I studied a gown such as the one I envision in the most recent copy of *La Belle Assemblée*. You will look your best, Doro. I will promise you that."

Dorothea's eyes began to sparkle. "How will you dress my hair, Lissa?"

"I'll fashion it in a twist, wound round with streamers of the same ribbon. You will be all the crack, Doro."

Dorothea's smile was joyful as she turned to her mother. "Isn't Lissa wonderful, Mama? Oh, I am so glad you thought to bring her along as our dresser!"

"Yes, indeed." Jane had the grace to look slightly embarrassed, but she quickly regained her composure. "Come along, Dorothea, and we shall examine my jewels. You may choose something to wear with your gown tonight . . . perhaps the emeralds would be appropriate."

"Oh, Mama." Dorothea's eyes were shining. "I should like to wear the emeralds above all things."

Regina and Melissa exchanged a speaking glance as Jane swept up the staircase with Dorothea following closely at her heels. When they had disappeared from sight, Melissa turned to Regina with a question. "Do you think your mother will give her permission for Dorothea to wear the emeralds?"

"I am certain that she will not." Regina shook her head. "Mama values the emeralds too highly and though they should look lovely with the gown you have described, she is not well known for her charity. I wager to say that if Doro wears any of Mama's jewels, they will be the pearls."

There was a bit of color in Regina's cheeks by the time the postilions had brought in their baggage and placed it according to their directions. After the men had been dismissed, Regina rang for the maid-of-all-work and asked her to bring them some light refreshment. Once the tray had been delivered and they had availed themselves of its contents, they climbed the staircase to their bedchambers.

"Do come in for a moment, Lissa." Regina opened the door to her bedchamber and motioned Melissa inside. The small room was filled with bandboxes and trunks and Melissa perched on the largest of them while Regina sat on the edge of the bed. "I do wish Mama would see fit to excuse me tonight. I fear I am not pleasantly anticipating this engagement."

Melissa nodded. She knew how reluctant Regina was to begin her second Season. "I understand, Gina, but you are obliged to attend. Is it not true that Lady Farthington's dinner unofficially opens the Season?"

"You have the right of it." Regina sighed. "Tonight's entertainment serves as the proving ground for this Season's debutantes. Any young lady who commits a *faux pas* tonight will be roundly snubbed by all the old tabbies for the remainder of the Season."

Melissa was perplexed at her stepsister's anxious tone. "But that will not affect you, Gina. You attended the dinner last Season and you were not snubbed . . . were you?"

"No. Mama cautioned us to be on our best behavior and we followed her advice to the letter. Both Doro and I came through unscathed."

Melissa was confused. "Then why do you appear anxious when you and Doro have already been accepted?"

"Perhaps I am so highly sensible to the feelings of others, that I cannot allow any comfort to myself. It distresses me to see the young hopefuls with their trembling hands and their distressed expressions. They live in fear that they will commit a social infraction and thus waste the money their families have spent on their Seasons."

Melissa crossed the room to give her stepsister a hug. "You must assume the best possible outcome, that no one will commit a blunder tonight and all will be well."

"Perhaps you are right." Regina did not sound as if she were convinced. "In any event, the Season will go on as it always does."

"Will you tell me why it is so distasteful to you?"

"Yes." Regina nodded. "Then perhaps you will understand why it would please me above all things were I not forced to take part."

Melissa settled down for a comfortable coze. Her stepsister seemed inclined to converse and it might serve to put her mind at ease.

"I must caution you, Lissa. Others do not regard the Season in the same manner as I do. There are some young ladies, Dorothea among them, who actually profess to enjoy it."

"I understand, Gina. Do go on." Melissa gently encouraged her stepsister.

"Doro and I will be expected to compete with the other young ladies to attract the attention of the eligible gentlemen. The whole thing is shameless, Lissa, and it reminds me of nothing so much as Market Day."

"Market Day?" Melissa was confused. "Whatever do you mean?"

"Mama will commence to put us on display, like prize piglets in a stall, to be sold to the highest bidder."

"Gina!" Melissa did her utmost not to fall into a fit of the whoops at the visual picture that her stepsister presented. "Surely it is not as bad as all that!"

"But it is. Remember that the object is to make an exemplary match. We shall be groomed within an inch of our lives and gowned in the finest the London modistes can offer. Our hair shall be dressed in the latest fashion and we shall perform our prettiest manners and assume our most attractive poses while the gentlemen peer at us through their quizzing glasses and put us through their tests."

"What comprises these tests?" Melissa noticed that Regina looked exceedingly blue-deviled and not at all impressed with the inner workings of London society.

"Dancing, beauty, conversation, and comportment. What may be in our hearts and our minds does not signify in the slightest; they are solely concerned with our appearance, our breeding, and whether or not our families have adequate means for a generous dowry. They will discuss us behind the closed doors of their private clubs and decide whether or not we are to take. If we meet with their approval, we will receive the appropriate offers of marriage, but if we do not, we will be placed on the shelf to be tortured again, the following Season."

"Surely you are bamming me, Gina!" Melissa was shocked. She had anticipated her own Season with a great deal of pleasure, but perhaps she had been misled. If Regina's description was accurate, she was not at all certain she would choose to experience the social whirl in London!

"Every word I've spoken is the truth, Lissa, and it's all so terribly unfair. The most disturbing fact of all is that we have no choice but to comply with their silly rules. If an eligible gentleman should declare for me and gain my mother's approval, there is little I could do to discourage the match."

Melissa nodded. What Regina had described had the ring of truth. Perhaps a Season *was* like Market Day.

"It is the very reason I pray every night that no one will offer for me." Regina's voice was low and she raised stricken eyes to Melissa's face. "Do you think badly of me for that, Lissa?"

"No, I do not. I should feel the same, Gina. If I am to marry, I should prefer that it be for love."

"By virtue of your birth, you have that luxury." Regina cast her an envious glance. "Since our mother is but your step-mother, she cannot force you to marry a gentleman of her choice."

"She cannot force you to marry either, not if you refuse to do so. You *do* have a choice, Gina."

Regina looked sad as she shook her head. "No, Lissa. If I refuse, Mama shall wear me down with her continual harangues. She'll make my life a misery if I fail to do her bidding. She'll tell me I'm a ninnyhammer, that she knows what's best for me, that's it's my duty to marry well and provide for her. Rest assured, I shall hold to my principles for as long as I am able, but you know how persuasive Mama can be. When she sets her heart on something, she simply won't take no for an answer."

Later that afternoon, when the altering of the gowns had been accomplished and Regina, Dorothea, and Jane were engaged in looking over the invitations and cards that had awaited them, Melissa spent a few quiet moments in the garden that adjoined the townhouse. A high brick wall confined the beautifully planted area and provided privacy from passersby in the street. The garden was accessible from both the Breakfast Room and the Drawing Room and provided a pleasant aspect to view when one was seated in either chamber.

The garden wall fence was planted with ivy that effectively hid its structure on two sides, but the surface that faced the street had been recently cleared and the area beneath it was planted with hawthorne that had not yet reached waist-height. There was a tall wooden gate, marred by several large knotholes and Melissa pressed her face to the largest of these to peer out.

The house was situated in a residential area and there was no sign of the bustling traffic that had so astounded Melissa when they had driven through the busier districts of London.

She had enjoyed the constant stream of carts, carriages, and coaches that had been much too numerous to count. Sedan chairs, borne by sturdy carriers, had inched slowly forward and footmen dressed in the fine livery of their masters had strolled along proudly, looking down their noses at the common servants. There had been beggars holding out their cupped hands in the hope that a more-fortunate citizen might be drawn to an act of charity, and ragamuffin urchins chasing each other along the streets. The windows of the stores had displayed wares for all to admire and delicious smells had drifted out of pastry and confection shops.

Now, as Melissa peered out at this quiet street, only one coach rumbled slowly past. The absence of noise was a virtue for those who were resting of an afternoon, but Melissa sorely missed the excitement of the wondrous sights she had seen.

The park was directly across the street, and Melissa spied two young children at play. Their young nurse, who looked barely more than a child herself, had taken a seat on one of the benches and was gently rocking a baby.

Melissa smiled as the children ran through the grass, enjoying a lively game of make-believe. The older boy, who appeared to be about six years of age, was chasing his younger brother. His expression was fierce and his arms were waving wildly. Growls and howls, faintly audible even at this distance, were emanating from his throat and Melissa surmised that he was pretending to be some sort of dragon. His younger brother was squealing in glee as he ran from the pretend monster. From his occasional burst of laughter, it was readily apparent that he was not frightened, and both boys seemed to be enjoying their romp.

The baby began to cry and the young nurse lifted the child to her shoulder. At that exact moment, the two boys reached the edge of the park, but their nurse was so intent on the care of her smallest charge, she failed to notice that the younger boy was much too close to the street.

Melissa gasped as she saw a carriage rounding the corner. She called out a warning, but she was too far away for either the boys or their nurse to hear her. The younger boy was perfectly oblivious of the danger, running out into the path of the approaching equipage before his brother could do more than shout out for him to come back.

It was at this point that a gentleman on horseback appeared, riding neck-or-nothing toward the disastrous event that was only scant seconds from occurring. As Melissa held her breath and prayed for the child's safe deliverance, he leaned dangerously low in his saddle and snatched the young boy from certain tragedy.

Melissa gave a glad cry of relief. The danger had been averted. The young boy seemed no worse for wear as the gentleman walked his horse up to the bench and lowered the child onto the bench where the nurse sat. Though Melissa was too far away to hear his words, his countenance was fierce and she suspected that he was admonishing the nurse for failing in her duties.

From their respective expressions, Melissa surmised she could imagine their conversation. The gentleman wore a grim look and he was undoubtedly cautioning the nurse that if he had not happened upon the scene, her young charge could now be requiring the services of a surgeon. The young nurse appeared most penitent and as Melissa watched, she began to cry. This caused the man's grim expression to fade, and it was clear he was now offering words of comfort, vowing that he could appreciate the difficult task of supervising two healthy active boys and a baby.

The nurse gave him a timid smile and the gentleman smiled back. It was apparent that now that the danger was behind them, they were speaking of more mundane matters. Melissa studied the gentleman as he spoke and her heart began to beat more rapidly in her bosom. He was exceedingly handsome with a lean, rugged face whose color testified to his love of the outdoors. His hair was the color of ripe wheat and it was cut in a natural manner, a far cry from the affected *a la Brutus* which Melissa had noticed on several young pinks they had passed on the London streets. He was well dressed for an afternoon ride through the park, and his clothing was exquisitely tailored to his tall, athletic frame. His horse was the finest that Melissa had ever had the pleasure to observe, a noble beast of apparently impeccable breeding that appeared to be a full sixteen hands high to accommodate his master's size. Taking into account the man's appearance and manner, and the obvious value of his magnificent steed, Melissa had no doubt that he must be a wealthy and titled gentleman.

The older boy tugged at his hand and the gentleman turned his attention towards him. A moment later, he had picked up the child, placed him securely in front of him on his saddle, and was treating him to a ride astride his powerful horse. Melissa smiled with delight at the sight. Being no stranger to the ways of children, she was sure that the older boy had argued that since his younger brother had gone for a ride, he should be given the same consideration.

In a few moments, the gentleman was back and he lowered the boy to the ground once again. He smiled at the nurse and spent a few moments conversing with both children before he took his leave.

Melissa sighed as he rode away. He had undoubtedly been the finest gentleman she had ever seen, not to say the bravest. A cow-hearted rider might have let the child run under the wheels of the coach, rather than risk his own skin by attempting a rescue.

The image of the fine gentleman remained in Melissa's mind as she quit the garden and entered the house. She greatly desired to see him again so that she might compliment him on his selfless act, but the chances of that meeting coming to pass were so slim as to be nonexistent. He was the type of gentleman to attend the best *ton* parties, but Melissa would not be present. She would come into contact only with the gentlemen who came to call upon her stepsisters, and it was extremely unlikely that either Regina or Dorothea would attract such a distinguished suitor.

As she climbed the staircase to her bedchamber, Melissa smiled wistfully. The gentleman she'd seen was the pattern card of her fondest dreams, the perfect match she'd imagined that someday she might be fortunate enough to make. But if such a perfect gentleman were unmarried, he would not remain so for long, and even if Jane permitted her to have her Season next year, he would be gone, brought up to scratch by some beautiful young lady and firmly caught in the parson's trap. She would never set eyes on him again and the best Melissa could do was to tuck his image close to her heart and be content to let him live on in her memory.

Three

Melissa turned away from the window with a smile of satisfaction as Jane and her daughters pulled away in the carriage. Regina had looked much prettier than usual in the pink gown that Melissa had altered and Dorothea had been lovely in the white with the green ribbons that Melissa had used to trim it. True to her word, Jane had given her youngest daughter a set of her jewels to wear, but exactly as Regina had predicted, they had been the pearls, not the emeralds.

"Begging your pardon, miss, but where would you want me to begin?"

Melissa turned to smile at the timid maid that the owners of the townhouse had left behind for their convenience. "Begin what, Mary?"

"The unpacking, miss. Her ladyship said that I am to help you with the trunks. She told me that everything must be put in place before they return."

Melissa's face mirrored her disappointment. She was exhausted from their early-morning journey, the altering of the gowns for her stepsisters, and the time she'd spent helping her stepmother and stepsisters dress.

Regina had been at her most obliging, admiring the gown that Melissa had altered and confessing that she thought it much too grand for a person such as herself. She had pleaded with Melissa not to bother any further with her, insisting that she had no wish to appear any other than her own plain self. It had taken Melissa several minutes to convince her dear stepsister that the fashioning of a complimentary hairstyle would not cause her any undo effort and, after she had dressed Regina's hair in a style that added height to her diminutive stature, Regina had been ready for the evening's engagement.

Dorothea had been impressed with the trim on her plain white gown, declaring it quite the most elegant thing she had ever seen. She had wished for additional ribbons in her hair and perhaps a few clusters of curls, but Melissa had managed to convince her that she appeared much more sophisticated without them. When Dorothea had declared that she was most pleased with Melissa's efforts, Melissa had gone to Jane's dressing room to attend to her stepmother.

Jane had been at her most demanding, setting standards for her appearance that had been impossible for Melissa to achieve. She had been critical of everything that Melissa had done for her, complaining that Melissa was clumsy and unskilled at enhancing a lady's appearance, and bemoaning the fact that they had no funds with which to engage a proper dresser.

One item of contention had been the condition of Jane's evening gown. Jane had protested that it was not pressed to perfection, even though Melissa had taken particular care with the task. She had also complained that she did not care for the manner in which Melissa had arranged her hair and insisted that it be twice done over. Only the lateness of the hour had spared Melissa from a third attempt and after a glance at the clock in her dressing room, Jane had allowed that it would simply have to do.

From the comments that Jane had made, Melissa had begun to suspect that her stepmother's age, not Melissa's untrained ministrations were the cause of her dissatisfaction. Regina had confirmed this suspicion in a private word with Melissa, begging her not to take Jane's criticisms to heart. She had explained that her mother had been regarded as an Incomparable during her first London Season and though well over twenty years had passed since she had taken London by storm, Jane still had aspirations of achieving a similar effect. Regina had also confided that during their last London Season, Jane had dismissed two abigails even though both of the women she'd engaged had come with the highest of recommendations.

Through it all, the only thought that had kept Melissa from despair was the knowledge that her stepmother and stepsisters would have to leave eventually or risk offending their hostess. Once the carriage had departed, Melissa had happily anticipated several hours that she could call her own, to sit quietly in the garden or perhaps, to read. Unfortunately, the quiet and peaceful evening she had planned for herself was not to be. Even with Mary's help, it would take them until long past midnight to accomplish the task that Jane had set for them.

Mary must have noticed the expression of dismay that crossed Melissa's face, for she spoke up quickly. "I can do it myself, miss, if you tell me where you want the things to go."

"No, Mary." Melissa smiled at the girl kindly. "We'll accomplish it together and do our best to make short shrift of it."

The work went smoothly, once they'd begun. Within the hour, the baggage that belonged to Dorothea and Regina was unpacked and properly stored in their rooms. Mary hurried off to prepare a cold supper for them, and while she was busy in the kitchen, Melissa entered her stepmother's rooms to begin the work there.

Though Melissa had attended to her stepmother in her dressing room, she had entered through a door off the hallway and had not yet viewed Jane's bedchamber or private sitting room. Jane had taken the largest suite of rooms and as Melissa stepped into her stepmother's sitting room, she gasped at the lavish furnishings. Light blue satin draperies adorned the windows and the room contained a settee, covered in matching blue satin. There were four white chairs that were edged with gilt, several low tables of the same design, a fireplace with a white marble mantelpiece, a white, gilt-edged writing desk with a small matching chair, and wall sconces in the shapes of cherubs and flowers. The walls, themselves, were covered with pale blue

satin and there was a lovely silk carpet of a slightly darker hue
that was liberally sprinkled with a design of white flowers.

The blue and white theme was carried into the bedchamber,
which connected to the sitting room by an arched doorway. The
focal point of the large room was the bed, a massive affair of
white and gilt that was carved with cupids and flowers. A white
lace canopy, over the bed, was woven to resemble a field of
flowers and gave the effect of a romantical bower.

Melissa did her utmost not to break into a fit of the whoops
as she imagined her stepmother reclining on this particular bed.
The decorations clearly bespoke a charming innocence and the
first sweet flower of young womanhood. It was obvious that the
bed had been designed for a shy and gentle young lady who
might retire to her bedchamber to peruse a slim volume of love
poetry or to dream of a perfect match. That her scheming stepmother, the pattern card of jaded sophistication, should sleep
in such innocent and chaste surroundings seemed but a step
away from a travesty.

Melissa crossed to the armoire which was of the same design
and also laden with carved cherubs and flowers, and took a
moment to marvel at the placement of the oval mirrors that
were set into the doors. There was a second set of mirrors on
the inside of the doors, and by opening them and adjusting the
angle, it was possible for a lady to view the back of her gown,
as well as the front and the sides.

The postilions had piled Jane's baggage under the windows
and Melissa opened one of her stepmother's portmanteaus.
When the contents had been placed to her satisfaction, she lifted
the lid on a large trunk and gave a small gasp of dismay. The
trunk was filled with papers and ledgers from her father's desk.
Since Jane would have no reason to bring the contents of the
baron's desk, Melissa could only surmise that a servant had
packed this trunk by mistake.

Melissa was about to close the lid and shove the trunk out
of the way, under the windows, when she noticed a small package inside that was addressed to her. The writing was in her

father's hand and Melissa removed it to examine it more closely. A letter was affixed to the top of the package. As Melissa opened it and read her father's words, tears of sadness for the kind and gentle man that she had loved gathered in her sea-green eyes.

This package is for you, my darling daughter, on the eve of your first formal ball. If you are reading these words, I will not be here to wish you well and to admire your lovely appearance. Rest assured that your mother and I wish you the greatest happiness.

Melissa smiled as she gazed down at the small package. She was almost certain she knew what was inside. On her deathbed, Melissa's mother had extracted a promise from her husband. He was to give Melissa her diamond earrings to wear on the eve of her first formal ball.

Her fingers trembled, itching to tear open the package and examine the earrings. Her mother had told her that they had originally belonged to her grandmother and had been passed down to her mother in the same manner. Would she ever have the opportunity to wear them? A frown replaced the smile on Melissa's face. Perhaps not, but if she ever married, she would give them to her own daughter to wear on the eve of her first ball, and carry on the tradition for another generation.

Melissa glanced down at her father's letter again. His handwriting seemed to swim before her eyes and she blinked to clear her vision.

I must apologize to you, Melissa. My concerns at finding myself solely responsible for a growing daughter led me to a decision that I fear has been a grave disservice to you. I pray that you can forgive my foolishness. My only excuse is that I held your welfare uppermost in my heart. Do not settle for less than you deserve, my darling daughter, and be assured that you deserve the best.

Though your mother and I are now gone from this earth, you may be certain that our love will remain with you always.

Tears threatened to overflow from Melissa's eyes and she wiped them away so that Mary should not be privy to the extent of her emotions. She had known that her father was not sublimely blissful with his choice of a second wife, but he had never spoken ill of Jane. Now, in this letter, he had come very close to admitting that he had grievously erred when he had married her. For such a proud man to humble himself thusly, caused Melissa's tears to start anew. Brushing them away a second time, she hurried to her bedchamber to hide the package amongst her belongings where it would be safe from prying eyes.

The unpacking had been accomplished at shortly past midnight and Melissa had dismissed Mary from any further duties and sent the girl off to bed. After a walk through the house to ascertain that all was in perfect order, Melissa had retired to her own bedchamber and prepared for bed. She was about to settle down in front of the small hearth for a soothing cup of tea before climbing beneath the covers, when she heard the sound of carriage wheels below. Jane and her stepsisters had returned.

Melissa sighed and hoped that they would have no further need of her. She was exhausted and though she knew she would enjoy hearing their accounts of the party, the prospect of sleeping appealed much more at this small hour of the morning.

There were three sets of footsteps upon the stairs and Jane's voice carried to Melissa's ears. Though Melissa was unable to hear the words her stepmother spoke, it was apparent from the tone of Jane's voice that she was displeased. The conversation continued for several minutes and then Melissa heard the door to Jane's bedchamber close with finality. Her stepmother had retired for the evening, obviously still in a bad taking.

There was a soft murmuring in the hallway and Melissa knew that her stepsisters were still discussing the party. Then the door to Dorothea's bedchamber closed and a scant moment later, there was a light tap upon Melissa's door.

Melissa sighed. She had no doubt that her visitor was Regina and though her eyes were aching from lack of sleep, she crossed quickly to the door and opened it.

Regina looked concerned as she noticed that Melissa was dressed in her night rail and a wrapper. "I wished to tell you of the party, Lissa, but perhaps it would be best if I wait until morning."

"Nonsense." Melissa observed the unhappy expression on her stepsister's face and motioned her inside. It was apparent that Regina sorely needed a friendly coze. "I was enjoying a cup of tea before bed. Please join me, sister."

Regina smiled and entered the room, taking a seat in one of the two chairs in front of the fire and accepting the cup of tea that Melissa poured for her. "The dinner was lovely, Lissa. They had six removes."

"Six!" Melissa raised her eyebrows. "It was a feast, then?"

Regina nodded. "We began with turbot with lobster and Dutch sauces, and red mullet with cardinal sauce. Then we had sweetbread *au jus,* lamb cutlets with asparagus, venison, roast saddle of mutton, and a turkey poult."

"However did you remember all that?" Melissa was impressed.

"A bill of fare was placed next to every person and I must admit that I perused it at every opportunity, committing it to memory in lieu of conversing with the gentleman on my right."

"Oh, dear." Melissa choked back the urge to laugh. "He was so undeserving then?"

"Worse than undeserving. He was a rake of the first order! He actually tried to . . ." Regina's voice faltered and heated color rose to her cheeks. "If he is indicative of the manner in which gentlemen are to behave this Season, I would prefer to be anywhere but London!"

Melissa's curiosity rose. It was apparent that Regina was in a state of nerves. Her color was high and her normally gentle countenance was as fierce as a mother vixen defending her den. "I am sensible of the fact that you are overset, Gina, but what, exactly, did this gentleman *do?*"

"He . . . Oh, it is most embarrassing, Lissa!" The color in Regina's cheeks rose ever higher. "When the first course commenced, he turned to converse with the lady on his right. That is the proper etiquette, you know. But during his converse with her, he reached down his left hand, beneath the table linen, and . . . and . . ."

Melissa's mouth gaped open as she realized what her stepsister was attempting to impart. "He *touched* you?"

"He did." Regina drew a deep, calming breath. "I would venture to say that *groped* would be a more accurate description for the action he intended to accomplish. And all the while, his attentions appeared to be directed towards the lady on his right."

"No one else at table observed his rude action?"

"No." Regina shook her head. "One cannot help but feel that he had done this deed before and had learned to accomplish it undetected."

Melissa took a moment to digest this latest revelation. "But what of the gentleman on your left, the one who was conversing with you? Did he not notice?"

"No, he did not. He was perfectly unaware of the reason for my discomfort, or even that I *was* discomforted. You would have liked him, Lissa. He was a nice young man who was enjoying his first Season and I have no doubt he thought me a poor conversationalist as it was exceedingly difficult for me to give his subject my full attention."

"I should say it must have been." Melissa began to frown. "What did you do about the gentleman on your right, Gina?"

"What could I do? I moved to the very edge of my chair and that served to stop him for a time. To complain overtly would have been unthinkable, considering his ranking."

"He was a nobleman, then?" Melissa's frown deepened.

"An earl. When it was his turn to converse with me, he told me that he had once been acquainted with your father."

"Did he give you his name?"

Regina nodded. "It was Stonehill and I shall not forget it as long as I live!"

Melissa fell into a fit of the whoops as she realized which particular gentleman had been seated on her stepsister's right. "The Earl of Stonehill?"

"The very one." Regina nodded. "Did your father speak of him, Lissa?"

"He did, but with no affection. He told me that Stonehill was a rake of the first order and that no lady could be in comfort around him. He chose to visit us once, shortly after my mother died, and my father packed me off to the rectory until he had left. It's a pity you didn't spear him with your fork, Gina. If I'd been in your place, I fear that is precisely what I would have done."

"I'm not nearly so unkind as you, dear Lissa. During the third course, when his hand commenced to wander once again, I merely spilled my goblet of wine in his lap." Regina began to laugh, her good humor restored. "The others at table may have thought me clumsy, but it served to cool his ardor."

The two shared a moment of light-hearted laughter and then Melissa's thoughts turned towards the consequences of her stepsister's action. "Did your mother observe your behavior, Gina?"

"Yes. She brought me to task the moment our carriage rolled away from the Farthington mansion. According to Mama, this was but the first of my infractions for the evening and she was so kind as to enumerate them."

Melissa raised her eyebrows. "La, Gina! What else did you do?"

"There were six infractions in all." Regina's lips were twitching with laughter. "Mama kept my accounts very well this evening and I fear she concluded that I am sadly deficient in the comportment befitting a lady of quality."

Melissa burst into laughter again. She thoroughly enjoyed

her stepsister's droll wit. "Tell me and I shall decide if you behaved badly."

"The first infraction was the incident at table."

Melissa nodded. "I have already exonerated you of that. Which came next?"

"While conversing with several ladies I had met last Season, I had occasion to make the acquaintance of a gentleman who had attended Oxford with the Reverend Mr. Watson. His tales of their student life were so entertaining, I fear I declined to dance with a gentleman that Mother had chosen for me."

"Oh, dear!" Melissa did her best to look dismayed. "He was an *eligible* gentleman?"

"Quite eligible, but scarcely out of the schoolroom. He joined our discussion when he learned that my companion had attended Oxford with his older brother."

"Then you failed to dance with either of the two gentlemen and conversed with them instead?"

Regina sighed as she nodded. "Those comprised my second and third infractions. The fourth came when Mama sent yet another gentleman in my direction and I confessed that I would much prefer a glass of orgeat over standing up for the Quadrille."

"Why ever did you suggest that?" Melissa was confused. She knew that her stepsister loved to dance and was both competent and graceful.

"His left foot appeared to be painful to him. He had a pinched look about his mouth and he was limping slightly. I was certain he'd asked me to stand up with him in deference to Mama and I wished to save him the agony. We sat beneath a potted palm instead and had a productive discussion about footwear. When he told me he was thinking to try a new bootmaker, I suggested Hoby and said that your father always claimed him to be the best."

"That makes four infractions, according to your mother." Melissa counted them off on her fingers.

"The fifth was quite unavoidable." Regina sighed deeply. "The young lady standing next to me had ripped her hem and she was highly mortified. I accompanied her to the ladies's withdrawing room and found a maid to repair it. In doing so, I missed the next gentleman that Mama sent my way."

"Are you saving the most grievous infraction for last?" Melissa's eyes were bright with laughter.

"Indeed, I am." Regina nodded. "You see, Lissa, I failed to sparkle."

Melissa managed to look properly devastated. "No sparkles at all?"

"Nary a glimmer. Mama warned me that if I fail to sparkle at the next event, she will be quite put out with me. Doro, however, did very well, much more so than Mama had anticipated."

"Doro met someone eligible?" Melissa held her breath.

"A gentleman of consequence, according to Mama. He's an elderly viscount, rich in the purse and widowed some three years. He stood up with Doro twice and he seemed quite taken with her. The *on-dit* is that he's seeking a wife, and no one but Doro has caught his fancy."

"But what are Doro's feelings for him?" Melissa couldn't hide her concerned frown.

"You may smile again, Lissa, for Doro favors him very well indeed. She confided that he puts her in mind of your father and she much prefers him to the younger gentlemen she's met."

Melissa breathed a sigh of relief. Dorothea might rub along well with an older viscount for a husband, especially one who could afford to buy her gowns, jewels, and any gewgaws that took her fancy. "Your mother is pleased then?"

"Very pleased, indeed. She was so delighted at Doro's success that her scolding of me tonight was quite tame. Mama has given him permission to pay a morning call, so we must be ready to receive him. I fear that will make more work for you, Lissa."

Melissa waved her concerns aside. "That does not signify. I shall be delighted so long as I know that Doro is happy in his attentions."

"She was fairly glowing when I left her." Regina smiled fondly. "It seems Lord Chadwick was most appreciative of her charms and she, of his."

After a few more moments of conversation, Regina bid Melissa a good night and took her leave. When Melissa was alone, she got into bed at long last and sighed wearily. It appeared that Dorothea could well have found her match and she wished her stepsister happy. In the course of the Season, it was also possible that Regina would meet a gentleman who would capture her heart. Melissa smiled as she thought of Regina. With her stepsister's kind and gentle ways, she would make a good wife for some fortunate gentleman and an excellent mother for their happy children.

Though she scarcely dared hope that it could happen, would she also meet her match? Melissa conjured up the image of the gentleman who had saved the young boy in the park. Was there a possibility that she might meet him and capture his heart? No, she was merely blowing smoke if she expected the goddess of chance to place him anywhere near her. Melissa was certain that she was doomed to the life of a spinster and she would do well to come to terms with her fate.

As she closed her eyes, Melissa attempted to imagine what her life would be like when her stepsisters married. She had not considered this possibility before and the very thought of being alone with her stepmother at Harrington Manor, spending the rest of her life catering to Jane's every whim, was enough to make her heart heavy and her sleep fraught with unease.

Four

Melissa stood in the hall, under a portrait of a young man with bushy eyebrows and a fierce scowl who appeared to be looking out at the world with extreme disapproval. She was holding a cream-colored velum paper with a heavy seal and debating whether or not she should open it. It was addressed to her stepmother, but Melissa was alone in the house and there had been no one else to receive it. Jane had left with Regina and Dorothea several hours ago, having secured a coveted appointment with Madame Beauchamp, one of London's most fashionable modistes. Though Regina had asked that Melissa be permitted to go along, Jane had denied that request.

Jane had not been pleased with Melissa's work on the previous evening. She'd complained that her gowns had not been arranged to her satisfaction and she'd ordered Melissa to press them again and rearrange them so that the evening gowns would hang on the left side of the armoire and the morning dresses on the right. Jane had also demanded that they be ordered by color, the lighter hues first and then the darker. It was not the sort of task that Melissa believed to be necessary and indeed, she suspected that her stepmother was merely making work for her so that she would have to forgo their journey to Madame Beauchamp's establishment.

Aided by Mary, Melissa had accomplished all according to her stepmother's dictates. When the time-consuming task was finished, Mary had rushed out in search of several items that

Jane had requested from the shops, among them a special type of tea that she declared she much preferred, and Melissa had been left alone in the house. She had been seated in the drawing room, preparing to peruse a small, leather-bound volume of poetry that she'd been particularly anxious to read, when she'd heard the sound of an approaching carriage.

As Melissa watched through the window, the carriage had pulled up in front of their rented house and a liveried footman had disembarked to deliver the very paper that she now held in her hand. The word "urgent" was written across the face of the missive in a bold hand and it had been heavily underscored. If not for this word and the fact that the footman was waiting for an answer, Melissa would have placed the message on the silver salver to await her stepmother's return.

After another moment of indecision, Melissa decided that the footman's continued presence, coupled with the heavily under-scored word, outweighed what might very well be the personal nature of this correspondence. Opening the envelope with trembling fingers, she unfolded the single sheet of velum inside and read the brief message.

It was from Lady Beckworth, an esteemed member of the *ton*. Lady Beckworth was hosting the ball that evening, a grand affair that would officially open the London Season. Lady Beckworth wrote that several of her staff had suddenly taken ill and she requested that Jane send over one of her most capable servants to help with the preparations.

Now Melissa was truly in a quandary. Jane had no servants save Mary, and though the girl was friendly and willing, Melissa had observed that she was sadly inexperienced and could, by no means, be described as capable. To send Mary to help Lady Beckworth would be tantamount to an open admission that Jane had no capable servants. This sad state of affairs was certain to be the subject of speculation and would inevitably result in a series of *on-dits* concerning Jane's finances or lack thereof among the tabbies of the *ton*.

Lady Beckworth's footman had presumed that Melissa was

a servant. It was not an unreasonable assumption considering her serviceable gown and the fact that she had opened the door to him. He was currently waiting outside in the carriage for Jane's answer, and Melissa was aware that she must act quickly. She would be Jane's servant, Lissa. It was a role her stepmother frequently expected her to assume and she was certainly as capable as any servant that Jane could engage. Her action would save the family the embarrassment of admitting that they were lacking in funds and Jane was certain to be gratified at Melissa's timely ruse.

Melissa hurried to the escritoire, penned a hasty note to her stepmother to explain the situation, and placed it on the silver salver with Lady Beckworth's message. Then she rapidly dressed in a clean, recently pressed gown and hurried out to join Lady Beckworth's footman before she could further debate the wisdom of her actions.

"The bouquets you've fashioned for the sconces are perfection, Lissa." Mrs. Collins, Lady Beckworth's housekeeper, turned to smile at her.

"Thank you, Mrs. Collins." Melissa bobbed a quick curtsy, the way she'd seen Mary do. This was the second compliment the stiff-backed model of grey-haired efficiency had given her since she'd arrived but an hour ago. Melissa would not have thought this unusual, but a serving maid had confided that Mrs. Collins seldom complimented any member of her staff.

"How long have you been with Lady Harrington, Lissa?" Mrs. Collins smiled at her kindly.

Melissa took a moment to consider the question. It would not serve to number the years as she had not prepared Jane for that eventuality. The only option Melissa could think of was to tell the truth. "All my life, Mrs. Collins. I was born at Harrington Manor."

"And your mother and father are still there?"

"No, Mrs. Collins." Melissa shook her head. "My mother died long ago and my father more recently."

"I fear your talents are wasted in the employ of Lady Harrington." Mrs. Collins sighed deeply. "She is not the type of mistress to appreciate your skills. When I speak with Lady Beckworth next, I shall mention that we are in need of someone of your caliber."

"Thank you, Mrs. Collins." Melissa bobbed her head again and did her best to look grateful. This was difficult, as she was struggling not to laugh and thus give her ruse away. She could picture Jane's discomfort should Lady Beckworth attempt to lure her servant, "Lissa," away.

"I daresay you'd find a position with us much more to your liking." Mrs. Collins cast an admiring glance at the lengthy garland that Melissa was fashioning from glossy, dark-green ivy. "Where will this go when you finish, Lissa?"

"I had thought to drape it between the bouquets of roses in the sconces."

"That would be perfect." Mrs. Collins nodded her agreement. "How did you learn this skill, Lissa? It's quite unusual for a lady's maid to have your way with flowers."

"My mother took great pleasure in her garden, Mrs. Collins." Again, Melissa told the simple truth. According to the stories her father had related to her, her mother had enjoyed her pleasure garden and had often gathered blooms to grace the sconces at Harrington Manor.

"Then your mother taught you to make these garlands?"

"No, Mrs. Collins." Melissa settled for telling the truth once again. "The parson's wife was fond of using them to dress the church for weddings. When I was a child, I was set to help her."

Mrs. Collins nodded, apparently satisfied with the answers to her queries, and went off to supervise several servants who were arranging chairs along the walls of the ballroom. Melissa worked alone until she had finished the garlands and then she enlisted a friendly maid to help her drape them between the sconces.

Melissa and her helper had just completed draping the last

ivy garland when an imposing woman entered the room. She was dressed in a fashionable gown of vivid blue silk and she wore a necklace of sapphires that glittered in the soft rays of afternoon sun that streamed through the windows. Only one aspect of her appearance spoiled the effect of total elegance. Her silver hair was piled in untidy curls at the top of her head, obviously fashioned by a person who was not accustomed to the task of arranging it.

"Lady Beckworth." Mrs. Collins dipped her knee in a curtsy and the other servants in the room did the same. "How kind in you to come to observe the progress we have made."

Lady Beckworth smiled, bringing warmth to her otherwise stern features. "The ballroom looks lovely, Mrs. Collins, and it shall do famously. I daresay it will be the talk of the *ton* on the morrow. I am especially fond of the garlands you've draped between the sconces. I don't believe I've ever seen anything like it before."

"Nor have I, my lady." Mrs. Collins motioned to Melissa. "Lissa made them for us. She's the girl Lady Harrington sent to help."

Lady Beckworth's smile grew as she peered at Melissa, who had bobbed her head in deference to the mistress of the house. "They are very pretty, Lissa, just what this old barn needed to dress it for the evening. Perhaps I should turn you loose in the dining hall to see what wonders you can work there."

"I shall be happy to do whatever you wish, my lady." Melissa bobbed another curtsy.

"Thank you, Lissa. It is most gratifying to meet one so young who is both able and willing."

"Lissa is a gem," Mrs. Collins spoke up. "Now that she has finished the flowers for the ballroom, I will set her to fashioning centerpieces for the table."

Lady Beckworth nodded. "Excellent. You are indeed a gem, Lissa. And I declare that if you could only work a miracle with this hair of mine, I would pronounce you a diamond of the first water."

"I would be happy to attempt it, my lady." Melissa bobbed her head again. "One of my duties is as Lady Harrington's dresser."

Lady Beckworth blinked once in astonishment and then she gave a delighted laugh. "How wonderful! My dresser has also been taken ill and I have need of another. When you have finished with the centerpieces, Mrs. Collins shall send you to my chambers. If you are as talented as I believe you are, I shall be the envy of every woman here tonight!"

Melissa was smiling as the footman escorted her to the servants' door of the rented house. Lady Beckworth had been most appreciative of her efforts, declaring that her toilette had never been accomplished with such style and fashion and bestowing upon "Lissa" several lovely gowns that she claimed were no longer in mode. Melissa planned to alter them to augment her own sparse wardrobe and she was eagerly looking forward to the task.

"I shall arrive promptly at seven to convey you." The footman surveyed Melissa with new interest. He had heard that she had been elevated in status and was now quite the apple of Lady Beckworth's eye. Indeed, Lady Beckworth had ordered him to carry her home in her own conveyance and to fetch her again, without fail, before the party commenced. Any servant his mistress regarded as this indispensable was bound to be worthier than he had originally thought, and he had come to regard Lissa as a girl of no ordinary consequence.

"Thank you." Melissa dipped her head to the distinguished footman. "I shall be ready when you arrive."

The house was empty when Melissa entered and she sent a grateful prayer heavenward for this respite. She knew that she would not be alone for long. Her stepmother and stepsisters must arrive in short order for they had not many hours before the ball commenced and they would need time to complete their toilettes. Melissa took a moment to fetch a hot cup of tea to revive herself, and then she hurried up to her bedchamber with the clothing that Lady Beckworth had given her. She had just hung the new gowns in her wardrobe when a carriage pulled up in front of the house and her stepmother and stepsisters disembarked.

"Lissa! Come and put yourself to good use!"

Jane's voice was a shrill demand and Melissa fairly flew down the staircase. Her stepmother was standing beside a growing pile of parcels which were being unloaded from the carriage.

"Carry these in and be quick about it. We have no time to waste if we are to look our best tonight." Jane pointed to a large parcel at the bottom of the heap. "That gown will have to be pressed before Dorothea can wear it."

The next hour was a whirl of frenzied activity that found Melissa at the hub. She stored away all the items they had purchased, pressed Dorothea's new gown, removed a spot from the pair of gloves which Jane wished to wear, located a misplaced slipper, brushed the nap of Dorothea's blue velvet pelisse, and assisted all three women in their toilettes. During this time, the opportunity to tell her stepmother of the ruse she had affected did not present itself. It was not until her stepmother and stepsisters were sitting down to a light refreshment that Melissa had a moment to inform Jane that she had played the role of her servant, Lissa, at the Beckworth Mansion.

"Clever girl!" Jane put down her teacup and favored Melissa with a rare smile. "And you say they were pleased with you?"

Melissa nodded. "I believe so. Lady Beckworth asked that I return to assist her housekeeper at the ball."

"But how are you to get there?" Jane's lips tightened. "It would not be proper to permit a mere servant to ride with us in the carriage."

Melissa stifled a sigh. It was apparent that Jane had no compunction whatsoever about regarding her as a servant. "There is no need to disoblige yourself. Lady Beckworth is sending a carriage to carry me to the mansion."

"How very odd!" Jane's eyes widened. "Lady Beckworth is sending a carriage for you?"

"Yes. If there is nothing further you wish of me, I must put on a clean gown so that I am ready when it arrives."

Melissa was almost at the door when her stepmother called her back. "There is one other thing, Melissa. If we should meet by chance at the ball this evening, you must needs remember to treat us with the proper deference."

"Yes, my lady." Melissa bobbed her head in the manner of a servant and was gratified to see that both Regina and Dorothea were stifling their amusement at her parody. "I shall be certain to do so."

This reply seemed to satisfy Jane for she waved her dismissal. "Off with you then. It would be very bad *ton* to keep Lady Beckworth's coachman cooling his heels in her carriage."

Robert Whiting, Duke of Oakwood, was not enjoying a pleasant afternoon. His day had begun at half past noon when he had awakened blurry-eyed and with a frightful pain in his head. His valet had hurried to fetch a vile potion that he guaranteed would put his grace to rights again and Robert had choked it down. Either the libations at Boodle's were not up to scratch, or his person was rebelling against several consecutive nights spent gaming at that gentlemen's club. If he were not careful, he should turn into a tosspot in his effort to avoid the other, more genteel amusements of the current London Season.

The message from his mother had come shortly before tea time and it had not been the usual polite request to join her, his elder sister and her husband, and his uncle for refreshment and social converse in the Drawing Room. It had been a summons, pure and simple, and by the particular words the duchess had chosen, Robert knew that his presence was not only required but also demanded.

Robert sighed, approaching the Drawing Room door with heavy steps. He surmised he knew precisely what turn this meeting would take and he did not like it. There had been enough gentle hints, over the past two years, and Robert was no fool.

It was true that it was past time for him to marry. Most of his friends had married long ago, and only the most hardened bachelor could resist much longer. He was two-and-thirty, still unmarried, and quite the most eligible catch of the past six Seasons. There was no doubt whatsoever, in Robert's mind, that the members of his family had gathered together for one sole purpose, to apprise him once again of his ducal obligations and to urge him to take a wife before the year was out and to set up his nursery in short order.

Robert squared his shoulders, wiped the scowl off his handsome face, and ran his fingers through his wheat-colored hair. He prayed his eyes were not as bloodshot as they felt and took a deep breath for courage. His mother undoubtedly had some young lady in mind for him. He had met the previous three, very nice girls if the truth were told, and had neatly arranged to discourage their interest without causing them any pain. How much longer he could continue to perform such a feat, Robert wasn't certain. The last young lady had been most persistent and only by making a spectacle of himself at a gaming hell her brother was wont to frequent, had he managed to thwart her desire to marry him.

Robert had searched his heart and found it empty of love for anyone other than his family. He could honestly claim that he had never been pierced by cupid's arrow or found himself drawn inexorably to a particular young lady. That he liked the young ladies was well evident, and he enjoyed himself greatly in their company. But as far as settling down with one in particular, he had never found himself inclined of the slightest desire to do so.

There was no help for it. He was obliged to listen to his family's concerns. Robert approached the door to the Drawing Room with a heavy heart and wondered in what manner he could extricate himself from their well-meaning advice. He had duly met a bevy of young ladies and had found them wanting. To blatantly say so would be cruel and Robert was never cruel. He preferred to discourage the hopefuls in other ways, by pretending to be a gamester, or a rake, or whatever would cause them to lose interest in him.

"Robert, dear." His mother spied him in the doorway and motioned for him to come in. "How kind in you to have come at last. Sit here beside me. We have something we wish to discuss with you."

"Mother." Robert dropped a kiss on her cheek and took the proffered seat. He had been correct in thinking that the whole family would be here. His sister, Lucinda, was seated on the sofa with her husband, and his uncle Lawrence, the Marquis of Pembrook, was resting his heavy bulk in the oversized chair in front of the window.

Social pleasantries were exchanged for several minutes. Yes, Robert was aware that this was a lovely day. No, he had not as yet sampled cook's strawberry tarts. And yes, he had noticed the new team of matched bays that his uncle had purchased at Tattersol's, high-steppers to be certain and not a penny too dear for such remarkable cattle. When the political news of the day had been discussed and the Regent's newest escapades had been cited, the conversation had turned to the entertainments of the current Season and Robert sensed that the true subject of this gathering was about to be broached.

"You are aware that Lady Beckworth's ball is this evening?" His mother looked up at him with guileless eyes.

"Yes, Mother." Robert nodded. There had been talk of nothing else for several days. It was the reason his sister and her husband had journeyed to London from Trelane Manor, their country estate. Lady Beckworth had been his mother's bosom bow and attending "Aunt Sarah's" ball *en masse* had become an annual family event. Robert had begged off this year, much to his mother's distress, but he had held firm in his wish to avoid the first big event of the Season. On the day following Lady Sarah's ball, Robert's mother, his sister and her husband, and his twin nephews would depart for Oakwood Castle where they would stay the summer months.

"Unfortunately, your uncle is unable to attend the ball."

Robert's mother sighed deeply. "Since he has already tendered his acceptance, it will be an awkward situation, I fear. Dear Sarah has planned the seating to perfection and she will be quite overset to have a lady without a partner. I suppose I must forgo the pleasure of attending so that her numbers will be even."

Four pairs of eyes turned to gaze at him and Robert sighed. He knew exactly what was expected of him, but the last thing he wished to do was to attend Aunt Sarah's ball.

"And I had been so looking forward to this evening!"

His mother sighed quite convincingly and Robert found himself the object of close scrutiny again. To refuse to escort his mother would be churlish.

"You win, madame." Robert grinned down at her. "I'll partner you. But if you try to introduce me to one more young hopeful, I'll—"

"Why, Robert! I had no intention of doing any such thing!" His mother interrupted, assuming an expression of outraged innocence.

Robert smiled down at her and tweaked her nose. "Of course not, Mother. I have no reason in the world to suspect you. It's not as if you've attempted to accomplish similar introductions in the past."

His mother burst into laughter and his sister followed suit. Soon everyone in the room was laughing and while they were all merry, Robert took his leave. It was not until he was back in his bedchamber, considering which attire to don for Aunt Sarah's ball, that he realized he had played very neatly into his mother's hand. Though he had vowed to take no part in the current Season, he had willingly agreed to attend the Season's first entertainment and by doing so, everyone of consequence would assume that he was once again in the petticoat line.

Five

When Melissa had arrived at the Beckworth Mansion, Mrs. Collins had put her to work immediately, stationing Lissa at a position near the ladies' withdrawing room. The trusted servant who regularly assumed this position had taken ill and the other servants were needed elsewhere. Mrs. Collins had also confided, in an undertone that none of her staff could hear, that Lady Beckworth, herself, had suggested Melissa for this sensitive duty. Lissa was in charge of assisting the ladies in repairing their toilettes and taking charge of their outer garments.

The position in which she found herself was much to Melissa's liking. Her vantage point enabled her to view the guests as they arrived in all their finery and afforded her the opportunity to see with her own eyes precisely which styles were in the first stare of fashion.

Melissa had been rushing to and fro for the better part of an hour when her stepmother and her stepsisters arrived. Regina was wearing her new cloak and Melissa thought it suited her very well indeed. It was made of a particularly beautiful embroidered silk and Jane had purchased it for her eldest daughter at the shop of the fashionable modiste they had patronized earlier in the day.

Both Dorothea and Regina smiled at Melissa in a friendly manner, but Jane quickly gave them a warning glance. Both girls immediately assumed neutral expressions and nodded slightly, the proper greeting from a lady of quality to a servant.

After Melissa had taken charge of her stepmother's evening cloak, Jane took a moment to speak with her.

"I have need of you, Lissa." Jane's manner was condescending and her voice had the tone she assumed to direct their servants. "A passing coach has splattered the hem of my daughter's cloak. See that it is cleaned before the stain becomes set."

"Yes, my lady. I should be happy to do so." Melissa bobbed a quick curtsy, but inwardly she was fuming. There had been no others nearby to hear their converse and provide a reason for Jane's curt treatment of her. This incident caused Melissa to suspect that Jane took perverse enjoyment in regarding her as merely a servant. As such, Jane would have no reason to feel the slightest amount of guilt for squandering the funds that had been allocated for Melissa's Season.

Jane swept off, followed by Dorothea, but Regina lagged behind for a private word with Melissa. "I do apologize for Mama's perfunctory treatment of you, Lissa. Though she does not see fit to thank you, Doro and I are appreciative of the sacrifice you have made on our behalf."

"Thank you, Gina." Melissa smiled. "And it is not such a sacrifice, after all. I possess the perfect vantage point to commit all the latest styles to memory and I have already planned how to alter several of your gowns."

Regina nodded, but she still appeared anxious. "But you should not be required to do tasks like that, Lissa. Doro and I had a brief moment alone to speak of it, and we both hold the opinion that Mama's treatment of you is shameful."

"It is kind in you to tell me, Gina, but you must not concern yourself on my account."

"But we *are* concerned, Lissa." Regina took a deep breath. "Doro and I have joined in a promise. The first of us to marry will invite you to be a part of her household. There you will be regarded as a dear sister and not an unpaid servant!"

Melissa smiled, cast a quick glance around to make certain they were unobserved, and gave Regina a fond hug. "Thank you, Gina. And please thank Doro for me as well. Now you must go. Your mother will be expecting you to join her."

When Regina had left, Lissa was presented with what appeared to be an endless parade of cloaks, pelisses, hats, and coats. At long last, the final guests arrived and the evening's entertainment commenced. Melissa took a moment to return her cap and apron to the servants' cupboard and then she hurried to fetch Regina's cloak.

A large balcony overlooked the formal gardens. Melissa opened the doors to the balcony and took Regina's new cloak out to the rail to brush it thoroughly. Fortunately, the splattered mud had not damaged the delicate silk material and it was a simple matter to brush it out with a soft cloth until no trace remained.

The night was growing chill and Melissa slipped her stepsister's cloak over her shoulders. She was certain that Regina would not begrudge her the use of it for a few moments. Though she had completed her assigned tasks for the evening, Melissa was loath to return to the town house and her solitary pursuits.

Under the wrap of protective darkness, Melissa gave free rein to her favorite dream. Standing on the balcony at the Beckworth Mansion, dressed in her stepsister's exquisite cloak and listening to the strains of music from the ballroom that floated through the still night air, Melissa felt almost as if she were a debutante enjoying this glittering evening.

The soft black night was enticing and Melissa leaned against the rail, gazing up at the stars. The orchestra was playing a new waltz, and she hugged herself tightly in the darkness. How she should love to be a part of the merriment and gaiety in the ballroom! Though she had not been formally trained in the figures of this dance, Melissa had observed her stepsisters at lessons with their dancing master and she had no doubt that she could perform the waltz to satisfaction.

As Melissa stood there, imagining that the handsome gentleman she had seen in the park had asked her to stand up with him, her feet began to move in the patterns of the waltz. They

would dance for a moment and then he would smile down at
her, praising her for her grace and style. She would accept his
compliment modestly, remarking that any grace he attributed to
her must be due, in full measure, to his own expertise. He would
be taken with her ways and request a second dance. And when
the orchestra had stopped playing, he would request a third. She
would be required to remind him, with her lips curving upwards
in a lovely smile and her eyes glinting with delightful amusement, that a third dance with the same gentleman should be
considered most improper. He would forgo dancing for the remainder of the evening, standing against the wall with a yearn-
ing countenance, observing her closely as she danced with other
young gentlemen. Before the night was over, his heart would
be firmly engaged and he would offer for her at the first opportunity.

Melissa sighed softly as her feet moved to the soft strains of
the orchestra. Fully engaged in this most wondrous dream of
her own making, reality faded to a brief flicker and after a time
she became perfectly oblivious to the world around her.

The Duke of Oakwood found he quickly had his fill of pretty
young ladies and waltzes. This Season's opening ball was no
different from last Season's, or the one before it. Perhaps Robert
was too jaded to appreciate the beauty of the elaborately decorated ballroom with its glittering chandeliers containing thousands of candles, the superb orchestra, and the lovely flowers
that seemed to be everywhere. Once he had dutifully stood up
with his mother and performed his turn around the dance floor
with his sister, he found himself adamantly wishing that he had
not fallen prey to his mother's scheme and had, instead, insisted
upon remaining at home. The lovely young debutantes held no
charm for him. Indeed, their postures seemed more tiring than
usual and their attempts to flatter him, absurd. True to her word,
his mother had not performed any introductions, but Robert
knew this respite would not last the length of the evening for

he had observed the chaperones of several young ladies desperately attempting to catch his mother's eye. The introductions would be made, the amenities duly observed under his mother's close scrutiny, and he would be required to ask each of them to stand up with him.

After escorting his mother to a comfortable chair beside a potted palm and fetching a glass of champagne for her, Robert bowed and made his excuses. He had left his favorite snuffbox in the pocket of his cape. It would only take a moment to retrieve it and he promised to be back almost before he was missed.

"Excuse me." Robert caught the eye of a maid in the hallway. "I fear I've left something in the pocket of my cape. Could you please direct me to the proper chamber?"

The serving maid bobbed a curtsy and looked up at him boldly with a saucy smile. "Yes, sir. It's down the grand staircase, the second door to the right. Would you be liking me to help you fetch it, sir?"

"No, that's not at all necessary." Robert favored her with a smile. She was a comely wench and obviously eager for his attentions, but he desired no passing dalliance with one of Aunt Sarah's maids.

Robert soon found the cloak room and began to look for his cape. It took him several minutes, but he found it at last and drew the snuffbox from his pocket. He harbored no desire for this item. His excuse to his mother had been merely a ploy to escape the confines of the ballroom, but he dropped it into his pocket in the event that she should quiz him on whether or not he had located it.

He was engaged in seeking out a deserted chamber where he could enjoy a few moments of solitude before rejoining the crush in the ballroom, when he noticed a young lady on the balcony that ran the length of the house. She was standing alone, wrapped in a cloak, gazing up at the stars overhead. Though he had no wish for social converse at this particular moment, Robert found that he was most curious. Perhaps some young lady had also grown disenchanted with the ball and was seeking a moment of refuge.

As Robert's curiosity drew him in her direction, a wealth of scenarios played out in his mind. She could not be one of Aunt Sarah's maids, taking a respite from her duties. Aunt Sarah's housekeeper was demanding with her staff. One of her maids would not be so foolish as to stand by idly contemplating the stars where she could be so easily observed.

If she was not a servant, the woman before him must be a lady of quality and it was likely that she had come here to collect her thoughts. If she were in some sort of distress, his duty was clear. As a gentleman of good breeding, it was his obligation to offer his assistance.

Robert's thoughts turned to the possible cause of her distress. If he found that she had quarreled with her spouse, he would quickly make his excuses and depart. It was never wise to take sides in a squabble between husband and wife. On the other hand, she could be unmarried and distressed over some slight that had been given her.

It was even possible that she was someone of his acquaintance. Robert peered at her intently, but he was unable to reach any positive conclusion. The balcony was in darkness, she had pulled up the hood of her cloak, and it was impossible to discern her features. In any event, he was now only inches from the balcony door and he decided that he must satisfy his curiosity before he took his leave.

Melissa was lost in a perfect dream when reality intruded at the sound of footsteps behind her. Before she could whirl and dash back into the safety of the chamber, a deep voice spoke.

"Are the stars in the heavens more interesting than the company in the ballroom?"

Melissa turned to peer at the tall gentleman who had joined her on the balcony. The moon had not yet risen and she could not see his face. It quickly occurred to her that if she could not discern his features, he would be at the same disadvantage. Since his voice had held a liberal hint of laughter, Melissa found herself responding in kind. "The stars are indeed preferable, sir. I have enjoyed a most delightful conversation with Cassiopeia."

"And what did the mother of Andromeda tell you?"

Melissa experienced a jolt of pleasure. Her uninvited companion knew the old myth. She considered her words for one brief moment and then she divulged one of her deepest and most private thoughts. "The stars are timeless, eternal and infinite, qualities we cannot claim as mere mortals. They change slowly, in a predictable manner. She felt that we should take a lesson from their constancy."

"A bit of wisdom from one glittering Incomparable to another?"

"Hardly, sir!" Melissa laughed softly. "I am a mere speck in the grand scheme of things, scarcely worthy of notice."

"You are far too modest, madame." There was a teasing note in his voice. "Tell me your name so that I may know you, and I shall decide whether your assessment of your character is accurate."

Melissa considered her reply very carefully. It was best that he remain in ignorance of her identity. Her stepmother would never approve of converse with a gentleman to whom she had not been properly introduced and quick to chastise her severely for such an improper action. "Souls in the darkness possess no names. I am merely a voice with no shape to tether it to this earth. Perhaps I am not human at all. You would be none the wiser. Indeed, I can and will be anyone I choose."

"And who will you choose?"

He sounded intrigued and Melissa smiled into the darkness. "I shall be one of my favorite mythical beings, come to life on this very evening to taste the pleasures of mortality."

"A lovely sentiment and well stated, but you must tell me which particular mythical being I am addressing."

Melissa recalled that magical time, so long ago, when her

father had introduced her to the wonder of myths and legends. The baron had told her the old tales and little Melissa had been enthralled. "I shall be Diana, the huntress."

"Ah! And I am the hunted?" His voice sounded suddenly wary.

"You flatter yourself, sir!" Melissa gave a merry peal of laughter. "Perhaps I shall choose to dally with you for a moment, but I should not bother to hunt you!"

"Others have hunted me and I have successfully escaped their lures." His words were again light and teasing and Melissa thought he sounded much relieved. "Oh, great Diana, do you not regard me as a worthy catch?"

"Hardly, sir! You must remember that the company I keep is exalted and my mythical companions would regard you with a sad lack of esteem. Their regard is limited to those who have slain armies with a single blow, tamed the lightning to do their bidding, and ridden on the back of the wind."

He laughed again. "Give me your hand, my goddess, and I shall escort you back to the ballroom. Once there I will show you how to tame the tabbies of the *ton*. It is said to be a far greater task than slaying dragons or commanding the waves."

"Alas, I cannot go with you, sir." Melissa sensed that he was about to reach out to grasp her hand and she pulled back quickly. "I am certain I should enjoy it immensely, but my time on this earth is fleeting and my duties are many. I fear you must leave me now."

The orchestra began to play another waltz and he shook his head. "Not quite yet my famed goddess. Dear Diana, will you give me the pleasure of being my partner in this waltz?"

Bowing low, he extended his arm to Melissa. She hesitated for only the briefest of moments and then she took his arm. There could be no harm in dancing with this delightful stranger. He did not know her identity, nor she his.

Melissa's heart began to beat faster as he held her in the darkness and they began to dance, fitting into each other's arms and matching their steps perfectly. It was a magical moment and Melissa was certain that she would remember it for the remainder of her life. This wonderful stranger was her partner in her very first dance. They did not speak, but moved as one, dipping and swaying across the balcony in flawless rhythm, guided by the lovely strains of the music.

Time seemed to stand still for Melissa. She wished to remain in this stranger's arms forever. But the music ended, as all music eventually must, and their dance was over.

As the last strains of the waltz faded away on the still night air, the tall stranger held her for a long breathless moment. Melissa's heart fluttered rapidly at his nearness and she held her breath in anticipation. Was he about to kiss her? She longed to stay in his arms, but she had been trained as a lady and, reluctantly, she slipped away.

"Wait!" He called after her desperately. "You have not told me your name and I must see you again!"

Her emotions in thorough disarray and her mind in utter turmoil, Melissa picked up her skirts and ran as if her life depended on it. She rushed out of the chamber and down the corridor, where she found a place of refuge in a deserted alcove. The stranger hurried out of the chamber a scant moment later in pursuit, and Melissa held her breath and prayed that he would not discover her hiding place.

As he ran past her, on his way to the staircase, Melissa caught a glimpse of his features. She gasped and swayed, catching hold of the wall for support. She had been dancing with the gentleman from the park, the perfect match who made up the fabric of her fondest dreams!

Six

Melissa drew a deep shuddering breath and stepped out of the alcove into the corridor. There was no one else in sight and for that fortunate circumstance, she was most grateful. If someone should suddenly appear to ask her what was amiss, she would be sorely at a loss for words. Realizing that she had so recently been in the arms of the gentleman of her dreams had left her senses reeling.

Once she had returned Regina's cloak, Melissa returned to the chamber she had so hastily vacated. She glanced once more at the balcony and reached up to touch her lips. He had been about to kiss her, she was certain of it, and now that the moment had passed, Melissa found herself wishing that she had remained in his arms. Two strangers, sharing a stolen moment of bliss, never to discover each other's identities.

It was at this exact moment that a distressing possibility occurred to Melissa. What if her handsome stranger should describe her features and make inquiries about her? It would be a source of many an *on-dit,* should she be identified as Lady Harrington's maid! Jane would be certain to hear of it and Melissa should be confined to the house for the remainder of the Season to insure that she would never have the opportunity to behave so improperly again!

Melissa quickly pushed these concerns aside and forced herself to view the situation with a rational bent. If she had not observed his features in the light of the corridor, she would not

have recognized his countenance. He had not enjoyed that advantage. The balcony had been in darkness and he had caught no glimpse of her face. And when she had fled through the lighted chamber to the corridor, he had viewed only her back. Melissa was certain that he was in total ignorance of her appearance. He could not describe her, and the secret of her identity was secure.

After a quick glance in the mirror to make certain that her dress and hair were tidy, Melissa left the chamber to seek out Mrs. Collins. To her immense relief, she encountered no guests as she took her leave and soon she was again seated in Lady Beckworth's carriage, riding through the streets with a large hamper at her side.

Melissa arrived at the house in short order and after she had thanked the coachman for carrying her there, she placed the hamper on a table and called for Mary. Mrs. Collins had told her the hamper contained a few delicacies from the party and she had instructed Melissa to open it the moment she arrived at home.

"Oh, miss!" Mary's eyes were round with delight when Melissa lifted the lid. Inside was a sampling of each and every sweet that had been served at the ball. "I have never seen so many treats before! Begging your pardon, miss, but however did you come by such a feast?"

Melissa laughed gaily. "It seems I have pleased Lady Beckworth's housekeeper and I have been rewarded for my troubles. Sit down, Mary, and we'll have a feast of our own. And while we're indulging our appetites, I shall tell you what you must say if anyone inquires about 'Lissa,' Lady Harrington's abigail."

There was a pleased smile on the Duchess of Oakwood's face as she watched her son dance. For one so reluctant to attend Lady Beckworth's ball, Robert appeared to be enjoying himself immensely. He had stood up for every dance since he had come back to the ball, partnering a different young lady in each.

Though her son had denied that he was in the petticoat line, his mother recognized the symptoms. There was no doubt in her mind that Robert was searching for one particular young lady. And when he found her, he would make her his bride.

Robert's mother smiled in anticipation of that happy event. To her way of thinking, she had been a prisoner at Oakwood Castle for far too long. It had been very different when Robert's father was alive. Then she had not minded the winters she had recently come to think of as dreary and isolated. Then their children had filled the castle with laughter and there had been frequent parties of visiting noblemen and their families. Though Oakwood Castle was far from London, it had become a popular place in winter as well as summer and the *haute ton* had eagerly sought invitations. Indeed, there had been very little time when they had been without a houseguest or two as her husband had relished entertaining.

All that had changed when they had laid the seventh Duke of Oakwood to rest in the family plot behind Oakwood Cathedral. As custom dictated, she had been in deep mourning for one full year, wearing black gowns and a somber expression. After that time, she had donned her grays and lavenders and the rigid social strictures had permitted her to once again entertain guests other than family. To her disappointment, she had found that entertaining without her husband was not the same joyful experience it had been while he was alive. House parties had seemed dull and lifeless, the guests more a bother than a welcome diversion, and she had missed her husband's presence exceedingly. In the quiet moments after the guests had retired for the night, she had rattled around, like a stone in a cask, in chambers that had seemed suddenly empty. It was then that she had vowed to leave Oakwood Castle as soon as her son had taken a wife.

The duchess anticipated her freedom with delight. She would hand over the keys to the new duchess gladly and only return for an occasional visit. Her duty would be done and she would be free to move, not to the dower house to live out her days in a rustic and peaceful environment, but to London where most of her old friends resided. She would not be lacking in funds. Her husband had settled a generous portion on her, more than ample to meet her needs for the remainder of her life. She would instruct her solicitor to purchase a house situated close to the residence of her old bosom bow, Lady Beckworth, and enter into the social world of London where there were parties and assemblies that would engage her interest and lift her heart.

The duchess turned to observe her daughter who was laughing and conversing with her husband. Lucinda had made a good match. James Trelane had already come into his uncle's inheritance and had taken his place as a viscount. Trelane Manor was lovely. She had visited there on several occasions and enjoyed herself thoroughly. Though she loved her daughter dearly, and delighted in her grandchildren, she had no intention of seeking to join Lucy's growing family. She was still a relatively young woman and many pleasurable years remained on her plate. She wished to live them in a place and manner of her choosing. Only one duty remained before she could cut the cords that bound her to Oakwood Castle. She must see that Robert was neatly settled with his bride.

Robert was smiling at the young lady he held in his arms and his mother sighed softly. She was a lovely young woman with an acceptable family, an impeccable manner, and a faultless appearance. The duchess had observed her dancing with several young gentlemen who had been obviously taken with her charms, but Robert did not appear to be so engaged. As she watched, the dance ended and her son escorted the young lady back to her chaperone. He conversed for a moment, observing the proprieties, and then he bowed and took his leave. It had been thus all evening, one polite dance and when it was concluded, Robert had gone on to seek a new partner. It was clear that he had not yet found his match, but the duchess was hopeful that he would be successful before she, along with the evening, grew much older.

* * *

There was a pleasant enough smile on Robert's face, but inwardly he was frowning. It was imperative that he locate the young lady who had so inauspiciously fled from his arms. She was the first young woman that he had been taken with since he had become the eighth Duke of Oakwood. Robert knew he must see her again and learn her identity. This was not a whim or a curiosity that he wished to indulge. It was a compulsion that could not be denied.

When he had reentered the ballroom, Robert had searched in vain for the lady he had come to think of as his Diana. In the beginning, he had hoped that his heart might recognize her and an invisible attraction would pull him inexorably to her side. This had not come to pass. Either she was no longer in attendance at the ball, or his heart was not so cooperative an ally as he had hoped it would be.

Robert had gone on to his second plan. He had held her in his arms on the balcony and he was certain that he would recognize her if he could but hold her again. For this reason, he had danced with every young lady who had made herself available to him, but he had come to the regrettable conclusion that none of them were his Diana.

It was not until the last dance of the ball, when he was again partnering his mother, that he remembered the cloak his Diana had been wearing. It had been distinctive and when she had rushed from the sitting room, he had observed it clearly. This prompted Robert to formulate a new plan, one that could not fail him. He determined to tarry late at the ball so that he could observe the cloak of every young lady who departed.

It was indeed fortunate that Robert had driven to the Beckworth Mansion in his own curricle, leaving his mother's party to follow in the family coach. After the ball had officially ended, he bid his mother's party to depart without his escort, claiming that he had met someone with whom he wished further converse, and promising to rejoin them within the hour. When they had safely departed, he took his own leave of Aunt Sarah and ordered his curricle brought round to the entrance.

While Robert was waiting for his curricle, he kept his eyes trained on the parties who departed before him, hoping to spy his Diana in her distinctive cloak. Since neither the cloak nor his Diana had appeared by the time his curricle arrived, Robert wheeled his team of matched bays to a position where he could observe the guests as they left. The flambeaux on either side of the entrance afforded adequate illumination and Robert watched anxiously as a bevy of young ladies, wearing an assortment of cloaks, pelisses and shawls, took leave of their hostess and were handed into their equipages.

Diana's cloak had been fashioned from gold-colored silk and Robert was on the alert for any cloak of a similar color. As the moments passed, he was astounded at how many ladies of the *ton* favored gold-colored cloaks this Season. Robert carefully scrutinized every one, but none was graced with the rich, multi-colored embroidery that he had observed on his Diana's cloak.

Robert felt his spirits plummet as the press of guests, waiting for their equipages, began to thin. His vigil was coming to an end and he had not yet found his Diana. He was almost certain that he had not missed her. He had examined every party with close attention and she had not been among them. Either she had left the ball early, or she was still inside the Beckworth Mansion.

Robert held his breath as the last party prepared to depart. His heart began to beat a rapid tattoo in his chest. One of the three ladies who made up the party wore a gold-colored cloak. Was she his Diana? He would not be certain until she had walked past the flambeaux and he had observed the back of her cloak.

Their good-byes were not swift. Robert waited impatiently, tapping his foot against the floorboards of his curricle, as Aunt Sarah conversed at length with one of the ladies. At last their conversation was concluded and all three ladies stepped outside to wait for their carriage to be drawn up to the entrance.

Robert cursed softly. The young lady in the gold cloak was in the front, the two other ladies so close behind her that he could not see the back of her cloak. He concentrated on the other two ladies, willing them to move to the side so that he would be afforded a glimpse of her back. It seemed to take forever but at last, his wish was granted.

"Diana!" Robert breathed her name like a prayer. The back of her cloak was embroidered in the exact manner he recalled. She was his Diana and he must hurry or she would once again escape him.

Without another thought, Robert jumped down from his curricle, leaving his man to hold the horses, and striding across the drive so rapidly, he almost stumbled in the darkness. He slowed to a walk as he approached their party and arranged a suitable smile of greeting on his countenance. He recognized the elder of the three ladies. Aunt Sarah had made the introduction herself, shortly before the ball had concluded. She was Lady Harrington, widow of Lord Harrington, and he had also been introduced to her daughters. Robert searched his memory, but he found that he could not recall their names.

Though his desire to take his Diana in his arms was so acute as to be almost overpowering, she was not alone. If he failed to observe the proprieties, her reputation with the *ton* would be in jeopardy.

"My apologies, Lady Harrington." Robert approached her and bowed politely, hoping that his voice did not betray the desperation he felt. "I had intended to speak with you further at the festivities this evening, but the opportunity did not present itself."

Lady Harrington seemed pleased at his intrusion and she favored him with a smile. "How kind in you to take such notice of us, Duke. I believe you have already made the acquaintance of my daughters, Regina and Dorothea?"

"Yes, indeed I have had that pleasure." The duke was filled with wonder at learning her name at last and he turned to Regina with a smile. "What a lovely cloak, and very unusual. I do not believe I have ever seen its like before. The manner in which it glitters in the starlight rivals the constellations in all their glory."

"It is most kind in you to say so, Duke." Regina seemed surprised at his lavish compliment, but she smiled politely.

The smile remained on Robert's face, but he felt a sharp stab of disappointment. There had been no answering gleam in her eye, no acknowledgment of the intimate moments they had shared on the starry balcony. Could it be that she was not his Diana? But no, that was impossible. She was wearing the cloak and it was proof of her identity.

Robert was about to tender a further comment, to attempt to tease her into revealing that she had been the lady on the balcony, when he became aware that her mother was keenly observing their interaction. It was likely that Lady Harrington was protective of her daughters and would take his Diana to task if she suspected any impropriety. If this were indeed the case, Regina would be reluctant to admit that she had spent long intimate moments on the dark balcony, dancing with a man to whom she had not yet been formally introduced.

"Lady Harrington," Robert turned to her with a smile. "I should like to request permission to call upon your daughter, Regina."

Lady Harrington's eyes gleamed with satisfaction as she nodded. "You will be most welcome, Duke."

"You may expect me tomorrow morning if that is acceptable."

"Most acceptable." Lady Harrington motioned for her daughters to enter the carriage. "Until tomorrow then."

Robert glanced at Regina, hoping for a smile or some small signal that this plan met her approval, but she steadfastly refused to meet his gaze. It was apparent that his Diana was most reticent in the company of her mother and sister, and Robert vowed to spirit her away at the first opportunity so that they might continue the delightful conversation they had shared on the balcony.

* * *

Melissa was waiting in her bedchamber when her stepmother and stepsisters came home from the ball. A tea service with two cups sat on the table by the fire in preparation. Melissa hoped that Regina would tap on her door again, desirous of a comfortable coze so that she could discuss the ball. If fortune favored her, Regina might describe the gentlemen who had attended the ball and Melissa could learn the name of her charming partner on the balcony.

Jane sounded in good spirits as she bid her daughters goodnight and Melissa breathed a sigh of relief. Regina and Dorothea must have acted in accordance with her expectations. The two sisters conversed for a brief moment and then the anticipated knock sounded on Melissa's door.

"Come in, Gina." Melissa pulled open the door. "I was hoping you would come to tell me of the ball."

Regina smiled and settled into one of the two chairs that flanked the grate. "But you were there, Lissa . . . at least in the beginning."

"This is true." Lissa laughed and poured a cup of tea for her stepsister. "I spent the greatest share of my time in the hall and saw nothing more exciting than Lady Farleigh pulling loose a button from her pelisse."

Regina's countenance sobered quickly. "I'm so sorry, Lissa. You should have been a guest at Lady Beckworth's ball. Indeed, it was only by trading on your father's rank and position that Dorothea and I were invited to attend. Mama may very well delude herself into believing that we would have been accepted on our own merits, but I fear she is sadly mistaken. And to make matters even more inequitable, it is her continued extravagance that keeps you from taking your rightful place in society."

"Let us not worry about those matters which we cannot control." Melissa reached out to pat her stepsister's hand.

"You are so good, Lissa." Regina sighed again. "Whenever I attend an entertainment or assembly, I am keenly aware that I am assuming the position of an impostor by taking your place.

If our positions were reversed, I fear I should be filled with hatred and envy."

Melissa shook her head. "No one who knows you as I do could ever suspect you of harboring any but the purest of emotions. And you are indeed a goose, Gina, if you entertain the notion that I am jealous of your good fortune."

Regina reached out to hug her stepsister. "I did have good fortune tonight, Lissa, though I am at a loss to understand it. The Duke of Oakwood asked Mama for permission to call upon me."

"The Duke of Oakwood?" Melissa tucked her feet up and settled back to listen. "Tell me of him, Gina."

Regina sighed happily. "He is the pattern card of a handsome and sophisticated gentleman, every mother's dream of a match for her daughter, and every young lady's aspiration. Why he should have chosen me, I have not the slightest notion."

"You sell yourself too cheaply, Gina." Melissa gently admonished her stepsister. "You have many qualities that a man of his stature should admire."

"I should be hard pressed to name one."

Melissa was not surprised at the skeptical tone of her stepsister's voice. Regina was modest to a fault. "Then I shall name them and you shall listen."

"Please do not." The color rose in Regina's cheeks.

"But I insist. Truly you are a paragon, Gina! You are loving, devoted, obedient, and most sensible to the emotions of others." Melissa stopped speaking suddenly and clamped her hand over her mouth to stifle a giggle. "Oh, dear! I did not intend to make you sound like a . . . a loyal dog!"

Both girls fell into a fit of the whoops that did not abate for some moments. When they had again composed themselves, Melissa continued in the same vein. "The duke would not have asked to call on you if his interest had not been engaged. It stands to reason that some action of yours must have apprised him of your good character. Think on it, Gina. What was the thrust of your conversation when you stood up with him?"

"I did not stand up with him. He danced with others, but never with me."

Melissa frowned thoughtfully. "Perhaps Dorothea said something that piqued his interest in you?"

"He did not speak with Dorothea. We were introduced quite formally by Lady Beckworth, and then she took him off to another introduction. Prior to his approach to us at the conclusion of the ball, we had not exchanged more than a word with him."

Melissa considered this for a moment and then she shrugged. "Someone of his acquaintance must have paid you a compliment that caused him to wish to know you further. Do you remember what he said when he spoke with your mother?"

"Yes. He said that he had wished to speak with us further, but had not been afforded the opportunity."

"And your mother was flattered by his attention?"

Regina laughed. "She was more than flattered. The moment Mama realized who he was, her eyes gleamed like those of a starving child gazing into a gingerbread stall. Even if the duke calls upon me but once, Mama's status with the *ton* will increase."

"Then your mother is delighted with this turn of events, but she is as puzzled as you are by the duke's interest in you?"

"Yes. It is indeed strange, Lissa. He paid me no attention at the ball. I dare say he did not even notice me. And later, when he came up to converse with us, the only words he spoke to me were to compliment me on my appearance. I have you to thank for that, Lissa."

Melissa smiled. "Did I not tell you that you looked beautiful?"

"You did, but I did not put much stock in your compliment. I assumed that you were merely attempting to give me courage for the ordeal ahead. And to think that I had anticipated this particular ball with dread! It was truly wonderful, Lissa. Mama did not scold me once during our journey home!"

"That gives me reason to think kindly of the duke." Melissa

smiled. "His request to call upon you has saved you from your mother's reprimand."

Regina smiled back, but suddenly an anxious expression spread over her countenance. "I had almost forgot to tell you, Lissa. Mama is writing a list of tasks for you. She will leave them on the table in her sitting room and she asks that you accomplish them in the early morning."

"I shall be certain to do so."

"I fear the duke's visit will make more work for you, Lissa." Regina appeared concerned. "Mama is all in a flutter concerning the arrangements and she will wish everything be done to perfection."

Melissa nodded. "I do not mind, Gina. And rest assured, I shall do my best to make certain that the duke is properly entertained."

When Regina left to go to her own bedchamber, Melissa sat thoughtfully for a moment. Unlike Jane and Regina, she did not find it strange that the duke had requested permission to call upon her stepsister. Regina was a proper young lady with a sweet temperament, a keen intelligence, and a kind heart. If the duke had recognized her worth and it was the source of his interest, Melissa had every intention of treating him with the highest regard. Any gentleman who was kind and attentive to Regina would find favor with her.

After another few moments of contemplation, Melissa arose and made ready for bed. She extinguished the candles, crawled under the covers, and sighed up into the shadows. Tomorrow would be a busy day. Lord Chadwick was expected to call upon Dorothea and the duke was arriving to pay his respects to Regina. Once the other young gentlemen realized that her stepsisters had gained the attention of such exalted personages, they would flock to their house in droves. Regina and Dorothea would be inundated with visitors and such an event could not suit Melissa more. With calls from so many members of the *ton,* she might be fortunate enough to make the acquaintance of the gentleman who had danced with her on the balcony after all!

Seven

"If you have no further need of me, miss, I'll begin the dusting now."

"Go ahead, Mary." Melissa turned to their maid-of-all-work with a smile. "I can finish these cakes by myself."

Melissa was in the kitchen, standing beside a table littered with bowls and supplies. Jane had asked her to bake lemon seed cakes and Melissa was complying with her stepmother's request. The recipe lay on the counter and Melissa glanced down at it to make certain that she had followed the instructions exactly and missed none of the ingredients. A note that had been added at the end of the instructions made her smile. This recipe had belonged to Elise, their family cook, who had retired when Lord Harrington had taken Jane for his wife. Melissa's own mother had brought Elise to Harrington Manor from her family home and Melissa harbored many happy memories of the hours she'd spent in the kitchen with Elise, watching her prepare the excellent food that had been served at their table.

Elise had been in the habit of writing notes on all of her recipes and this one was no exception. It said, "These cakes are Lissa's favorites. Remind her not to eat too many, else she will no longer fit through the little manor's door."

Melissa gave a happy laugh as she read the words. She had been exceedingly fond of the lemon cakes and only Elise's admonition regarding her little manor house had kept her from taking more than her share. Her mother had designed a playhouse for her, a miniature replica of Harrington Manor. Lord Harrington had engaged a carpenter to build it from the sketches Melissa's mother had made and they had given it to Melissa on her fourth birthday. Young Melissa had been enthralled with this child-sized version of her home and she could still remember her cries of delight when she had spied it under a tree in the garden. She had spent many pleasant hours ensconced in her playhouse, entertaining her dolls with tea parties and banquets, and dreaming of the day when she would grow up to be mistress of her own grand manor.

After a final stirring of the batter, Melissa prepared it for baking. She had no sooner put the cakes on the baking shelf when Regina appeared in the kitchen doorway. Her cheeks were flushed with high color and she looked very excited, indeed.

"Which dress would you advise me to wear, Lissa? The duke will be here in less than two hours."

Melissa considered it for a moment. "I should choose the sprigged muslin, Gina. It will do very well for a morning call. If you could find Mary and ask her to press it, I will come to arrange your hair just as soon as these cakes are baked."

"You are making your lemon seed cakes!" Regina smiled as she sniffed the air appreciatively. "Oh, thank you dear Lissa! I do love them above all things. And the duke will be so impressed with the quality of our refreshments!"

Melissa laughed. "I am certain that the duke has tasted lemon seed cakes before."

"Perhaps, but all others pale in comparison. It will be a test of my will to enjoy only one, but I would not have the duke think me greedy. When the refreshments are served, you must sit by my side and keep me from taking a second."

"I will put a plate aside for us to enjoy later." Melissa smiled at her stepsister. "But I cannot sit by your side, Gina. Your mother has asked that I serve the refreshments."

"You are to be our waiting maid?" Regina began to frown.

"I fear that I have been bested by my own cleverness, Gina. By passing myself off as your mother's servant to Lady Beckworth, I am now obliged to assume that position for the entire Season."

"But why?" Regina looked dismayed. "Surely none of the guests who attended Lady Beckworth's ball will remember who took their cloaks."

Melissa sighed and shook her head. "There is one who will remember me well. It seems the duke was so impressed with the flower arrangements in the ballroom, he asked Lady Beckworth who had done them. That kind lady pointed me out to him, and she confided to your mother that he took careful note of my appearance."

"This is most unfortunate!" Regina's frown deepened. "And it is also most unfair! Could we not make a clean breast of it to the duke? From all I have heard, he is a kind man. Surely he will not give us away!"

"Your mother would never agree to any action that might jeopardize her good standing with the *ton*. There is naught to be done about it now, Gina. It is exactly as Mr. Shakespeare wrote; I have been hoisted on my own petard."

Somehow everything was accomplished in time. When Jane, Dorothea, and Regina were seated in the Drawing Room, prepared to receive their first callers, Melissa took up her position at the door. She did not have long to wait.

Lord Chadwick was the first to arrive. Melissa relieved him of his stylish coat and escorted him to the Drawing Room where Dorothea was eagerly awaiting his company. She had not much opportunity to converse with Lord Chadwick on the short journey to the Drawing Room, but Melissa was impressed with his kindly, almost paternal manner. She had no doubt that the servants in his home were a happy lot as the viscount seemed inclined to treat his social inferiors with both kindness and civility.

Only a few moments passed before there was another knock at the door. When Melissa opened it to give access to the gentleman who was standing there, her face drained of color and her limbs grew suddenly weak. A wave of dizziness threatened to overwhelm her senses, and it was all she could do to force her trembling hands to receive his coat. He was the same handsome stranger who had danced with her on the balcony and Melissa's heart fell as he introduced himself. The man of her dreams was none other than the Duke of Oakwood. And he had come here not to seek her out, but to court her stepsister, Regina!

Robert could not help but feel bewildered as he conversed politely with Regina. She was a lovely young lady, he had none but the highest regard for her, but he could catch no glimmer of the mystic sprite that he had held in his arms on the previous evening.

Though he could not be faulted for failing to take part in the conversation around him, Robert's polite comments engaged only a portion of his mind. The remainder attempted to solve the puzzle that his Diana had presented to him. Perhaps her reticence was due in large measure to the fact that her mother and sister were in attendance. Under such constraints, she might feel obligated to behave in a manner of total propriety and give no hint to the lively personality he had witnessed only a few short hours ago. If this were the case, he would be well served to seek a few moments alone with her, but this could not be achieved on a first call unless he were to bodily remove her from the Drawing Room and spirit her off in his curricle.

When no answer to his conundrum immediately presented itself, Robert turned his full attention to Lady Harrington. His mother was exceedingly fond of the old adage, "To know the mother is to know the daughter." After several moments of keenly observing Lady Harrington, Robert found himself sincerely hoping that his mother was in error and the old saying had no merit.

Lady Harrington motioned to the maid who hovered at the

far side of the room. "We wish for more lemon seed cakes immediately."

"Yes, my lady."

After the serving girl had bobbed her head and quickly disappeared, Regina turned to the duke. "Please have the last lemon seed cake, Duke. There are more in the kitchen."

"Thank you." Robert took the last lemon seed cake and after he had taken a bite, he smiled at Regina. "These are excellent! Indeed, I believe I have never tasted any that are their superior!"

"How kind in you to say so." Lady Harrington smiled, accepting his compliment graciously, but before she could continue with the conversation, Regina spoke up.

"Lissa made them this morning. They are even better on the second day, but they seldom last that long."

Robert laughed. "If our pastry cook made lemon seed cakes like these, they should not even have the time to cool. Did you say that *Lissa* made them?"

When Regina nodded, Robert turned to Lady Harrington. "Then I was not mistaken in believing that I recognized your maid. Lady Beckworth told me that she arranged the flowers in her ballroom?"

"Yes. It seems that Lissa has a way with flowers, a skill she has not seen fit to exhibit for our enjoyment on this morning." Lady Harrington dismissed the arrangement of flowers that graced the mantelpiece with a haughty sniff.

Robert turned his attention to the vase of flowers. Though they were not arranged in an elaborate manner, they seemed quite pleasing to him.

"I arranged those flowers, Mama." There was the barest hint of laughter in Regina's voice. "And I freely admit they do not come close to Lissa's standards. I thought to free her for tasks of greater importance like—"

"Making lemon seed cakes!"

The duke, Lord Chadwick, and Dorothea joined Regina in speaking the remainder of her sentence. There was a moment of shared laughter, and even Lady Harrington was forced to smile. But Robert observed that she still appeared discomfited by the praise that was being lavished on her servant.

"Well said!" Lord Chadwick seemed to be enjoying himself thoroughly. "If Lissa were a member of my staff, I should assign her one task only, to make thousands upon thousands of lemon seed cakes!"

Dorothea shook her head. "I think you would quickly change your opinion, Lord Chadwick, if you knew of Lissa's other skills. She can stitch a seam as well as any mantua-maker, she can always supply the proper turn of phrase when one is struggling with a difficult correspondence, and she is perfection as our dresser."

"Lissa is exceedingly talented." Regina's voice was warm. "We are indeed fortunate that she was able to come to London with us. Do you not agree, Mama?"

Lady Harrington appeared quite unsettled by her daughter's question, but she nodded pleasantly. "Yes indeed, Regina. Good servants are difficult to find."

"As are good friends." A smile hovered about Regina's lips. "And our dear Lissa is a friend as well as a servant. Indeed, I often find myself regarding her as a sister."

Robert observed the speaking glance that flashed between mother and daughter. Then Regina dropped her eyes quickly and the color rose in her face. Both Regina and Dorothea appeared to be quite protective of their maid, and Robert wondered whether Lady Harrington had treated her ill in the past. It was another mystery that intrigued him and one that he should not fail to solve.

"What think you of Wellington's latest maneuver, Lord Chadwick?" Lady Harrington turned the conversation neatly. "I fear that as a woman who is unacquainted with military matters, I have not the slightest understanding of his strategies."

As Lord Chadwick commenced to explain the intricacies of Wellington's military tactics to Lady Harrington, Robert bit back a smile. He had followed Wellington's campaigns closely and had come to believe that the highly-touted general lacked even the simplest strategy.

Robert's attention was diverted as Lissa re-entered the room. He watched as she set a full plate of cakes on the table and faded back to the edge of the room to await further instructions. Robert had often observed his own servants and there was nothing unusual about Lissa's manner. But he did notice that she was listening to the conversation with interest and, at one point, she seemed about to object to one of Lord Chadwick's remarks before she remembered her place and remained silent.

Lissa was correct. Lord Chadwick's statement was in error. Robert had recognized that at the onset, but he had not expected a servant to be so discerning. It seemed that in addition to her other accomplishments, Lissa possessed a keen mind. Vowing to put his supposition to the test at a later time, Robert again immersed himself in the conversation.

Melissa could hear perfectly from where she stood, and she listened with interest to the conversation. It seemed that Lord Chadwick had a long-standing acquaintance with some distant members of the duke's family and he inquired politely after them. When the duke told him that his family had departed for Oakwood Castle that morning and the very relatives that Lord Chadwick had so kindly inquired after were planning to visit them there, Jane was prompted to ask of the castle and how far it was situated from London. This led to a discussion of travel and the rigors thereof, and Jane recounted her journey to Bath where she had enjoyed the entertainments of both the upper and the lower rooms.

Lord Chadwick remembered an incident that had occurred when he was in Bath and they all shared a laugh at his recollection. He had attended the theater one evening and an altercation had broken out in the front row of the audience. The leading lady, a woman of no small stature, had picked up a spindle-legged chair from the stage and coshed both combatants on their heads. When the ushers had carried the insensible brawlers away, she had gone on with her performance without missing a line, much to the delight of the spectators.

There was a brief discussion of the exhibition of watercolors that had recently opened, the safety precautions one must take against pickpockets when attending the Pantheon Bazaar, and the magnificence of the fireworks at Vauxhall Gardens. After the proper interval of pleasant conversation had been observed, the viscount arose to take his leave.

"Have you plans to attend Lady Ashford's assembly this evening?" Lord Chadwick quite properly addressed Jane, though Melissa knew that his attentions were clearly directed towards Dorothea.

Jane nodded. "Yes, indeed we do, Lord Chadwick. I hear that Lady Ashford has a voice to rival the angels, and her skill at the pianoforte is said to be unparalleled. We should not miss it for the world."

Melissa raised her eyebrows. One of Lady Beckworth's maids had told her that Lady Ashford had a voice like a crow, but as she was such a respected member of the *haute ton,* no one dared offend her by speaking the truth or refusing to attend one of her assemblies. Her staff was rumored to draw lots to ascertain which unlucky servants would be required to be in attendance when their mistress was performing and several had sought new positions after their first experience in the music room. Lady Beckworth's maid had also confided that the sole reason Lady Ashford hosted these assemblies was to secure a captive audience.

"I shall send my coach for you if you so desire." Lord Chadwick offered quickly.

"That is most obliging in you." Jane nodded her assent. "We should be pleased to accept your kind offer."

Melissa hurried to fetch Lord Chadwick's coat and when she had seen him to the door, she returned to the Drawing Room to find that the duke was also taking his leave. She crossed her fingers behind her back, a gesture she had learned from a superstitious maid they had once employed, and wished fervently that this was not the last they would see of him.

There was a moment of silence in which the duke seemed to be contemplating his words and then he turned to Jane. "If it meets with your approval, Lady Harrington, I would seek permission to escort your daughter on a ride through the park tomorrow afternoon."

"I am certain that Regina would enjoy such a lovely excursion, Duke."

Melissa almost burst into laughter at the gratified expression on her stepmother's face. Indeed, she resembled the cat that had emptied the cream pot as she bid the duke farewell and ordered Melissa to fetch his coat.

When Melissa returned to the hall with the duke's coat, he turned to her with a most disarming smile. "Tell me the truth, Lissa. Do you think she favors me?"

"Most certainly, your grace." Melissa nodded quickly. "Miss Regina is most appreciative of your kind attention."

The duke laughed. "Not her, Lissa. I was speaking of Lady Harrington."

"Indeed she does, your grace!" Melissa's eyes crinkled with laughter and she found she had to struggle to maintain her composure. Jane would favor anyone who was a suitable match for one of her daughters.

"Tell me what you are thinking, Lissa. I can see that you are fairly bursting with laughter."

"It does not signify, your grace." Melissa did her best to compose herself in the demeanor befitting a loyal servant.

"Were you thinking that I could be blind, deaf, and dumb and Lady Harrington would still favor me so long as I possessed a title and the blunt to go with it?"

"No, your grace." Melissa glanced up at him and it was almost her undoing. The expression he wore was that of a mischievous boy. "The thought of blindness never once occurred to me."

The duke threw back his head and laughed for a long moment. When he had recovered sufficiently, he sighed and wiped his eyes. "I hope we will be friends, Lissa. There are times when I tire of propriety and I long for irreverence."

"I understand, your grace." Melissa bobbed her head. "Irreverence is difficult to come by when you are a duke. Most people equate it with a lack of respect."

"And you would not equate it thusly?"

"Indeed I would not, your grace. Lord Harrington used to say that irreverence stems from a sense of the ridiculous, carried to its extreme. He also claimed that it was a sad day indeed, when one could not laugh at the folly of the human condition."

"A wise man, Lord Harrington." The duke nodded, carefully considering her words. "You knew him well?"

"Yes, your grace." Melissa blinked back the tears that threatened to well up in her eyes. "He was like a . . . a father to me."

"Then you were lucky, indeed. I never had the pleasure of meeting Harrington, but I have heard nothing but praise of him."

They shared a moment of silence in which Melissa was strangely content. Then the duke smiled again. "I must tell you again, Lissa. The lemon seed cakes you made were delicious."

"Thank you, your grace. Elise, our cook, taught me to make them on the first day I became tall enough to reach the table. If they were not served to the guests we entertained at Harrington Manor, it was regarded as a slight."

"Then you were trained to be a cook?"

There was an expression of surprise on the duke's face and Melissa shook her head. "No, your grace. Elise said that everyone who lived at the manor should learn to do a few simple things in the kitchen. She set up classes and taught us all."

"Were the master and mistress included in this instruction?"

Melissa nodded, her eyes twinkling. "Why even my . . . that is . . . Lord Harrington occasionally set foot in the kitchen!"

"Perhaps we should have had an Elise when I was a boy."

The duke looked thoughtful. "The kitchens at Oakwood Castle are a greater mystery to me than the pyramids."

"There is a single important difference between the kitchens and the pyramids, your grace." Melissa's eyes sparkled with laughter. "If a dead Egyptian king should be discovered in the kitchens, the cook should be certain to be dismissed without references."

The duke laughed in delight for a moment and then he took his leave. When Melissa closed the door behind him, she leaned against it weakly. He was just as she had remembered, but the memory of their dance was now bittersweet. The duke was no longer hers to dream of. He belonged to another. Melissa loved Regina and wished her happy, but her heart ached for the perfect match that she had lost forever.

Eight

Melissa was out early the next morning with another long list of errands. By midmorning, she had already accomplished the greater share of them and she glanced down at the remainder of her list with a sigh. Dorothea's new gown was ready to be collected. She would do that errand next, as she was only a few streets from the modiste's small establishment. Then she would step next door to the milliner's shop and fetch the bonnet that Regina was to wear on her ride through the park with the duke. Once she had accomplished those two errands, only one task remained.

The last errand on the list was most specific. On Melissa's journey home, Jane had instructed her to stop to procure a bottle of fine brandy. She was to use the remainder of the purse that she had been given for this purchase. The brandy must be of a high quality since it would be offered to the duke when he next arrived to pay a formal call.

As she hurried down the street, Melissa remembered Regina's description of Lady Ashford's musicale and she smiled. The music room had been dreadfully overheated and Regina had claimed that the stuffy air and the escalating temperatures had saved her from grave embarrassment. When their hostess had begun to sing an Italian aria, Regina had been able to hide her amusement behind her fan. It appeared that Lady Ashford's voice was much as Lady Beckworth's maid had described, though Regina had compared it to the screeching of an owl, rather than a crow.

One by one, Melissa accomplished the remaining errands and she was emerging from the last shop with her arms heavily laden with packages when she spied a small puppy running into the street. At that instant, a coach careened around the corner, heading straight for the hapless little dog. Melissa did not stop to consider her own safety or the fate of the packages she carried. She let her bundles fall where they might and dashed out into the street. With nary a second to spare, she snatched the puppy from beneath the horses' hooves before he could be trampled and jumped back to a place of safety.

It was only then, as Melissa stood there holding the badly frightened puppy in her arms, that she realized the penalty her humane action had cost her. The expensive bottle of brandy had broken and she had no more money with which to replace it.

For one who had been in the habit of entertaining late and sleeping until the sun was midway in the sky, Robert was out uncharacteristically early. He had been to the flower stall to buy a bouquet to present to Regina, and he had also purchased token gifts for Dorothea and Lady Harrington. He had chosen a trinket for Dorothea, a small wooden carving of a squirrel since she had mentioned how the creatures scampered through the trees at Harrington Manor. For Lady Harrington, his offering was less whimsical. He had found a small silk bag, embroidered with flowers, which was filled with a delightful blend of potpourri.

As Robert wheeled his team around the corner, he came upon a sad sight. A young girl was standing by the side of the street, staring down at a pile of packages that she had dropped. She held a small puppy in her arms and Robert pulled up on the reins as he caught sight of her face. She was Lissa. And from the woebegone expression that flooded across her countenance, she was in no small distress.

* * *

Melissa looked up as a familiar voice hailed her. It was the duke! As she watched, he wheeled his curricle to the side, leaving his horses to the care of his man, and hopped out.

"Oh, dear!" Melissa held the puppy a bit tighter and buried her face in his soft fur. "We are indeed in a tangle, if he sees fit to tell Jane what I have done!"

"What happened, Lissa?" The duke arrived at her side and gestured toward the jumble of packages that were strewn about. "Did someone knock you down?"

Tears gathered in Melissa's eyes and she blinked them back. "No, your grace. I . . . I dropped them! And now Jane . . . I mean, Lady Harrington, will never trust me with her errands again. And I was so enjoying the morning air and being out of the house."

Robert reached out to scratch the little puppy under the chin. "You may leave Lady Harrington to me, Lissa. I will devise a way to tame her ire. But tell me, how did you come by this fine fellow?"

"He was about to be trampled by a speeding carriage. That's why I dropped the packages, your grace. I had to save him. I simply could not stand by and do nothing!"

"Of course you could not." The duke began to retrieve her packages but he ceased quickly when he came to one with a brown stain that was spreading over the paper. "What *is* this, Lissa?"

"I fear it's your brandy. The bottle broke when I dropped it. The other packages are intact. I examined them before you arrived."

Robert lifted a flap of the paper and winced at the label inside. "Perhaps that is all to the good. I shall replace this brandy with a bottle from my own cellars. It will be our secret, Lissa, and Lady Harrington will be none the wiser."

"Oh, thank you, your grace! You have no concept of how much this will mean to me!"

"Nor to me. Because of your timely mishap, I shall be allowed to sip my favorite brandy in Lady Harrington's Drawing

Room." The duke laughed as he picked up the remainder of Melissa's packages and rose to his feet. "Come along, Lissa. I will provide you with a bottle of brandy and then I will carry you home."

When Melissa reached the duke's curricle, she stared down at the puppy in her arms. He was curled up, fast asleep, and she could not bear the thought of leaving him here, on the dangerous streets. "But, your grace . . . what will I do with Perseus?"

"Perseus?" The duke raised his brows in surprise. "Then you've named him already?"

Melissa nodded. "Yes, your grace. I thought it appropriate for if I attempt to keep him, he will have to borrow the helmet of Hades to make himself invisible to Lady Harrington."

"And winged sandals so that he can fly out of her path." The duke laughed heartily. "Perseus it is then. What think you of your name, little fellow?"

Perseus opened one eye, sighed in contentment, and went straight back to sleep. This elicited a rumble of laughter from the duke, but Melissa was still too anxious about the puppy's reception to do more than smile as he helped her into his curricle.

The duke picked up the reins and turned to Melissa. "From your comments, I presume that Lady Harrington will not welcome Perseus with welcome arms?"

"No, your grace." Melissa sighed deeply. "Lady Harrington is a staunch proponent of the theory that any animal, kept in the house, is a hazard to the health of all who reside there. I daresay that if she lays eyes on Perseus, she will toss him out like yesterday's refuse."

The duke nodded. "I would have guessed as much. Does the rest of the family share in this sentiment?"

"Oh, no, your grace! Miss Regina loves animals and would gladly keep my secret, as would Miss Dorothea. This is the very reason I will not ask them to do so. Lady Harrington would severely chastise them if she suspected that they were aiding me in a deception."

"I see." The duke looked thoughtful. "What would you say, Lissa, if I told you that I knew of a home for Perseus? It is a place where he would have all the love and care he could wish for."

"I would change his name to Lucky and wish him God-speed."

The duke laughed as he nodded. "It is settled then. Lucky Perseus will make his home with me."

"Oh, thank you, your grace!" Melissa didn't think, she simply leaned over and bestowed a kiss upon the duke's cheek. Then, realizing the social blunder that she had committed, she gasped in sudden alarm. "Your grace! I am so terribly sorry! Please say that you will overlook my rash behavior and accept my abject apologies! My only excuse is that I was so . . . so grateful!"

"Do not concern yourself, Lissa." When the duke turned toward her, his eyes were twinkling. "Your action was quite spontaneous and entirely appropriate for the circumstances that prompted it."

"Yes, your grace." Melissa dipped her head in a nod, but color still stained her cheeks. It would constitute a grave breech of etiquette for the daughter of a nobleman to kiss a duke in broad daylight on a public street. For a mere servant to do so was totally unthinkable!

The duke must have noticed that she was still anxious for he reached over to pat her hand. "Let us go on as if nothing out of the ordinary has happened. You must promise not give it another thought."

"Yes, your grace." Melissa agreed readily enough, but she knew that she would not forget the kiss that she had given him. She would think about it again when she was alone. It was as close as she would ever come to the man of her dreams, and she would not forget it so long as she drew breath.

* * *

The next few days were a delight for the duke and he found that he did not mind in the slightest when Lissa accompanied Regina on their outings. The ride they had taken through the park had been most enjoyable. Regina had explained that was Lissa's first view of society on parade and Robert had found himself laughing frequently as Regina had attempted to explain the proper etiquette for such an excursion. When one met a person of a higher ranking, one did not speak unless spoken to. One inclined one's head, assumed a friendly countenance, and took direction from the manner of the other. If another carriage pulled abreast and a conversation ensued, one was permitted only the briefest of discourses before moving on to let others pass by. And if, heaven forfend, one chanced to spot a gentleman of one's acquaintance who was accompanied by his mistress, one expressed an abiding interest in the view from the opposite direction and pretended not to notice so as not to embarrass the gentleman.

There were other rules and Robert had listened as Regina had explained them all. A lady did not remove her gloves for any but the most necessary reason and kept her face shielded from the sun by a bonnet. She never pointed at things of interest, laughed too loudly at her escort's quips, or otherwise made a spectacle of herself. Stopping the carriage to climb out when one desired a closer view of a lovely flower or a tree filled with blossoms was never permitted on the Promenade, and one's dignity must be maintained at all times.

"What a lot of bother, having to remember all that!" Lissa's eyes had been wide with amazement. "It removes all the enjoyment from riding through the park!"

Regina had nodded in complete agreement. "I fear that you have the right of it, Lissa. But unless a lady observes these rules, she is not accepted."

"Given the choice, I should prefer not to be accepted!" Lissa had sighed deeply. "I, for one, will be glad when I am back at Harrington Manor. There I can stop to pick all the flowers I wish, and point to my heart's content. And even more enjoyable, I can run through the grass in my bare feet!"

"Have you truly done that, Lissa?" Regina had appeared surprised at Lissa's confession.

"Yes, indeed I have! It fills me with a delicious sense of freedom, as if I am part of the wild things that live in the wood. One must be cautious, though, and not choose to indulge this pastime in a field where cattle have recently grazed. There are some objects that are most unpleasant for one's foot to encounter."

"Lissa!" Regina had collapsed into laughter, but when her initial burst of merriment had passed, she had turned to Robert with an anxious expression. "Please excuse us, Duke. I fear that Lissa and I have sadly forgotten our manners."

Robert had smiled with amusement. "Indeed you have, and I find that I am very grateful. I have been bored to tears by previous rides through the park with proper young ladies. Escorting the two of you has been a most enjoyable exception."

"Then you don't mind, your grace?" Lissa had appeared remorseful for her lapse.

"Not in the slightest. And if ever you find yourself longing for a run through the grass without the benefit of shoes, I will dismiss the servants, clear the house, and offer my garden for your pleasure."

The remainder of the ride had passed enjoyably and when they had returned to Lady Harrington's Drawing Room, Robert had indulged in a snifter of the excellent brandy he had provided to replace the bottle that Lissa had broken. There had also been lemon seed cakes. Lissa had made them that very morning and when Robert had asked, she had promised to copy the recipe for Henri, his French chef. Before taking his leave, Robert had surprised himself by asking Lady Harrington's permission to escort Regina to the watercolour exhibit the next afternoon.

On the following afternoon, Lissa had again accompanied them as they perused the paintings that covered the huge walls of the gallery. Regina had stopped to admire a still life of a bowl of fruit.

"What a lovely apple!" she had exclaimed. "It appears to be as delicious as it is perfect, and I should partake of it with the greatest of pleasure."

Lissa had frowned. "I should not let you eat it, for I fear that this particular apple should present a grave danger."

"But why?" Regina had turned to Lissa. "The apple is perfection, itself!"

"Exactly so and that is precisely the problem. It is much *too* perfect. A perfect apple must be suspect, as nature itself is imperfect."

Robert had begun to smile for he surmised that Lissa was enjoying this argument immensely. "Go on, Lissa. Explain your reasoning to us."

"You must think about the apples you have eaten. I daresay they have all had some quality to keep them from approaching perfection. Perhaps it was a wormhole, or a spot of blight, a color that faded at the top or the bottom, or a shape that was slightly uneven. The apple in this painting is perfection itself, and I cannot help but be reminded of the perfect poisoned apple that the witch presented to Snow White."

Robert had laughed, but he had been puzzled by Lissa's knowledge of the story. Jacob and Wilhelm Grimm had but recently published their collection of fables, and *Nursery and Household Tales* had been written in German. "You astound me, Lissa. How did you come to know of this tale?"

"It is simple, your grace." Lissa had exchanged a speaking glance with Regina and then she had given him a disarming smile. "I am certain you have heard mention that Lord Harrington was a scholar of no small repute."

Robert had nodded. His father had mentioned that aspect of the baron's character.

"His lordship was used to enjoy the pleasures of Paris and it was there that he made the acquaintance of Mr. Jacob Grimm. They met in the libraries where Mr. Grimm was working with

Savigny. His lordship was pleased to find that they had a common interest in fables and folklore, and they spent many an enjoyable evening exhausting this topic. When Lord Harrington returned to England to take up his duties at Harrington Manor, they deepened their acquaintance through frequent correspondence, and his lordship was among the first to receive a volume of *Fables and Household Tales*. Though it was written in German, Lord Harrington was fluent in that tongue, and he would often translate the stories for us in the schoolroom."

"You were in the schoolroom, Lissa?" Robert had been surprised. It was highly unusual that a servant be allowed access to that chamber of learning.

"Yes, your grace." Lissa's face had colored quickly and Robert had not missed the anxious glance that she had cast at Regina.

"My stepfather believed that education should be made available to all who lived under his roof." Regina had spoken quickly. "He was a wonderful man, and I carry the memory of his charity in my heart as an example of what I hope I may someday achieve."

Robert had turned to gaze down at Regina. Her face had been glowing with inner purpose and he remembered thinking that she had never looked lovelier nor more ethereal.

"You are far too modest." Lissa had smiled at Regina and then she had turned to Robert. "Miss Regina has begun lessons at the parish to teach the children of the tenants to read. She is a wonderful teacher, your grace, and all the children love her. If not for her mother's insistence, she would have forgone her Season to stay at Harrington Manor and continue her lessons."

"Then I am indeed fortunate that Lady Harrington intervened." Robert had smiled at Regina and his estimation of her character had risen another notch. Most young ladies of her station would have been more concerned with their wardrobes than the welfare of the tenants' children.

Looking back on that moment, Robert decided that it had been a turning point in his relationship with Regina. It was then that he had begun to seriously entertain the notion of declaring for her. While it was true that the magic of their first meeting had vanished, Robert thought they rubbed along very well indeed. Though Regina no longer stirred his blood nor caused his senses to reel with excitement as they had at their first, clandestine meeting, according to his married friends, it was a rare wife indeed who fully engaged her husband's passions.

There was no doubt that Regina would be perfection as a wife. Her character was impeccable and Robert was assured of her loyal devotion. She would honor her husband and never dream of betraying him in any manner, large or small. Regina loved children. Robert had seen it in her eyes when she had described the reading classes she had introduced for the tenants' children. She would be an adoring and dedicated mother.

His house would be kept in good order. Regina had been well trained in the management of a household and Robert had no doubt that she was thrifty and conscientious. She had been raised as a gentle lady and he could find no fault with her comportment. Regina also possessed a pleasing countenance, an intelligent mind, and a generous heart. She would be charitable to those who relied on him for their livelihood and fair and pleasant in her dealings with his servants.

Robert sighed. Regina was perfection itself, a veritable paragon who would meet with approval from every quarter. His mother and his sister would embrace her warmly, his staff would welcome her gentle direction, and he, himself, would enjoy her company on long winter evenings at Oakwood Castle. Regina was utterly and completely suitable to be the next Duchess of Oakwood. She would assume the duties of that exalted position gladly and perform them admirably. There was only one small impediment that stood in the path of the proposal that Robert was contemplating. This impediment had a name, and the name was Lissa.

Robert frowned as he sank down in a chair by the fireside and poured himself a small snifter of brandy. Though he knew it was utter foolishness on his part, he found himself strangely attracted to Lady Harrington's servant. When he had first made her acquaintance, on the morning he had paid his initial call on Regina, he had experienced the uncomfortable sense that he had met her previously in another time and at another place. At first, he had attempted to dismiss it out of hand, but it disturbed him greatly because he could not identify its origin. This uncomfortable sensation still lingered to this very day. Lissa put him in mind of someone very dear, but he could not think of who it could be.

One late night, ensconced in his library in front of a dying fire with an empty snifter of brandy in his hand, Lissa had invaded his thoughts. In that half-awake state, her imagined presence had prompted him to indulge his wildest imaginings. He had pictured himself offering for Lissa and taking her to wife to the utter horror of his friends and family. It had been a nonsensical notion, but it had pleased him immensely to imagine her life entwined with his for all eternity. Such was Lissa's strange power over him, and Robert suspected that a similar passion had caused lovesick young swains in previous generations to do battle against insurmountable odds for a favor from their beloved.

Robert had attempted to dissect this emotion, but he had failed miserably. While Lissa was lovely, there were others who possessed greater beauty. Her wit was sharp and her mind was keen, but those attributes could be found elsewhere. Still, there was an attraction that Robert could not deny. Merely the image of her face or the memory of her laughing eyes conjured up a relentless fascination that Robert could not dismiss until he had escaped into a fitful sleep.

In the clear light of morning, Robert had realized that there must be a reasonable explanation for the affinity that drew him to Lissa. It was then that he had vowed to spend more time with her, to listen to her words as she conversed with him, and to observe her every action. Perhaps, by using all the wits at his disposal, he could solve this compelling mystery.

Nine

"Miss Regina hoped that you would call, your grace."
Melissa smiled as she took the duke's coat and hat, and accepted
his card. The corner was turned down to signify that he was
calling in person, but there was no need to ask him to wait while
she carried it to the Drawing Room. Jane had anticipated his
call and had instructed Melissa to show him immediately into
her presence.

The duke had come to call every day in the two weeks that
had passed since Lady Beckworth's ball, and Melissa had found
herself anticipating his arrival with the greatest of pleasure.
While other young gentlemen might ignore her, or give her, at
the most, a polite nod, the duke always stopped to chat with her
before he took his leave.

In the past fortnight, the duke had provided Regina with many
hours of entertainment and he had invited Melissa to accompany
them on every occasion. Included in a party made up of Jane,
Dorothea, Regina, Lord Chadwick, and the duke, Melissa had
enjoyed the tragedian Edmund Kean's performance as Shylock
in Drury Lane. She had accompanied the duke and Regina to
a watercolour exhibition, a tour of the British Gallery, and an
evening at Vauxhall Pleasure Gardens. At Vauxhall, under the
lights from a thousand lamps, Melissa had been treated to a
vocal concert, a daring performance by a tightrope walker, a
display of equestrian feats, and a lavish array of fireworks.

There had also been several rides through the park and an

afternoon stroll in Kensington Gardens. And just yesterday afternoon, the duke had invited Regina and Lissa to partake of a surprise he had planned for them. When they had joined him in his carriage, he had promptly driven them to Carlton House, where Henry Holland had almost completed his commission to remodel the Prince Regent's London residence.

Melissa had smiled with delight as Henry Holland, himself, had granted them entrance. From his converse with the duke, she had learned that he was a friend of the duke's family, and he had appeared quite eager to convey them on a tour. He had explained that the style of the remodeling was predominantly French, and he'd confided that the Regent had spared no expense to decorate his residence with dazzling silver and gold.

Following in Regina and the duke's wake, Melissa had enjoyed a lengthy perusal of the interior. Their tour had encompassed the fan-vaulted observatory, the round second drawing room, the dining hall, and the forty-foot library. The great chandelier in the center of the Crimson Drawing Room had so taken her fancy that Melissa had stood gazing up at it for several minutes while her thoughts had turned fanciful. She had imagined herself as an invited guest, seated in one of the heavily upholstered chairs which stood in two opposing rows on either side of the intricately woven round carpet. The Crimson Drawing Room would be filled with famous personages, and Melissa imagined that the famous authoress, Miss Jane Austen, might be among them. Henry Holland had permitted them to examine the three volume edition of *Emma* which had been presented to the Regent. Melissa had thought she had never seen books more handsomely bound, and she had observed that it had been "most respectfully dedicated" to His Royal Highness the Prince Regent "by His Royal Highness's dutiful and obedient humble servant The Author."

"Lissa." The duke had touched her on the shoulder, startling her out of her pleasant reverie. "You have been gazing up at that chandelier for an exceedingly long time. I will grant that it is lovely indeed, but what, in particular, is there about it that you find so fascinating?"

Melissa had quickly remembered her assumed station and she had turned to him with an apologetic expression. "I am indeed sorry if I have delayed our progress, your grace. It is merely that I fail to see how any one person could ever clean it properly without risking a broken neck."

The duke and Regina had laughed delightedly and even Henry Holland had chuckled. Then he had explained how he had devised a system to facilitate that undertaking and was awaiting the approval of the Regent to install it. It consisted of hidden levers, winches, and pulleys that would lower the heavy cascade of fine crystal to a height where it could be more easily cleaned.

In addition to including her in his outings with Regina, the duke had been kind in other ways. When he had presented small gifts to Jane, Dorothea, and Regina, he had also thought to bring something for her. Melissa knew these small favors had been selected with great care as to her preferences. When Regina had mentioned that Melissa was skilled as a seamstress, the duke had presented her with a lovely silver thimble and several papers of pins. There was also a box of brightly colored paper on which she could copy her recipes, a slim volume containing a collection of fables, and a packet of seeds to grow her own kitchen garden of herbs.

They had reached the door to the Drawing Room and Melissa was startled out of her memories by the duke's voice.

"Have many other visitors arrived before me?"

"Yes, your grace. There is quite a crush."

"Tell me who is in attendance, Lissa." The duke reached out to stay her hand as she prepared to open the door. "I shall be better prepared to be charming if I know the identity of the persons I must charm."

Melissa laughed. "I am certain that you will be charming without that knowledge, your grace, but I shall be happy to name them."

As Melissa conveyed the names to the duke, she thought back
to their arrivals. The first to call had been Lord Chadwick, another daily visitor. When Melissa had left him, he was sitting
next to Dorothea on the settee, laughing at some comment she
had made. Melissa found she liked him very well indeed, as he
always had a friendly word for her. And his attentions towards
her stepsister had Melissa's full approval. Lord Chadwick
seemed truly appreciative of Dorothea's charms, and Dorothea
had confided that she found him very personable, indeed. She
seemed relaxed and happy, basking in the light of the viscount's
admiration, and much less fearful of her mother's disapproval.

The next coach to arrive had carried Lady Beckworth and
her cousin, Lady Jennings, who had been accompanied by her
two daughters. Though the young girls would not be formally
presented until the following Season, Melissa had noticed that
they had already caught the attention of two young pinks who
had come in after them. One was the second son of an earl and
the other was in line to inherit his uncle's title. Both had come
to call upon Lady Harrington in the hopes of currying favor
with the duke and Lord Chadwick.

Lady Ashford had also come to pay a call, and she had been
accompanied by her *cicisbeo,* Lord Wheeler. Lord Wheeler was
a large man with a florid countenance that was heightened even
further by the vivid red and yellow patterned waistcoat he wore.
In the guise of a servant, Melissa had been privy to the latest
on-dit about the strange coupling. It was bandied about that
Lord Wheeler was tone deaf, and it was due in whole to this
particular infirmity, that he could tender sincere compliments
regarding the quality of Lady Ashford's musical performances.

When Melissa came to the end of her list, she glanced up at
the duke. "Shall I announce you now, your grace?"

"Just a moment, Lissa." The duke turned to her with a twinkle
in his eye. "Your Drawing Room does not contain a pianoforte
on this day, does it?"

"No, your grace. It most certainly does not."

"You may announce me then." The duke stayed her hand

again, just as Melissa was preparing to pull open the pocket door. "But if Lady Ashford should take it into her mind to sing *acappella,* I should like you to most surreptitiously provide me with two small bits of cloth to stuff into my ears."

They shared a smile and then, at a nod from the duke, Melissa opened the pocket doors that gave access to the Drawing Room and stepped aside for him to precede her. When he had entered, she also stepped into the room and assumed her customary place at the far corner, where she should be available for Jane's instruction.

"I am delighted that you should join us, Duke." Jane smiled and extended her hand in greeting. "We have many callers upon this day."

The duke conveyed her hand to his lips. "You are indeed popular with the *ton,* madame. One can only assume that your reputation as a consummate hostess has engendered this crush. I trust this morning finds you well?"

As the amenities were observed between hostess and guest, Melissa turned to glance at Regina. There was a welcoming smile on her stepsister's face and it was clear that Regina was eagerly awaiting the duke's notice. Melissa quelled a sudden stab of envy and cautioned herself to maintain a pleasant expression. Envy was an emotion that ill-suited her and she would not indulge in it.

"Lissa?"

Melissa turned and observed that the viscount was motioning for her. She hurried to do his bidding and arrived at his side in short order. "Yes, my lord?"

"Miss Dorothea has urgent need of your assistance." The viscount valiantly attempted to hide a smile. "She has had a small misfortune."

"From the manner in which you described it, Charles, I would say that it is a *large* misfortune!"

Melissa turned to her stepsister who was a study in contrasts. The color of embarrassment was bright in Dorothea's cheeks, but her eyes were merry with laughter.

"I fear I have made a goose of myself, Lissa." Dorothea giggled softly. "When I arose to greet Lady Beckworth, I trod upon the hem of my gown and the back of my skirt tore loose from the waist. Lord Chadwick observed my misfortune and bid me to sit back down, but now that I am seated, I find I dare not move from this spot."

Melissa did her best not to laugh. "I shall think of a solution, Miss Dorothea. I would not wish for you to come undone in the presence of everyone here."

"Thank you, Lissa." Dorothea nodded, her lips twitching at the corners. "That would be most unladylike, indeed, and I fear poor Charles should be thoroughly shocked."

"Never, my dearest Dorothea." Lord Chadwick patted her hand. "But I freely admit that I should not care for any other gentlemen to share in the delightful *dishabille* that I alone witnessed."

"You forget yourself, my lord!"

The smile that hovered round the corners of Dorothea's lips belied the sincerity of her reproof and the fond look she bestowed upon the viscount made Melissa smile. Only a blind person would fail to realize that they had developed a *tendre* for each other.

Melissa considered the problem for a moment and then she turned to enlist the viscount's aid. "I shall bring you a cup of tea, my Lord. Wait for my signal and then spill it on Miss Dorothea's gown."

"But it will stain, will it not?" Lord Chadwick appeared anxious. "I should not care to cause the ruin of such a lovely gown."

Melissa nodded. "This is precisely the excuse that we shall tender. The gown will not stain if it is cleaned quickly and this will give us leave to quit the Drawing Room in a rush. I shall escort Miss Dorothea to the door, holding up her gown as I do so. You shall follow her, very closely, preventing any from viewing her back."

"I knew you'd think of something, Lissa." Dorothea looked

greatly relieved. "Let us get on with it quickly before I lose what little courage I possess."

The deed was done according to plan, and all three conspirators burst into laughter as they gained the safety of the hall. When their mirth had subsided, Lord Chadwick returned to the drawing room to proffer their excuses and Melissa and Dorothea hurried up the staircase.

"Do you not think that Charles is perfection?" Dorothea turned to Melissa the moment they had gained the sanctuary of her bedchamber.

"Indeed I do." Melissa replied honestly, choosing another dress for her stepsister to wear. "He is your perfect match, Doro."

While Melissa cleaned the tea from Dorothea's ill-fated gown, Dorothea donned another. A final check to make certain that the buttons were all fastened, and Melissa gasped in shock. "This gown was fitted perfectly at the beginning of the Season, but now it is much too loose. You have lost weight, Doro."

"This is true." Dorothea nodded. "I did not set out to do so, but sweets no longer hold the pleasure for me that they once did. I suspect that I gained flesh only to spite Mama. It was the one aspect of my life that she could not control."

"And you no longer wish to spite her?"

Dorothea laughed gaily. "There is no reason to do so any longer. Soon I shall be rid of Mama and her mean-spirited ways."

"La, Doro!" Melissa began to smile. "Do you mean that—"

"Yes, dear Lissa!" Doro interrupted, throwing her arms around Melissa and hugging her tightly. "Charles has confided that he wishes to offer for me!"

"This is indeed, wonderful news!" Melissa smiled, not at all surprised. "I am most happy for you, Doro. When will this happy occasion occur?"

"I have asked him to wait until the Season has ended and he has agreed."

Melissa was puzzled. "But why, Doro? If he were to declare for you now, any number of people would host parties for the two of you. You would be touted as the first bride of the Season and everyone would compliment you on the splendid match you made."

"That does not signify." Dorothea shook her head. "I should prefer to wait to save my dear sister from embarrassment."

"I fear that I do not understand, Doro. Why should your good fortune cause Gina to be embarrassed?"

"Because she is the eldest and, as such, she is expected to marry before me." Dorothea frowned slightly.

"But I am certain that Gina would wave your concerns aside and wish you happy."

"This is true." Dorothea nodded. "But it is also true that my impending nuptials would place her in a most uncomfortable position. You have seen several of the old tabbies, Lissa. Can you deny that there is not one among them who would regard Gina with pity and regale her with condolences were I to be betrothed first?"

Melissa sighed and shook her head. "You are right, Doro. There are several old tabbies who would relish the prospect."

"Exactly!" Doro nodded. "There is also the matter of the duke. Charles has confided that he is as skittish as a new colt when the mere whisper of an impending alliance is made. It is possible that others may urge him to offer for Gina if it is known that I am to be wed. I should not like to be the cause of frightening him away."

"I appreciate your concerns, Doro." Melissa was thoughtful as they stepped out into the hallway and walked down the staircase. When they were again outside the Drawing Room door, Dorothea turned for one last word.

"I should like it above all things if Gina were to receive an offer before me, but if this does not come to pass, Charles and I have agreed to a second plan. We should like Regina and you to come to live with us. We shall be a family together, three sisters and my dear Charles."

Melissa smiled. "That is very kind of you, Doro."

"If you think me kind, it is to Charles's credit. He believes me to be an Incomparable, Lissa. And because of his high estimation of my character, I find it is not at all difficult to be exactly as he imagines me."

Melissa nodded and glanced around to make certain no one was about. Then she gave Dorothea a loving hug and patted an errant curl into place. "I am proud of you, Doro. And I find that I agree with Lord Chadwick. You are, indeed, an Incomparable."

After Dorothea had re-entered the Drawing Room, Melissa went to fetch more refreshments. When she had placed them on the table, she stood at the side of the room again, listening to the conversation that flowed around her.

"I shall never forget the dinner party your mother held last Season." Lady Jennings claimed the duke's attention. "I swear I have not tasted such exquisite delicacies since. Is that marvelous French chef still in your employ?"

The duke nodded politely. "Yes, Lady Jennings. Henri is still with us."

"It is unfortunate, indeed, that your mother is not in residence at Oakwood House." Lady Ashford sighed. "I had hoped that we might enjoy Henri's talents again, this Season."

"Have you also a preference for French cuisine?" The duke turned to Regina.

"I am not certain." Regina smiled up at him. "It is an impossible query for me to answer, since I have not partaken of it."

The duke looked thoughtful for a moment and then he laughed. "It appears that my mother has whetted everyone's appetite for French cuisine and then conveniently taken herself off to Oakwood Castle. Perhaps it is my duty to host a dinner party."

"There is no need to feel obligated on our account." Jane spoke up quickly. "It would be a difficult undertaking, especially since you are currently without a hostess."

"This is true, but it is also a situation that can be rectified." The duke smiled at Jane. "Will you do me the honor of acting as my hostess for the occasion, Lady Harrington?"

Melissa could tell that Jane was surprised, but she recovered quickly and favored the duke with a brilliant smile. "The honor is entirely mine, Duke."

Speaking glances shot around the room like balls from cannons, and Melissa was sensible of their meaning. The subject concerned the duke's reason for singling out Lady Harrington to be his hostess. Some would claim that he curried her favor because he had formed a *tendre* for Regina. Others might propose that the duke had simply chosen the closest woman at hand and it was sheer coincidence that it had been Lady Harrington. Still others might suspect that the duke did so out of charity, since Lady Harrington had voiced no plans to entertain any social functions, and the *on-dit* was that she was regrettably short of purse. Whatever his true reason, the duke had chosen her stepmother for his hostess, and Melissa sighed as she realized that as Lissa, Lady Harrington's favored servant, she would be responsible for overseeing the preparations to make certain that the duke's dinner party was a success.

Alone in her bedchamber, Melissa wrestled with her problem until the wee hours of the morning. Though she had been loath to address her feelings for the duke, the time had arrived to deal with them. She was in love with the Duke of Oakwood. There could be no other explanation for the way her heart beat faster when she opened the door to his presence, or the manner in which her hands trembled when his hand brushed hers while taking his coat. Her mind was filled with the conversations they had shared. Indeed, she could remember every word. She had memorized all of his gestures, the way he brushed back his hair when he was searching for something to say, the straightening of his shoulders when he prepared to enter a crowded room, and the extra breath he took when he picked up the reins and gave his team the signal to start.

In the past two weeks, Melissa had made a study of his preferences and she felt she knew him as no other. Even Gina, who might very well become his duchess, did not know that he fancied the Greek versions of classical myths over the Roman, enjoyed falling asleep to the sound of the wind soughing through the pines outside his window at Oakwood Castle, and preferred black tea to green. In their brief private meetings, Melissa had learned that he liked a spoonful of gooseberry preserves on a slice of fresh bread, could wiggle his right ear but not his left, and thought bonnets that were decorated with fruit were silly. She knew he liked to rise early to ride through the forest, had once fallen through the ice when he'd attempted to cross a frozen lake, and did not care at all for marzipan. She also knew that he had plagued his poor nanny by putting crickets in her pockets, that he had been fond of climbing up to the parapets when he was a child, and that his sister had extracted all manner of services from him by threatening to divulge that he had used the best china bowl for a receptacle in which to keep his pet worms.

Melissa sighed as she gazed at the little gifts he'd given her, gifts that she cherished as tokens of his friendship. If he offered for Gina, would that precious friendship have to come to an end?

With a shake of her head, Melissa dismissed that dire possibility. If the duke married Gina, he would become a part of her family and their friendship could stand intact. She could visit Gina at Oakwood Castle and enjoy the duke's company as Gina's husband. They could still converse and laugh together, exactly as they did now. There was only one way to put a period to their friendship.

If she should choose to reveal her *tendre* for him, the duke would be obliged to disassociate himself from her company. Her admission would gravely injure Regina and this Melissa vowed she would never do. Their affections must continue as fond sister to fond brother and she would never step beyond that line. Her abiding love for the Duke of Oakwood would be a secret that Melissa would take to her grave.

Ten

"Thank you, my lord." Melissa hopped down from Lord Chadwick's curricle and waved until the viscount was out of sight. He had been out very early, accomplishing an errand, and had come upon her on her way to Oakwood House. It was the morning of the duke's dinner party and Jane had instructed Melissa to spend the day there to make certain that all the preparations were accomplished. Since her stepmother had not seen fit to give Melissa the use of her own equipage or to hire one for the purpose, Melissa had found herself trudging the two-mile distance between their rented house in Belgrave Square and the duke's home.

This was not the first occasion that Melissa had walked this route. Jane had sent her to Oakwood House on almost every day of the past sennight. In truth, Melissa did not mind her frequent presence at the duke's home as his servants were pleasant and on several occasions, she had enjoyed brief visits with the duke, himself. Now, as she traversed the walkway leading up to the front of the house, Melissa mentally reviewed the preparations that had been made. She had written out the invitations from her stepmother's guest list, collected the acceptances, and carried the menu the duke's French Chef had provided to Jane for her approval.

After a survey of the duke's gardens, Melissa had chosen the flowers she wished to arrange for the party and the head gardener had promised to have them cut this morning. She had engaged the orchestra to provide music for dancing after the formal dinner, and made certain that tables of cards had been arranged for the convenience of any gentleman who might prefer the pleasures of whist to those of the Quadrille.

During her very first visit to Oakwood House, Melissa had solicited the good offices of the duke's housekeeper. When the duke had introduced her to the robust woman in black bombazine who had controlled his household for so many years, Melissa had thrown herself on Mrs. Parker's mercy. She had explained that she was merely a country servant in Lady Harrington's employ, and she had expressed great dismay at being ordered to take charge of such an august affair.

To Melissa's surprise, Mrs. Parker had laughed and said that Lissa's reputation had preceded her. It seemed that Lady Beckworth's housekeeper was Mrs. Parker's cousin and she had already heard what a gem Lissa was. Instead of being affronted by Lissa's presence, Mrs. Parker had been delighted to meet the girl who had so taken her cousin's fancy.

The sun had just risen over the housetops when Melissa made to approach the elaborately carved front door. But just as she was about to knock for admittance, she remembered her station and an amused smile spread over her countenance. Lissa should not be granted entrance at that portal. The servants' entrance was in the back. She had best be more cautious or she would surely give her ruse away.

Melissa hurried down the flagstone path that led around the side of the house and entered the servants' door. No sooner had she set foot inside, than a small black and brown bundle came flying at her and jumped up, into her arms.

"Perseus!" Melissa laughed down at the little pup whose tail thumped merrily as he bestowed a series of wet kisses on her face. He was not so little as he had been three weeks ago. Indeed, Perseus was now an armful and it was abundantly apparent that he was receiving tidbits from the kitchens.

"He remembers you, Lissa." Emmy, the youngest of the scullery maids, smiled as she took Perseus from Melissa's arms.

"Perseus has the run of the house and he is even allowed in his grace's bed."

"I would expect no less." Melissa grinned. She had first made Emmy's acquaintance when the duke had taken her to Oakwood House to fetch the brandy that had replaced the ill-fated flask she had broken. At that time, the duke had given Perseus over to Emmy's care and it was most evident that the pup was thriving.

"I am so glad that you are here, Lissa." Emmy put the pup down and he scampered away, his tail wagging in excitement. "Mrs. Parker took ill with the fever last night, but she has refused to take to her bed. She attempted to come down the stairs this morning, this being the day of the party and all, but she was so weak, she could scarcely stand."

Melissa frowned. "Has someone told his grace of her condition?"

"Oh, yes. Mr. Oliver went in to wake his grace immediately."

Melissa nodded. She had met Mr. Oliver, the duke's valet. "And what did his grace do?"

"His grace went to see Mrs. Parker straight away, not even taking the time to dress. He said Mrs. Parker's health was more important to him than observing the proprieties. Once he had seen her, his grace sent Mr. Harley to fetch his personal physician."

"Has Harley returned with the physician?"

"No, Lissa." Emmy shook her head. "But he has been gone for near to an hour and we expect him back at any moment."

Melissa nodded and her estimation of the duke rose even higher. Most employers would have summoned the apothecary or his assistant, but the duke had sent his head footman to bring in his personal physician. "I shall try to make her comfortable while we wait for the physician to arrive. Take me to her, Emmy, and I will see what I can do."

When Melissa entered Mrs. Parker's bedchamber, she found that good woman attempting to dress. One touch of her fevered brow and Melissa ordered her back to bed. She sent Emmy to

We'd Like to Invite You to Subscribe to Zebra's Regency Romance Book Club and Give You a Gift of 4 Free Books as Your Introduction! *(Worth $19.96!)*

If you're a Regency lover, imagine the joy of getting 4 FREE Zebra Regency Romances and then the chance to have these lovely stories delivered to your home each month at the lowest prices available! Well, that's our offer to you and here's how you benefit by becoming a Zebra Home Subscription Service subscriber:

- **4 FREE Introductory Regency Romances are delivered to your doorstep**
- **4 BRAND NEW Regencies are then delivered each month (usually before they're available in bookstores)**
- **Subscribers save almost $4.00 every month**
- **Home delivery is always FREE**
- **You also receive a FREE monthly newsletter, *Zebra/Pinnacle Romance News*** which features author profiles, contests, subscriber benefits, book previews and more
- **No risks or obligations...in other words you can cancel whenever you wish with no questions asked**

Join the thousands of readers who enjoy the savings and convenience offered to Regency Romance subscribers. After your initial introductory shipment, you receive 4 brand-new Zebra Regency Romances each month to examine for 10 days. Then, if you decide to keep the books, you'll pay the preferred subscriber's price of just $4.00 per title. That's only $16.00 for all 4 books and there's never an extra charge for shipping and handling.

It's a no-lose proposition, so return the FREE BOOK CERTIFICATE today!

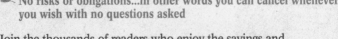

the kitchen for cold compresses and when they had arrived, Melissa and Emmy took turns bathing Mrs. Parker's face.

"Thank you, Lissa." Mrs. Parker struggled to sit up after a few minutes had passed. "I feel much relieved now and I believe I shall be able to dress."

Melissa shook her head and pushed the housekeeper kindly, but firmly back against the pillows. "No, Mrs. Parker. You must rest until the physician arrives."

"The physician?" An expression of dismay crossed Mrs. Parker's countenance. "Am I indeed so ill that I should have need of a physician?"

Melissa reached out to touch her brow again and then she smiled. "I think not, Mrs. Parker. Lady Harrington was afflicted with a similar malady only last winter and she recovered very well indeed."

Emmy looked worried. "Did her ladyship have a physician to attend to her?"

"No." Melissa sighed. "I fear there were none who could traverse the roads at that time of year. Lady Harrington had to make do with my nursing and a mixture of herbs that I steeped for her."

"Tell me the herbs and I will fetch them." Emmy offered eagerly. "If her ladyship recovered her health with them, so shall Mrs. Parker."

Melissa considered it for a moment and then she shook her head. "His grace's physician has already been summoned and his knowledge far exceeds my simple remedy. It would be best to wait upon his arrival."

The words had no sooner left Melissa's mouth, then there was a knock upon the door. Emmy went to answer it, and when she came back she was frowning. "Mr. Harley has returned without the physician. His housekeeper said that he was called out early this morning, and he's not expected back until nightfall."

"Perhaps it is just as well." Mrs. Parker looked greatly relieved. "I must confess that I have a fear of the physician, and I have no need of him now that Lissa is here to attend to me."

Lissa nodded and turned to Emmy. "Bathe Mrs. Parker's brow with the compresses, Emmy, and replace them with fresh when they are warm to your touch. I will gather the herbs I need from the kitchen garden."

With the aid of the head gardener, Melissa located the herbs and barks she needed for her medicinal tea. Once they had been pounded to a pulp and steeped in boiling water, she carried a steaming cup to Mrs. Parker and assisted her while she drank the bitter brew.

"Emmy, dear. Will you please fetch more cold water for those compresses?" Mrs. Parker smiled at the youngest of her scullery maids.

"Yes, ma'am." Emmy bobbed her head. "I'll be back afore the cat can lick her ear, ma'am."

"*Before,* not *afore.* You must always take a caution to speak properly." Mrs. Parker corrected her gently. "And thank you, Emmy, for taking such care with me."

When Emmy had left, Melissa turned to Mrs. Parker. She was certain that the duke's housekeeper had wished for a private word as the compresses were quite cold enough for their purpose. "What is it you wish, Mrs. Parker?"

"It's Henri." Mrs. Parker sighed. "On the day of a dinner party, he regards himself as an artist and his temper is legendary. I fear he will have the whole household at sixes and sevens if I am not there to calm him."

Melissa nodded reassuringly. "I will make certain that does not occur. What is it that you do for him in particular?"

"I regale him with compliments." Mrs. Parker gave a tired smile. "I swear that the particular dish he is preparing would be certain to please even the Prince Regent, himself, and I assure him that no household, however grand, has ever possessed a chef more worthy. I spin Banbury tales of his greatness at every turn and thus prevent Henri from stalking off in a fit of pique."

"Then there is no cause for anxiety, Mrs. Parker." Melissa wrung out the compress and replaced it with a fresh one. "I will appease Henri for you."

"That is good in you, Lissa. My cousin had the right of it. You are a gem."

Mrs. Parker smiled and then her eyes fluttered closed. Melissa sat silently until the housekeeper's breathing was deep and even and then she rose to tiptoe to the door. The herbal potion she had administered would reduce Mrs. Parker's fever and cause her to sleep for most of the day. While she was resting, her body would mend and Lissa was certain that the services of a physician would not be needed. She would instruct Emmy to continue with the compresses until the fever had abated, sit with Mrs. Parker for the remainder of the day to assure that her sleep was undisturbed, and send word to her immediately if there was any change in the housekeeper's condition.

"You say that her fever has gone?" The duke frowned slightly as his gentleman's gentleman finished tying his neck cloth in a perfect waterfall. "How can this be? Harley has reported that he was unable to locate my physician."

"It is Lissa's doing, your grace. The medicinal tea she made for Mrs. Parker has done wonders for her condition."

Robert raised his eyebrows at the smile that spread over his valet's customarily staid countenance. It seemed that Lissa had made another conquest among the members of his staff. "And the preparations are proceeding without Mrs. Parker?"

"Yes, your grace. Lissa has taken charge."

"Then all will be well." Robert answered his valet's smile with one of his own as he was helped into his coat. "I shall remain at home today. Inform me at once if any problems arise and I shall deal with them personally."

"Yes, your grace. If you have no further need of my services, I shall place myself at Lissa's disposal."

"An excellent suggestion. Please convey my appreciation to Lissa and inform her that I am available should she need me."

An amused chuckle escaped Robert's throat as his gentleman's gentleman quit the room. His valet had certainly never offered to assist a member of the household staff before, but he seemed more than eager to do Lissa's bidding. In the past sennight, Lissa had charmed his staff, from the lowest scullery maid to the most elevated retainers who had been in his father's employ. Robert wasn't certain how she had accomplished this feat, but he was extremely grateful that Lady Harrington had seen fit to send her to Oakwood House.

As Robert traversed the hall and opened the door to the chamber he had refurbished for his private sitting room, he wore a broad smile. The knowledge that Lissa was in his home, organizing his servants and overseeing the preparations for the elaborate dinner party that he would host tonight, made him feel content. She was undoubtedly the most capable young woman he had ever had occasion to meet, and though she was a servant, he regarded her as an equal. It was a strange turn of affairs that would be certain to send his mother into the boughs if she caught wind of it. That the young Duke of Oakwood should enjoy such an informal relationship with a mere servant would set tongues wagging in the best of households. Indeed it was scandalous, and the duke's grin widened as he considered dropping a hint of his warm feelings for Lady Harrington's servant. He would not care a whit if his friendship with Lissa became the topic of the latest *on-dit,* but his action could do the dear girl a great disservice. It might also serve to embarrass Regina and that was certainly not his intention. He would be wise to keep his emotions close to his chest and not divulge them to a soul. But how tempting it was to consider making a clean breast of his fascination with Lissa and let the matter end as it would.

Lissa had just finished arranging the last of the flowers when she heard a horrendous crash from the regions of the kitchen.

As she hurried down the hallway to the source of the distur-
bance, there was another crash and then another. Someone was
shouting, the words almost indistinguishable, but Lissa recognized the language. It was French and Lissa remembered Mrs.
Parker's warning. The duke's chef, Henri, was on a rampage
and it was up to her to settle him down.

"La!" Lissa stopped short at the kitchen door, her eyes wid-
ening at the sight that greeted her. The diminutive Frenchman
was brandishing a pot and chasing a poor kitchen maid who
looked about to succumb to an attack of the vapors.

"What is amiss, Monsieur Henri?" Lissa approached him
calmly and took the pot out of his hand.

"These lobsters, they are dead!" Henri kicked at the large
barrel that sat in the center of the kitchen. "This stupid girl,
she leave them outside and the water to cover them, it has
gone!"

Lissa turned to the kitchen maid, who was cowering behind
a wooden counter, and motioned for her to make herself scarce.
Then she walked over to the lobster barrel and peered inside.

"You see?" Henri walked over to join her. "Dead! And how
is it possible that I accomplish the lobster course with no lobsters?"

"Here is a live one." Lissa reached into the barrel and pulled
out one active crustacean. "And I see another near the bottom
of the barrel."

Henri rolled his eyes at the ceiling. "Two lobster will not be
sufficient to serve forty guests and I cannot make them live
again!"

"No indeed, though if anyone could accomplish such a feat,
I am convinced it would be you." Lissa smiled at him. "Your
reputation as a miracle worker precedes you, Monsieur Henri."

"Miracle worker?"

Lissa smiled at the astonished expression on his face. "It is
said that your soufflés are as light as the clouds themselves,
and your confections melt into supreme goodness the instant

they touch the lips. These are rivaled only by the delicious sauces you create to grace tender morsels of meat and fowl."

"Who is it who says these things?" Henri looked pleased, but doubt still lingered on his countenance.

"Why everyone who is anyone!" Lissa smiled. "Every one of Lady Harrington's callers has praised the delicious and unusual feasts you create. At least four ladies have told her ladyship that they intend to fast for an entire sennight so that they may indulge their appetites at your table this evening."

Henri laughed. "Is this so?"

"It is." Lissa leaned closer to impart a confidence. "I have heard tell that the Prince Regent, himself, turned green with envy when he learned that you were in his grace's employ. It is a test of their enduring friendship that he has not attempted to engage you for himself."

Henri looked even more pleased, but then he began to frown again. "But no one will praise me when I fail to serve the lobster."

"You will not fail." Lissa was at her most convincing. Calming Henri was much like appeasing a petulant child, but there was still a problem to be solved. "Let me think for a moment, Henri, and I shall figure a way out of our difficulty."

As Melissa stared down at the lobsters in the barrel, she was put in mind of the wonderful lobster bisque that Elise had prepared for her mother and father. It would not do to suggest a recipe that had been served in a mere baron's household, but perhaps she could spin a Banbury tale that would satisfy the little Frenchman's sense of pride.

"I shall share my secret with you, Henri." Melissa began to speak in French, explaining that she did not wish the kitchen maids to carry tales of what she was about to say. "I had occasion to meet a woman who was once a kitchen maid in King George's employ. When she left the castle, she took with her the instructions for preparing the royal bisque. She confided to me that it had not been prepared for a number of years. The recipe was lost and she was the only one left alive who had the knowledge to make it."

Henri's eyes began to sparkle at the story that Melissa had spun. "This royal bisque you speak of, is it lobster?"

"Yes, and very little lobster is needed to prepare it. I daresay that we shall have ample."

"Fantastique!" Henri's smile was like a shaft of sunlight. "You will give this recipe to me?"

Melissa frowned. "I only wish that I could do so, but I gave my promise never to speak of the ingredients."

"What good is it to have knowledge of a recipe that you cannot say?" Henri threw his hands upward in a helpless gesture.

"I vowed never to *speak* it to another, but I did not promise not to *prepare* it. I shall do so and you shall watch and take careful note of the ingredients. If we proceed in this manner, I will not break my vow."

Henri laughed, and the kitchen maids began to smile. It was a most welcome sound after the screaming and crashing that had taken place only moments earlier.

"I would caution you to dismiss the kitchen maids." Melissa turned to glance at the maids who were observing their every movement. "They may return when the royal bisque is completed."

Henri nodded and turned to the maids. "You may go, all of you. I shall call for you when you are needed."

The maids filed out, casting grateful glances at Melissa. The moment they were alone, Henri turned to Melissa. "I am at your disposal, Lissa."

Melissa bid Henri to help her separate the dead lobsters from the live. When that task had been completed, she proclaimed that there were just enough. Henri, himself, gathered the ingredients for Melissa as she prepared the bisque.

While Melissa stirred the large soup pot, Henri sliced and shredded the ingredients. When it came time to prepare the lobsters, Melissa begged off, admitting to some weakness when it came to plunging live creatures into boiling water, and Henri duly accomplished the deed. The cooked lobster and the fish would not be added until the bisque was served, but Melissa asked Henri to taste the completed broth to tell her if it needed additional seasoning.

"Magnifique!" The diminutive Frenchman took a taste and a blissful smile spread over his face. "The strands of saffron you have added to the broth is exquisite! Thank you, Lissa. You have saved Henri from certain embarrassment!"

"You must vow never to give this recipe to another." Melissa cautioned the chef as she prepared to leave the kitchens.

"I so vow it." Henri nodded solemnly. "I shall take this secret recipe for the royal bisque to my grave."

Melissa left Henri smiling and calling for the kitchen maids. Despite her detour to Henri's domain in the kitchens, she had the preparations well in hand. The china was ready, rubbed to a high gloss that would mirror the guests' certain smiles, and the silver was polished to perfection. The chairs were arranged at the side of the duke's ballroom and the dais for the orchestra had been festooned with flowers.

After a brief meeting with the household staff to make certain that they knew of their duties for the evening, Melissa made a final visit to Mrs. Parker's quarters. She found the housekeeper much improved under Emmy's tender ministrations and smiling at the antics of Perseus, who had gained admittance to the housekeeper's bedchamber. She presented Perseus with a bone that Henri had given her from the kitchens and took her leave, assuring Mrs. Parker that everything for the duke's party was well in hand.

The sun was lowering in the sky when Melissa departed for Belgrave Square. She had just stepped out, through the servants' entrance, when Harley intercepted her.

"I'm to take you in the carriage, Lissa." Harley took her arm. "His grace ordered me to carry you home and wait there to bring you back."

Melissa frowned slightly. "That is most kind of his grace, but I fear I shall be at Belgrave Square for upwards of an hour, assisting her ladyship and her daughters. Are you certain his grace said that you were to wait?"

"I am certain, Lissa." Harley nodded. "When you have finished with your duties, I am to carry you back to Oakwood House. Only when I have delivered you safely, am I to return for Lady Harrington and her daughters."

Melissa frowned. "But Lady Harrington should arrive before me. She is to be his grace's hostess for the evening and I am merely her servant."

"I took the liberty of making mention of that, but his grace was most definite." Harley lowered his voice and leaned closer. "He knows that Lady Harrington did not lift a finger on his behalf and assigned every task to you, instead."

A delighted smile spread over Melissa's countenance. It was obvious that the duke appreciated her efforts and held her in high regard. "Thank you for telling me this, Mr. Harley."

"It was my great pleasure, Lissa." Harley smiled as he helped her into the carriage. "His grace also instructed me to tell you that if he could devise a way to introduce you as his hostess without causing a scandal that would embarrass Lady Harrington's daughters, he would be certain to do so."

Melissa leaned back against the comfortable squabs of the duke's carriage and smiled. Though it was gratifying to think of the comeuppance that Jane would suffer at the hands of the *ton* if the duke introduced her servant, Lissa, as his hostess, Melissa did not actively wish for that event to occur. It would cause a rift in their family that could never be mended and sides would have to be taken to the distress of them all. It was, however, the stuff that happy dreams were made of and the smile remained on Melissa's face all the way to Belgrave Square.

Eleven

"You look lovely, Gina." Melissa stood back to survey her handiwork with a proud smile. Regina was wearing a new gown made of burgundy silk that set off her pale complexion to advantage. The gown had a wide skirt that would swirl prettily when Regina danced and puffed sleeves that disguised her thin arms. The delicate Belgian lace that overlaid the bodice made her figure appear much fuller, and the back was cut low to show her smooth, lightly powdered skin. The skirt was draped in the front and fastened higher with lace rosettes on both sides, allowing an enticing glimpse of her dainty lace underskirt.

Regina smiled as she glanced in the mirror. "I believe this coiffure suits me, Lissa."

"Yes, it is perfection." Lissa reached out to fluff the curls that crowned Regina's head. "This style makes you appear taller."

Regina laughed. "That is all to the good. The duke is tall and I am so short of stature. When we stand up together, our disparity in height brings a smile to everyone's countenance."

"I am sorry, Gina, but I cannot arrange your hair to a sufficient height to correct that contrariety." Melissa laughed. "It would be such a high and mighty tower, it would surely topple before the dance was finished and pull you over with it."

Regina laughed for a moment and then she took on a serious mien. "I fear that stature is not the only disparity in my relationship with the duke. We are hopelessly ill-suited, Lissa."

"In which way?" Melissa sat down on the side of Regina's bed and prepared to listen.

"He is forever introducing subjects that are beyond the scope of my knowledge. Mama has told me to smile and listen as he talks, pretending to agree with everything he says, but I am certain he will soon discover my ignorance and hold me in less regard."

Melissa was puzzled. "What subjects are those, Gina?"

"Mythology, for one. He is highly enamored of it. I have managed to turn the conversation quite neatly several times in the past, but yet he urges me to tell him the tales of the gods and goddesses."

"That is most strange." Melissa frowned slightly. "But perhaps he just wishes to pique your interest and further your knowledge."

Regina nodded. "No doubt you have the right of it, Lissa. Perhaps I should learn these tales for him since it seems to interest him so highly. Could you impart them to me, Lissa? I know that you studied them with your father."

"I shall be happy to do so. Listen carefully and I shall tell you the story of Apollo, the son of the Greek god Zeus, who drove the chariot of the sun across the skies."

Melissa told the tale while Regina listened, a rapt expression on her face. When it was finished, Regina smiled. "I shall do my utmost to remember all that you have told me and perhaps that will satisfy the duke."

"I am certain it will." Melissa nodded. "I shall tell you a tale every evening and soon you will know the old stories well."

Regina appeared much relieved. "Thank you, Lissa. There is but one further thing I must learn. Do you know of a woman named Diana? The duke has referred to me by that name on several occasions and I am at a loss to know whether it is a compliment or a criticism."

"Diana?" Melissa turned away and busied herself arranging the brushes and curl papers so that Regina should not see the sudden color that flooded her countenance. Diana was the name that the duke had called her when he'd danced with her on Lady Beckworth's balcony. "It is indeed a compliment, Gina. Diana was a goddess in Roman mythology. She was known as the huntress and is said to have been very powerful, formidable, and utterly fearless."

Regina laughed. "I fear the duke is in grievous error to make such a comparison. I am not in the least part fearless as well you know. The very sight of a mouse scampering across the floor causes me to stand on a chair."

"Perhaps he does not mean that you are fearless in precisely that way." Melissa searched her mind for a way to explain the duke's reference without giving a hint as to the clandestine moments that they had shared. "His intention may have been to commend you on your dealings with your mother."

"Mama?" Regina looked completely mystified. "Whatever do you mean, Lissa?"

"Do you recall the first time that the duke came to call? Your mother made a disparaging remark about the flowers in the sitting room and you openly admitted that you had arranged them. That act took a good bit of courage, Gina."

Regina burst into a delighted peal of laughter. "The expression on Mama's countenance was worth every word of the scolding she delivered to me later. I have never seen anyone blush so rapidly or so colorfully. Mama was most discomfited."

"I recall it well." Melissa smiled. "That same day, you told the duke that your feelings for me were more deserving of a sister than a servant."

Regina nodded. "And I spoke the truth, Lissa. Though we are not related by blood, you are as much my sister as Doro is. This deception Mother forces us to perpetuate serves us ill. Each letter I write to the Reverend Watson, describing our life in London, must be carefully worded so as not to let our acquaintances know what we are truly about. Though I have not asked that kind gentleman's advice, I am certain he would tell me that it is a sin to deceive others merely to make us seem more than we are."

"No doubt you are entirely correct."

Regina looked thoughtful. "What would be the consequence, Lissa, if I made a clean breast of it to the duke and begged his forgiveness?"

"Heaven forfend!" Melissa's heart beat rapidly in alarm. "Our ruse has gone too far to be set aright by mere words. If you should confess all to the duke, the Harrington name would surely suffer. We should earn the reputation of liars and braggarts and thus lose the good will that my father spent his lifetime fostering."

Regina sighed, acknowledging the truth of Melissa's statement. "Will there ever be a way to set it aright, Lissa?"

"I am certain there will be." Melissa forced a smile that she did not feel. "We will think on it and do our best to devise a solution at the conclusion of the Season. In the meantime, it would serve us well to continue as we have been and not breathe word of our duplicity to anyone."

Robert smiled as he gazed around his table. The guests all appeared to be enjoying themselves immensely. His hostess, Lady Harrington, was seated at the opposite end of the long table, accepting the compliments from the guests as her due. He found her airs nettlesome, but Robert was grateful that they were separated by the widest margin possible, alleviating the necessity for him to make polite converse with her.

"To look at Mama, one might think she accomplished all this herself."

A gentle voice spoke very close to his ear and the duke turned to smile at Regina, who was seated in a place of honor at his side. "Precisely what I was thinking! Are you a mind-reader as well as a beauty?"

"A beauty?" Regina laughed. "Far from it, I fear. If I present a pleasing appearance on this evening, it is entirely to Lissa's credit. I am only sorry that she could not take my place and enjoy this lovely dinner that she toiled so long to effect."

The duke nodded. "My sentiments exactly, though I should not wish to lose your company. If Lissa were allowed to attend, where should you choose to seat her?"

"At my mother's place, as it is Lissa who is truly your hostess."

"Excellent!" The duke gave her a warm smile as he gestured toward a servant who had arrived at her elbow, bearing a silver platter heaped high with the next offering. "Would you care to partake of Henri's delicious *escargo?* "

Regina was about to nod her assent when she remembered Melissa's discussion of the menu with her mother. *"Escargot* are snails, are they not?"

"Yes, with butter and garlic. They are quite delicious and I recommend them highly."

Regina shuddered slightly. The concept of eating a creature that had crawled its way up the garden wall, leaving behind a glistening trail of slime, was repugnant in the extreme. "I think not, thank you just the same. I shall content myself quite nicely with the aspic."

The duke shook his head. "The aspic is quite ordinary. You will forfeit one of Henri's best achievements if you do not sample the *escargot.* Have you never tasted them before?"

"No, never. We did not have such delicacies in the country."

"Then you must try them now." The duke smiled, a teasing glint in his eyes. "Unless, of course, you are less adventuresome than I had assumed."

The duke's tone was teasing, but Regina sensed that he was testing her. The goddess Diana would not have been put off so easily by the mere thought of eating a garden grub. The famed huntress might indeed have cracked one open and popped it into her mouth while the creature still wiggled with life!

"If it pleases you, Duke, I will taste one gladly." Regina smiled up at him bravely. "But I fear you must instruct me. I have not the least notion of how to get it out of its shell."

"Allow me, my dear." The duke was smiling as he drew the

snail from its shell with a practiced motion and then held it out to her.

Regina took a deep breath and popped it into her mouth before she could consider which garden it had last inhabited. She chewed, swallowed, and then she laughed. "It is precisely as Lissa told me, merely an excuse for a delightful excess of butter and garlic with no taste of its own to speak of."

"Lissa said that?" The duke laughed long and hard. "She did not make that statement in Henri's presence, did she?"

"I fear that she did, but she confided that Henri also laughed, especially when she told him that he could save a fortune on your accounts by cleaning the shells and using a bit of tough meat with which to stuff them."

The duke laughed again. "I must watch Henri carefully, or he will do exactly that. Lissa is correct. There would be few who would be the wiser."

When the next course was served, the duke turned to Aunt Sarah, who was seated on his left, with real regret. Regina was a delightful dinner companion and he had enjoyed their repartee. He had not meant to coerce her to eat the snail, but she had met his challenge well and had made him laugh in the bargain. It was apparent that she was beginning to relax around him and no longer felt so subjugated by his title and station.

"Do not you agree?"

Aunt Sarah was gazing at him expectantly, and the duke nodded quickly. "Indeed I do, Aunt Sarah."

This seemed to satisfy her and when she went on to describe an exhibit at the Royal Academy that she had attended last Season, the duke's mind returned to his assessment of Regina. His feelings for her had grown during the past few weeks, but not precisely in the way that he had hoped. He found he regarded Regina as a friend, one with whom he would be content to share many happy hours. He enjoyed her wit, found her most personable, and sought out her company to the exclusion of all others. His mother and sister might claim that these attributes were sufficient to make a successful marriage, but Robert was not so certain. He had wished to develop a true *tendre* for Regina, to enjoy once again the emotions he'd harbored when they'd first met on Aunt Sarah's darkened balcony. Until that happened, he would hold his tongue in check and refuse to utter the words which Lady Harrington wished so desperately to hear.

Lissa smiled as the ladies retired and the gentlemen prepared to enjoy their cigars and port. Her work was finished and she was free to return to Belgrave Square. She would wait until the dancing had commenced, take one last tour of the premises to make certain that nothing had been neglected, and then she would take her leave.

Henri was seated in the kitchen, his face flushed with success. The duke, himself, had entered the kitchens to compliment his French chef. When Henri saw Lissa, he jumped from his chair and kissed her soundly on both cheeks.

"Mon enfant!" Henri gazed at her fondly. "It is because of you that his grace entered my kitchens!"

Melissa was surprised. "But why is that, Henri?"

"He came to tell me that the royal bisque was a grand success and to warn me of the ladies who would attempt to steal my recipe."

Melissa nodded. "And you assured him that no one save you knew how to make it?"

"Precisely! His grace wagered that it would be the talk of the *ton* on the morrow and that many others would try to lure me away from his kitchens."

Melissa frowned slightly. "But you would not leave his grace, would you, Henri?"

"Never!" Henri shook his head dramatically. "When I assured his grace that my loyalties were solely his, he made me the gift of a generous gratuity for what he termed a most exquisite feast."

Melissa nodded, hiding a grin. "I am most happy to hear that, Henri."

"I am preparing a hamper for you." Smiles wreathed Henri's face as he regarded Melissa. "I have located my recipe for a chocolate confection that you will be certain to enjoy and I shall have packed a sample of all that was served tonight. Why do you not go out to the gardens and breathe the cool air for a few moments? It will be finished when you return."

"Thank you, Henri. I shall do that."

Melissa was smiling as she left the kitchens and slipped out into the gardens. There was no danger of meeting any of the guests. The ladies were still in the withdrawing room and the gentlemen were conversing over cigars and snifters of brandy or port.

The garden was peaceful and lovely. Melissa found a marble bench by a huge tree whose low-hanging branches screened her from view. She seated herself on the cool smooth surface and breathed in the night air gratefully. She had not taken a moment to rest this entire day and she was indeed weary.

Melissa sat, deep in thought for long moments, staring up at the brilliant stars overhead. The moon was a thin slice of silver on the horizon and the air was perfumed with the scent of sweet flowers in bloom. The night and the aspect were so romantic, Melissa could not keep her thoughts from turning to the duke and the dance they had shared on Lady Beckworth's balcony. Oh, how she wished that she could feel his strong arms around her once more as their feet moved in rhythm to the lovely strains of the waltz!

As if in answer to her unspoken desire, the orchestra began to play. The French doors of the ballroom were open to the warm night air, and the music wafted out, carried by the gentle night breeze, to surround Melissa's bench with its rich melody. It was the opening dance and the duke would partner his hostess. Melissa could imagine her stepmother sweeping across the length of the ballroom in the duke's arms, smiling and nodding at the guests as she graciously accepted their compliments for the evening's successful entertainment.

Melissa was not certain how long she sat there, listening to the music by the light of the glittering stars. The second dance, in which the duke would partner Regina, started and ended, and then the third. Melissa was aware that it was long past time for her to take her leave. The hamper that Henri had prepared for her would be filled by now, and Mary would be awaiting her company at the house on Belgrave Square.

Still Melissa sat on, the gentle night breezes drifting through her hair and easing her exhaustion away. She was completely alone, far from the eyes of the duke's staff and his guests, and there was no one to observe her as she shed her servant's role and dreamed of taking her rightful place in society. As the daughter of a nobleman, she would have been an invited guest at the duke's table, laughing and conversing with the guests while she freely sampled Henri's culinary delights. Perhaps she might even have been seated at the duke's side, privy to his smiles and private converse as Regina had been. And perhaps, just perhaps, he would have chosen to court her, instead of Regina.

Melissa wiped her tears away with the back of her hand and attempted to clear her mind of traitorous thoughts. Regina was entirely deserving of the duke's attentions and to deny it would be unworthy of her. She was truly happy for her stepsister's fortune and it would serve her well to put her jealous feelings aside and accept whatever the fates decreed with good grace.

They were playing a waltz! A smile turned up the corners of Melissa's lips and she rose to her feet. The lovely strains of music served to soothe her and carry her bleak thoughts away. She swayed gently to and fro and then her feet began to move on the lush green grass. She would dance this waltz with the memory of the duke's dear features in her mind and then she would vanquish his image from her heart. It was as her father had always told her; there was no cause to turn into a watering pot over a situation that she could not change.

The duke slipped away through the French doors and gave a sigh of relief. He had completed his dance with Lady Harrington, though it had not been pleasant. The widow was a superb dancer, as light as a feather in his arms, but he had found himself bristling with outrage each time one of his guests had paid her a compliment on the evening's arrangements. The second dance with Regina had been most pleasant as had the third, with her sister, Dorothea. It seemed a miracle that Lady Harrington had given birth to two daughters, both who differed in such a pleasant manner from their mother. During the fourth dance, he had stood up with Aunt Sarah who had done her utmost to persuade him that her chef was in dire need of the recipe for Henri's lobster bisque. Then Robert had sought out Regina again, intending to ask her if she would care to step out on the balcony with him for a bit of fresh air.

But Regina had not been in attendance. After a word with Dorothea, Robert had learned that she had exited the ballroom shortly after a vigorous dance with Lord Ulmann who was known far and wide as a clumsy partner who had ruined more pairs of satin slippers than the London rains. No doubt Regina had retired to enlist the aid of one of the maids to repair some damage Lord Ulmann had caused to her *ensemble*.

The balcony was deserted and Robert leaned against the rail, remembering his first dance with Regina. In all his dealings with her since, she had not engaged his heart as she had done on that fateful night. He found himself wishing that she would see him standing here and come to his side, transforming herself into the sprite that he had once held in his arms.

The dance ended and Robert sighed again. Perhaps it had been the magic of the night or the sense of freedom that Regina had felt, dancing in the darkness with an unknown partner. If only he could re-create that moment, he would be the happiest of men!

The deserted garden beckoned and Robert made his way down the path. Duty dictated his presence in the ballroom, but he would not be missed in the crush of guests if he tarried a bit longer in the soft night air. Perhaps he would sit on his favorite bench for a moment and gather his jumbled thoughts.

If the fates were with him on this lovely evening, his mind would clear and he would reach a decision regarding his future.

As Robert approached the marble bench, he saw a flicker of movement in the distance. A young lady was dancing on the grass, moving gracefully to the strains of a waltz. Robert's breath caught in his throat and he made not a sound as he moved closer. Could such magic occur twice in a single lifetime? Could the dancer be his Diana?

The darkness was deep, under the trees, as Robert bowed and offered his arm. There was a moment of perfect stillness, when time seemed to cease its forward march, and then she accepted his offer.

Robert could not see her face as they danced, but the feel of her in his arms was seductively familiar. It was his Diana and his heart beat fast as he held her much closer than propriety allowed.

She made no protest, melting against him as their feet moved to the music. It was magic and Robert's smile grew to consume his whole being as he held the woman he loved in his arms.

Melissa's happiness knew no bounds as they danced across the thick carpet of grass. It was the duke and she was in his arms once again! No thought crossed her mind, no care pierced her heart as they moved in a perfect rhythm. The moment was magical and she wished with all her heart that it could last forever.

But the music ended and with it came the unwelcome return of reality. She was in the arms of Regina's intended. Oh, he had not yet declared for her stepsister, but her action was improper nonetheless. Melissa made to withdraw but his arms tightened around her.

"My dear, Regina." The duke's voice was low and filled with tender feeling. "I've found you again, my darling Diana, just like that first night on Lady Beckworth's balcony. I have loved you since the moment I held you in my arms."

Melissa's mind whirled in shocked circles. The duke thought she was Regina! When he next saw her stepsister he would be certain to mention the two dances they had shared in the darkness! Regina, the soul of honesty, would deny that they had ever danced in such a manner and the duke would come to realize that Regina was not the woman that he had held in his arms. His sense of honor would demand that he find this mystery woman and he would search for her, leaving Regina heartbroken!

Suddenly a solution occurred to Melissa and she breathed a sigh of relief. All would be saved if she could keep the duke from mentioning these magic moments to Regina.

"Diana, my goddess, I must be certain. Do you love me as well?"

Melissa blinked back tears of sadness and reached up to touch the duke's face. "Yes, I love you. I love you more than you will ever know."

The duke bent his head and as his lips touched hers, Melissa sighed in blissful surrender. How she wished that she could reveal herself, but that was not to be. She would not be the cause of tragedy for her beloved stepsister. The duke must continue to think that she was Regina. It was best for all concerned.

All the longing that filled her soul, all the pathos at the thought of relinquishing the only man she had ever loved, was contained in this single kiss. Melissa gave the duke her heart, knowing full well that it would be broken beyond any mending.

The duke's arms tightened around her and their kiss deepened. It was as if he could sense that all her hopes and dreams, her solemn vow that she would belong to no other, were his for the taking.

Melissa sighed, her breath warm against the duke's lips. She was nearly undone in this magical moment as they clung together in a circle of love. This was the beginning and the end of Melissa's joy and she held fast to the duke as if he were a lifeline tossed to a sailor in a troubled sea.

The stars whirled above them, the wind caressed them, the

very leaves on the trees whispered endearments. Melissa's resolve threatened to fade as the kiss consumed her and she trembled and sighed in her love's arms. But Melissa's concern for her stepsister was strong and at last she ended the kiss. She pulled the duke close, for the last time, and whispered in his ear. "This must be our secret moment. You must give me your promise never to speak of it again, even when we are alone."

"But what purpose would this serve?" The duke's voice was trembling slightly. "My dear Diana, I do not understand."

Melissa choked back a sob. This was indeed, the most difficult moment of her life! "You must give me your vow or . . . or I shall never see you again."

"Regina, my love, I will promise as you ask, if it means this much to you. But please tell me why, my darling."

"I cannot." Melissa's eyes were swimming with tears as she whispered her answer. "Perhaps someday, when we are old and gray, but I beg of you never to mention it again."

The duke nodded, giving his promise, and Melissa reached up to touch his cheek with her lips. Then slipped from his arms and fled through the garden on feet that did not feel the stab of sharp stones. She ran until she reached the safety of the servants' entrance and then she took a moment to dry her eyes. When she felt that she was fully composed, she forced a smile and went to pick up the hamper that Henri had packed for her.

The ride through the deserted streets was an agony as she dared not give way to her tears. She bid Harley a pleasant evening and climbed the steps to the town house with legs that trembled with exhaustion. Mary was waiting, as she had expected, and Melissa gave her free reign to explore the hamper and partake of the delights within. Pleading exhaustion, she climbed the stairs and sought the privacy of her bedchamber.

It was not until after she had washed her face and changed to her night rail that Melissa released a shuddering sigh. Now that she was safely ensconced in her own bedchamber, she could allow herself to give way to the full measure of her emotions.

The light from the candle on her bedside table was soft and soothing, but Melissa took no comfort from the cheerful little light. She extinguished it with a single breath and crawled under the covers to seek the comfort of a good cry. But when the chamber was as dark as a moonless night, Melissa found that she could not indulge in the time-honored release of tears. Her eyes were dry as she stared up at the darkness and vainly attempted to banish the duke's memory from her mind. Melissa had heard said that if one experienced immense grief, tears would dry in the searing pain and could not fall from one's eyes. Reluctantly, she came to the conclusion that this must be true. The pain that consumed her at the loss of her love had burned her tears away. She was certain that she had made the right decision to assure her stepsister's happy future, but the price she had paid was very dear, indeed!

The duke was in great confusion as he rejoined the crush in the ballroom. Though he had considered it long and hard, he still did not glean the reason for Regina's strange request. He had given his promise and as a gentleman, he was required to honor it. This he would do, but the mystery of why she had asked for his vow intrigued him greatly.

Robert located the lady in question in short order. She was seated next to her sister and Lord Chadwick and he approached the small party with some difficulty as he was waylaid by several of his guests who requested a word with him. Once he had observed a few moments of polite converse with each, he arrived at Regina's side.

"I compliment you on your appearance." The duke favored her with a smile that was slightly risqué. "The exertions of this evening do not seem to have affected you adversely."

Regina returned his greeting with a calm and peaceful countenance. "You would not say as much, Duke, if you had observed my dance with Lord Ulmann. I fear I was quite out of breath and immensely grateful when the music ended."

The duke observed her closely, but no heightening of color stained her cheeks. As her gaze met his, there was no hint of the passion that they had shared only moments before.

"Shall we take a turn through the gardens, my dear?" The duke's eyes glinted dangerously as he extended his arm.

"That would be most enjoyable." Regina smiled and rose to her feet. "But I fear that we must observe the proprieties and first avail ourselves of a chaperone."

The duke stifled the urge to throw back his head and laugh. He was most impressed with Regina. She was the pattern card of the proper young lady when they were in company and a passionate woman when they were alone. It was a combination he found utterly charming and he smiled as he turned to ask her sister and the viscount if they would accompany them.

Robert was not unaware of the picture they presented as the two couples crossed the room at a sedate pace and entered the gardens. Several of the old tabbies had been smiling behind their fans and *on-dits* would spread through the *ton* on the morrow. The young Duke of Oakwood had never been known to take leave of a party to stroll through the gardens with a young lady before. The *tendre* that all would assume he had formed for Regina would be the topic of conversation in dozens of drawing rooms, and the gentlemen at White's would be laying down pounds for pence that he would declare for her before the Season was concluded.

"Are you quite all right, Duke?"

Robert turned to find Regina gazing up at him and he became aware of the bemused smile that had spread across his face. "I am most content, my dear. It is a lovely night, is it not?"

"It is lovely, indeed." Regina smiled happily. "Your gardens are exquisite. I could not imagine a more beautiful setting. I should like it above all things if you would take us to your favorite spot."

Robert grinned as he led them toward the marble bench and

the rolling green lawn where he had shared a kiss with his goddess Diana. What a little minx Regina was! If he had not come to know her so very well, he would swear that she had never set foot in this particular section of his gardens before!

It was when they were seated on the marble bench that Robert came to a decision. He would ask for Regina's hand in marriage. She was perfection itself, and he found himself most eager to make her his duchess.

But how should such a proposal take place? Robert suspected that a simple declaration would not satisfy. Regina had made her tender feelings known to him in a most courageous way. She had slipped into his gardens most improperly unescorted, and invited him to waltz with her in the darkness. She had initiated their kiss and enjoyed it most passionately, declaring her love for him. This highly regarded and seemingly decorous young lady had flouted convention and risked censure from every member of the *ton*. It had been a daring ploy for one of so gentle a heart and it was only after she had elicited his promise never to speak of their interlude, that her modesty had returned.

Robert glanced at Regina, who was engaged in conversation with her sister and Chadwick, and sighed. It was clear that he must tender his proposal in a like manner, one that would captivate her sense of intrigue and romance. Perhaps it would aid him if he knew more of her preferences. He waited until there was a break in the conversation and then he turned to Regina.

"What is the one entertainment that you would like most to enjoy this Season? I wish to know the type of affair that would intrigue you the greatest."

Regina considered it for a moment and then she smiled up at him. "I should very much like to attend a costume ball. Mama has told me of the splendid costumes and the grand unmasking at which prizes are awarded for the most beautiful and unusual attire."

Robert smiled back, but his mind was busy. A costume ball

would be the perfect setting to tender his proposal. "Then you have never attended such a ball before?"

"No, and I do hope that one will be held this Season, and that I shall receive an invitation to attend."

"What a fortuitous coincidence!" The duke's eyes crinkled with mirth. "Just moments ago, I decided to host a costume ball."

"Oh, how wonderful!" Regina clapped her hands together like a schoolgirl. "I do hope that you shall invite me to attend."

"Gina!" Dorothea chided her gently.

"Please accept my apologies, Duke." Regina's voice was contrite. "It is just that I was so excited at the prospect of attending my first costume ball that I forgot myself."

The duke laughed and patted her arm. "There is no need for apology, my dear girl, for I was about to ask if you would be my honored guest."

"Oh, yes!" Regina's voice was high and breathless. "I should be delighted!"

Robert smiled as they strolled back to the ballroom. His grand costume ball would be the pinnacle of the Season with hundreds of guests in their costumed finery and a buffet that would tempt even the most discriminating of palates. They would dance to the strains of the finest orchestra and enjoy excellent wines and spirits. Then, at the time of the unmasking, he would make his declaration for Regina in full hearing of all his guests. Such a spectacle was bound to please her and the *ton* would speak of his unique proposal for years to come.

"Are you intending a large affair?" Lord Chadwick inquired politely.

"Excessively large." Robert smiled. "I plan to invite every member of the *ton* who is in residence for the Season."

"It will be such a grand crush!" Dorothea's voice was merry. "What think you, Gina? Shall I be an historical figure or a simple shepherdess?"

While the two ladies discussed costumes with Lord Chadwick, Robert chuckled softly in amusement. The moment the news of his proposed ball was spread among the members of the *ton,* the odds would change at White's. If he knew of a deserving, but destitute, lad, he would send him there with a purse tonight to make his fortune.

Twelve

Melissa nodded as she sampled the lemon confection that Henri had made. "This is delicious, Henri. You must not hesitate to serve it at his grace's ball."

"If it pleases you so, why are you not smiling, *mon enfant?*" Henri's gaze was anxious. "You have not smiled once in the time that you have been here. Are you feeling not quite the thing?"

Melissa frowned. "It is nothing of importance, Henri. I am a bit tired, that is all. The fact that I have failed to smile truly does not signify."

"Perhaps it is the fault of *l'amour,* eh?" Henri leaned over to peer at her closely. "When one has formed a *tendre* for another and the other does not return this affection, one often fails to smile."

A heated blush rose to Melissa's cheeks and she shook her head quickly. "Oh, no, Henri. That is not at all the case! I have not formed a *tendre* for anyone."

"I am grateful to hear you say that, for there is no one who is worthy of my Lissa." Henri winked at her. "If you doubt my words, you must ask Harley, or Emmy, or Mr. Oliver, or even Mrs. Parker. We all are in complete agreement. Not even His Majesty, himself, would be a suitable match for our Lissa!"

Melissa laughed at Henri's words. The little chef was doing his utmost to coax her out of her brown study, plying her with delicious tidbits from the kitchens and complimenting her to the point of absurdity. She must shake herself from the doldrums and present a cheerful demeanor for those in the duke's employ.

On the pretext of perusing the flower gardens to learn which varieties would bloom in time for the duke's costume ball, Melissa made a hasty exit from Henri's domain. There, in the lovely gardens, she could be safe from prying eyes until she had managed to compose herself. Melissa sank down on a bench near the roses and sighed as she drank in the sweet scent of their perfume. In less than a sennight, the duke's costume ball would be a *fait accompli* and Regina would be his betrothed.

Melissa thought back to the day following the duke's dinner party when Jane had summoned her for a private audience. Every word that her stepmother had spoken had added to Melissa's distress.

It was the morning following the duke's dinner party and Melissa had been summoned to Jane's private sitting room. It was the first that Melissa had heard of the costume ball and her eyes were wide as Jane described it.

"It is to be the grandest event of the Season and I am to be his hostess again." Jane's eyes sparkled with excitement. "It will be held in two week's time so we must begin the preparations immediately."

Melissa nodded, but she barely managed to stifle a groan of distress. The prospect of another grand affair following so closely on the heels of the dinner party that Melissa had worked so arduously to arrange was daunting. Perhaps it would not be so difficult if her stepmother were willing to help, but Melissa was certain Jane would rely solely on her servant, Lissa, and not inconvenience herself in the slightest.

"It is to be a costume ball unlike any the *ton* has ever seen before." Jane preened in front of the mirror, not unlike a peacock admiring his own plumage. "I am convinced that the Duke of Oakwood intends to declare for Regina before the entire assembly."

Melissa forced a smile, arranging her countenance in the manner that Jane expected. "That would be a wonderful occurrence, indeed, but what is it that makes you so certain?"

"He has asked Regina to be his honored guest." Jane seated herself gracefully on the settee, smoothing her skirts around her. "The duke has hinted to me of a magnificent surprise that is to take place on that evening. What else could it be?"

Melissa fought to keep the pleasant expression on her face, as if the prospect of the duke declaring for Regina did not cause her heart to break even further. "I daresay you are correct. I can imagine no other surprise that would be as magnificent."

"Regina must be dressed to perfection for the event." Jane lowered her voice, as if she were imparting a delicious secret. "I have secured an appointment with Madame Beauchamp and that good woman has agreed to fashion a spectacular *ensemble*. We shall consult with her on the morrow."

Melissa nodded, trying not to betray her true emotions. While she was happy for her dear stepsister, a wave of longing for the man she had lost made her cast down her eyes lest her stepmother catch a hint of the sadness that consumed her.

"This is to be the grandest ball the *ton* has ever seen." Jane's excitement was evident in her heightened color and the way she clasped her hands. "Everyone who is come to London for the Season will receive an invitation."

"Everyone?" Melissa felt a small glimmer of hope pierce the gray fog of depression that had settled around her like a heavy cloak.

"Everyone." Jane nodded emphatically. "All will be invited from the lowliest *debutante* to the Prince Regent, himself!"

"Am I to be invited then?" Melissa hardly dared to speak the words. How wondrous it would be to dress in costume and mingle with the others in the duke's ballroom!

"You?" Jane gave a mirthless laugh. "Of course not, you

silly chit! All who know you regard you as my servant and servants do not attend *ton* parties."

"But if I were to dress in costume, no one should discern my true identity. Surely you know that I should never betray you and I shall promise to take my leave long before the unmasking. Please say that you will give me your leave to attend!"

"No, I forbid it." Jane shook her head, putting an end to the matter. "It would be foolish to take such a risk merely to afford you a few stolen moments of pleasure."

Melissa glanced up into the beautiful but unyielding face of her stepmother. Seeing no charity in Jane's countenance, she quickly dropped her eyes again.

"It is not as if I am depriving you to the slightest degree." Jane pursed her lips in displeasure, obviously out of sorts with the direction that her interview with Melissa had taken. "You will be in attendance as part of the staff. I shall even let you stay until the duke declares for Regina so that you may witness their happiness. I am certain that you will have ample opportunity to view the festivities from a secluded corner and to enjoy it thusly."

Melissa was shocked into complete silence. Viewing the ball from the corner of a darkened balcony, or peeking in through a partially closed door, could in no way be compared to attending as an invited guest. She wished to rebel, to remind her stepmother that she was not a servant, but it would be wise to wait until she had carefully considered her options. She clamped her lips together tightly, took the list of tasks to be accomplished for the day, and left her stepmother's sitting room without a further word.

In the end, Melissa had not protested. There was nothing to gain and much to lose. Her very livelihood depended on Jane's charity for she had no money of her own. If Jane were to turn her out from Harrington Manor in a fit of pique, she could expect no one to come to her rescue. Though Dorothea had generously invited her to join her family once she was wed, and Melissa had no doubt that Regina would offer the same should she marry the duke, Melissa did not choose to be a burden to either of her stepsisters. She must seek another way out of her difficulties.

"Lissa?"

A cheery voice startled Melissa out of her thoughts and she smiled as Emmy ran toward her down the garden path, Perseus at her heels. In light of the excellent care that Emmy had given Mrs. Parker when she was ill, the housekeeper had relieved her of her scullery duties and promoted her to the position of under house maid. "Hello, Emmy. Has Henri sent you here to chase away my gloom?"

"No." Emmy looked concerned. "I did not know that you were in a taking, Lissa, else I would not have disturbed you."

Melissa smiled. "It does not matter in the slightest, Emmy, as I am no longer blue-deviled. One glimpse of your smile and I find myself quite cheerful once again."

"I have come to tell you a secret, Lissa." Emmy threw a stick for Perseus to chase and flopped down on the bench beside Melissa. "I have discovered what his grace is to wear!"

Melissa turned to look at Emmy. The girl's eyes were shining with excitement. "And what is that, Emmy?"

"He is to be King Arthur!"

"Such a costume would be perfect for his grace." Melissa nodded quickly, envisioning the duke in elaborate medieval garb. "However did you learn this, Emmy?"

A rush of color stained Emmy's cheeks and she twisted her hands nervously. "I did not mean to overhear, but I was just outside the door when his grace consulted with Mr. Oliver. His grace has received a summons from his mother and he must journey to Oakwood Castle. He has entrusted Mr. Oliver with the task of obtaining his costume while he is away."

"How long will his grace be gone?" Melissa frowned slightly. It would be unfortunate, indeed, if the duke were not able to return in time for the ball.

"I am not certain, but he assured Mr. Oliver that he will return on or before the day of the ball. Mr. Oliver is to have all in readiness for him."

Melissa breathed a sigh of relief. The duke was a man of his word and he would make certain to be here for the ball.

"You must promise not to tell what I have learned, Lissa. Mrs. Parker would be most upset if she thought that I had been listening at keyholes and she might send me back to the scullery."

"I will not divulge your secret, Emmy." Melissa smiled at the nervous maid.

"Thank you, Lissa." Emmy gave a sigh of relief. "I told you about his grace's costume because I could not help but imagine how romantic it would be if her ladyship's daughter should dress as Queen Guinevere."

Melissa nodded. "That would indeed be propitious, but I fear Miss Regina has already commissioned her costume. I cannot tell you what it is to be, but I assure you that it does not even remotely resemble Lady Guinevere."

"I do hope *someone* dresses as Queen Guinevere." Emmy sighed deeply. "I should so love to see King Arthur leading Queen Guinevere in the dance."

Melissa was silent for a long moment, a daring scheme taking form in her mind. Then she reached out to squeeze Emmy's hand and bid her to go back to her duties before her absence was noted.

"Thank you for telling me your secret, Emmy." Melissa smiled as Emmy rose from the bench and whistled for Perseus. "Perhaps some fortunate lady will choose to dress as Queen Guinevere, and you shall see the dance you desire, after all."

It was nearing midnight when there was a soft knock on Melissa's door.

"Lissa? Are you awake?"

It was Regina's voice and Melissa hastily threw a cover over the clothing on her bed and crossed the room to open the door. "Come in, Gina. There is tea if you would care for some."

"How kind in you to have tea waiting for me at this hour!" Regina crossed to the chairs by the brazier and sank down gratefully. "Though I daresay I could do with something stronger after the reception I enjoyed at tonight's entertainment."

Melissa frowned as she took her place in the other chair and poured a cup of tea for her stepsister. She knew that Jane had received vouchers for Almack's and they had attended this evening. "You were not well received?"

"Oh, our welcome was most proper." Regina nodded quickly. "Indeed, Lady Cowper was most ingratiating. But I found that I deeply resented the comments that several of the other young ladies made to me."

"What did they say?"

"It was not so much the content of their speech, but the implications that they made. One young lady, a Miss Harper, was so unkind as to hint that I must have entrapped the duke in some way."

"Miss Caroline Harper?"

"Why, yes!" Regina noticed that Melissa was smiling. "Are you acquainted with her, Lissa?"

"Only by reputation. I have not met Miss Harper personally, and I do not think I should wish to. The duke's housekeeper, Mrs. Parker, told me that Miss Harper used trickery to attempt to trap the duke into declaring for her."

Regina's eyes widened. "I am aware that it is not seemly of me to ask, but . . . do you know precisely how she accomplished this?"

Melissa laughed as she nodded. "It seems that Miss Harper gained access to Oakwood House through a rear entrance and secreted herself in the duke's bedchamber. When her mother came to call, several hours later, she planned to be discovered there."

"Her mother was part of this scheme?"

Melissa nodded. "And their plot might well have succeeded, had the duke been in residence. Fortunately, he was visiting one of his country estates at the time and all the young lady gained for her efforts were a few moments of painful embarrassment."

"Good heavens!" Regina's mouth dropped open. "I cannot believe Miss Harper went to such lengths!"

"She is not the only young lady to attempt such a trick. Mr. Oliver told me of another, a Miss Amanda Truesblood."

Regina nodded. "Miss Truesblood was in attendance this evening and she also made several inferences as to my character. What did she do, Lissa?"

"She enlisted the aid of her groom to sabotage the duke's carriage. Her father, Lord Truesblood, begged the duke to carry his daughter to their country estate, pleading some type of family emergency. In this case the duke's sister received warning of their trickery and followed them in the family coach. The duke's carriage broke down in the late afternoon, exactly as the Truesbloods had planned, but the duke's sister arrived long before nightfall and delivered Miss Truesblood to her country estate, much to her father's chagrin."

Regina burst into laughter. "Is there no end to the tricks the young ladies and their families will attempt to trap the duke into marriage?"

"I daresay there is not." Melissa shook her head and smiled at Regina. "But all their attempts have been foiled. Perhaps if they had set out to earn the duke's respect rather than to trick him, they would have been better served."

Regina was thoughtful for a moment and then she met Melissa's eyes. "Mama is certain the duke will declare for me, Lissa. Do you think this is true?"

"I do." Melissa nodded. "The duke thinks very highly of you, Gina, and his staff all agree that he has never shown such an interest in any other young lady before."

Regina sighed. "What shall I do, Lissa, if Mama is correct and he does declare for me? You must give me the benefit of your advice."

"First you must tell me of your feelings for the duke."

Melissa took a deep breath and vowed to do right by her dear stepsister.

Regina took a moment to ponder that question and when she spoke her voice was soft. "He is all that is good, Lissa, and the most worthy of men. I delight in his company and find myself captivated by his charm and his knowledge. I find that he has fine sensibilities and his behavior is most honorable. I should gladly trust him with my life and the lives of those I hold dear."

Melissa nodded. It was quite obvious that Regina respected the duke highly and harbored tender feelings for him. Perhaps this was so close to love as to be indistinguishable. "Then you would not regard your life as his wife with aversion?"

"Oh, no!" Regina seemed truly shocked. "Marriage to the duke would be most wonderful, indeed! His declaration would send Mama into raptures and thus I would gain my freedom from her continual censure."

"You would marry the duke for that reason only?" Melissa held her breath.

"Of course not, Lissa." Regina laughed. "I am not such a goose as to marry solely to gain Mama's approval! There are many other considerations and I am aware of them all. The duke has indicated to me that he finds my work commendable and I am certain he would not have any objection if I chose to continue in my charitable endeavors. In fact, I truly believe that he would encourage me greatly in these pursuits."

"I am certain that you are correct on that account." Melissa nodded quickly.

"The duke has also told me that he is fond of Lord Chadwick and Doro. After they are wed, as I am most certain they are to be, I will be free to invite them to visit Oakwood Castle as often as I wish. He is also sensible of the fact that Mama and I do not share a close affection and I am convinced that he will arrange matters so that she can live comfortably on her own."

Melissa nodded. "You seem to have thought of every aspect, Gina."

"There is more." Regina's eyes were sparkling. "I have saved the best for last. Marriage to the duke would enable me to carry out my fondest wish."

"And what is that, dear Gina?" Melissa held her breath, expecting her stepsister to speak of the children she would have with the duke, or the delight she would experience at sharing his love.

"I will be free to tell the duke who you really are!" Regina's smile was tremulous. "At long last the truth will triumph and I am certain the duke will appreciate the reason for our deception and forgive us in an instant. Then I shall invite you to live with us, dear Lissa, not as a servant but as my beloved sister. The duke, himself, will sponsor your Season and you shall have all the pleasures that Mama has denied you all these years."

Melissa smiled at the sight of her stepsister's glowing face, but she was oddly discontent. Regina's reasons for accepting the duke's proposal were all satisfactory and most important, but the critical reason was completely lacking. Her stepsister had made no mention of love.

Regina reached out quite suddenly and took Melissa's hand. "Thank you for listening to me tonight, Lissa, but I find I have no further need for your advice. I have come to a decision and I truly believe that it is right. If the Duke of Oakwood should offer for me at his costume ball, I shall accept him with a glad and joyous heart."

As Regina hugged her, tears filled Melissa's eyes. She was not yet convinced that her dear stepsister would be accepting the duke's proposal for the right reason.

As Regina pulled away, she noticed the tears in Melissa's eyes. "What is it, Lissa? Are you not happy for me?"

"I am most happy!" Melissa blinked furiously to clear her eyes of unwanted tears. "Have you never heard tell of tears of joy?"

Regina laughed gaily and picked up a linen napkin to wipe the tears from Melissa's cheeks. "Of course I have! My only desire is that you will not turn into a watering pot on the day of my wedding for I wish you to attract the eye of every young nobleman there."

When Regina had left, Melissa pulled back the cover on the bed and stared at the array of clothing that she had arranged there. Lady Beckworth had given her several gowns and they contained the materials Melissa would need to fashion her costume for the ball. Perhaps it was wrong, in light of Regina's decision to accept the duke's proposal, but Melissa planned to share one more dance with the duke. It would be their last dance, the final time she could be in the arms of the man she loved, before he would become Regina's husband.

As Melissa busied herself with the shears and then plied her needle with shaking fingers, she took care that her tears would not stain her work. When her duties as Lissa were finished for the evening, she would dress in the costume she had fashioned. Then she would slip into the ballroom with the invited guests and Queen Guinevere would dance with King Arthur. The memory of this shining moment was all she would have to keep her warm in the cold and lonely nights to come.

Thirteen

Robert Whiting, the eighth Duke of Oakwood, sat at his father's desk in his father's library, feeling every ounce of the weight of his duties resting against his shoulders. This was now Robert's desk and his library, the chamber in which he would conduct his ducal business. Robert only wished that he might prove worthy of the title he now held.

The library had been closed since his father's death and there were holland covers over some of the larger pieces of furniture. In the two years following his father's death, Robert had conducted all the estate business from a small study on the second floor, intending to take charge of the library when the grief at his father's passing had lessened. This chamber had been his father's domain and Robert had been sensible of the fact that his mother would certainly be saddened to see him sitting at his father's desk and making use of his father's private possessions so soon after his death. He had been intending to open the library on the third anniversary of his father's death, but his mother and sister had decided that the time was now right and had ordered it opened and cleaned for his use.

The duchess had cleared the desk herself, removing the mementos she wished to keep in her possession. It was while she was emptying one of the drawers that she had come across a sealed packet addressed to Robert with the caveat that it be opened by no other. Deciding that the contents could be of some importance, she had sent a message to Oakwood House, requesting his immediate presence.

Robert gazed down at the package in his hand. His name was written in his father's bold hand and he took a deep breath as he broke the seal. He was anticipating directions concerning unsettled estate business, or a final word of advice on assuming his title and duties. But the words his father had written were as shocking as they were unexpected and Robert found his hands trembling as he examined his father's letter.

It seemed that Robert's father had enjoyed the company of a childhood friend, a Miss Anne Hathaway who had lived with her grandmother on a neighboring estate. The two had grown up together, fallen in love, and planned to marry when they were of an age. There was only one problem; Anne was the by-blow of an earl, not a suitable match for a duke's heir. When Robert's grandfather became aware of the couple's intentions, he spoke to Anne's grandmother and Anne was sent away to marry an elderly vicar in the north country.

Robert's father saw Anne only once more, on the eve of her departure. He wrote that he had pleaded with her to run away with him, but Anne had refused. She knew that Robert's father would be disinherited if they married and she loved him too much to be the cause of his ruin. Anne had one item of value, a set of fine jewelry made of rare blue diamonds that her mother had left to her. They had been a gift from the earl who had fathered her, presented to Anne's mother when she had become his mistress. Anne gave the necklace to Robert's father and elicited his promise to present it to his firstborn son. She kept the earrings for herself and made a like vow, that she would bequeath them to her firstborn daughter. It was Anne's hope that someday their children might fall in love and the set would again be complete.

Robert sighed. He was touched by his father's letter and curious that he had never heard the tale before. His father went on to write that he had married Robert's mother several years later and that their match had been a happy one. He had no regrets and he loved Robert's mother dearly, but he was haunted by not knowing what had happened to his childhood love. When he had become duke, he had hired investigators to find out where Anne had gone, but Anne's grandmother had taken that secret to her grave. Rumor had it that Anne's elderly husband had died shortly after their vows had been spoken and that Anne had subsequently remarried. There was also a rumor that Anne had given birth to a daughter and had died several years later, but the duke's investigators were unable to substantiate either story.

The final paragraph of his father's letter brought tears to Robert's eyes. The old duke pleaded with Robert to carry on with the search and to find Anne Hathaway if she were still alive. If not, he should do his utmost to locate her daughter. If Robert succeeded in this last request, he should present the necklace to Anne's daughter and tell her of the love Robert's father had shared with her mother.

Robert opened the packet and gasped at the splendor of the necklace. It was both exquisite and unusual, quite obviously the gift of a wealthy lover. He slipped it into his pocket and went to find his mother who had asked him to come to her in her sitting room after he had examined the packet.

The duchess bid him to enter and patted the chair beside her. "Robert, dearest. Are you most distressed at this belated word from your father?"

"No, Mother. It was not in the least distressing." Robert smiled and accepted the cup of tea that she poured for him. On his way to his mother's sitting room, he had decided he must choose his words with caution. It would not do to divulge the full extent of his father's final request. If his mother learned that the old duke had harbored a secret love all these years, she could very well become overset.

"Well?" The dowager duchess peered at him over the rim of her cup. "You must not keep me in suspense any longer. I have been imagining all sorts of dire possibilities."

Robert laughed. "It was of little consequence, Mother. Father merely wished me to locate a childhood friend and return a gift that was given him long ago. It is a trifling request, but it had great significance for him and I shall see that it is done."

"You are a good son, Robert." The dowager duchess patted his hand. "Perhaps you will be so kind as to grant me a request also?"

Robert nodded. "Certainly Mother, if it is within my power. What is it that you wish?"

"It is my desire to take leave of Oakwood Castle at the first opportunity. I dearly loved this drafty old place when your father was alive, but now I find that I am most eager to quit it. I beg you to marry soon so that I may be free to leave."

"Where will you go?"

"To London." A smile spread over the duchess's face. "I have missed my old friends and they seldom venture out this far to visit. I should like to establish myself in a small house and partake of the excitement that the city has to offer. I am certain that if you put your mind to it, you shall find a suitable bride and release me from my duties here."

Robert's lips turned up in a mischievous smile. "I sense that this is another of your attempts to marry me off. Where have you hidden her, Mother?"

"Hidden whom?" The duchess looked bewildered for a moment. Then she caught her son's meaning and began to chuckle. "I am hiding no one, Robert."

"Are you certain?" Robert rose to his feet and crossed to the drapes, lifting them aside to ascertain that no one was hiding there. Then he peeked beneath the cloth that covered the table and searched behind his mother's settee.

The duchess laughed at his antics for a moment and then her expression sobered. "There is no need to search, Robert, for I have ceased my matchmaking pursuits. If the truth be known, I have run out of suitable young ladies to present to you."

"After so few?" Robert chuckled. "If I recall correctly, there have been only three dozen or so, over the past two years."

The dowager duchess raised her eyebrows. "That many? Perhaps I was better at the game than I thought I was."

"It was a valiant effort, Mother." Robert reached out to take her hand. "Father would have been proud of your tenacity."

"And yours as well, for you resisted every young lady that I brought forward. You must choose your own bride, Robert, for none of my suggestions have borne fruit. All I ask is that you make your choice quickly before I become so old and decrepit that I can no longer enjoy dancing at parties."

Robert nodded, taking the seat beside her and patting her hand. "I shall do that, Mother, perhaps sooner than you expect."

"You have met someone then?"

Robert laughed at the eager expression on his mother's face. "Yes, Mother, and I am certain that you will approve of my choice."

"Oh, Robert! She is not an opera girl, is she?"

Robert was shocked until he gazed into his mother's teasing eyes. "No, Mother, she is not an opera girl, and it is unseemly of you to even know of such things. In your exalted position as duchess you must concern yourself with loftier matters."

"Like counting the china that remains unused in the cupboards, or seeing that the linen is in readiness for the guests who never arrive? Or would you prefer I do needlework for hours on end, or paint charming likenesses of the birds in the trees?" The duchess laughed at the image she presented. "I am more sophisticated than you think me to be, Robert, and I have never been sheltered. You forget that I had four elder brothers who did not guard their speech around me, and a husband who believed that his wife should be an equal, not a delicate creature to cosset from reality. I heard of opera girls long before I attended my first performance of the same name, and your father, himself, told me of the mistress to whom he gave *conge* when he married me."

"But . . . Mother!" Robert felt the heat rise to his face.

"Do not pretend that such a side of life does not exist, Robert. I am certain that you have attended a Cyprian ball or two, and perhaps even ventured to Harriet Wilson's of an evening when you were alone and wished for feminine companionship."

Robert's mouth fell open and he found himself utterly speechless. That his gentle mother should not only know of such things, but speak of them in such a nonchalant manner was a surprising revelation to him.

The duchess gave a mischievous giggle and reached out to take her son's hand. "I see by your expression that you are shocked to hear me speak of such things. Your father was not a saint, Robert, and you must not regard him as such. He was quite a charming rake, in his day, and I think it unlikely that the apple should fall that far from the tree!"

Robert whooped with laughter at her comment and then he sobered quickly. "Put your fears to rest, Mother. I have not decided to seek a wife from among the ranks of the fashionably impure. The young lady I have chosen is a most suitable match, one that would satisfy even the most discriminating of the old tabbies who hold court at Almack's. She is the eldest daughter of Lord Harrington's widow and as pleasing as she is proper."

"Well done, Robert!" The dowager duchess clapped her hands in delight. "Though I do not know the girl personally, I am so glad that you have reached a decision. When shall you declare for her?"

"As soon as I get back to London, Mother. And once the formalities have been observed, I will bring her here to meet you. You should not mind receiving her, should you?"

"Mind?" The duchess laughed so merrily, the tea sloshed from her cup. "My darling Robert, you do not know the extent to which this pleases me. I shall be so delighted to meet your future wife, I may hand her the keys and take leave for London before you have even spoken your vows!"

Fourteen

It was the night before the duke's costume ball and Melissa was exhausted as she was handed down from the carriage in front of the house in Belgrave Square. She had not left Oakwood House until she was assured that all was in readiness and darkness had fallen several hours ago. The duke had not yet returned from Oakwood Castle, but he had sent word that he would arrive on the morrow. In his absence, Harley had ordered that she be carried home, insisting that it was much too dangerous for her to walk in the dark, and Melissa had gratefully availed herself of the convenience.

As she entered the house, Melissa was thankful to see that only Mary was there to greet her. The young maid reported that Jane and her daughters had left upwards of an hour ago, to attend the opera with Lord Chadwick. This news suited Melissa perfectly as she needed an uninterrupted hour or two to add the finishing touches to her costume. After a few words with Mary, she went up to her bedchamber and busied herself with needle and thread.

At last the elaborate medieval costume was finished and Melissa pressed it carefully. The flowing velvet and brocade of the gown would compliment her figure and she had made a matching headdress and a mask so that her face would not be recognized. Almost everyone who had received an invitation had responded in the affirmative. There would be a veritable crush in the duke's ballroom and Melissa was certain that she could slip in amongst the throng without anyone noticing one more guest or questioning her presence at the affair.

It was past midnight when Melissa retrieved the packet that her father had addressed to her. With great excitement, she opened it and gasped as she examined the contents. She had not dreamed her mother's earrings would be such a lovely treasure. They were fashioned of glittering blue diamonds and Melissa had never seen stones to equal their beauty. A single sheet of velum lay inside the casket that held her mother's treasure. Melissa's hands were shaking as she removed it and realized that it was a missive from her mother, written in a lovely but faltering hand.

> My Darling Daughter, I hope that you shall never have cause to read this for it will mean that I did not survive my illness. Your father has promised to give you my earrings on the eve of your first formal ball. Before you wear them, I must tell you the story of the set of jewelry my mother gave to me.

Melissa blinked back tears as she read the sad story of her mother's childhood love and how she had given him the necklace that matched the earrings. Her mother's letter told of her first marriage to a pleasant, but elderly vicar who had died shortly after they had exchanged their vows. She described her first meeting with Melissa's father and how kind he had been to the lonely young widow, forced by circumstances to live off the charity of her eldest stepson. Melissa's father had rescued her from a grim life of genteel poverty and made certain her future held nothing but happiness.

The letter spoke of Melissa's birth and what a joyous event it had been. But in spite of the contented days her mother had spent with a man she described as generous, loyal, and loving, one small portion of her heart had not been engaged. She had longed for her childhood love though she knew she could never see him again, and she had treasured her fond memories of the short time they had spent together.

Melissa sighed. She knew her parents' marriage had been happy. She remembered the tender looks they had exchanged and the fond words they had spoken. Her mother had been a devoted wife and Melissa was certain her father had never known of the love she had relinquished. The letter ended with a poignant request from mother to daughter.

> My first love and I had hoped that someday our children should meet and continue the affection we shared for each other. Wear the earrings for me, darling, at your first formal ball and pray that you shall meet your true love.

Why had her mother not mentioned the man's name? Melissa read the letter again, but there was no clue as to his identity. It was quite obvious that her father had never known of his existence and it was far too late to ask. With a heartfelt sigh, Melissa slipped the earrings in the bottom of the basket she would carry to Oakwood House in the morning. Perhaps it was not exactly as her dear mother had intended, but this would be her first formal ball and she was determined to wear them.

It seemed as if Melissa had just closed her eyes when she was rudely awoken by a series of loud, distressed cries. At first she was confused and thought the noise came from one of the peacocks that Jane had imported to Harrington Manor. The birds were indeed beautiful, but they possessed disagreeable dispositions and were bad-tempered, vicious and prone to frequent squabbling amongst themselves. But she was no longer at Harrington Manor and Melissa blinked in the strong sunlight that streamed into her chamber. This was the rented house in Belgrave Square and the cries that came from below stairs were emanating from her stepmother.

Melissa threw back the covers and jumped to her feet. She had barely managed to slip into her wrapper before Jane burst into her bedchamber.

"It is a disaster of the first magnitude!" Jane pressed the back of her hand to her brow in a classical pose and sighed theatrically. "Whatever are we to do?"

Melissa crossed the room and took her stepmother's arm, leading her gently to one of the chairs near the brazier. "Please sit down and calm yourself. If you could but tell me what is the matter, I may be able to help."

"There is no help at this late date!" Jane took the lavender-scented handkerchief that Melissa offered and dabbed daintily at her face. "Madame Beauchamp has failed us!"

In spite of her stepmother's distraught state, Melissa immediately assessed her meaning. "Gina's costume is not finished?"

"No, and that horrible French woman, who is much too high in the instep to my way of thinking, has sent round a useless apology. She writes that regrettable and unforeseen circumstances have kept her from completing her commission!"

"I see." Melissa nodded quickly. "Perhaps it may be possible to—"

Before Melissa could finish her thought, Jane emitted a joyous cry. "You dear child! How glad I am to have brought you here to serve as our dresser! You are indeed brilliant to have saved us from this utter disaster!"

Melissa frowned slightly. Had her stepmother slipped from the bounds of normalcy? She turned to look where Jane was pointing and gasped as she realized that the costume she had fashioned was draped over the clotheshorse in plain view.

"I shall be sure to tell everyone of your merits, Melissa." Jane leapt to her feet and snatched the costume up in her hands. "How clever of you to have fashioned another costume in the event that one should be delayed! I must take this to Regina immediately to make certain that it suits her."

As Jane rushed from the room, Melissa opened her mouth to call her back. Then she closed it again, in utter defeat, as she realized that she could offer no reasonable objection. She could not admit that she had intended to wear the costume herself. Jane would never allow her to slip in amongst the guests if she were aware of Melissa's plan.

Melissa used the word she had heard the duke's stable boy utter when he had been kicked by one of the horses. Use of profanity did not serve to lighten her spirits, but she said it several more times as she dressed for the day and stuffed a clean apron into her basket. If the recipient of her costume had been her stepmother, Melissa might have torn out the stitches in a fit of pique. But she could not begrudge its use to Regina.

As she hurried down the staircase, Melissa did her utmost not to think of what might have been. The duke was intending to declare for her dear stepsister, and it was only fitting that Regina be Queen Guinevere to his King Arthur. The costume was merely a costume. There had been nothing magical about it and it would not have served to change her life. But oh how Melissa wished that she could have been the one to wear it!

"What would you have me do first, Mrs. Parker?" Melissa addressed the duke's housekeeper the moment she entered Oakwood House.

Mrs. Parker slipped a companionable arm around Melissa's shoulders and gave her a welcoming hug. "You have accomplished the preparations so well in advance that there is little to do upon this day. The flowers will need arranging, of course, but I can think of little else."

"Tell me of Henri." Melissa's lips turned upwards in a smile. "Is he in a taking yet again?"

Mrs. Parker laughed. "But of course, Lissa. Henri is forever in a taking on the day of an important affair. He began asking when you would arrive as soon as the sun peeked over the rooftops. I doubt that he truly needs your services, but it is apparent that he desires your company."

"I will go and find him then." Melissa turned toward the kitchens. "Please send for me if I am needed elsewhere."

Melissa found Henri working busily, the kitchens in a predictable state of disarray. When the French chef looked up to see her in the doorway, a broad smile crossed his face.

"Lissa! *Mon dieu, mon enfant!* I thought you should never arrive! I have been waiting for your opinion of the decorations I made last night."

Melissa took a seat on the stool at the counter as Henri sent a kitchen maid to fetch the decorations. When the girl returned with a long platter filled with miniature confections, she gasped in delight. *"Magnifique,* Henri. You have outdone yourself!"

"And now we must assemble the *piece d'resistance,* the grand finale of our banquet!" Henri's eyes sparkled at Melissa's obvious delight. He turned to another of the kitchen maids. "Fetch the cakes."

Melissa waited anxiously. The marvelous dessert had been her conception. The idea had occurred to her shortly after Emmy had told her that the duke planned to dress as King Arthur. It was to be a massive cake in the shape of a medieval castle with turrets, a drawbridge, and a moat. When she had mentioned it to Henri the concept had caught his fancy and he had declared that he could make such a cake with the appropriate trimmings, every one of them completely edible. Now it was time to turn their dream into reality. If their assembly succeeded and the cake was as wondrous as Henri and Melissa anticipated, it would be a credit to the duke's ball and the subject of *ton* legend for years to come.

Melissa nodded as several kitchen maids carried in platters filled with cakes of various sizes and shapes. There were small, round cakes for the turrets, long, thin cakes for the walls, and several cakes that were dense and nearly flat for the roof and the drawbridge. Seeing the pieces thusly gathered and resting upon their platters reminded Melissa of a complicated puzzle and she prayed that they would be able to assemble them in a manner that resembled a castle. The materials were ready and

Henri had prepared a large bowl of sticky icing that they would use as an edible mortar to affix the pieces together. Once the castle took shape, Henri's frosting would harden and then their cake would be ready to receive decoration.

"Come, Lissa. Let us begin." Henri cleared a large space on one of the long tables and referred to the drawings she had made. "The pieces are here. All we must do is fit them together."

Melissa sighed. It seemed an insurmountable task, but Henri appeared much more confident than she had expected. "Have you done something similar before, Henri?"

"Not of this magnitude, *mon enfant.*" Henri chuckled. "But I once created a cake to resemble a box tied up with a ribbon. How much more difficult can this be?"

Melissa's mouth dropped open in surprise. A cake was naturally shaped like a box. It would be no great feat to wrap a ribbon about it. She turned to Henri to ask him how this would compare with the task they had set for themselves on this day, and noticed the twinkle in the French chef's eyes. He was bamming her, but she could give as well as she could get.

"Thank you for telling me this, Henri." Melissa's eyes twinkled back at him. "As you are so experienced in this art, I will step aside so that you may lay the first piece."

Robert wore a smile as he stepped from the carriage. It was late morning and he had made much better time than he had anticipated. After he had greeted the members of his staff who had come out to welcome him home, he went directly to his bedchamber where he found his valet waiting.

"Your grace." Mr. Oliver favored him with a rare smile. "Your costume was delivered in your absence. Would you care to examine it?"

Robert nodded and his valet hurried to fetch the costume. One look, and a satisfied smile spread across Robert's countenance. His costume had been fashioned exactly according to the directions he had left. "It is precisely as I had envisioned it. It will do admirably."

"Very good, your grace." Mr. Oliver looked pleased as he whisked the costume off to the dressing room. When he returned, he was surprised to see his master standing pensively at the window. "Do you require further need of my services, your grace?"

Robert nodded as he turned. "I should like water brought up for my bath. When I have washed off the dust of the road, I shall require a light nuncheon in my private sitting room. Please ask Mrs. Parker to join me. I wish to hear of the preparations that have been made in my absence."

"I shall see to it immediately, your grace." Mr. Oliver made ready to exit the bedchamber, but he halted as the duke held up his hand.

"One other thing. Is Lissa in attendance?"

"Yes, your grace." A broad smile spread over Mr. Oliver's face. "She arrived shortly after daybreak and I believe she is with Monsieur Henri in the kitchens. Shall I call for her?"

"No. I merely wished to know, that is all. Precisely what is she doing in the kitchens?"

"Assembling the cake, your grace. Monsieur Henri and Lissa have barred all from the kitchen until it is completed, for its appearance is a secret. She did, however, confide to me that it is to be a most elaborate affair."

Robert smiled. He knew of the nature of the cake, he had discussed its contents with Lissa at length, but he had left its appearance to her. Now it seemed that Lissa had concocted another mystery to pique his curiosity. "Am I to be barred from the kitchens as well?"

"You, your grace? Surely you do not wish to venture to the kitchens."

Robert laughed at his valet's shocked expression. "Not at the present time, no. It would not do to intrude upon Lissa's surprise."

"No, your grace." Mr. Oliver nodded emphatically. "I am

certain the staff would be quite distressed if any were to ignore
Lissa's instructions."

Robert waited until his valet had left and then his shoulders
quaked with suppressed laughter. Though it was *his* staff, and
his residence, it appeared that Lissa commanded more loyalty
than he did himself!

"Oh, Henri! It is indeed, remarkable!" Lissa stood back to
survey the cake with a proud smile. "I am certain that this is
the finest creation that you have ever fashioned. Now everyone
will know that you are truly the finest chef in London!"

Henri nodded. "It is *magnifique,* but I did not create it alone.
You must also claim credit for our feat, *mon enfant."*

"But I did no more than assist you, Henri." Lissa's eyes were
warm. "And while it is true that you fashioned it in response
to my suggestion, I had not the slightest knowledge of how to
go about it by myself."

"What of his grace? Do you believe that he will be impressed?"

"How could he not be completely overwhelmed with its
magnificence?" Lissa gestured toward the cake. "I wish I
could be there to see his enraptured expression when it is presented."

Henri rolled his eyes heavenward and slapped the side of his
head with his palm. "I am an idiot, *mon enfant!* If I had but
thought, I should have found you a costume so that you could
slip inside with the guests. This would have enabled you to see
the presentation with your own eyes."

"I, too, thought of this scheme, Henri." Lissa sighed deeply.
"I planned to do exactly as you suggested, but I no longer have
the costume I made in secret."

Henri frowned. "Where is this costume? I shall have someone
fetch it immediately!"

"It is far too late for that, Henri." Lissa blinked back the tears
that suddenly formed in her eyes. "Lady Harrington discovered

it in my room and now Miss Regina is to wear it. Her costume was not finished in time and I gave it to her freely, Henri. She is a fine lady who regards me as a sister and I do not resent that she is to wear it. Perhaps it is just as well. I should not have presumed that I could masquerade as a fine lady."

Henri led her over to a stool and handed her a bit of clean linen to wipe her eyes. "Fustian! You *are* a fine lady, Lissa, much finer than the ones who will attend the ball this evening! Perhaps you are not of noble birth, but you are the finest lady, all the same."

"I am sorry to turn into such a watering pot." Lissa dabbed at her overflowing eyes. "It is just that I had so wished to dance at his grace's ball. I was even so foolish as to imagine that I might find the man of my dreams!"

Henri patted her shoulder awkwardly. "There is no need to cry. Many hours remain until time for the ball to commence. Perhaps you could fashion another costume to wear."

"No, Henri." Lissa shook her head sadly. "My dream was sheer frivolity and I do not choose to indulge in it again. This sad day has served as a lesson for me. It is imprudent for me to aspire to put myself above my station."

Fifteen

The Duchess of Oakwood broke the seal of the letter that had arrived in the morning's post. It was from her old friend, Lady Jennings, who was visiting Lady Sarah in London.

"What is it, Mama?" Lucy looked up from the firescreen she was embroidering for Trelane Manor.

"A letter from Lady Jennings. No doubt it will be filled with all the latest *on-dits* from London, for she has always shown a fondness for gossip."

Lucy peered over at the letter. "Why does the woman cross her lines so? It is devilishly difficult to read!"

"Indeed it is, and Lord Beckworth has franked the letter so there is no need for her to be frugal. It is a habit she developed in the schoolroom when she was used to correspond with an aunt who had little money for the post. It was a great kindness in that case, but now it is simply a nuisance." The duchess gave a merry laugh. "Did you know, Lucy, that the cost of the post can be a useful weapon?"

Lucy's eyes began to sparkle. Now that she was a married lady with twin boys of her own, her mother had begun to share more confidences with her. "No, indeed, I did not. Tell me about it, Mama."

"When I was but a school girl, I developed a *tendre* for the older brother of a classmate. I was visiting her at her parents' country estate at the time and I must admit that I was regrettably naïve. We kissed away several summer afternoons and I assumed that he intended to declare for me when I was of an age. I mentioned this happily anticipated event to my classmate and she informed me that it was impossible for her brother was already engaged to another. It seemed that he had merely sought to relieve the boredom of a family visit by trifling with my affections."

"Poor Mama! To endure a broken heart at such a tender age!" Lucy's tone was teasing, once she had noted the sparkle in her mother's eyes. "What did you do when you learned that the object of your young affections was a rake?"

"I made use of the post as my revenge. I knew that he had not yet come into his inheritance and was forced to live on a small allowance. I penned a letter to him containing but a single word and signed my name to it."

"What was the word, Mama?"

"Cad." The dowager duchess laughed at the memory. "Then I wrapped my letter around several heavy stones and sent it off on the next post. I daresay he has not yet forgiven me as his sister reported that he paid a small fortune to retrieve it."

"That is delightful, Mama!" Lucy laughed. "I shall keep it in mind if I have the need to seek revenge."

"Perhaps I should not have told you." The duchess looked slightly worried as she picked up her letter again.

"Do not fear, Mama. I was simply bamming you. I am happily married and well past that foolish age." Lucy put her embroidery aside and smiled at her mother. "Please read Lady Jennings's letter to me. A juicy bit of gossip is just what I need."

The dowager duchess turned the letter and attempted to read the crossed lines. "Lady Jennings reports that we will miss the most important ball of the Season. It is to be a costume ball held at . . . I do not believe it, Lucy! Lady Jennings must be mistaken!"

"What is it, Mama?" Lucinda frowned as she glanced at her mother's shocked expression.

"She says *Robert* is to host the ball!"

"Robert?" Lucinda appeared equally shocked. "But how is this possible, Mama? Robert is unmarried and has no hostess!"

The duchess read the next line with a frown on her face. "It seems that Jane Harrington is to be his hostess for the occasion!"

"But why would Robert choose Lady Harrington?"

The duchess seemed to hesitate for a moment and then she sighed. "Perhaps it is wrong in me to divulge a confidence, Lucy, but you will know soon enough. When Robert was here, he confided to me that he intended to declare for her eldest daughter."

"Oh, dear!" Lucy reached out to take her mother's hand. "I have not made the acquaintance of her daughters, but I have heard distressing tales of Lady Harrington."

The duchess narrowed her eyes. "You must tell me what you have heard, Lucy. It is best that I be informed."

"It is said that she trapped Lord Harrington into marriage while he was still grieving for his first wife. I have also heard that the woman is an opportunist and she made her husband's life a misery with her constant demands for money and jewelry."

The dowager duchess frowned. This news did not bode well for her son. "I assume that Lady Harrington has not reformed in her ways, now that Lord Harrington is dead?"

"She is even more foolish, Mama. James knows of the family. His uncle and Lord Harrington were well acquainted and he is the source of the information I have given you. Uncle Frederick told James that she is living the life of a merry widow and has squandered the revenues from her portion of the estate for the past two years in an attempt to launch her daughters with the *ton*."

"And has she succeeded?" The duchess searched her daughter's face.

"Not yet, Mama. Her daughters were presented last Season, but they did not take. Uncle Frederick said that Lady Harrington is even more determined this Season. He claims that she will stop at nothing to assure that her daughters marry titled noble-men with heavy purses."

The dowager duchess nodded. "Of course. If she has light pockets, she must make certain that her daughters marry wealth. It is her only hope to continue in her extravagant ways."

"And Robert told you that he intends to declare for one of Lady Harrington's daughters?"

"Yes, indeed." The duchess sighed as she nodded. "Tell me of these daughters, Lucy. Do they emulate their mother?"

"I have no knowledge of that, Mama. Uncle Frederick does not speak ill of them, but he has said that they follow their mother's lead."

"Like sheep." There was derision in the dowager duchess's voice.

"Exactly, Mama. Uncle Frederick says that Lady Harrington controls them completely and that they appear to obey her in all things."

"Thank you for telling me of this, Lucy." The dowager duchess sighed heavily. "Would James be overset were you to accompany me to London?"

Lucy shook her head. "Not at all, Mama. He would think it a capital idea, as he has been urging me to take a respite from the children. When shall we leave?"

"Within the hour. There is no time to waste." The duchess rose to her feet. "We shall travel light and arrive in London on the morrow. If luck rides with us, Lucy, we will be in time to warn Robert of Lady Harrington's scheme."

Melissa's heart was heavy as the carriage rolled away from Belgrave Square. She had assisted her stepmother, Dorothea, and Regina to dress in their costumes and they were now on their way to Lord Chadwick's house. There they would meet the viscount's sister and brother and partake of a light refreshment before forming a cortege for their brief journey to Oakwood House.

"You'd best hurry, miss." Mary tapped her shoulder. "His grace's carriage should arrive at any moment."

"Thank you, Mary." Melissa smiled at the girl and rushed up the stairs to change her dress for the ball. When she opened the door to her bedchamber, the sight of the empty clotheshorse brought moisture to her eyes. Melissa dashed it away with the back of her hand and busied herself with her preparations. Her dream was not to be and she would not waste her time on regrets.

She had helped her stepmother dress as Cleopatra in a thin silk gown that had displayed her figure to full advantage. Jane's gown, itself, had been deceptively simple, but Melissa knew that the delicate gold sandals, the elaborate gold and jeweled headdress, and the gold filigree girdle that fit snugly around her waist had been very dear, indeed. Melissa had dressed Jane's hair in a shining curtain that fell straight to her shoulders and Jane had declared, quite charitably, that Melissa's effort was far superior to the wig that she had planned to don for the occasion.

Dorothea had chosen a lovely blue shepherdess costume with a frilly white underskirt. She had confided to Melissa that she had known the style would not be flattering when she had chosen it, but since Lord Chadwick had complimented her on her most delightfully rounded figure, she had indulged her passion for ruffles, flounces and furbelows to her heart's content.

Regina had been a vision of loveliness in the costume that Melissa had fashioned. Melissa had dressed her hair in clusters of soft curls and added a touch of rouge to her cheeks. When she was finished, Regina had made a perfect Queen Guinevere and Melissa had wished her happy on this fateful night that would assure her future.

"Miss! The carriage is here!"

Mary's excited voice floated up the staircase and Melissa grabbed her basket. She raced down the stairs and ran the length of the hallway to arrive at the door breathless.

"Oh!" Melissa gasped as she threw open the door and came

face to face with a stranger. His hand was raised, as if he had been surprised in the act of knocking for admittance.

"Excuse me, miss." He gave her a friendly smile. "I have recently taken leave of the Reverend Mr. Watson and he has entrusted me to bring a letter to Miss Regina."

Melissa returned his smile. "She will be most pleased, sir. But she is not here at present."

The young man frowned. "But Mr. Watson has instructed me to deliver it to her hand and no other."

"I do not think the gentleman would object if you gave it over to my keeping. I am Melissa, Miss Regina's stepsister, and I shall present it to her this evening."

The young man looked relieved as he reached out to hand her the letter. "I am certain Mr. Watson would approve. He has the highest opinion of your character."

"And I, of his." Melissa smiled and took the letter. "Miss Regina shall have his letter before the night is out. I promise you that, sir."

After Melissa was ensconced in the duke's carriage, she stared down at the letter for a moment. There was no doubt that Regina would be delighted to receive a communication from Mr. Watson. Her mother, however, would be most overset. Jane had often remarked that she did not approve of that gentleman's influence on Regina, and Melissa was certain that her stepmother would regard his letter as a most unwelcome intrusion.

Melissa slipped the letter inside her basket and covered it securely it with a cloth. She would slip it to Regina in secret, when her stepmother was not present to object.

A blush rose to Regina's cheeks as she hurried to the ladies' withdrawing room. She had made her excuses to the duke and her mother, asking for their leave to repair a minor tear in the hem of her costume. The tear had been accomplished by Regina's own hand, only moments before, in an attempt to gain a few moments of privacy. While one of the duke's maids stitched

up the tear, she would read the letter Mr. Watson's young col-
league had so propitiously given to Lissa.

All went according to plan. A maid was summoned, needle
and thread were duly fetched, and Regina broke the seal on the
letter. Lissa had told her that the young man had been most
cautious, lest the missive fall into the wrong hands.

"I shall have this repaired in a moment, miss." The maid
bobbed her head. "There is no need to remove it."

"Thank you." Regina smiled as the maid pulled up a stool
and began to ply her needle. Then she unfolded the letter to the
rhythm of a heart which was beating much too rapidly for comfort, and began to read the words.

"Oh, my!" Regina was not aware that she had spoken until
the maid looked up at her inquiringly.

"Did I prick you, miss?" The maid's voice was filled with
distress.

"No, most certainly you did not." Regina hastened to reassure
her. "You may continue."

As the maid bent over her work once more, a heated blush
rose to Regina's cheeks. Mr. Watson loved her! He had written
as much in a decidedly frank and undeniably sincere manner.
And he intended to declare for her the moment she returned from
London!

What bliss it should be to be married to such a gentle and
dedicated man! Regina sighed softly and considered the delight
she should surely experience in regarding him as her husband.
She had never permitted herself to think of Mr. Watson in such
a manner before. Indeed, she had purposely banished all
thoughts of the Reverend Mr. Watson, the man, from her mind.
Perhaps once or twice, in the privacy of her bedchamber, she
had entertained the notion that it should be rapturous, indeed,
to touch his dear face, or to brush back the errant lock of hair
that occasionally fell over his forehead. But Regina had attributed the source of those traitorous thoughts to the "temptations
of the flesh" that Mr. Watson's predecessor had been so fond

of sermonizing about and had roundly chided herself for giving way to them.

Mr. Watson loved her! A blissful smile spread across Regina's countenance. And she loved him, with all her heart. It was all as clear as crystal to her now. Every aspect of her behavior that had so puzzled her in the past, was now explained. It was her love for Mr. Watson that had caused her hands to tremble whenever she was near him and her heart to race at several times its normal rate. Her love was responsible for the manner in which she could remember every word that he had ever spoken, and this same love had induced her to see his dear countenance in every one of her dreams. Of course she would marry him! Indeed, Regina could imagine being wed to no other.

Regina's thoughts turned to the wonderful life she would be certain to share with the Reverend Mr. Watson and she sighed with supreme happiness. What joy it should be to stand at his side in the small church, greeting the parishioners after the conclusion of one of his excellent sermons. What satisfaction would be hers when they provided comfort to the sick and made life a bit less dreary for the more unfortunate members of his flock. She should not have to beg for his permission to continue her charity work for he embraced her same sensibilities, and had devoted his life to the enrichment of others, precisely as she wished to do.

But their work together would not be the only happiness that Regina should enjoy. They would share a deep and abiding love that would shine from the very windows of the small parsonage. All who saw them would know that theirs was truly a match made in heaven. Their life would not be easy. Regina was well aware of the hardships that awaited her as Mr. Watson's wife. No maid would lighten her load for they should not be able to hire one from the small salary he received. She should have to clean, and cook, and care for their children without assistance. But this was not in the least daunting to Regina. The contemplation of long hours spent in housewifery merely filled her with additional joy. She should be willing to endure any hardship with Mr. Watson at her side.

Regina's thoughts turned to the private life they should lead and a warm glow suffused her countenance. When their children were tucked in their beds and the long winter nights stretched out before them, they should sit by the fire in perfect companionship. He would read to her, in his wonderful voice, as she mended a shirt from the charity box or stitched a new article of clothing for one of their many children. Perhaps she would tell him the latest news of the schoolroom, where he should encourage her to teach any and all children who expressed a desire to learn, regardless of their station. There would be a cozy tea tray between them and he would compliment her on the excellent cakes she had baked. And then, when it was time for them to retire to their chamber above the stairs, they would embrace warmly and—

"It is finished, miss." The maid removed her stool and smoothed out the hem of the costume, bringing Regina out of her perfect dream with a jolt. "It was only a small tear and I have stitched it so that no one shall ever notice when you lead the procession with his grace."

Regina gasped in shock as the full force of the maid's words reached her startled mind. The duke! In her blissful excitement over the Reverend Mr. Watson's declaration, she had forgotten that she was all but promised to the Duke of Oakwood!

"Is there something amiss?"

"No, indeed." Regina gave the maid a shaky smile that she prayed was convincing enough to set the girl's suspicions to rest. "You have done excellent work and I thank you for it. If you will leave me now, I shall take a moment to compose myself and then I shall return to the ball."

When the maid had departed with a smile and a nod, Regina dropped her head in her hands and gave a most uncharacteristic groan. Whatever would she tell the duke? If her mother was correct and he was intending to declare for her tonight, she would cause a dreadful scandal by refusing!

Panic threatened to consume her, but Regina pushed it back with firm resolve. Her path was clear and she must not falter. She could not marry the duke, not when her heart truly belonged to Mr. Watson.

Regina rose to her feet, shook out her skirts, and marched firmly to the door. She had been so foolish as to mistake the warm friendship she had shared with the duke for love, and she had come within a hairsbreadth of making a dreadful mistake. She would have to find some way to tell the duke her true feelings for him before he made his formal declaration.

With her heart beating fast with anxiety, Regina opened the door and stepped into the hallway. She would ask the duke for a private moment before the conclusion of the ball. And then she would inform him that she could not marry him, even though that would take every ounce of courage that she could muster.

Sixteen

"Look at the harlequin, Melissa!" Emmy's eyes were shining as she pointed to the gentleman in a shining gold and purple satin costume.

"I see him, Emmy." Melissa smiled at the excited young girl. "Take care not to move too close to the rail. We must not let anyone see us."

Emmy nodded and moved back several steps. They were standing on the interior balcony that overlooked the ballroom, hidden in the shadows of a potted tree. From this vantage point, both Melissa and Emmy could observe the guests as they entered the ballroom and prepared for the grand promenade to the sumptuous buffet that had been arranged in the duke's solarium.

"Where is your mistress, Lissa?" Emmy searched the array of brightly costumed guests below. The glittering chandeliers that hung from the high, vaulted ceiling provided a soft glowing light that flooded the ballroom and left no dark corner unexposed.

"Do you see the gentleman dressed as Pan with his magic flute?"

Emmy took a moment to survey the scene below and then she shook her head. "No, Lissa."

"He is to the right of the French doors leading to the gardens, next to the lady dressed as a gypsy princess. Lady Harrington's party is about to greet them."

"I see her!" Emmy smiled as she successfully identified Lady

Harrington in her Cleopatra costume. "And the shepherdess is her daughter?"

Melissa nodded. "Miss Dorothea. Her escort is Lord Chadwick. He wears the costume of a pirate."

Emmy nodded quickly. "But where is Miss Regina?"

Melissa searched the crush below and then she shook her head. "I do not see her. She must have taken leave of Lady Harrington's party for some reason."

There was the sound of scattered applause below and Lissa and Emmy watched as the guests turned toward the entrance to the ballroom. It was apparent that someone of great consequence was about to arrive.

"Miss Regina is at the entrance, with his grace." Lissa wore a proud smile as she spied her stepsister on the arm of the duke. Regina was lovely and her costume was more elaborate than any other at the ball.

"Miss Regina is beautiful, Lissa!" An expression of awe crossed Emmy's face. "And her costume is the finest that I have ever seen!"

Melissa smiled. Emmy had confided that this would be the first costume ball that she had ever observed. She had seen no costumes before this evening and thus had no range of comparison. All the same, Emmy's compliment came from the heart and Melissa was pleased at her words.

Emmy began to smile. "If another costume ball is to be held this Season, all the grand ladies will be asking for your services. They will squabble and peck like a gaggle of geese to see who will be the first to wear a costume fashioned by Madame Lissa, the famous modiste."

"Madame Lissa?" Melissa turned to Emmy in surprise. "But I do not pretend to be a modiste, Emmy, and I am certain the ladies who are present here this evening do not regard me as such. Indeed, not one of them knows that I fashioned Miss Regina's costume."

"But they *do* know, Lissa. Mrs. Parker said she heard Miss Regina tell his grace that you had sewn her costume. And Mr.

Harley was present when she conversed with Lady Beckworth and Lady Jennings. At that time she told them that all the credit for her appearance belonged solely to you."

"But what of Lady Harrington? Surely she did not credit Miss Regina's costume to me!"

Emmy giggled. "Not her! That one would not credit God for the beauty of the trees and the sky! But Mrs. Parker heard Miss Regina's sister mention it to several ladies, and his grace, himself, told more than a few gentlemen of your talents. Everyone knows by now, Lissa. Mrs. Parker says that such an exciting discovery cannot remain secret for long among the members of the *ton*."

"Thank you for telling me this, Emmy." Melissa reached out to take the girl's hand. "I did not expect to be praised thusly."

The guests were forming a line for the opening promenade and as Melissa watched from her position on the balcony, her depression began to lift. While it was true that she had lost her opportunity to dance once more with the man she loved, perhaps some good had been served when Jane had discovered the costume that she had fashioned and had appropriated it for Regina's use. Her generous stepsisters had told all that she was the creator of the lovely costume. If Emmy was correct and the ladies of the *ton* would seek out her services as a modiste, perhaps she could establish a small shop for herself in London. It would be a way to escape from the life of servitude her stepmother was certain to require of her without imposing on either Regina or Dorothea.

When the lines of guests had been formed, the duke raised his hand and the orchestra began to play. Melissa watched as the duke took Regina's arm and began to lead the procession to the banquet that awaited them.

"We must go, Emmy." Melissa guided Emmy away from the rail. "The banquet is about to begin and we will be needed elsewhere."

They had just entered the corridor, on their way to the kitchens, when Harley intercepted them. "Mrs. Parker requests a word with you, Lissa. You come along, too, Emmy. She sent me to fetch both of you."

"Is something amiss?" A worried frown appeared on Melissa's brow.

"No, Lissa." Harley gave her a reassuring smile. "Mrs. Parker merely wishes to speak with you on a matter of some importance."

As they followed Harley to Mrs. Parker's quarters, Melissa still wore an anxious expression. It was highly unusual for the housekeeper to be in her quarters at this hour. Perhaps Mrs. Parker had fallen ill and needed Melissa and Emmy to tend to her. But Harley had stated that nothing was amiss and he would surely have told them if the housekeeper were unwell.

When they arrived at Mrs. Parker's chambers, Harley knocked once and then opened the door. Melissa stepped in and her mouth dropped open in surprise as she saw Mrs. Parker, Henri, Mr. Oliver, and several other members of the staff in attendance.

"There is no need to be concerned, Lissa." Mrs. Parker laughed merrily as she noticed the worried frown that was still present on Melissa's face. "I have sent for you to present you with a gift."

"A gift? But . . . why?" Melissa was thoroughly mystified.

"Henri has told us of your dream, my dear, and we wished to help." Mrs. Parker took Melissa's hand and led her to a clotheshorse that had been draped with linen. She whisked off the drape and smiled in delight at Melissa's astonished expression.

"It's . . . it's a costume!" Melissa blinked at the sight of the lovely gown. "But how did you . . . ?"

"You must credit Henri with the concept." Mrs. Parker laughed. "You are to be the Princess of Winter at the ball this evening."

The gown was made of flowing white silk and fine Belgian lace, and Melissa reached out to touch the delicate material. "It is lovely! However did you fashion it in so little time?"

"You remember my cousin, Mrs. Collins, do you not?"

Melissa nodded quickly. "Indeed I do, Mrs. Parker."

"When I sent word to her of our plans, she presented us with her wedding dress. The bodice was trimmed with pink rosebuds, but those were easily removed. At Henri's suggestion, we replaced them with lace."

"Bridget did that." Henri nodded, beaming broadly.

Bridget smiled and dipped her head in a nod. "And Mrs. Parker sewed the cape, herself."

"Oh!" Melissa gasped as Mrs. Parker revealed the cape. It was fashioned from ice blue velvet with snowy white fur around the hem and the neck. "This is lovely material! Wherever did you find it on such short notice?"

"There is an abundance of it in the Blue Drawing Room." Mr. Oliver chuckled as Melissa's eyes widened. "Perhaps the draperies are not as full as they were this morning, but Mrs. Parker has assured me that none will notice."

"And the beautiful fur to trim the cape?" Melissa's eyes began to sparkle. No doubt that had been purloined in some manner from the duke's furnishings.

"It came from one of his grace's carriage robes." Harley spoke up. "He has many so you have no cause to be anxious."

"The robe was large and there was enough fur to fashion a cap for you to wear." Tina, another of the maids, stepped forward to present Melissa with the cap.

"Does this costume meet with your approval?" Mrs. Parker looked anxious. "We know it is not as fine as the one you made, but we all did our best."

Melissa rushed over to hug the housekeeper. "It is perfection, Mrs. Parker! Indeed, I have never seen one as delightful, or as imaginative!"

"You must dress now, Lissa." Emmy's eyes were shining. "The dancing will begin in less than an hour and you must be ready to take your place in the ballroom."

Melissa's heart was beating an excited rhythm as Mrs. Parker and her maids helped her to dress. Mr. Oliver, himself, saw to her coiffeur, claiming that he had arranged his grace's hair for a number of years and insisting that there could not be that much difference between the hair of a gentleman and the hair of a lady. When the cape was settled around her shoulders and the cap on her head, Melissa entered Mrs. Parker's small sitting room where Harley and Henri were waiting. Once they caught sight of her, they broke into applause, announcing that they had never seen a lovelier sight than their Princess of Winter.

"Magnifique!" Henri blinked several times to dispel the moisture that had gathered in his eyes. "You will be the belle of the ball, *mon enfant.*"

Harley nodded. "Well said! It is a pity that the duchess is not in residence, for I might have borrowed a gem or two for Lissa to wear."

"I am so glad you have reminded me, Harley, for I have the perfect earrings to wear with this lovely costume!" Melissa hurried to her basket to remove the packet that was hidden in the bottom. She uncovered the earrings and there was a collective and appreciative gasp from all in attendance as she clasped them on.

"Perfection!" Mrs. Parker nodded, gazing at the glittering blue diamonds in awe. "Wherever did you get them, Lissa?"

"They were a gift from my grandmother to my mother. When Mama died, she left them to me."

"Gorblimey!" Emmy was so shocked, she lapsed into the speech of her ancestors. "Be they real diamonds, Lissa?"

Melissa was about to reply that indeed they were, when she remembered that the servant, Lissa, was highly unlikely to possess something of so great a value.

"They could not possibly be real, Emmy." Henri pronounced, saving Melissa from the necessity of answering the question. "No doubt they are a clever imitation."

Mrs. Parker nodded. "They are indeed an excellent forgery, the best I have ever had the pleasure to see. Even I was taken in at first sight, Emmy, and I have seen many precious gems in my day."

"They are a superb copy." Mr. Oliver gazed closely at the jewels. "But I am certain that Lissa's grandmother would have sold them long ago to provide for her family, had they been genuine diamonds."

Emmy sighed. " 'Tis a pity they are not real, Lissa, but you must not be sad about that. They are a gift from your dear mama and that makes them precious. I am certain she will watch you from heaven tonight and be happy to see you wearing them."

"You are right, Emmy." Melissa smiled. Both her mother and father would be pleased that she was wearing the earrings, but this was not how either one of them had envisioned their daughter's first ball. They would be most distressed if they knew that she was there as her stepmother's servant who merely pretended to be the lady of quality, rather than an invited guest.

Regina clapped her hands together as the duke's chef wheeled in the cake. It was every bit as impressive as Lissa had promised it would be.

"La! It's a castle!" Lady Jennings cried out in delight. "There is even a courtyard with fruit trees!"

The guests formed a line to file past the table, admiring the clever beauty of Henri's creation. They were even more impressed when Henri informed them every part on the castle was edible, from the roof right down to the chocolate sauce that floated in the moat. There were many exclamations over the walls and turrets, and all agreed that the marzipan trees in the courtyard, trimmed with miniature sweets shaped like flowers and fruit, were utterly delightful and unlike any that had ever been seen before. When all had viewed the pastry to their satisfaction, the duke gestured for them to again take their seats.

"Your cake is a masterpiece, Henri!" The duke bowed to his French chef. "Without a doubt, you have outdone yourself."

Henri bowed back, a proud smile on his face. "Thank you, your grace, but I cannot claim all the credit for myself. The cake was Lissa's design and she assisted me in its assembly. I could not have done it without her help."

Low murmurs of appreciation came from the guests and Regina glanced quickly in her mother's direction. There was a scowl on her mother's face that did much to mar her beauty.

"Lissa again?" The duke turned to his guests with a smile. "It seems we must all thank Lissa tonight. Not only has she fashioned the elaborate costume my guest of honor displays with such beauty and grace, she has also ventured to my kitchens to help with the preparation of this marvelous work of culinary art. What say you we ask her to come out and accept our congratulations for a job well done?"

The guests broke into applause at the duke's suggestion. Many of them had made Lissa's acquaintance when they had called at the house on Belgrave Square. Of those, none had failed to like her and more than a few had remarked to friends that Lissa's talents were sorely wasted as Lady Harrington's servant. For those who had not encountered Lissa personally, they had heard Lady Beckworth's comments regarding her. That good woman had been quick to sing Lissa's praises and every member of the *ton* knew the tale of how Lissa had saved the opening dinner of the Season from certain disaster when Lady Beckworth's servants had fallen ill.

As the shouts for Lissa grew more insistent, Mrs. Parker made her appearance. She whispered a word in her employer's ear and an expression of dismay clouded the duke's countenance as he turned to address his guests once more.

"I fear we are to be denied Lissa's presence on this evening. It seems she has already gone to seek some well-deserved rest. I am certain you will all agree that her efforts on this day have been Herculean."

"Hear, hear!" Lord Chadwick rose to his feet. "Perhaps a small gratuity would not be amiss for the girl who has made our evening such a delight . . . unless, of course, it would offend Lady Harrington?"

Before her mother could do more than gasp, Dorothea stood

up to join Lord Chadwick. "How could this possibly offend Lady Harrington? It is a compliment to her wisdom in entrusting these critical tasks to Lissa."

Regina glanced at the duke who gave her a most improper wink. Before she could think, Regina winked back and then the duke spoke again.

"Let us pass the hat for Lissa. If you have no coins, personal notes will be accepted and redeemed upon the morrow."

The guests applauded this idea and there were several cries to second it. In view of this positive response, the duke reached up for his hat, but his costume had only an open crown.

"It seems my crown is unsuitable for the purpose." The duke laughed along with his guests. "Who among us will provide the hat?"

Henri swept off his gleaming white chef's toque. "I shall be happy to oblige you, your grace."

"And I shall pass it." Regina stood up to take the toque from Henri, beaming in delight despite her mother's disapproving glare. "Call out if you wish to contribute to this highly worthy cause."

As Regina passed the toque, Robert glanced at Lady Harrington. At first her expression was carefully guarded, but as the toque began to fill with notes and coins, her lips turned upwards and her eyes sparkled with greed. He would make certain that Lady Harrington did not take possession of Lissa's bounty. If it were given into that avaricious lady's keeping, the duke doubted that Lissa would see more than a penny or two of the money.

Henri's toque began to overflow before Regina had attended to even half of the assembly and a man dressed as a sultan offered his bejeweled turban. When the turban was full, a dairy maid donated her straw bonnet and that was half-filled by the time Regina arrived at the duke's side, her eyes shining with success.

Mrs. Parker had brought out a hamper for their use and the duke emptied the contents of Lissa's collection into its roomy interior. Then he handed the hamper to Mrs. Parker, instructing her to take it to his private sitting room, and smiled at the look of disappointment in Lady Harrington's eyes. When the toque, turban, and bonnet had been duly returned to their owners, the duke stood up once again.

"I thank you all for your generosity and now I have a small gift for you. Only last week, Lissa told me of a cake her family used to bake for special celebrations. Several small mementos were wrapped inside pouches of cloth and baked into the batter. Each guest received a portion of the cake and the lucky ones discovered that they had received gifts as well. Henri has duplicated this delightful custom on this evening, so I must warn you all to use caution lest you bite into a trinket."

There was a murmur of excitement as Henri picked up a knife to cut the cake. There were several protests that the cake was truly too beautiful to eat, but the duke gave Henri the signal and the cake was cut into portions to be distributed by the staff.

"Thank you, Duke!" A young lady dressed as a wood nymph cried out in delight as she uncovered a cloisonné ring. "This is lovely, indeed!"

"I have a watch fob shaped like a stag." A court jester held up his prize for all to see.

"My prize is a miniature jade dragon." A gypsy princess was the next to find her gift. "Thank you, Duke."

"This is utterly delightful!" Lady Beckworth held up a rose made of silver filigree. Then she turned to Lady Jennings, who had just found a set of dainty earrings in her portion, and exclaimed over them.

Regina watched the proceedings with amusement. Even the guests of mature years were behaving like children as they found their prizes. And wonder of wonders, it seemed that everyone had found a prize and not a single guest would go home empty-handed.

"Exactly how did you accomplish this feat?" Regina turned to the duke with a smile. "It appears that no one will be disappointed on this night."

The duke laughed and raised his brows in a rakish manner. "It was merely the luck of the draw, my dear. Do look . . . your mother is about to uncover her prize."

Regina turned and her eyes widened as her mother unwrapped a gold sovereign. With a smile of immense satisfaction, Lady Jane Harrington bit into the coin to test its authenticity and then slipped it into her bodice. Without even glancing round the table to see if she had been observed, she returned to ply her fork with even greater vigor to see if there might be another.

"Her efforts are wasted. There is but one." The duke winked at Regina. "Henri baked it into one of the turrets and that is the piece your mother received."

"Then you knew in advance where the prizes were hidden?"

"Of course." The duke favored her with a warm smile. "Henri marked the locations with bits of clean straw that stuck up above the batter. When the batter was baked, he removed the straws and marked them again with a drop of colored fondant. He used white for the ladies and chocolate for the gentlemen. It was all arranged in advance."

"And Lissa told you of this trick?"

The duke nodded. "She thought of it herself once I told her I wished for everyone to receive a prize."

"Where is this bit of colored fondant?" Regina stared down at her portion of cake.

"Flip it over with your fork and you shall see."

Regina did as he bid her and looked up in surprise as a dollop of pink frosting appeared. "Did you not tell me that the ladies' pieces had white fondant?"

"Yes, but I wished to make certain that no other would receive your portion. Cut into it, my dear. I should like to see if you are pleased by your prize."

Regina's heart was beating frantically as she extracted her trinket. She had assumed that the duke would save his declaration for the conclusion of the ball, but perhaps she had been mistaken. Her hands were trembling as she loosened the cloth.

Was this the moment the duke had chosen to propose to her and would she find the ring to pledge his troth as her prize?

"Oh! How . . . how beautiful!" Regina stared down at the tiny gold statue in her hand as relief washed over her in waves. "It is a likeness of Diana, the huntress, is it not?"

The duke nodded, apparently pleased at her enthusiastic response. "I wished to give you a private token on this most special of evenings."

"Thank you, Duke! I shall treasure it always!" Regina smiled up at him. She was not certain why he regarded this token as private. Indeed, it could have been given to any lady at the ball.

The duke took her hand and patted it gently. "I have not forgotten the evening we met and I promise that I shall always think of you as my goddess Diana."

Regina received his comment with a warm smile, but inwardly she was puzzled. She had known nothing of the goddess Diana before Melissa had told her the story, and neither she nor the duke had mentioned it on the evening they had met. For some reason, unknown to her, the duke seemed to equate her with this ancient goddess and Regina wished she had the courage to ask him to explain the reason he did so.

"Come, my goddess. It is time to lead the procession to the ballroom." The duke rose and held out his arm.

As Regina rose and waited for the other guests to form a queue behind them, she felt a flutter of regret for the news she would soon have to impart. The Duke of Oakwood was a charming gentleman and she hoped that he would not be too disappointed when she told him that she intended to marry another.

Seventeen

"God bless his grace." Mrs. Parker looked up to smile at Melissa. They were in the duke's private sitting room and the housekeeper was totaling the contributions the guests had made. "I have never heard tell of a host taking up a collection for a deserving servant before. Now that his grace has initiated the custom, no doubt it will become quite the rage at *ton* affairs."

Melissa held her breath as Mrs. Parker made the final tally marks and proceeded to add the column of figures. When the housekeeper turned to her there was a gratified smile upon her face.

"La, Lissa! You have enough and more to open your own shop as a modiste!"

Melissa shook her head. "But this largess was given for the tasks that were accomplished, and your staff worked by my side. It is only right to divide it amongst them equally, so all will benefit."

"Attempt it and you shall soon see that none will accept so much as a penny." Mrs. Parker laughed. "We have all agreed that this purse is for you alone, Lissa."

"But is it right for me to keep it?" Melissa's brow furrowed in an anxious frown.

"Of course it is, child!" Mrs. Parker smiled. "The contributions his grace's guests have made are but a mere trifle to them. It would be mean-spirited indeed, to deny them the pleasure they receive by gifting one who is not as fortunate as they are."

"You are doing it up much too brown, Mrs. Parker." There was a teasing note in Melissa's voice. "But I do believe that you are, for the most part, correct. I shall accept this kind contribution with gratitude."

Mrs. Parker nodded and then she cupped her ear to listen to the sounds that came to them from above. "The guests are entering the ballroom, Lissa. You must make ready to slip inside once the dancing has begun."

"Thank you, Mrs. Parker." Lissa reached out to hug the housekeeper who was now her good friend. "I truly believe that this is the happiest night of my life!"

Robert was dancing with Regina when there was a murmur of excitement in the ballroom. The noise swirled around them and he turned his head so that he could see the source of the commotion. A young lady had just entered, and Robert's eyes widened in appreciation as he caught sight of her. She was dressed as the Princess of Winter and she was so lovely, she took his breath away.

"She is beautiful!" Regina looked up at the duke, who appeared mesmerized. A faultless dancer, he had come close to missing a step. "I do not believe I have seen her before. Do you know who she is?"

Robert shook his head, attempting to calm his rapidly beating heart. "I do not know. Perhaps she is someone's house guest. I issued several open invitations to accommodate friends and relatives who had arrived unexpectedly."

"I do not recall seeing her at the banquet." Regina frowned slightly. "Perhaps she was delayed and has but recently arrived."

"Yes. That is a distinct possibility. I shall greet her after this dance has concluded and attempt to discover her identity."

The dance seemed endless and Robert did his utmost to concentrate his full attentions on Regina. Despite his best efforts, his eyes were drawn to the Princess of Winter and he found himself scowling as several young gentlemen approached her. He had no doubt that they were inviting her to stand up with them. How could any man resist the prospect of partnering the loveliest woman at the ball? But Robert was gratified to observe that though the Princess of Winter smiled charmingly at all who sought out her company, she accepted no offers and appeared quite content to stand close to the doors and observe the dancers.

"I am to partner Lord Chadwick in this dance."

Robert gazed down at Regina, fully aware that he had been distracted and hoping that she had not noticed. "Of course, my dear. I shall escort you to him straight away."

"One moment, please." Regina's voice trembled slightly as they approached Lord Chadwick. "I . . . I wish to know if there will be the usual intermission."

Robert nodded. "Yes, indeed. It will take place immediately following the second Quadrille."

"If it pleases you, Duke, I wish to request a private moment with you at that time."

Robert looked down at Regina in some confusion. All the color had left her cheeks and she appeared greatly distressed. "Is something amiss, my dear?"

"Oh, no. That is . . . I am not at all certain. I wish to discuss a matter of some importance with you. Indeed, it is of *supreme* importance and we . . . we must be alone."

"Then I shall ask your mother's permission to escort you to the observatory." Robert smiled to set her at ease. "Despite its name, no one will observe us there."

Regina laughed at his quip and a bit of color returned to her cheeks. "I thank you for agreeing so readily to our rendezvous and I pray you do not think me improper for requesting it. I assure you that were it not necessary, I should never have presumed to ask."

"None could accuse you of impropriety, my dear." Robert smiled down at her warmly. "And I shall make certain that no one ever shall."

When he had safely delivered Regina to Lord Chadwick's side, Robert sought out the Princess of Winter. He told himself that as her host, it was his duty to greet her and bid her welcome to the festivities. But Robert knew that his role as a proper host was not his sole motivation for seeking her company. There was something about this young lady that was hauntingly familiar and he was eager to discover who she was.

"I bid you welcome to the ball, Princess." Robert was surprised to find his voice was thick with emotion as he took her hand. "Would you do me the honor of standing up with me for this dance?"

"I should be delighted, Sire."

Her voice was low and musical, and Robert was certain that he had heard it before. But her words confused him for she had called him Sire. Surely she did not think that His Majesty, himself, approached her! Then he remembered that he was dressed as King Arthur and he laughed in amusement as he led her to the dance floor.

She fit into his arms as if she belonged there, following his lead faultlessly. His mind whirled as he held her and gazed at the portion of her face that was not covered by her mask. He knew her, he was as certain of it as he was of his own name. But the puzzle of her identity remained, and though he tried his utmost, he could not place her amongst his acquaintances.

Melissa sighed in utter contentment, her eyes sparkling to rival the diamonds that dangled brightly from her ears. She was in the arms of the man she loved once again, on this wondrous night of nights. None had recognized her or even questioned her right to attend the ball. Her ruse had been successful and she had been accepted as one of the invited guests.

Her lips parted slightly and a feeling of blissful happiness filled her being. Her dream had come true and she would not think of the morrow. This moment was magic and she would relive it, time and time again, for the rest of her life!

* * *

Damme! He knew her! Robert pulled her closer as they moved to the graceful steps of the waltz. He could remember the feel of her in his arms, the faint but compelling scent she wore, the way her hand rested so trustingly in his. He had danced with her before, he was certain. He had even kissed her on a warm summer's eve, he could recall the sweet taste of her lips. It had been a magical moment with the stars shining brightly over their heads and the soft breeze caressing the shining curtain of her hair.

Robert stepped back, into that moment, allowing his memories to guide his mind. They had danced to the strains of a far-away orchestra and the grass had been soft and fragrant beneath their feet, a green carpet that had been recently clipped. Light streamed out from windows in the distance, but it had not reached so far as to reveal her face. She had asked him for a promise on that magical night and . . .

The scales fell from Robert's eyes and he gazed down at the lovely young lady in his arms with astonishment. She was the lady that he had partnered on Aunt Sarah's balcony and kissed in his own gardens on the night of his dinner party. She was his very own goddess Diana!

Robert's startled gaze swept the ballroom until he located Regina, dancing with Lord Chadwick. Regina was not his goddess Diana. His true ancient huntress was in his arms in the guise of the Princess of Winter!

Perhaps he had tightened his arm around her, Melissa wasn't certain. Some instinct, some premonition of disaster, made her glance up into the duke's face. What she saw there caused her heart to pound and then miss a beat. He knew!

They were nearing the French doors to the garden. Melissa prayed that her expression would not give her away as she waited for her opportunity. She must leave, and quickly, or she would ruin her dear stepsister's life!

As if in answer to her prayer, the final strains of the dance were played. As everyone turned to applaud the orchestra, Melissa tore herself from her love's arms and slipped through the crowd so swiftly, the duke was not able to follow.

The cool night air revived the sudden wave of faint-headedness that threatened to overcome her. Melissa took a moment to slip off her dancing pumps and then she ran through the gardens, as if the furies were pursuing her, winding her way through the maze of walkways. She knew the paths well as she had come out to admire the blooms on almost every day that she had spent at Oakwood House. In very short order, she arrived at a spot on the garden wall where the stones were low enough to allow her to climb over and gain access to the street.

The street was deserted, but Melissa would not have noticed had it been filled with carriages. The tears in her eyes blinded her to her surroundings as she slipped on her shoes and wearily trudged the distance to Belgrave Square.

Once she had arrived home, Melissa began to think more clearly. Mary would be certain to mention it if she answered the door and saw Melissa garbed in the costume of the Princess of Winter. Rather than enter in the usual way, Melissa let herself in the side gate that led directly into the garden. From there it was possible to open the doors that led into her stepmother's Drawing Room and gain access to the hall.

Her heart beating rapidly, Melissa crept noiselessly up the staircase. Only when she had gained the safety of her bedchamber without discovery, did she sink down on the side of her bed and give way to her anguished sobs.

Robert returned to the ballroom in a brown study. His Diana had disappeared once again. He had followed her into the gardens, hoping that he could capture a glimpse of her, but all he had found were several embarrassed couples who had been taking full advantage of the darkness.

It was not until Robert stepped into the ballroom and caught sight of Regina, dancing with Lord Beckworth, that he realized he was in a distressing tangle. He had led dear Regina to believe that he would declare for her. Indeed, he had even been so foolish as to intimate to her mother that it was his true purpose for hosting the ball. In view of his actions, Regina's expectations had been raised to the highest level and if he failed to offer for her, she would be understandably overset.

Robert sighed. He could not offer for Regina when he was in love with another. It would be unfair to the delightful woman he had come to respect so greatly. There was no doubt that their marriage would be happy. Robert was quick to admit that they would rub along famously together. But Robert wanted more than commodious companionship. He wanted his Diana and no other, not even Regina, would do.

Regina arrived at his side, her color high from the figures of the Quadrille. "The intermission is about to begin."

Robert nodded, well aware of his obligations to this lovely young lady. "You are right, my dear. I shall address your mother straight away."

The request was duly made and answered in the affirmative. Robert sighed as he led Regina to the staircase that led to the observatory. From the predatory gleam in Lady Harrington's eye, he knew she fully expected him to discuss marriage with her daughter.

The moment the door to the observatory closed behind them, Regina turned to him with a sigh. "There is something of great import that I must tell you. I most fervently wish that we might be friends at the conclusion of our discussion, but I am prepared to take full blame for what I am about to say."

"You must sit down, Regina." Robert led her to a chair and pushed her down gently. The dear girl looked ready to crumple at his feet. "I shall light the candles."

"No! Please, I beg of you not to do so. This will be easier said if I cannot see your features."

Robert pulled a second chair close to hers and when he had settled himself, he took her hand. "Come now, Regina. What you are to tell me cannot be so drastic as to ruin our friendship."

"Yes, it can! My mother has told me that you plan to offer for me this evening. Is this true?"

Robert hesitated for a moment and then he nodded. "Yes, Regina. It is true."

"Please do not follow your plans! For you see . . . I . . . oh, Robert! I cannot bear to disappoint you so!"

Robert felt himself start with surprise. This was the first time that Regina had used his Christian name. Then the full impact of her words struck him and he realized why she had requested this private moment with him. "Are you about to tell me that you will not accept my offer?"

"Yes! I am so sorry, Robert! I know that I have appeared to return your affections, but . . ."

"Yes, Regina?" Robert smiled into the darkness. If Regina could be coaxed into speaking the words he anticipated, his dilemma would be solved. "You must not be afraid to tell me, my dear. I promise you that nothing you can say will cause me to regard you with less affection."

"I . . . I cannot marry you because I am in love with the Reverend Mr. Watson."

"Mr. Watson?" Robert repeated the name. "The young cleric with whom you do your charity work?"

"Yes. I truly did not mean to mislead you, Robert. I did not know my true feelings for him until he wrote to say that he wished to declare for me. The letter arrived only this evening and . . . I am so dreadfully sorry, Robert!"

"Hush, my dear." Robert gathered the shaking girl into his arms. "All will be well. You shall see."

"Then you are not upset with me?" Though Regina's voice was tearful, a current of hope ran through it.

"How could I be? You have entrusted me with your deepest emotions and that is as sacred a bond as the one we came so very close to making."

Regina sighed and laid her cheek upon his chest. "You are so good, Robert, and I feel so terribly guilty for causing you this distress. If I did not love Mr. Watson, I should be so very proud to be your wife."

"And if I did not love another, I should be so happy to have you."

"Oh, Robert!" Regina sat up quickly. "You are also in love with another?"

Robert sighed. He had not meant to tell her, but the confession had sprung from his lips before he could call it back. "Yes. And like you, dear Regina, I did not know of it until this very evening. I am so very grateful that you had the courage to tell me of your love for Mr. Watson."

"The Princess of Winter!" Regina breathed the words. "I know I have the right of it, Robert. I saw how you gazed down at her before your dance with her ended. Who is she? And does she know that you love her?"

Robert sighed and lit the candles. He called for refreshments and when they were seated comfortably again, he told Regina all about the mystery woman whom he had mistaken for her. In the end, both of them were laughing at the dreadful mistake they had come so dangerously close to making. Regina promised to go over the guest lists to identify the lady for Robert. She was certain that they could find Robert's Diana if they both set their minds to it.

"This is indeed a remarkable evening!" Regina's voice was filled with joy. "We are both to follow our hearts and no one is to be disappointed."

Robert shook his head. "You are forgetting about your mother. She will be in quite a taking over this whole affair."

"Mama!" Regina gasped. "What am I to do, Robert? Mama expects me to marry you. She has her heart set on making a match for me with a wealthy, titled nobleman. She will never accept the Reverend Mr. Watson in your stead."

Robert thought for a moment and then he took Regina's hand. "Your mother does not know it but she has already arranged one successful match. Chadwick has confided that he intends to declare for your sister at the closing of the Season. Do you think that will be enough to satisfy her?"

"Perhaps." Regina did not sound convinced. "But she will not accept Mr. Watson in any event. She will say that he has nothing to offer and she will be correct. While it is true that his parish is poor and we will have little to sustain us, I am of an age to marry without her permission and I vow I shall do so."

Robert reached out to hug her. "Perhaps you are my Diana, after all. It will take great courage to disobey your mother. She is a very determined woman."

"Yes, indeed." Regina giggled. "Mama is every bit as formidable a force as Wellington's best troops!"

"What would your mother say if you were to marry a vicar who is certain to become a bishop?" Robert began to smile as a plan occurred to him.

"Why . . . I am not certain. But I should think that would meet with her approval. It is a high office with much prestige and those qualities matter greatly to her."

"Then that is what you shall tell her. The vicar of Oakwood is about to retire and it is my duty to name his replacement. Your Reverend Mr. Watson shall become the new vicar."

Regina threw her arms around his neck and gave him an enthusiastic hug. "Oh, Robert! You are indeed the kindest of men! I shall write to him tonight and tell him how good you are! You have fulfilled one of my fondest dreams!"

"One of them?" Robert smiled down at her. "You have others?"

Regina nodded. "There is but one more and it concerns Lissa. You see Lissa is not truly our servant. She is my stepsister, the daughter of Lord Harrington."

As Regina told the story of how Lissa had been trapped into performing the role of their servant, the duke felt his anger rise. Lady Harrington deserved to be punished roundly for the anguish and humiliation she had caused dear Lissa to endure. He had long suspected that all was not as it seemed with Lissa and now the puzzle was solved at last.

"You are not to concern yourself any longer, Regina." Robert smiled as he guided her to her feet. "Now that I am aware of your mother's duplicity, I promise you that I shall make certain that your dear stepsister's life is set aright."

More than an hour had passed before Melissa felt capable of rational thought. She had prayed that she had been mistaken, that the duke had not guessed that she was his Diana. But even if he had realized that Regina was not the woman he had held in his arms on Lady Beckworth's balcony or kissed passionately in his own gardens on the eve of his dinner party, Melissa knew that he would uphold his honor as a gentleman. He had courted Regina and given her reason to assume that he would offer for her. He would not cry off from that duty.

Somewhat relieved, Melissa removed her costume and folded it carefully. She was gratified to observe that the delicate Belgian lace was intact. Mrs. Collins's wedding gown could also be restored to its original state. All Melissa need do was to reattach the pink roses that had been clipped from the bodice.

Clothed in her night rail and a wrapper, Melissa sat down by the brazier to remove her precious earrings. It was only then that she noticed that one was missing.

Heart pounding in alarm, Melissa retraced her steps, hunting frantically for its mate. Though her search was diligent, it was in vain. Her missing earring was not in her stepmother's townhouse, nor anywhere in the immediate vicinity.

Melissa sighed as she crawled under her covers and blinked back tears of remorse. It would be useless to continue her search in the darkness. Early tomorrow morning, she would set out for Oakwood House, walking the route she had taken in reverse. If she failed to find her precious earring, she would ask for Mrs. Parker's assistance in searching the ballroom and the duke's gardens.

Eighteen

Melissa attempted to find a dry spot on her pillow, but her search was doomed to failure. After waking frequently during the night with disturbing dreams and a sense of desolation that she could not dispel, she wanted nothing more than to sleep the day away. She wished to remain hidden in her bedchamber, safe from the curious glances that Jane and her stepsisters would be certain to bestow upon her, once they observed the traces of her recent tears. But the sun was peeping over the horizon and there was no time to tarry. She had to inform Mrs. Parker that she had lost one of her earrings immediately so that the house-keeper could ask the staff to keep watch for it during the clean-ing and straightening of the duke's residence that was certain to take place this morning.

After performing her morning ablutions and dressing in one of her serviceable gowns, Melissa picked up the package that contained her costume and tiptoed down the staircase. The sun had barely risen and no one was awake to witness her departure as she let herself out the heavy front door. She simply had to find her missing earring. They had been her grandmother's most beloved possession and she had entrusted them to Melissa's mother. Now that they had come into Melissa's keeping, Melissa felt as if she would be violating her family's trust if she did not find the precious gems.

* * *

"My son did not declare for her at the ball?" The duchess looked greatly relieved as Lady Beckworth shook her head. They had reached London early this morning and had driven directly to Lady Beckworth's mansion to solicit her advice.

"This is wonderful news, Mama!" Lucy gave a heartfelt sigh of relief. "Our trip has not been in vain."

"You do not approve the match?" Lady Jennings, who was also in attendance in Lady Beckworth's sitting room, frowned slightly.

"It is not that Mama disapproves." Lucy made haste to explain. "We do not know Lady Harrington's daughter and can form no opinion of her character."

Lady Beckworth nodded and a smile crossed her face as she addressed her old friend. "I understand perfectly, Aurora. It is not the daughter, but Lady Harrington, herself, who concerns you."

"Precisely right!" the duchess agreed quickly. "You were always quick to catch my meaning, Sarah, even when we were in the schoolroom. Lucy and I have come to warn Robert of Lady Harrington's character, not to malign her daughter."

Lady Jennings leaned forward, as if she were about to impart the juiciest tidbit of *ton* gossip. "That horrible woman dismissed two highly suitable dressers last Season, turning them out without references. She wishes to recapture the glory of her first Season and refuses to admit that her beauty has faded. I engaged one of the dressers myself, after the woman was dismissed. She confided to me that her only fault was to call Lady Harrington's attention to several gray hairs and suggest that they be plucked out."

"Then vanity is another of the lady's failings?" Lucy asked the question.

Lady Jennings laughed. "But of course, my dear Lucy. I should put it near the top of the list, which is very long, indeed. Lady Harrington steadfastly refuses to admit that if one chooses to strut like a peacock, one should be certain one still has the plumage for it. After one reaches a certain age, no amount of damping one's petticoats will catch a gentleman's eye."

"She truly engages in that ploy?" Lucy looked properly shocked.

Lady Jennings shook her head. "Not recently, no, but her costume at last night's ball left very few of her charms unexposed. I suspect the lady must have doused herself with paste to prevent her from popping out of her bodice."

"If you were not my dearest cousin, I should chide you for shocking poor Lucy." Lady Beckworth laughed. "But I must admit that your assessment of the lady's character is correct. Jane Harrington is a silly woman, vain and avaricious. If one should poll the members of the *ton,* I venture to say that one should find few who hold even a modicum of respect for her."

"Then why has she been so well received?" Lucy began to frown. "I should think that such a lady would be given the cut."

Lady Jennings sighed. "It is only her status as Lord Harrington's widow that causes the *ton* to receive her. The gentleman was well respected and to refuse courtesy to his widow would reflect upon his good name. There are also Lady Harrington's daughters to consider. They appear to be well-bred young ladies and it is not fair to fault them for being born to such a despicable mother."

"Tell me about the elder daughter, Sarah." The dowager duchess addressed her old bosom bow. "What is your opinion of her character?"

Lady Beckworth appeared thoughtful. "I have had little converse with her, but I believe her to be of high principles. It is true that she has encouraged dear Robert's attentions, but there is no conspiracy on her part, I am certain. She is, however, quite firmly in her mother's pocket, obeying Lady Harrington instantly without the slightest whisper of protest. I would wager to say that she would not even attempt to breathe should her mother expressly forbid it!"

"The poor thing!" Lucy sighed. "To have a mother like that. I cannot imagine what distress it must cause her."

The dowager duchess smiled and patted Lucy's hand. "Thank you, Lucy, for that lovely compliment. But I fear the news that dear Sarah and Lady Jennings have given us is most distressing. Let us go immediately to Oakwood House and inform Robert of what we have learned."

"Will he believe us if he has formed a *tendre* for Lady Harrington's daughter?" A look of concern crossed Lucy's countenance. "The poets claim that love is blind and he may not see the influence this horrible woman has over her daughter."

Lady Beckworth nodded. "Your point is well taken, Lucy. Perhaps we should go *en masse*. Robert has always shown a fondness for me. Indeed, he has told me that he regards me as his Aunt Sarah, though we are not related. I am certain he respects my opinion on *ton* matters and will realize that I have no reason to falsely accuse Lady Harrington."

"An excellent suggestion!" The duchess reached out to take her old friend's hand. "Let us be off before any more harm can occur. It will be preferable for Robert to fail to declare for Lady Harrington's daughter than to cry off once he has done so."

"Good morning, Emmy." Robert stepped quickly to the side to avoid a collision with the young maid who was rushing down the hall. Emmy looked astonished to see him up with the sun on this morning, as the ball had ended only a few hours ago.

"Good morning, your grace!" Emmy bobbed a curtsy.

After he had waved Emmy on her way, Robert climbed the staircase to the ballroom. He had left instructions with Mrs. Parker that it was not to be straightened until he ordered it. His Diana had fled from his arms to the gardens and had not reappeared in the ballroom. Perhaps she had dropped some clue to her identity in her headlong flight.

Though he searched the ballroom for close to an hour, Robert found no trace of his Diana. There were several items the guests had left behind; a painted fan, a lace handkerchief, a string of glass beads, and an ivory snuffbox, but none of them had belonged to the Princess of Winter. His heart heavy, Robert opened the French doors that led to the gardens and resumed his search there.

There was nothing on the stone steps save a forgotten goblet containing an inch or so of champagne. Robert was alert as he walked down the steps and entered the gardens. Dew still clung to the petals of the roses and he sighed as he inhaled their sweet perfume. As he did not know which particular path his Diana had taken, he would examine them all.

A bit of black lace was caught on the thorn of a white rose bush. Robert was about to retrieve it when he remembered the colors of his Diana's costume. The lace belonged to another of his guests, perhaps the Spanish countess who had revealed herself as Lord Chadwick's sister.

Robert's search took him past the tree where he had danced with his love in the starlight. He stared at the stretch of perfectly manicured grass and sighed. What would he do if his search were fruitless? Regina had promised to provide him with the guest lists, but he doubted that he would find his Diana's name among the others who had been issued invitations. The Princess of Winter had not been present in the ballroom when they had formed the opening promenade, nor had she been seated in the solarium to enjoy Henri's excellent cuisine. Robert had relived those moments carefully, and he was certain that he would have noticed her, had she been among the other guests.

The path he was searching curved very close to the stone wall that bordered the street. Robert had never been in this particular section of the gardens before and he frowned as he realized that the mortar had crumbled and several stones had fallen from the top of the wall. He would have to tell his gardeners to repair the damage immediately, as it would be possible for someone to climb over the low spot and gain access without his permission. He was about to go fetch the head gardener to show him the damage, when he spotted something glittering brightly in the sunlight at the base of the wall.

Heart beating rapidly in excitement, Robert strode to the spot and retrieved the object. It was a lovely earring made up of a string of blue diamonds, bound together in a cleverly fashioned chain. Robert gasped as he examined it. The Princess of Winter had worn these very earrings, he was certain. He remembered thinking how well they suited her costume as they had reminded him of sparkling blue icicles.

A smile spread over Robert's face as he dropped the earring into his pocket. He had solved the puzzle of his love's disappearance. The Princess of Winter had fled through his gardens and climbed over the low spot on the wall. And even more important, he had found only one earring, not the pair. Even if they were *faux* diamonds, the settings were painstakingly crafted and they were worth a pretty penny. There was no doubt that she would be most distressed when she discovered her loss and would return, retracing her steps, in an attempt to retrieve it.

His Diana had provided him with a golden opportunity and Robert vowed to take full advantage. He would not repair the garden wall at present. Instead, he would station a team of gardeners to watch the wall from a hidden spot. If his Diana came back to search for her earring, he would have her brought to him straight away.

After giving Mrs. Parker leave to set the ballroom in order, Robert called for his head gardener and arranged for additional men to watch the low spot on the garden wall. He did not give his true reason for requesting this surveillance. Robert was aware that one careless word, spoken by one of his servants, might warn his Diana of the trap he had set for her. But he did make certain that anyone who entered his gardens in that fashion, be it gentleman, lady, or servant, be detained and brought into his presence.

It was not until he was back in his chambers that Robert realized the full significance of his find. With trembling fingers, he drew out the packet that his father had left for him and compared the necklace to the earring he had found. The blue diamonds were of a like size and cut, and the workmanship of the settings was identical. His Diana was the daughter of Anne Hathaway, his father's first love, and Robert vowed that he would not rest until he had found her again and fulfilled his father's dying request.

When Melissa arrived at Oakwood House, she was weary and dispirited. Though she had followed the exact route she had taken the previous evening, she had found no trace of her missing earring.

"Lissa! Whatever is amiss?" Emmy rushed up to greet her friend, but after one look at Melissa's distressed countenance, the smile quickly vanished from her face.

"I must see Mrs. Parker, Emmy. Would you be so kind as to find her for me? It is a matter of grave importance."

Emmy nodded and pulled up a chair for her friend. "Your face is the color of snow, Lissa. You had best sit down while I fetch her."

Mrs. Parker arrived in short order, wearing an expression of deep concern. "Emmy told me that you are overset, Lissa. Whatever is the matter?"

"I have lost one of my precious earrings!" Melissa's voice was trembling and she took a moment to compose herself. "I did not discover that it was missing until I was back in my bedchamber last night. I searched there thoroughly, and this morning I retraced my steps to your door. But I . . . I failed to find it!"

Mrs. Parker took Melissa's hands and squeezed them tightly. "You must not give up hope, Lissa. Do you remember when last you possessed it?"

"I . . . I am not certain!" Melissa sighed heavily.

Mrs. Parker thought for a moment. "Your earrings were both in place when you entered the ballroom. I remember noticing how lovely they looked in the light of the chandeliers."

"And you were wearing them when you danced with his

grace. Emmy spoke up. "I was watching from the balcony. You had both when you went into the garden. I am certain of that!"

Melissa gave a small heartbroken cry. "My earring is gone then, just as I feared! If I lost it in the garden, it may never be found!"

"Of course it will, child." Mrs. Parker patted Melissa on the shoulder. "I shall call the staff together and organize a search for your precious heirloom."

Emmy nodded. "Mrs. Parker is right, Lissa. With that many searchers it is certain to be found. Did you bring your other earring?"

"Yes, it is in the bottom of my basket." Melissa was surprised at Emmy's question. "Why did you wish to know?"

"Many members of the staff did not see you in your costume. You must show them your other earring so that they will know precisely what they seek."

"Well done, Emmy!" Mrs. Parker was beaming as she gestured for them to follow her. "Let us make haste to organize this search. We shall each take a small section of the garden and comb it thoroughly. Not a single blade of grass shall escape our notice. You shall see, Lissa. Our search shall be so meticulous, your missing earring will be certain to be found."

Robert frowned as he rang, once again, for his valet. He had intended to don the appropriate clothing to call on Regina. It was early but he was certain that she would receive him. Once he had secured the guest lists, they would peruse them together to see if they contained any names they did not recognize. He rang another time and began to pace the floor anxiously. His valet had been unfailingly prompt in all his years of service. Where in tarnation was the man?

Deciding that there was nothing for it but to locate the gentleman's gentleman himself, Robert opened the door and stepped out into the hallway. He found it deserted, which was also unusual. Not a sound reached his ears as he walked toward the staircase. It was as if he were alone in the house. Had there been some type of crisis that had demanded the services of his entire staff? If so, why had he not been informed?

Fearing the worst, Robert hurried down the staircase but he found no one in attendance on the first floor. It was as if his entire staff had suddenly deserted him. What in blazes was going on?

As he passed through the entrance hall, he heard the sounds of approaching carriages. Robert glanced out one of the tall narrow windows that flanked the front door and frowned as he observed two carriages arriving. He recognized the first. It was his mother's coach and it contained two occupants, the duchess and his sister, Lucy. A frown furrowed Robert's brow. Why were they here, in London? He had just taken leave of them not two days past!

A second carriage arrived on the heels of the first and Robert's frown deepened as he observed that the coachman was dressed in Lady Beckworth's livery. Aunt Sarah was here, too. And with her was her cousin, Lady Jennings.

At that exact moment, Robert heard a commotion at the side of the house. He rushed to the Drawing Room to look out the French doors, and he was astounded to see his entire staff gathered in his gardens.

Robert hurried to the doors and threw them open, just in time to see his housekeeper hold up a mate to the earring he had found. The staff was gathered around her and they were all staring at the earring, as if they wished to memorize its design.

"We are searching for another, precisely like this one." Mrs. Parker's voice was commanding. "Lissa is certain that she lost it in the gardens and there is no time to waste. We shall search until we have found it!"

With a murmur of agreement, the staff dispersed. The head gardener directed them to various sections of the gardens and all were so intent on the task before them, none saw their master standing at the open doors with a shocked expression on his face.

"Lissa?" Robert breathed the question. If Lissa had lost the earring, then she was his Diana, the Princess of Winter! The woman he loved, the woman he could not live without, had been right under his nose at Oakwood House for the past two weeks, and now she was only a few steps away in his gardens!

Robert rushed from the Drawing Room and threw open the front door, calling out for his mother and the rest of her party to join him in the gardens. Then he raced up to his bedchamber to retrieve the earring and necklace and raced out to the gardens to find Lissa.

Nineteen

"Whatever was Robert doing, throwing open the door himself?" Lady Beckworth turned to her old friend with a frown.

The duchess began to smile. "I have not the slightest notion, Sarah, but nothing Robert does shall ever truly surprise me, not after the pranks he pulled as a boy. I suggest we do as he directed and go to the gardens straight away."

After instructing their coachmen to drive round to the stables and see to their horses and equipages, the small party approached the door. It was fortunate that it was ajar for there was no one to grant them access.

"Where are the servants?" Lady Jennings surveyed the empty entrance hall with concern.

"They are obviously elsewhere." The duchess looked amused as she turned to her daughter. "Take Lady Jennings's cloak, Lucy, and find a convenient place for it. Sarah and I shall fend for ourselves."

After the ladies had divested themselves of their outer garments, the duchess took Lady Beckworth's arm. "Did you take notice of my son's unusual manner of dress?"

"How could I *not* take notice?" There was an answering twinkle of amusement in Lady Beckworth's eyes. "His shirt cuffs were not fastened correctly and it appeared to me that the buttons were in the wrong holes. And I am not certain, but I believe he had an untied cravat looped over his wrist."

The duchess nodded. "You are precisely right, Sarah. Robert

was in a frightful state of disarray, as if he had hastily dressed himself and failed abysmally at the task. And he wore a most puzzling smile, very like the one he used to wear when I caught him pilfering cakes from the ledge where cook had placed them to cool."

"It was a most mischievous smile, indeed." Lady Beckworth laughed. "I have not seen Robert enjoy himself so since he assumed his father's duties as the duke."

Lucy nodded in complete agreement. "Robert did look supremely happy. What could be the cause of it, Mama?"

"I am not certain, Lucy, but I do believe I sense a scandal in the offing."

"A scandal? How dreadful!" Lady Jennings fanned her face, her eyes wide with distress.

"You are doing it up too brown, cousin." Lady Beckworth laughed merrily. "We are all aware that you adore a good scandal. Do not bother to pretend otherwise for we shall not believe you."

Telling color rose to Lady Jennings's cheeks and she gave an embarrassed laugh. "I fear you are right, cousin. But scandal is exciting, is it not?"

"It is, indeed." Lucy giggled. "And I do believe Mama has the right of it. Robert is up to a good bit of mischief. Let us hurry to the gardens and see for ourselves."

The duchess marched toward the Drawing Room, a happy smile on her face. "I do declare, Sarah. I have not had so much fun since the night we attempted to run away from Mrs. Scarborough's Academy, intent upon becoming actresses!"

Melissa was searching the ground under a small hawthorne bush, when she became aware of the hush that had fallen over the garden. A moment later there was a shout, followed by a babble of excited voices.

"Lissa!" Mrs. Parker's voice carried clearly to Melissa's ears. "Come quickly! Your earring has been found!"

Melissa stood up and rushed toward the clearing where they had agreed to meet should her earring be recovered. Her steps slowed somewhat when she noticed Lady Beckworth and three other well-dressed ladies observing the process with some amusement.

"I am here, Mrs. Parker." Melissa brushed off her dress hastily and approached the housekeeper. "Who found it?"

"I did."

Melissa's eyes widened as the crowd of servants parted slightly and she caught sight of the Duke of Oakwood. He was holding up her earring for all to see and smiling broadly.

"Your grace!" Melissa's lips mouthed the words, but her voice was no more than a whisper. She stood there transfixed, staring at the glittering earring he held in his hand, her feet no longer capable of forward motion.

"Come to me, Lissa."

The duke beckoned her forward but Melissa's feet seemed affixed to the ground. Had the duke recognized her earring as one of the pair that the Princess of Winter had worn?

"Lissa?" The duke's eyes were warm and they seemed to twinkle in the sunlight. "Come here and I will return your lovely earring."

"Yes, your grace." Her legs were trembling so violently, they felt like a pair of thin sticks in a fierce wind. Melissa somehow managed to make them obey her and crossed the clearing to approach him. She reached out to take the earring from his hand and that was when the Duke of Oakwood did something so completely unexpected that Melissa could do no more than gasp. He reached into his pocket, drew out a glittering blue diamond necklace, and quickly clasped it around her neck. And then he pulled her into his strong arms and kissed her in front of the whole assembly!

Melissa felt her knees weaken and dissolve the way Elise's apple conserve had melted on freshly-baked bread. Her head spun in confused circles and she was only dimly aware of the shocked exclamations and the startled gasps that surrounded her. Her confusion lasted for no more than a moment and then she gave way to the bliss that filled every portion of her soul.

Robert felt passion overtake him as she began to return his kiss. He had found his Diana and nothing would keep him from making her his wife. He wished with all his being that their kiss could continue forever, but he owed an explanation to his staff and his family.

Reluctantly, Robert released his Diana. He took the precaution of clamping one arm firmly around her waist to assure that she would not escape him again, and he turned to face the crowd that surrounded them. "Now that I have thoroughly comprised this lovely young lady, I fear she has no choice but to marry me."

"You are bamming us, certainly!" Lady Jennings's voice was quavering with shock. "Surely you cannot mean that you are declaring for Lady Harrington's maid!"

Robert smiled. "But that is precisely what I am doing, Lady Jennings. I formally declare for this lovely young lady before this whole assembly. What say you, Mother? Will you indulge in an attack of the vapors and refuse to speak to me ever again if I marry dear Lissa?"

"Certainly not!" The duchess laughed. "You know that I have never given a button for social conventions! If you marry her, I shall welcome her as my daughter with open arms."

Lucy smiled. "Well done, Mama. I, too, will welcome her, Robert, if she is the choice of your heart."

"Aunt Sarah?" Robert turned to Lady Beckworth who was wiping a tear from her eye.

Lady Beckworth nodded quickly. "Of course I shall welcome her, Robert. And I shall do my utmost to assure that the *ton* does likewise."

"And I shall do my part, also." Lady Jennings spoke up. "I vow that I shall not breathe a word of what I have witnessed here today until you give me your leave."

"That is a sacrifice indeed, Lady Jennings." Robert favored her with a smile. And then he turned to his housekeeper. "Mrs.

Parker? I value your opinion and I wish to hear it. Will your staff accept Lissa as their new mistress?"

Mrs. Parker turned to her staff and one by one, they began to applaud. When they had quieted, Mrs. Parker nodded. "You have your answer, your grace."

"Now that you have informed me of your true feelings, I must answer the question that is uppermost in your minds." Robert smiled at them all. "Lady Harrington's daughter released me from my obligations last evening after we both had confessed that we loved another. My dearest friend, Regina, is to marry her young parson who is soon to become the vicar of Oakwood."

"Can this be true?" Melissa's voice was only a whisper but the duke heard her and nodded. A smile of joy spread over Melissa's face and she knew she had never been so happy. Regina was to marry the Reverend Mr. Watson! And he would be the vicar of Oakwood!

"Regina also confessed that Lissa is the daughter of Lord Harrington."

"Then Lissa is not a servant?" Lady Jennings looked greatly relieved when the duke shook his head. "But for what purpose did Lady Harrington introduce her as such?"

"Lissa must tell you the reason if she wishes to do so. It is not my secret to tell. And now, if you will all indulge me, I must have an answer from my intended bride." Robert knelt down on the grass, keeping a firm grip on Lissa's hand. "Will you marry me, my darling Lissa? Or would you prefer that I compromise you more thoroughly, right here in my gardens?"

"Oh, yes! I will marry you!" Lissa's eyes were shining as she gazed down into the dear face of her very perfect match. And then, when he had risen to take her in his arms once more, she whispered in his ear. "It would be well for us to marry at once, my darling duke. I should not like to wait longer for you to compromise me much more thoroughly, indeed!"

Epilogue

The aroma of freshly baked lemon seed cakes drifted up to tease Melissa's senses and she smiled at her reflection in the mirror. Henri, who had made the long journey from London for this special occasion, had seized Melissa's old family recipe with great enthusiasm. Indeed, the diminutive French chef had prepared it for five days running to make certain that there should be enough for the boisterous crowd that was soon to fill the dining hall of Oakwood Castle.

It was to be a grand Christmas celebration and Melissa was filled with delight at the prospect of spending the entire holiday season with the family she loved so dearly. Dorothea and her husband, Lord Chadwick, had arrived two days past and had immediately thrown themselves into the midst of the preparations. Indeed, Charles had barely taken a sip of the toddy that Robert had given to him upon their arrival before he had insisted that he be allowed to accompany Robert to the woods that surrounded the castle to oversee the procurement of the yule log.

Dorothea had set to work immediately, helping Melissa and her staff fashion decorations. She had taught all the maids the exact manner in which to tie bows of red and green velvet so that they could be easily affixed to the swags of green branches that adorned the ballroom.

That evening, dear Regina had come from the vicarage to help with the trimming. It had been a marvelous party.

Just when they had decided that the guests from London

should surely be delayed another day, the sound of horses stomping and grooms shouting had alerted them that a large party had arrived. Moments later, the dowager duchess had blown in with the snow, greeting her family with warm affection. Aunt Sarah had followed in her wake, brushing the snow from her cloak with a laugh, and declaring that she was delighted to be here at last. Her cousin, Lady Jennings, had seemed a bit flustered to arrive with her hair blown out of place by the wind, but her two daughters, Violetta and Helena, had quickly assured their mama that she looked quite fetching that way.

The next arrivals had come before the greetings had been properly concluded. Robert's sister, Lucinda had burst in with her two small boys, who had greeted their Aunt Lissa and Uncle Robert with sleepy mumbles and been promptly taken off to bed. Once Lucy's husband, Viscount Trelane, had tucked the boys in, he had joined the group and accepted a hot toddy with pleasure. Two of Robert's young nephews had then arrived, accompanied by their father, the Marquis of Pembrook. Uncle Lawrence, as he had urged Melissa to call him, had brought his two sons for the express purpose of meeting Lady Jennings's daughters. The girls had been delighted, of course, to meet such eligible young gentlemen and Melissa had noticed that Uncle Lawrence, a widower for the past three years, had shown a decided interest in making the acquaintance of their widowed mother.

When Melissa had observed that her two stepsisters were eyeing the entrance with ill-concealed anxiety, she had motioned to Robert to put them at ease. That was when her beloved husband had announced that Lady Harrington would not be joining them for this Christmas celebration as she had embarked on a trip to the continent and was at this moment, enjoying the delights of Paris. It had been an early Christmas present from Robert and the reservations he had secured had necessitated her immediate departure for this glittering capital of France, without the time to even take proper leave of her daughters and Melissa.

There had been cries of "Well done!" all around and Gina and Doro had appeared much relieved. Though they had all treated Jane with the respect that her position as mother and stepmother required, no one, not even her daughters, had been anticipating her arrival at Oakwood Castle with any degree of pleasure. They had all spent the remainder of the evening in contented enjoyment, knowing that they had been spared, through Robert's largess, any but congenial company.

"What a lovely sight!"

A deep voice from the connecting doorway made Melissa smile as she turned to greet her husband. He cut a dashing figure in his formal wear and as always, Melissa's heart quickened at the sight of the handsome gentleman that she had married.

"Robert, dear." Melissa rose to greet him. "How very kind in you to pay me a compliment when I know I must look a fright."

Robert reached out to wrap his arms around her and hugged her tightly. "You could not look more beautiful to me. Is that a new gown? I don't recall seeing it before."

"No. It is an old one and much too tight!" Melissa frowned slightly. "Emmy managed to button it properly, but I can scarcely breathe. And when I bent down to pat Perseus, I feared that I should split a seam."

"You look lovely in it, but you should not wear it if it causes you discomfort. You must change to something looser so that you will be able to enjoy Henri's excellent feast."

Melissa shook her head. "That is precisely what I planned to do, but this is the third gown I have tried. It seems none of my gowns are large enough and it is most distressing!"

"Hold still, darling." Robert turned her around and swiftly unfastened the back of the gown. "There. Is that better?"

"Much better. I can breathe again! But I cannot appear before our guests with my gown undone. Whatever am I to do, Robert?"

"I have just the thing to solve your problem." Robert dropped a quick kiss on the tip of her nose. "Wait here a moment and I will fetch it."

Melissa sighed as she waited for her husband to return. The exposed skin on her back tingled warmly where his fingers had brushed it. His touch never failed to stir her this way, even though they had been married for well over a year.

"Here you are, my love. This shall do the trick."

A happy smile spread over Melissa's face as she caught sight of the lovely shawl that her husband draped over her shoulders. It was woven of the finest cashmere and the design resembled a field of colorful spring flowers. "Oh, Robert! I have never seen such a beautiful shawl! Wherever did you get it?"

"I wrote to Mother and she commissioned a milliner in London to obtain it. The winters are dreary here at Oakwood Castle, and I wished that my dearest Diana should always be surrounded by a field of beautiful flowers."

Melissa stood on tiptoe to kiss him, but what she had intended as a simple kiss of gratitude soon became much more than that. When Melissa pulled away at last, with undisguised reluctance, she sighed deeply. "I promised to see my sisters when I was dressed, though I confess that I should much rather—"

"Your sisters." Robert interrupted her with a groan. "I completely forgot to tell you that they are waiting in the hall to see you."

Melissa laughed at the guilty expression on her husband's face. "It seems we must both take care to remember that we are entertaining and can no longer do *precisely* what we wish when we wish to do it."

"And *precisely* what would that be, my love?"

Robert's voice was teasing, and the color rose to Melissa's cheeks. "You know *precisely* to what I refer. And if you do not, I shall tell you when we are truly alone."

"I shall hold you to that promise, my dear." Robert was smiling as he crossed to the door to let her sisters in. "I will join the gentlemen and await your arrival."

"Lissa!" Doro rushed into the room to give her stepsister a hug. "You look enchanting!"

Gina nodded, following a trifle more sedately. "You do, Lissa. And that shawl is lovely! Dede and Lucy joined us while we were waiting for you. Shall I ask them to come in?"

"Dede?" Melissa was confused.

Gina laughed and hastened to explain. "It is the new name that Lucy's boys gave their grandmama. They are her initials, you see. Dede is for dowager duchess. She liked it so well, she gave us all leave to call her that if we wished."

"By all means, do ask Dede to come in." Melissa tried the name and smiled in delight. "I declare, it is perfect for her!"

Doro ushered in Dede and Lucy, and it turned into a merry party. Everyone declared that Melissa's new shawl was exquisite and there were bursts of excited chatter as hair was patted into place, skirts were smoothed, and jewelry was selected for Melissa to wear.

At least they were ready to make their entrance, and Melissa turned to Lucy. "Does my new shawl cover my back? Robert had to loosen the laces on my gown."

"Robert loosened your gown?" Dede gave Melissa a searching look. "Why did he do that, dear girl?"

"It was too tight. I fear that I have gained flesh, though I do not understand how such a thing could have occurred. I felt rather poorly for several days and I ate very little."

Dede began to smile in undisguised delight. "You felt poorly and ate very little, yet you gained flesh?"

"Yes." Melissa nodded. "But just recently my appetite has returned with a vengeance and I find I am so looking forward to this evening's din . . ."

Melissa stopped suddenly and stared at them in bewilderment. "Why are you all smiling in that particular manner? Every one of you resembles the cat that got into the cream pot!"

"My dear, Lissa." Lucy stepped forward to give her a hug.

"Could it be possible that you are increasing and well on your way towards giving my brother an heir?"

"Increasing?" Melissa looked completely astounded for a moment and then a telling blush rose to her cheeks.

"Ah, ha!" Lucy turned to her mother. "You were right, Mama, though I cannot for the life of me understand how you can tell so quickly!"

"You knew?" Melissa turned to Dede in astonishment.

"I suspected, and I certainly hoped, but I did not know." Dede smiled at Melissa. "There is a certain look in your eyes, a serenity I have not seen there before. Does Robert know?"

Melissa laughed merrily. "Of course not! How could he know when I did not even guess? Oh, I am such a ninny not to suspect it! I must tell Robert straight away!"

"It will be your Christmas present to him." Dede hugged Melissa tightly. "And never fear. We shall not give away your secret until you have chosen the proper time to tell him."

Melissa took Dede's arm and hurried to the door. "Let us go down, girls. If we tarry much longer, our husbands will come to discover what is keeping us."

Melissa led the way down the hall and paused at the top of the grand staircase. The gentlemen were waiting below and she smiled as she saw her dear husband. Robert closed one eye in a slow, almost devilish wink, and the color immediately rose to flood Melissa's cheeks. He possessed the power to fluster her in a most delicious manner, but she would be the one to knock him off balance when they retired to their chambers tonight. The Duke of Oakwood was going to have a most memorable Christmas celebration, one that he should remember with pleasure for the remainder of his life!

ABOUT THE AUTHOR

Kathryn Kirkwood lives with her family in Granada Hills, California. A MATCH FOR MELISSA is her first Regency romance and she is currently working on her second, A SEASON FOR SAMANTHA, which will be published in February 1999. Kathryn loves hearing from readers and you may write to her c/o Zebra Books. Please include a self-addressed stamped envelope if you wish a response. You may also contact her at her e-mail address: OnDit@aol.com.

WATCH FOR THESE ZEBRA REGENCIES

LADY STEPHANIE   (0-8217-5341-X, $4.50)
by Jeanne Savery
Lady Stephanie Morris has only one true love: the family estate she
has managed ever since her mother died. But then Lord Anthony Rider
arrives on her estate, claiming he has plans for both the land and the
woman. Stephanie soon realizes she's fallen in love with a man whose
sensual caresses will plunge her into a world of peril and intrigue . . . a
man as dangerous as he is irresistible.

BRIGHTON BEAUTY   (0-8217-5340-1, $4.50)
by Marilyn Clay
Chelsea Grant, pretty and poor, naively takes school friend Alayna
Marchmont's place and spends a month in the country. The devastating
man had sailed from Honduras to claim his promised bride, Miss
Marchmont. An affair of the heart may lead to disaster . . . unless a
resourceful Brighton beauty finds a way to stop a masquerade and
keep a lord's love.

LORD DIABLO'S DEMISE   (0-8217-5338-X, $4.50)
by Meg-Lynn Roberts
The sinfully handsome Lord Harry Glendower was a gambler and the
black sheep of his family. About to be forced into a marriage of convenience, the devilish fellow engineered his own demise, never having
dreamed that faking his death would lead him to the heavenly refuge
of spirited heiress Gwyn Morgan, the daughter of a physician.

A PERILOUS ATTRACTION   (0-8217-5339-8, $4.50)
by Dawn Aldridge Poore
Alissa Morgan is stunned when a frantic passenger thrusts her baby
into Alissa's arms and flees, having heard rumors that a notorious
highwayman posed a threat to their coach. Handsome stranger Hugh
Sebastian secretly possesses the treasured necklace the highwayman
seeks and volunteers to pose as Alissa's husband to save her reputation.
With a lost baby and missing necklace in their care, the couple embarks
on a journey into peril—and passion.

*Available wherever paperbacks are sold, or order direct from the
Publisher. Send cover price plus 50¢ per copy for mailing and
handling to Kensington Publishing Corp., Consumer Orders,
or call (toll free) 888-345-BOOK, to place your order using
Mastercard or Visa. Residents of New York and Tennessee
must include sales tax. DO NOT SEND CASH.*

WATCH FOR THESE REGENCY ROMANCES

LOOK FOR THESE REGENCY ROMANCES

n is the widely acclaimed author of such int
-selling books as *Your Kitchen Garden, Your Ind*
The Wholefood Book (also published by Mitch
has been both features editor and assistant editor
s well as being responsible for all gardening featur
en a regular contributor to *The Guardian*.

ledgements

phers
chael Boys 50, 55 *top*, 56 *top*, 58 *top left and right*, 59,
ger Phillips 49 *bottom*, 51 *bottom*, 52 *bottom*, 53,
56 *bottom*, 57 *bottom*, 60 *bottom*, 62.

p, 54 *bottom*, 63 *top*; Bruce Coleman 64 *top*;
leman/Eric Crichton 57 *top*; Eric Crichton 51 *top*,
; John Sims 60 *top*; Harry Smith 52 *top*, 54 *top*,
, 61, 63 *bottom*.

Barber, Ian Garrard/Linden Artists;
Box/Saxon Artists; Vana Haggerty; Peter Wrigley.

d and edited by
Beazley Publishers Limited
Mitchell Beazley Publishers Limited
f the material in this book has
appeared in *Your Indoor Garden*
Mitchell Beazley Publishers Limited
ted 1981, 1982, 1985 twice, 1986
hts reserved

0 85533 197 6
toset by Key Film (Trendbourne Limited)
gination by Photoprint Plates Limited
ted in Hong Kong by Mandarin Offset Int. Ltd.

nsultant Kenneth A. Beckett
ecutive Editor Susannah Read

litor Bobbi Mitchell
rt Editor Linda Francis
opy Editor Ken Hewis
roduction Julian Deeming

The Mitc...
pocke...
Indoor
George ...

The Author
George Seddo...
nationally bes...
Garden and ...
Beazley). He ...
The Observer ...
He has also b...

Acknow...

Photogra...
Photo: M...
Photo: R...
55 *bottom,*

A–Z **49** *t...*
Bruce Co...
64 *bottom...*
58 *bottom...*

Artists
Norma...
Leonor...

Design...
Mitchel...
©1979...
Some o...
already...
©1976...
Repri...
All rig...

No p...
any ...
record...
witho...
Mitc...
14–15...
Lon...

ISBN...
Ph...
Or...
Pri...

C...
E...

E...
A...
C...
P...

Mitchell Beazley

Contents

Introduction

This little book has been conceived to provide instant reference for the amateur and more experienced indoor gardener alike. Its compact size means that you can always take it with you when you go to buy plants, thus saving the all-too-common heartbreak of returning home with a plant that is thoroughly unsuitable for the spot you had in mind. When you do not need to have the book with you, keep it close to hand with your watering can and all your other essential indoor gardening equipment.

The heart of the book is a catalogue of some 350 plants listed alphabetically by Latin botanical name (there is also a common name index for easy reference). Each plant is clearly illustrated and described together with all the general plant care advice you need to keep it flourishing all year round. A system of symbols for essential requirements makes vital information available at a glance.

To help the indoor gardener choose the best possible plants for available conditions a comprehensive listing of specific plants for varying degrees of light and temperature is given at the beginning of the book, and a separate index of plant groups, with reference to the following catalogue of plants, enables you to explore the possibilities within a particular range of plants.

Caring for your plants

Times have changed for house plants. In fewer than a hundred years their environment has altered almost as much as when they were uprooted from their native lands. From the Victorian era of gloomy rooms with drawn curtains, smoking fires and poison gas lighting, the successors of the few potted plants that survived such treatment are likely to find themselves in a totally different world of light, airy and warm rooms. The difficulty now is to choose from the bewildering selection of plants available, making sure that the plants chosen will flourish in their new home.

When choosing an indoor plant, it is important to consider its individual needs in relation to the environment in which it will live, as well as its aesthetic appeal. Light, temperature, atmosphere and humidity must all be taken into account, and what is potentially damaging for one plant may be exactly what another needs.

Before choosing a plant, therefore, it is essential to know what conditions can be provided in the home, and even more specifically, to know in which position the plant will live. A plant must be chosen to suit existing conditions. Failure to observe these rules often ends in the slow or rapid death of the plant.

Plants for cool rooms (7–13°C)

Cool conditions are preferable for some of the most popular house plants, whose growing temperature requirements can be as low as 7–13°C (45–55°F). A cool light room suits such long-flowering plants as *Chrysanthemum*, the many varieties of *Pelargonium*, the beautiful *Campanula isophylla*, the pink and purple *Erica gracilis* and the perfumed *Heliotropium*. Some foliage plants also thrive in light and cool conditions: these include the graceful *Cupressus cashmeriana*, the aromatic *Myrtus communis* and *Chamaerops humilis*, Europe's only native palm. Some of the most indomitable and enduring plants, however, prefer partial shade, from the easier plants such as *Aspidistra* and *Hedera* to the more tricky Indian Azalea and *Cyclamen*.

Here is a selection of easy plants for fairly cold rooms, which can survive even without heat in winter, providing temperatures do not drop much below 3–4°C (38–40°F).

Direct light	Partial shade
Aporocactus flagelliformis	*Araucaria heterophylla*
Chlorophytum elatum	*Aspidistra elatior*
Fortunella margarita	**Aucuba japonica*
Myrtus communis	*Cissus antarctica*
Pelargonium x hortorum	**x Fatshedera lizei*
Rebutia kupperiana	**Fatsia japonica*
	Grevillea robusta
	*Hedera helix
	Nertera depressa
	Oxalis deppei
	*Saxifraga sarmentosa
	*Tolmiea menziesii

*These plants will even tolerate frost.

4

Plants for temperate rooms (13–18°C)

Most indoor plants thrive best in the temperate conditions also favoured by most people, where average room temperatures are 13–18°C (55–65°F). Among the light-loving plants in this category are many strikingly-coloured foliage plants, and if the brilliance of the colouring is not to fade, good light is essential. Two great favourites are *Euphorbia pulcherrima* and the modest *Impatiens wallerana*. Partial shade is preferred by the large number of variegated plants in this group, but if they are kept in too deep shade they may revert to green. Luxuriating in shade are palms, ferns and such flowering plants as the beautiful *Begonia*, *Fuchsia*, *Clivia* and *Gardenia*.

Some fairly easy plants to grow under temperate conditions:

Direct light	Partial shade	
Coleus blumei	*Asparagus densiflorus*	*Gynura aurantiaca*
Impatiens wallerana	*Asparagus setaceus*	*Howea forsteriana*
Phoenix roebelenii	*Begonia metallica*	*Pteris cretica*
Pilea cadierei	*Billbergia nutans*	*Sansevieria trifasciata*
Rhoeo spathacea	*Chamaedorea elegans*	*Tradescantia fluminensis*
	Cyperus alternifolius	*Zebrina pendula*

Plants for warm rooms (18–24°C)

Warmth and humidity are necessary if tropical plants are to thrive. Tropical flowering plants also require plenty of light. Although such conditions are more easily provided in a conservatory, these plants can be successfully cultivated in well-heated homes. Regular mist-spraying, however, will have to be provided to make up for the lack of moisture in the air. The striking scarlet and white climber *Clerodendrum thomsonae* thrives in the light, at a warm temperature of 18–24°C (65–75°F), while shade-loving plants in this group include the various *Ficus*, the delicate *Adiantum raddianum* and bold *Blechnum gibbum* ferns and the amusing *Mimosa pudica*.

Fairly easy plants to suit these warm conditions:

Partial shade	*Ficus elastica decora*
Beloperone guttata	*Hoya carnosa*
Cryptanthus acaulis	*Monstera deliciosa*
Cryptanthus bromelioides	*Philodendron scandens*
Ficus benjamina	*Vriesea splendens*

Plants needing special care and attention

The following plants need special attention as far as watering and room temperatures are concerned. They should generally be kept moist without overwatering otherwise they may rot at the base or the leaves may fall. Prescribed temperatures should be carefully followed if the plant is not to suffer. For the beginner this can often be a stumbling block, although the plants themselves are straightforward once the right conditions have been provided.

Acalypha hispida	*Ochna serrulata*
Alloplectus capitatus	*Pitcairnia xanthocalyx*
Begonia serratipetala	*Polyscias balfouriana*
Bertolonia marmorata	*Quesnelia liboniana*
Biophytum sensitivum	*Smithiantha zebrina*
Clianthus formosus	*Sonerila margaritacea*
Dichorisandra thyrsiflora	

Choosing a plant

Attractive flowering plants

*Hanging and trailing

Abutilon
  megapotamicum*
Abutilon striatum
  'Thompsonii'
Acacia armata
Acalypha hispida
Achimenes longiflora
Aechmea fasciata
Aechmea fulgens
Aeschynanthus
  speciosus*
Anthurium andreanum
Anthurium
  scherzerianum
Begonia boweri
Begonia coccinea
Begonia fuchsioides
Begonia metallica
Begonia semperflorens
Begonia socotrana
  'Hiemalis'
Begonia x tuberhybrida
Beloperone guttata
Billbergia nutans
Bougainvillea x
  buttiana †
Bougainvillea glabra †
Bouvardia x domestica
Browallia speciosa
Brunfelsia calycina
Calceolaria x
  herbeohybrida
Callistemon speciosus
Camellia japonica
Campanula isophylla*
Capsicum annuum
Celosia argentea
  Cristata
Celosia argentea
  Pyramidalis
Chrysanthemum
Citrus mitis

†Climbing and creeping

Clerodendrum
  speciosissimum
Clerodendrum
  thomsonae †
Clianthus formosus*
Clivia miniata
Convallaria majalis
Cyclamen persicum
Dipladenia splendens †
Duchesnea indica*
Episcia cupreata*
Episcia dianthiflora*
Euphorbia fulgens
Fuchsia magellanica
Fuchsia triphylla
Galanthus nivalis
Gardenia jasminoides
Guzmania lingulata
Heliotropium x
  hybridum
Hibiscus rosa-sinensis
Hoya bella*
Hoya carnosa†
Hypocyrta
  nummularia*†
Impatiens wallerana
Jacobinia carnea
Jacobinia pauciflora
Jacobinia suberecta*
Jasminum mesnyi †
Jasminum
  polyanthum †
Kohleria eriantha
Liriope muscari
Manettia bicolor*†
Medinilla magnifica
Myrtus communis
Nerium oleander
Nertera depressa
Ochna serrulata
Oxalis deppei
Pachystachys lutea

Passiflora caerulea †
Pedilanthus
  tithymaloides
Pelargonium crispum
Pelargonium x
  domesticum
Pelargonium x
  hortorum
Pelargonium peltatum*
Pelargonium
  tomentosum †
Pentas lanceolata
Primula malacoides
Primula obconica
Punica granatum
  'Nana'
Rechsteineria cardinalis
Rechsteineria
  leucotricha
Rhododendron simsii
Rondeletia roezlii
Ruellia macrantha
Saintpaulia ionantha
Salpiglossis sinuata
Sanchezia nobilis
Schlumbergera
  truncata*
Senecio cruentus
Sinningia speciosa
Smithiantha zebrina
Solanum capsicastrum
Sonerila margaritacea
Sparmannia africana
Spathiphyllum wallisii
Stephanotis
  floribunda †
Streptocarpus x
  hybridus
Tacca chantrieri
Thunbergia alata †
Tillandsia lindeniana
Vriesea splendens

Plants grown for their foliage

*Hanging and trailing

Acalypha wilkesiana
Acorus gramineus
Adiantum capillus-
  veneris
Adiantum hispidulum
Adiantum raddianum*
Aeschynanthus
  lobbianus*
Aglaonema
  commutatum
Aglaonema pictum
Alternanthera amoena
Amomum cardamom
Ananas comosus
  'Variegatus'
Aphelandra squarrosa
Araucaria heterophylla
Asparagus densiflorus*
Asparagus setaceus

†Climbing and creeping

Aspidistra elatior
Asplenium bulbiferum
Asplenium nidus
Aucuba japonica
Begonia masoniana
Begonia rex
Bertolonia marmorata
Blechnum gibbum
Caladium x
  hortulanum
Calathea insignis
Calathea makoyana
Calathea ornata
Calathea zebrina
Callisia elegans
Campelia zanonia
Carex morrowii
Chamaedorea elegans
Chamaerops humilis

'Elegans'
Chlorophytum
  elatum*
Cissus antarctica†
Cissus discolor*†
Cissus striata*†
Citrus limon
Citrus mitis
Citrus sinensis
Codiaeum variegatum
  pictum
Coffea arabica
Coleus blumei
Columnea
  microphylla*
Cordyline terminalis
Cryptanthus acaulis
Cryptanthus
  bromelioides

6

Ctenanthe
  oppenheimiana
Cupressus cashmeriana
Cyanotis kewensis*
Cyperus alternifolius
Cyrtomium falcatum
Dieffenbachia picta
Dionaea muscipula
Dizygotheca
  elegantissima
Dracaena godseffiana
Dracaena marginata
Eucalyptus globulus
Euonymus japonicus
Euphorbia pulcherrima
Fatshedera lizei †
Fatsia japonica
Ficus benjamina
Ficus elastica decora
Fittonia argyroneura
Fittonia verschaffeltii
Geogenanthus undatus
Graptophyllum pictum
Grevillea robusta
Gynura aurantiaca
Hedera canariensis †
Hedera helix*†
Hemigraphis colorata*†
Howea forsteriana
Hypoestes
  sanguinolenta
Iresine herbstii

Iresine lindenii
Jacaranda mimosifolia
Maranta leuconeura
Microcoelum
  martianum
Monstera deliciosa †
Nandina domestica
Neoregelia carolinae
Nephrolepis exaltata
Nidularium innocentii
Ophiopogon jaburan
Ophiopogon
  planiscapus
Oplismenus hirtellus*†
Pandanus veitchii
Pellaea rotundifolia
Pellionia pulchra*†
Peperomia argyreia
Peperomia hederifolia
Peperomia
  magnolifolia
Philodendron
  andreanum †
Philodendron
  oxycardium †
Philodendron selloum
Phoenix roebelenii
Pilea cadierei
Pilea muscosa
Piper ornatum*†
Pitcairnia xanthocalyx
Platycerium

bifurcatum*
Plectranthus coleoides
Plectranthus
  oertendahlii*†
Polyscias balfouriana
Polystichum
  acrostichioides
Pseudoranthemum
  kewense
Pteris cretica
Pteris ensiformis
Rhoeo spathacea
Rhoicissus
  rhomboidea †
Sansevieria hahnii
Sansevieria trifasciata
Saxifraga sarmentosa*
Schefflera actinophylla
Scindapsus aureus †
Scirpus cernuus*
Selaginella kraussiana
Senecio rowleyanus*†
Setcreasea purpurea*
Siderasis fuscata
Syngonium
  podophyllum †
Tetrastigma
  voinieriana †
Tolmiea menziesii
Tradescantia
  fluminensis*†
Zebrina pendula*

Bulbs

Amaryllis belladonna
Caladium x
  hortulanum
Canna x hybrida
Crocus vernus
Freesia x kewensis
Galanthus nivalis
Gloriosa rothschildiana
Habranthus robustus

Haemanthus multiflorus
Hippeastrum
Hyacinthus orientalis
Hymenocallis calathina
Lachenalia aloides
Lilium longiflorum
Lycoris aurea
Narcissus
Nerine flexuosa

Ornithogalum thyrsoides
Sparaxis tricolor
Tulipa
Vallota speciosa
Veltheimia viridifolia
Zantedeschia
  aethiopica
Zephyranthes
  grandiflora

Cacti and succulents

Agave americana
Aloe variegata
Aporocactus
  flagelliformis
Astrophytum
  myriostigma
Cephalocereus senilis
Chamaecereus silvestrii
Crassula argentea
Echeveria gibbiflora
Echinocactus grusonii

Echinocereus pectinatus
Echinopsis rhodotricha
Epiphyllum x
  ackermanii
Euphorbia milii
Euphorbia obesa
Faucaria tigrina
Gasteria verrucosa
Haworthia
  margaritifera
Kalanchoe blossfeldiana

Lithops lesliei
Mammillaria bocasana
Opuntia microdasys
Rebutia kupperiana
Rhipsalidopsis
  gaertneri
Schlumbergera
  truncata
Senecio rowleyanus
Trichocereus chiloensis

Bromeliads

Aechmea fasciata
Aechmea fulgens
Ananas comosus
  'Variegatus'
Billbergia nutans

Cryptanthus acaulis
Cryptanthus
  bromelioides
Guzmania lingulata
Neoregelia carolinae

Nidularium innocentii
Tillandsia lindeniana
Vriesea splendens

Bonsai	**Orchids**	
Acer palmatum	*Calanthe vestita*	*Miltonia vexillaria*
Cryptomeria japonica	*Coelogyne cristata*	*Odontoglossum grande*
Juniperus chinensis	*Cymbidium x Rosanna*	*Oncidium variocosum*
Rhododendron simsii	*Dendrobium nobile*	*Paphiopedilum insigne*
Zelkova serrata	*Epidendrum*	*Paphiopedilum*
	prismatocarpum	*venustum*
	Laelia pumila	*Pleione formosana*
	Lycaste deppei	*Vanda tricolor*

Plants from pips and stones

Citrus limon	*Litchi chinensis*	*Phoenix dactylifera*
Citrus sinensis	*Mangifera indica*	*Punica granatum*
Daucus carota	*Pastinaca sativa*	
Ipomoea batatas	*Persea gratissima*	

Herbs

Allium schoenoprasum	*Ocimum basilicum*	*Solanum melongena*
Capsicum annuum	*Origanum majorana*	*ovigerum*
Lycopersicon	*Petroselinum crispum*	*Thymus vulgaris*
esculentum	*Phaseolus aureus*	
Mentha spicata	*Salvia officinalis*	

Window-box plants

Antirrhinum	*Euonymus japonicus*	*Linaria maroccana*
Aster novi-belgii	*Godetia grandiflora*	*Malcolmia maritima*
Chamaecyparis	*Hebe rakiensis*	*Phlox drummondii*
lawsoniana	*Heuchera sanguinea*	*Primula auricula*
Dianthus chinensis	*Iris pumila*	*Tagetes patula*
Erica carnea	*Juniperus communis*	*Viola*

Pots and containers

Pots can be specially chosen to suit individual plants. Plastic, non-porous pots are ideal for plants which flourish in moist compost. The soil in them is kept at a more even temperature and requires watering less frequently than soil in clay pots, which lose moisture more rapidly through the sides. Because of their porous nature, waterlogging is less likely, but a glazed saucer helps to allow drainage and prevents excess water from collecting at the base of pots. New pots should be soaked for several hours before use.

When a plant appears to be pot-bound (i.e. roots are growing through the drainage hole and are matted together within too little soil) it must be repotted, preferably in late spring. Choose a slightly larger container and place a crock (a broken piece of clay pot) at the bottom, rounded side up over the drainage hole. Cover this with a layer of good compost. Place the plant, or cutting, on top of this and gently fill in around it with potting compost. The pot can then be placed within another larger or more attractive container and the space between filled with peat which should be kept constantly moist—the advantages of this are that the plant needs less watering, and the moist air rising from the peat is beneficial to many plants. There is also the aesthetic advantage that one can choose a suitable container from the wide range of shapes and materials available on the market. Pebbles are equally successful, and more suitable for transparent containers.

Common name index

9

10

Catalogue of plants

On the following pages you will find advice on how to care for approximately three hundred and fifty indoor plants. Listed alphabetically by Latin botanical name, entries are clarified wherever possible by the easy-to-read symbols below, which provide quick reference as to easy care, light and temperature requisites and humidity.

☆ Easy to grow

△ Difficult to grow

Ⓒ Cool conditions required (temperature range 7–13°C)

Ⓣ Temperate conditions required (temperature range 13–18°C)

Ⓦ Warm conditions required (temperature range 18–24°C)

◯ Direct light tolerated

⊘ Partial shade needed

Ⓗ Humid atmosphere required during the growing season (late spring to early autumn

Abutilon megapotamicum
BRAZILIAN ABUTILON,
FLOWERING MAPLE

Ⓣ ⊘

This versatile plant may be cultivated in a hanging basket or a pot and can grow to about 120 cm (4 ft). It has green or green and yellow variegated leaves and red and yellow, lantern-shaped flowers which open from spring until autumn. Water liberally in summer, less in winter and keep at a minimum temperature of 7°C (45°F). Spray in spring and feed weekly from February until August. Prune large plants in April and repot then using a moderate-sized pot. Propagate by stem cuttings in summer.

Abutilon striatum
SPOTTED FLOWERING MAPLE,
THOMPSON'S ABUTILON

Ⓣ ⊘ Ⓗ

This plant has green leaves covered with yellow blotches and bell-shaped, orange flowers with dark red veins. The flowers open from late spring to autumn. In winter keep at a maximum temperature of 13°C (55°F) and water sparingly, keeping soil just moist. Spray regularly in spring. From March until August water well and feed weekly. Prune in April to encourage bushiness and repot then in a moderate-sized pot containing proprietary potting compost. Propagate with stem cuttings in summer.

Acacia armata
KANGAROO THORN

This Australian native grows to
90–120 cm (3–4 ft) as a pot plant.
A profusion of tiny, fluffy yellow
flowers appear in spring, backed
by narrow, dark green, spine-
tipped phyllodes. Light and cool
conditions are ideal for this plant
which will grow well on an east-
or west-facing window-sill. In
winter it should rest at 4°C (40°F)
and be watered sparingly. Water
more liberally in spring but never
overwater. Feed fortnightly during
growing period from March to
August. After flowering in May
repot in potting compost.
Propagate by cuttings in March.

Acalypha hispida
RED-HOT CAT'S TAIL, CHENILLE
PLANT

The common names of this
plant from Papua New Guinea
perfectly describe the colour,
shape and texture of the dark red
flower spikes produced from
May to September. They grow
up to 50 cm (20 in) long. The
plant will thrive at a humid
minimum temperature of 16°C
(60°F). It dislikes standing in
water but its soil should be kept
moist at all times. Feed
fortnightly from February to
August. Prune side shoots the
first year, then top shoots annually.
Repot every February. Propagate
by basal or side-shoot cuttings.

Acalypha wilkesiana
'Thompsonii'
COPPER LEAF

The leaves of this plant may be
green, red, brown or copper-
coloured, with or without white
edges. If kept in heavy shade,
the leaves of the red, brown or
copper forms may revert to
green. Keep the plant at a humid
minimum temperature of 16°C
(60°F). Water sparingly,
keeping the soil moist, and feed
fortnightly from February to
August. Prune back side shoots
after one year and from the
second year onwards, cut back
top shoots annually. Repot
every February. Propagate by
cuttings of basal or side shoots.

13

Acer palmatum
JAPANESE MAPLE

The leaves of this deciduous
bonsai native to China and Japan,
turn orange, red and yellow in
autumn. It thrives best in good
light but tolerates a shady position.
Keep it outdoors except for short
periods in summer when it may
be brought indoors. Always
keep soil moist. If possible,
plunge pot into peat or sand in
winter to protect the roots from
frost. Prune the roots every
autumn or winter and repot in
bonsai or loam-based compost.
In summer trim side shoots and
pinch out growing point.
Propagate by seed in autumn.

Achimenes longiflora
HOT-WATER PLANT

This plant has narrow leaves,
green above and red-flushed
underneath, and provides a mass
of blue, pink, violet or white
flowers from June until October.
Water sparingly in spring and
autumn and more liberally in
summer, always using tepid
water. After late summer
flowering has finished, slowly
dry off, cut back stems and store
the tubers in dry sand at a
minimum temperature of 7°C
(45°F). Repot in an all-peat
compost and start watering the
following spring. To propagate,
separate the tubers before repotting.

Acorus gramineus
MYRTLE GRASS

A tufted, moisture-loving native
of Japan, this is one of the hardiest
of house plants. It is grown for its
attractive variegated cream and
green grass-like leaves, which can
grow to 25 cm (10 in), and not for
its insignificant flowers. This plant
likes plenty of light and some
direct sun. In winter leave in a
cold but frost-free room. It is a
thirsty plant and likes to be kept
moist, so water liberally in
summer but decrease the amount
slightly in winter. Repot in a
loam-based compost in March,
when it can be propagated by
division.

14

Adiantum capillus-veneris
MAIDENHAIR FERN

This species of Maidenhair Fern grows wild in many temperate parts of the world and its black stems grow to 20–25 cm (8–10 in) before its triangular and fragile-looking fronds curve over. A dry atmosphere is fatal so water well from March to August; water less in winter but never let plant dry out completely. The minimum temperature it will tolerate is 7°C (45°F). Feed every three weeks from March to August. Repot at the end of March, preferably in an all-peat compost. Propagate by division in spring.

Adiantum hispidulum
MAIDENHAIR FERN

Unlike the common Maidenhair Fern, this species originates in the tropics. Its fronds, forked at the base, grow to about 30 cm (1 ft); hairy leaflets appear as reddish-bronze and become mid-green later. Winter temperatures should never fall below 13°C (55°F). Water liberally in spring and summer but in winter keep soil just moist. Stand the plant on wet pebbles or moist peat to provide humidity. Feed fortnightly in summer. Repot every other spring in an all-peat compost. Propagate by division.

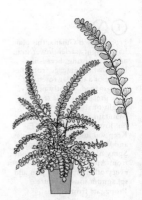

Adiantum raddianum
(A. cuneatum)
DELTA MAIDENHAIR

This plant often grows to 45 cm (18 in) and is a perfect fern for a hanging basket. Although indigenous to Brazil, it will tolerate a winter temperature as low as 10°C (50°F). Place it in a north-facing window or semi-shaded situation. Spray often, particularly from March to August, to ensure humidity. Water liberally during summer and never allow soil to dry out. Apply a very dilute fertilizer monthly from April to August. Repot in spring, preferably using a proprietary all-peat compost and propagate by division.

15

Aechmea fasciata (Billbergia rhodocyanea)
URN PLANT

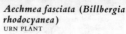

The silver-grey and grey-green striped leaves of this Brazilian plant form a funnel from which its magnificent flower head of pointed pink bracts protrudes. This dies after flowering. Water compost moderately in summer and sparingly in winter. Keep the leaf funnel filled with tepid, soft water from late spring to early autumn but dry in winter when a temperature of 10–13°C (50–55°F) should be maintained. Feed every 3–4 weeks from April to October. Propagate from side shoots in an all-peat compost.

Aechmea fulgens
CORAL BERRY

From French Guiana, this plant has a bright scarlet flower stem and long-lasting, berry-like bracts which emerge from the centre of a tubular rosette of strap-shaped, slightly prickly, dark green leaves. It reaches a height of about 38 cm (15 in). Maintain a winter temperature not lower than 10°C (50°F). Keep soil just moist at all times and water even less in winter. Spray often. Feed once a month from April to September. Repot every other April in a peat and sphagnum moss mixture. Propagate from offsets.

Aeschynanthus lobbianus
LIPSTICK PLANT

A native of Java, this trailing plant looks best in a hanging basket. It has shiny, dark green leaves and terminal clusters of scarlet flowers with purple-brown calyces. The flowers open from May to July. This plant will thrive best at about 13°C (55°F) in winter. In spring and summer water liberally, otherwise keep soil barely moist. From May to September feed monthly. Spray in hot weather. Repot every second or third spring in three parts peat compost to one part moss. Propagate by cuttings in spring or summer.

Aeschynanthus speciosus

A hanging basket is ideal for this Indonesian perennial which has long, trailing stems carrying terminal clusters of bright orange, tubular-shaped flowers from July to September. The winter temperature must not fall below 13°C (55°F). Maintain a humid environment during its growing season, spraying frequently with tepid water. Water sparingly from November to February; thereafter use tepid water to keep soil moist. Repot every two to three years in spring, using an all-peat compost. Propagate by tip cuttings in summer.

Agapanthus campanulatus
BLUE AFRICAN LILY

This lovely South African summer-flowering lily has long, strap-like leaves, which die in winter, and round heads of blue, funnel-shaped flowers on stout stems reaching a height of more than 60 cm (2 ft). Water moderately from May to October. Keep completely dry and cool at 2–4°C (35–40°F) from November to April or flowers will be disappointing. Feed weekly from May to July and look out for greenfly. Every fourth year divide roots and repot in separate pots, in good potting compost, preferably all peat.

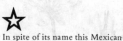

Agave americana
CENTURY PLANT

In spite of its name this Mexican succulent matures well before its hundredth year and is noted for its decorative rosette of grey-green, leathery, spine-tipped leaves. A young plant as small as 15 cm (6 in) across can reach a width of 120 cm (4 ft) if potted on in spring every two years. It prefers dry air and welcomes a well-lit position with a minimum winter temperature of 4°C (40°F). Water regularly in summer but sparingly in winter. Apply a liquid feed each month from April to September. Propagate from spring offsets.

17

Aglaonema commutatum
CHINESE EVERGREEN

Reaching a height of about 15 cm (6 in), this compact Southeast Asian perennial has lance-shaped leaves with silvery markings. Very small, waxy, white spathes appear in July. It will thrive if protected from direct sunlight at a minimum winter temperature of 10°C (50°F). It likes a moist atmosphere and will thrive on a tray of wet pebbles or moist peat. Water well from April to August, but sparingly in winter. Give a fortnightly liquid feed during the growing season. Repot every other spring. Propagate by cuttings in summer.

Aglaonema pictum
CHINESE EVERGREEN

Malaya and Borneo are home to this elegant plant whose leaves, up to 20 cm (8 in) long, are covered with irregular patches in three different shades of green. Creamy-yellow spathes are borne in August. This plant will not tolerate a temperature below 10°C (50°F) and needs to be shaded from direct light and kept away from oil and gas fumes. It thrives in a moist atmosphere. Water liberally and feed fortnightly from April to August but keep soil just moist in winter. Repot in April. Propagate by cuttings in summer.

Allium schoenoprasum
CHIVE

The slender, tubular leaves of this 15–25 cm (6–10 in) hardy perennial have a mild onion flavour and should be cut when about 10 cm (4 in) tall. Its pinkish-purple flowers which open in June and July should be removed to encourage leaf growth. Keep chives on a sunny outdoor window-sill. In March sow seeds in moist seed compost. When seedlings are large enough to handle, plant two or three in an 8 cm (3 in) pot with potting compost. Keep moist at all times. Repot every other year in winter and propagate by division.

Alloplectus capitatus
VELVET ALLOPLECTUS

The soft leaves of this South American plant are olive green on top and greenish-red below. Downy, succulent, red stems grow 60–90 cm (2–3 ft) tall and in autumn bear terminal clusters of yellow flowers with deep red centres. In winter a minimum temperature of 13°C (55°F) must be maintained and the plant should be watered sparingly. Water liberally at other times and spray regularly. Feed every fortnight from May to September. Repot every April. Propagate by cuttings of basal shoots in summer.

Aloe variegata
PARTRIDGE-BREASTED ALOE

Unlike most succulents, this South African species has a winter growing season and produces upright spikes of pale orange, tubular flowers in spring. It has a rosette of triangular, dark green leaves banded with white markings. The plant likes a sunny window-sill in dry air and needs a minimum winter temperature of 4°C (40°F). Water very sparingly in summer, moderately in winter and spring, never in the rosette. Repot every other year in spring. Propagate by removing offsets in summer.

Alternanthera amoena
PARROT LEAF

Indigenous to Brazil, this plant has broad, lance-shaped leaves marked with orange and red blotches. Insignificant white flowers open in summer. Although a perennial, it is more usually grown from annual spring cuttings in a heated propagating case. The old plant, if kept, needs a minimum winter temperature of 16°C (60°F) and can be repotted each spring. Water sparingly in winter. In spring and summer keep soil moist and spray regularly. Feed fortnightly from June to October.

19

Amaryllis belladonna
BELLADONNA LILY,
CAPE BELLADONNA

This South African plant grows
to 60 cm (2 ft) tall. Pink or
reddish-pink flowers are borne
on stout stalks in autumn before
strap-shaped leaves appear. In
October start bulb into growth
at a temperature of 13–16°C
(55–60°F). Keep in a sunny
position and water sparingly.
When leaves appear, water
liberally and feed once a week.
When the leaves turn yellow, keep
soil dry. Repot every other
October in potting compost
leaving the top half of the bulb
uncovered. Propagate by
removing offsets when repotting.

Amomum cardamom
CARDAMOM, CARDAMOM GINGER

A native of Java, this plant has
rather hairy, tough, lance-
shaped leaves which emit a spicy
odour when rubbed. While it
may reach a height of 3 m (10 ft)
in the wild, in a pot it is unlikely
to grow taller than 90 cm (3 ft),
and will not flower. In winter
provide a temperature of
13–16°C (55–60°F) and water
sparingly. In spring and summer
keep soil moist and spray on hot
days. In summer feed every two
weeks. Repot every spring in an
all-peat potting compost.
Propagate by division when
repotting.

Ananas comosus
'Variegatus'
PINEAPPLE

Indigenous to South America,
the centre of this Pineapple is
flushed red and the leaves are
striped creamy-white. It bears
dense spikes of purple flowers
that give way to fruit. It thrives
in a warm, draught-free room at
a minimum winter temperature
of 13°C (55°F). Keep moist all
year, but less so in winter. It
should flower when two or
three years old. After flowering,
use liquid fertilizer sparingly.
Suckers then develop while the
parent stem dies; these can be
removed with roots and repotted
in potting compost.

Anthurium andreanum
PAINTER'S PALETTE

This native of Colombia grows
about 45 cm (18 in) tall and has
large, heart-shaped, dark green
leaves. From May to September
it produces waxy, palette-
shaped, red or white flowers.
Ideally the plant should be kept
at a winter temperature of 16°C
(60°F) and be watered liberally
in spring and summer and
moderately in winter. From May
to August feed fortnightly.
Provide a humid atmosphere by
standing plant on a tray of wet
pebbles or moist peat. Repot
every second or third April.
Propagate by division.

Anthurium scherzerianum
FLAMINGO FLOWER, FLAME PLANT

Providing a burst of colour at
the end of winter, this plant has
curly, yellow flower tassels and
scarlet spathes which grow
singly on slender stems from
February to July. Its leaves are
shiny and leathery. It likes a
humid atmosphere and a winter
temperature of not less than
16°C (60°F). Water judiciously
all the year, keeping soil just
moist. From February to
December feed every three
weeks after watering. In spring,
repot in a wide, fairly shallow
pot with all-peat compost.
Propagate by division or seed.

Antirrhinum
SNAPDRAGON

Long-lasting, colourful and hardy,
this is an ideal window-box plant,
especially dwarf cultivated species
such as 'Floral Carpet' or 'Tom
Thumb'. Grown annually from
seed, the 15 cm (6 in) stems bear
narrow leaves and flowers of
various colours which open from
summer until early autumn. Sow
seeds in February or March at a
temperature of 16°C (60°F). From
March to May harden off seedlings
in a cool, frost-free room before
planting in a south-, east- or
west-facing window box. Water
liberally. Pinch out shoot tips of
the taller cultivated varieties.

21

Aphelandra squarrosa
ZEBRA PLANT, TIGER PLANT

This attractive plant has large, dark green leaves with creamy-white veins and cone-shaped, red-edged, yellow bracts from which its yellow flowers protrude. It blooms between April and August. Provide a humid atmosphere and a winter temperature no lower than 13°C (55°F). Water and spray liberally in summer, making sure soil is never waterlogged. Water sparingly in winter. Feed every fortnight from March to August. Pot on in March. Prune back top shoots after flowering. Propagate by cuttings.

Aporocactus flagelliformis
RAT'S TAIL CACTUS

Although frequently grafted on to a tall cactus, this Mexican species looks best in a hanging basket. Bright pink flowers open in spring. To ensure flowering, keep at a minimum winter temperature of 4°C (40°F), in plenty of light and a dry atmosphere. From April to August give a liquid feed monthly and water regularly, allowing compost to dry out completely between each watering. See that compost is just moist at other times. Repot annually when flowering has ceased. Propagate by cuttings between April and July.

Araucaria heterophylla (A. excelsa)
NORFOLK ISLAND PINE

A native of New Zealand, this conifer is usually kept indoors until it is about 120 cm (4 ft) tall, after which it loses its lower branches. In winter the plant likes light and a minimum temperature of 4°C (40°F). In summer it requires plenty of fresh air but should be screened from the hottest sun. From May to August water liberally with soft water and feed fortnightly. Pot on every other spring. Old plants which become leggy can be cut back to about 15 cm (6 in) and the resultant shoots used as cuttings.

Ardisia crispa
CORAL BERRY, SPEAR FLOWER

This shrub's reddish flowers open in June and are followed by bright scarlet berries which remain on the plant at least until spring. The plant grows about 60–90 cm (2–3 ft) tall and has dark green, glossy leaves. Water freely in summer and spray with tepid water. In winter the temperature should not fall below 7°C (45°F) and the soil should be kept fairly moist. Feed fortnightly from April to August. Repot in spring. Prune fairly ruthlessly in February. Propagate by seed in March or by cuttings of lateral shoots in spring or summer.

Asclepias curassavica
BLOOD FLOWER

This shrub from tropical America has glossy, spear-shaped leaves and orange-red flowers which account for its dramatic name. Growing to a height of 60–90 cm (2–3 ft), it flowers from June until October. Keep at a minimum winter temperature of 7–10°C (45–50°F), watering just enough to prevent the soil completely drying out. Cut back hard in March and water more liberally; feed fortnightly until October. Repot in a peat-based compost. Propagate by seed during February or March in seed compost. Young shoots may also be used.

Asparagus densiflorus 'Sprengeri'
ASPARAGUS

From Natal, this plant has trailing stems and stiff, green, needle-like leaves on branches which are often used in flower arrangements. In June it sometimes produces small, greenish-white flowers followed by red berries. Mature plants have rather prickly stems. Water liberally in summer and sparingly in winter when the temperature should not fall below 7°C (45°F). Feed every fortnight from May to September and cut off any yellowing branches. Pot on in April in any good potting compost. Propagate by division or seed in spring.

Asparagus setaceus (plumosus)
ASPARAGUS FERN

Although closely resembling culinary asparagus, this South African variety is completely inedible but is worth growing for the decorative effects of its elegant, feathery branches. Scarlet berries may develop. The Asparagus Fern likes a minimum winter temperature of 7°C (45°F). Water sparingly during this period. Water liberally in summer when the plant should also be fed every fortnight. Repot in April in any good proprietary potting compost and remove any yellowing branches. Propagate in spring by division or by seed.

Aspidistra elatior
PARLOUR PLANT, CAST IRON PLANT

Uprooted from its native China, this undemanding plant made itself at home in Victorian parlours, apparently impervious to smoke, gas fumes, cold and blatant neglect. After a period out of favour, it has staged a comeback. Water moderately in summer and less often in winter. It will not tolerate its roots standing in water nor does it enjoy direct sun. Feed monthly during summer. Overwinter at about 10°C (50°F). Do not be too eager to repot but when you do, use an all-peat compost. Propagate by division in spring when repotting.

Asplenium bulbiferum
HEN AND CHICKEN FERN,
MOTHER SPLEENWORT

Remarkable for its method of reproduction, this feathery fern has small plantlets or bulbils which develop on its larger fronds. In India, Australia and New Zealand, where it grows naturally, the plantlets pull the fronds down to ground level where they take root. Indoors, these plantlets may be removed and replanted in March. Water liberally in summer and less often in winter when the temperature should be at least 13°C (55°F). Feed weekly and spray regularly from March to August. Repot in spring. Propagate then by repotting plantlets or by division.

Asplenium nidus
BIRD'S-NEST FERN

(T) (N) (H)

From the tropics, this fern has tough, glossy leaves, about 60–120 cm (2–4 ft) long, which form a rosette at its base. In winter the temperature should not fall below 13°C (55°F) and the soil should be barely moist. It likes a humid atmosphere in spring and summer. Water freely in summer and feed with a weak solution of fertilizer fortnightly from March to August. Repot in spring, preferably using an all-peat compost. Propagation by spores is difficult for the novice. If offsets are formed they may be detached and potted separately in spring.

Aster novi-belgii 'Lady in Blue'
MICHAELMAS DAISY

These hardy perennials have daisy-like flowers which open in September and October in a wide range of colours. They usually have yellow centres. The best choice for a window box is the deep blue, dwarf 'Lady in Blue', which grows 25 cm (10 in) tall. In winter or spring plant in a south-facing window box which contains any good-quality potting compost. Set them at least 30 cm (12 in) apart. Water liberally in dry weather. Prune back hard after flowering. Replant every winter or spring and propagate by division then.

Astrophytum myriostigma
BISHOP'S CAP, BISHOP'S MITRE

This globular, spineless Mexican cactus has an arrangement of five, sharply edged ridges and an overall covering of small tufts. Yellow flowers develop from the centre of the plant which grows to 15 cm (6 in). It is well suited to indoor culture because it thrives in full light and plenty of air. See that winter room temperature does not fall below 5°C (41°F). Water only when the soil is dry from March through to October. Do not spray. Repot in early spring using equal parts of coarse sand or grit with compost. Propagate by seed in spring.

Aucuba japonica

SPOTTED LAUREL

This bushy evergreen from Japan has insignificant brownish or greenish-purple flowers which open in March and April, and glossy, dark green leaves which look better for being sponged regularly. Tolerant of deep shade and capable of growing to about 180 cm (6 ft) or more in a large pot or tub, this is a good plant for a hallway or landing. It likes cold but frost-free conditions in winter. Feed every fortnight from May to September. Prune lightly and repot in any good potting compost in spring. Propagate by cuttings in late summer or autumn.

Begonia boweri

MINIATURE EYELASH BEGONIA

This small Begonia grows about 15 cm (6 in) high. Its small white or shell-pink flowers open from February to May and its emerald green leaves have purple-brown markings on their hairy margins. This plant requires a humid atmosphere in summer. In winter a temperature of 13–16°C (55–60°F) is required and the soil must be kept only just moist. Spray, water liberally and feed fortnightly during growing period from February to August. Repot every April in a shallow pot or pan. Propagate by division when repotting.

Begonia coccinea

ANGELWING BEGONIA

This plant has green leaves with fine red margins and bamboo-like stems which grow to 180 cm (6 ft). Drooping light red flowers open from May to October. The hybrid 'President Carnot' has silver-spotted leaves and larger pink flowers. Provide a humid summer atmosphere. Keep at a minimum winter temperature of 10°C (50°F) in barely moist soil. From April to September water liberally, spray regularly and feed fortnightly. Cut out two-year-old stems in March. Repot each April in a large pot with potting compost. Propagate by cuttings in summer.

Begonia fuchsioides
FUCHSIA-FLOWERED BEGONIA

As its name implies, this bushy variety has fuchsia-like, red or pink flowers which open from October to March. The plant has glossy green leaves, grows about 120 cm (4 ft) tall and needs a humid atmosphere in summer. During its winter resting period it should be kept at a temperature of 10°C (50°F) and watered sparingly. From May to September spray and water liberally, but do not allow soil to become waterlogged; feed fortnightly then. Cut out two-year-old stems in March. Repot every April. Propagate by cuttings in summer.

Begonia masoniana
IRON CROSS

This unusual plant has hairy, grey-green, puckered leaves marked centrally with a purple-brown cross. Older leaves take on a silvery tinge. This variety grows to about 25 cm (10 in). It rarely flowers. Like all *Begonia*, it requires a humid atmosphere in summer when it should be sprayed often and watered liberally. In winter the temperature must not fall below 13°C (55°F) and the soil must be kept just moist. Feed fortnightly from April to September. Repot every April in a shallow pot with potting compost. Propagate by leaf cuttings in summer.

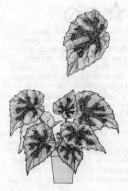

Begonia metallica

This plant grows to a height of about 1 m (40 in). Its olive green leaves have a metallic sheen, with crimson veins on their undersides. Pink flowers appear in September. Provide a humid atmosphere in summer and a winter temperature of not less than 10°C (50°F). Water liberally but do not allow the soil to become waterlogged. Feed fortnightly from April to September. In winter keep soil just moist. In March pinch out top shoots to encourage bushiness. Repot in April, preferably in an all-peat compost. Propagate by stem cuttings in summer.

27

Begonia rex

This plant has dark green leaves with silver markings. Although it is seldom seen today, many hybrids and cultivated varieties are sold under this name. Their wrinkled leaves have silver, cream, pink, red, purple or copper markings. Mature plants may produce pink flowers in summer when a humid atmosphere should be provided. In winter supply a minimum temperature of 13°C (55°F). Water liberally and feed fortnightly from April to September. Keep compost just moist in winter. Repot every April. Propagate by leaf cuttings in summer.

Begonia semperflorens

This is a low, bushy plant with glossy green or brown-purple-flushed leaves and small, white, pink or red flowers opening mainly from May to October. There are many hybrids, ranging in height from 15–45 cm (6–18 in). Water freely, ensuring the compost never becomes waterlogged, keep humid and feed fortnightly from May to September. In winter this plant needs a temperature of about 10°C (50°F). Keep soil just moist. Pinch out top shoots in March. Repot in April in a loam-based compost. Propagate by seed in spring or stem cuttings in summer.

Begonia serratipetala

This bushy plant rarely exceeds a height of 30–45 cm (12–18 in) and has pink flowers with serrated or notched edges which open from spring to autumn and contrast well with its glossy, pink-spotted, dark green leaves. In summer keep in a humid atmosphere, water liberally and feed fortnightly. In winter do not let the temperature fall below 10°C (50°F), and water sparingly, keeping the soil just moist. Prune the plant in March. Repot in April in any good proprietary potting compost, preferably in an all-peat one. Propagate by stem cuttings in summer.

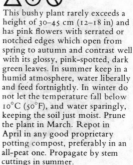

Begonia (socotrana hybrids) Hiemalis

With their pink, white, yellow or orange flowers which open in winter, the Hiemalis group of *B. socotrana* are the most attractive. Water sparingly after flowering has finished in January. When the green leaves discolour, prune and move to a cool position at 7°C (45°F). In April give more water and warmth. When new shoots are 8 cm (3 in) long, cut off at the base and plant in separate pots. Discard the parent. Pot cuttings on, pinching out top shoots to encourage bushiness. Feed fortnightly, spray and water freely until flowering ends.

Begonia x *tuberhybrida*

These tuberous hybrids have rose-like or pendulous flowers of many colours. When they have stopped flowering, in September, water sparingly. After their stems wither, keep tubers in dry peat at a winter temperature of 7°C (45°F). In April, repot, start to water gradually and move to a warmer temperature of about 18°C (65°F). Water more liberally when the plant is in full leaf and once its buds are just visible, feed fortnightly until the flowers are over. Propagate from newly sprouted tubers or by cutting the tubers into two or more pieces.

Beloperone guttata
SHRIMP PLANT

Down-curving flower heads composed of overlapping, pinkish-brown bracts, from which narrow white flowers emerge, give this bushy, evergreen shrub its common name. It flowers from April to December and rarely exceeds 45 cm (18 in). It can survive a temperature of 7°C (45°F) but prefers more temperate conditions. Water liberally from April to November and sparingly in winter. Feed fortnightly from May to September. Prune hard in February. Repot in March. Propagate by stem cuttings in spring or summer.

Bertolonia marmorata
JEWEL PLANT

The bright green leaves of this small Brazilian plant are heavily splashed with silvery-white on top and flushed with purple underneath. Tiny purple flowers sometimes appear in summer. Keep at a temperature not lower than 16°C (60°F) at all times. Water moderately in spring and summer. In winter keep soil barely moist. From April to September feed once a month. Repot every second May or June in an all-peat potting compost. Propagate by careful division or by cuttings in summer; a heated propagating case gives best results.

Billbergia nutans
ANGEL'S TEARS, QUEEN'S TEARS

Indigenous to South America, this plant has silvery-bronze-tinted, arching leaves for most of the year but from winter until early summer exhibits violet-blue and green flowers protruding from pink bracts. The plant grows about 45 cm (18 in) tall. Ideally, it needs a temperature around 16°C (60°F) in winter, when it should be watered sparingly, but can endure a temperature as low as 2°C (35°F) for short spells. Water liberally and feed fortnightly from May to October. In June or July repot in an all-peat compost and propagate by division.

Biophytum sensitivum
LIFE PLANT

The oval, green leaves of this umbrella-shaped, tropical plant fold back if touched or if exposed to bright sunshine or sudden blasts of air. Cup-shaped flowers, which are pale purple at first, become yellowish-orange and open in summer. It grows about 15 cm (6 in) tall. The winter temperature should not fall below 16°C (60°F) and the plant should be watered sparingly. In spring and summer keep soil moist and spray regularly. From April to September feed fortnightly. Repot each spring. Propagate by seed in spring, at a temperature of 18°C (65°F).

30

Blechnum gibbum

This fern from New Caledonia in the Western Pacific may reach a height of about 1 m (40 in) and its large fronds are divided into narrow, stiffly-held segments that give the appearance of a palm-like crown. It is accustomed to a warm climate so the winter temperature should not fall below 13°C (55°F). This plant benefits from a humid atmosphere in spring and summer. From March to July feed fortnightly with dilute liquid fertilizer and water liberally; at other times water sparingly. Propagate by offsets or by spores in spring or summer.

Bougainvillea x buttiana 'Mrs Butt'
BOUGAINVILLEA, CRIMSON LAKE

This shrubby climber with thorny stems has beautiful, bright crimson-pink bracts which surround the plant's insignificant flowers. Water liberally in summer and sparingly in winter, when the plant should be kept at a temperature of 4–7°C (40–45°F). It likes a humid atmosphere and fresh air in warm weather. Feed weekly in summer. When young, repot each February; older plants may be repotted every other year. This can be a difficult plant to propagate, but a small percentage of stem cuttings, taken in spring or summer, will take root.

Bougainvillea glabra 'Variegata'
BOUGAINVILLEA

A native of Brazil, this is a thorny shrub which flowers from March to July. Its insignificant cream-coloured flowers are enclosed by purple and red bracts. This is a natural climber which can reach 3 m (10 ft), so train it around hoops or a trellis in front of a south-facing window; a smaller, bushier plant is achieved by regular pruning. In winter the temperature should not fall below 7°C (45°F). Water well from March to August but keep drier in other months. Feed weekly from February to September. Repot in January. Propagate by cuttings in spring.

Bouvardia x domestica
TROMPETILLA

This evergreen shrub of garden origin has clusters of white, pink or red tubular flowers which open from June to December. Provide a minimum temperature of about 7-10°C (45-50°F) all year, keeping the plant in front of an east- or west-facing window. Water and spray from spring until flowering stops, then keep plant fairly dry until the following March. Feed weekly from April to September. Repot in spring in equal parts of peat and sand. Cut back main shoots hard in early February. Propagate by cuttings in spring. Discard after two years.

Browallia speciosa
BUSH VIOLET

This bushy South American plant grows to a height of about 50 cm (20 in) and has deep violet, white-centred, tubular flowers which look superb against its dark leaves. If sown in spring it flowers in summer and in winter if sown in July or August; winter-flowering plants require a minimum temperature of 18°C (65°F). Water moderately, never allowing soil to dry out completely. Feed fortnightly after the flowers bud until fully bloomed and remove them as they die to encourage new blooms. Discard the plant after flowering. Propagate by seed.

Brunfelsia calycina
YESTERDAY, TODAY AND TOMORROW

This Brazilian shrub has tough, rather glossy leaves and sweet-smelling, purplish-violet flowers which fade to almost white and are profuse from March to September. It can grow to a height of about 60 cm (2 ft). It likes a lot of light in winter, when it should be kept at a temperature no lower than 10°C (50°F) and watered sparingly. In summer keep in the shade, water liberally and spray. Feed monthly from March to September. If potbound, repot in spring using an all-peat compost. Pruning is seldom needed. Propagate by cuttings in summer.

Caladium ✕ *hortulanum*

(H)

This South American foliage plant grows to 38 cm (15 in) and has long-stemmed, arrow-head-shaped leaves which are usually two-coloured and grow from a tuber. In March pot the tuber in potting compost. Keep at a temperature of 21°C (70°F) and water sparingly. When the leaves develop, move the plant to a cooler room, water liberally, spray daily and feed weekly. Gradually stop watering as leaves wilt in autumn. Keep tuber at a winter temperature of 13°C (55°F) in barely moist soil. Propagate by removing offsets from the tuber when repotting.

Calanthe vestita

(H)

From October to February, this deciduous Malaysian plant bears 90 cm (3 ft) spikes of up to 25 white flowers, each with a pink or red lip. It needs shade from hot summer sun and a minimum winter temperature of 13°C (55°F). Water well as leaves expand but stop when foliage turns yellow. Water sparingly during flowering. When the leaves are half grown, apply a dilute liquid food fortnightly until they mature. When flowering stops, repot pseudobulbs singly, preferably in a loam-based compost. Propagate by separating offsets then.

Calathea insignis
RATTLESNAKE PLANT

(T) (⊘) (H)

The wavy-edged, lance-shaped, velvety leaves of this Brazilian plant have oval, olive markings and undersides the colour of port wine. To prevent discoloration, they should always be shaded from direct sunlight and will rarely exceed 15 cm (6 in) in length if the plant is kept in a small pot. In summer keep it in a humid atmosphere and water liberally. Keep at a minimum winter temperature of 13°C (55°F) and water sparingly. Feed fortnightly from May to September. Repot in early summer and propagate by division when repotting.

Calathea makoyana
PEACOCK PLANT

The long-stemmed leaves of this
Brazilian plant are silvery-green
with dark green markings along
the main veins. This pattern is
repeated on their undersides but
the dark areas are a purplish colour.
In a small pot the plant rarely
exceeds 23 cm (9 in). Always keep
it in the shade. In summer a humid
atmosphere and plenty of water
are welcome. In winter keep at a
temperature of not less than 13°C
(55°F) and water sparingly. Feed
fortnightly from May to
September. Repot in early summer
in an all-peat potting compost.
Propagate by division then.

Calathea ornata

Pairs of pink stripes, gradually
fading to cream, curve between
the main veins of this plant's dark
green leaves. Their undersides are
dark purple. In its natural habitat,
it will grow to 250 cm (8 ft) but
as a pot plant is unlikely to be
taller than 45 cm (18 in). Shade
from the sun and keep in a humid
atmosphere in summer. In winter
the temperature should not fall
below 16°C (60°F). From March
to September water liberally,
keeping the soil just moist, and
feed fortnightly from May to
September. Repot in early
summer. Propagate by division.

Calathea zebrina
ZEBRA PLANT

Boldly striped with bands of dark
green, the emerald-green leaves of
this Brazilian plant are purplish on
their undersides. It usually grows
to 45 cm (18 in) tall but in a large
tub or pot may reach 90 cm (3 ft).
Protect from bright sun. Keep in a
humid atmosphere in summer and
at a minimum temperature of
16°C (60°F) in winter. Water
liberally except in winter when the
soil should be kept barely moist.
Feed fortnightly from May to
September. Repot in early
summer, using an all-peat
compost. Propagate by division at
the same time.

Calceolaria x herbeohybrida
SLIPPERWORT, SLIPPER PLANT,
POCKET-BOOK PLANT

This group of hybrid annuals
produces a mass of colourful,
pouch-shaped flowers which open
from May to July and are yellow,
red or orange with crimson
blotches or spots. The leaves are
soft and hairy. Some hybrids grow
45 cm (18 in) tall but dwarf
varieties are more suitable as house
plants. Grow first in an open cold
frame or well-ventilated green-
house until September then place
in a light, partially shaded position
indoors while it flowers. Keep
moist. Discard after flowering.
Propagation should be left to
professional horticulturalists.

Callisia elegans
(Setcreasea striata)
STRIPED INCH PLANT

This native of North America
grows to a height of about 30 cm
(1 ft), and has dense and decorative
foliage whose green-and-cream-
striped leaves have purple
undersides. Small white flowers
open from May until October.
Water well in summer. During the
winter months keep the soil just
moist and feed once a week from
March until October. Repot in
any good-quality potting compost
every April. Whilst the plant may
be past its prime after a couple of
years, it is very easy to propagate
by cuttings which should be
planted in spring or summer.

Callistemon speciosus
ALBANY BOTTLEBRUSH

This Australian shrub grows to
60–90 cm (2–3 ft) indoors and its
flowers, resembling brilliant red
bottle brushes, open from May to
August. It tolerates direct sun but
prefers light shade during extreme
heat when it benefits from fresh
air. In winter the temperature
must not drop below 7°C (45°F).
In early spring bring it into a
warmer, bright room. From
March until August feed fortnightly
with liquid fertilizer and water
well with soft water. Keep the
plant drier in winter. Repot in
early March in lime-free compost.
Propagate by stem cuttings in June.

Camellia japonica
'Adolphe Audusson'
CAMELLIA

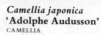

This native of Japan has glossy leaves and rose-like single or double flowers which open from February to May and may be white, pink, red or variegated. The plant grows to 60–90 cm (2–3 ft). It needs varying temperatures: 10–13°C (50–55°F) when in bud, no more than 16°C (60°F) when in flower and not less than 7–10°C (45–50°F) at other times. Water liberally from May to July, otherwise keep just moist. Feed fortnightly from December to July. Prune lightly and repot in May. Propagate by stem or leaf-bud cuttings in summer.

Campanula isophylla
BELL FLOWER

This plant, from the mountains of northern Italy, can be trained up a small trellis or allowed to trail from a hanging basket. Take care of its fragile stems. It sometimes produces so many blue or white star-shaped flowers in late summer that its downy, grey-green leaves are almost hidden from view. Water well in summer and sparingly at other times. Feed weekly from April to August. Keep in a cool but frost-free room in winter at about 4–7°C (40–45°F). Repot every February, ideally in a loam-based compost. Propagate from cuttings in spring.

Campelia zanonia
'Mexican Flag'

Green- and cream-striped leaves with red margins grow on this Mexican plant's erect stems. Small white flowers, sometimes spotted or flushed with purple, appear in summer. Never let the temperature drop below 10°C (50°F) and supply a humid atmosphere. In spring and summer water moderately. In winter keep soil just moist. From April to September feed fortnightly. Discard the plant after one or two years when it is about 90 cm (3 ft) tall and bare at the base. Take cuttings in summer and keep humid until rooted.

Canna x hybrida
CANNA

Developed from several species, these hybrids grow from tuber-like rhizomes and reach a height of 90–120 cm (3–4 ft). They have green, bronze or purple leaves and clusters of long-stemmed, orchid-like yellow, orange or red flowers. In spring start the rhizomes into growth by providing a temperature of 13–16°C (55–60°F). Keep in good light and water sparingly. When shoots appear, water liberally and feed fortnightly. In autumn cut plant back, move to a cool but frost-free room and keep almost dry. Repot each spring. Propagate by division.

Capsicum annuum
ORNAMENTAL CHILLI PEPPER

This native of Central and South America is grown for its brightly coloured fruit, some of which is edible and some purely decorative. Although technically a short-lived perennial it is cultivated as an annual and usually discarded after its fruit ripens in autumn and winter and then fades. Provide fresh air and light. When flowers form, spray daily to set fruit. Water liberally from March to September. Decrease slightly at other times but do not let soil dry out or both fruit and leaves may drop off. Propagate in spring from seed.

Capsicum annuum acuminatum
RED OR GREEN PEPPER

Although normally grown under glass for culinary use, the many varieties of pepper with their attractive fruit can also make decorative house plants. They require plenty of light but some shade during the hottest weather. Water liberally and feed weekly with liquid fertilizer once flowering starts. Daily spraying is beneficial. Encourage bushiness by pinching out growing tip when the plant reaches 15 cm (6 in). Propagate by seed during March at a temperature of 16–18°C (60–65°F) and pot seedlings singly in 8 cm (3 in) pots.

37

Carex morrowii 'Variegata'
JAPANESE SEDGE

This tufted, grass-like plant from Japan is related to the Papyrus and is one of the very few sedges that is suitable for growing indoors. Its slender arching leaves have a white central area and green margins and can grow to 30 cm (1 ft) long. Whilst it is easy to grow and fairly undemanding, it will nevertheless thrive best if kept at a cool temperature which should not exceed 7°C (45°F) in winter. The soil must always be kept moist. Feed monthly from April to September and repot every other year in any good potting compost. Propagate by division.

Carissa grandiflora
NATAL PLUM

This large shrub – 150–210 cm (5–7 ft) – has tough leaves and white, fragrant flowers which open in May and may be followed in July by scarlet berries. This plant likes plenty of fresh air and light and should be kept in front of an airy, south-facing window. Protect from sun on very hot days. Maintain a minimum winter temperature of about 13°C (55°F). Water well in summer but keep drier in winter. Feed fortnightly from April to August. Repot in spring and pinch out young shoot tips. Propagate by seed in spring or cuttings in summer.

Celosia argentea Cristata
COCKSCOMB

This is an annual from tropical Asia which grows to a height of about 30 cm (1 ft) and has crimson, yellow or orange flowers. It likes plenty of fresh air when the weather is warm but does not take kindly to too much strong sunshine. The plant should be watered fairly frequently but not allowed to get waterlogged. Discard it when the flowering season in autumn is over. In spring propagate by seed at a minimum temperature of 18°C (65°F). When the resultant seedlings are large enough to handle, prick them out and pot in a peat-based compost.

  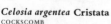

Celosia argentea Pyramidalis
PLUME CELOSIA

☆ ©○

This Asian annual has feathery, plume-shaped, yellow or scarlet flowers and enjoys warm, fresh air and protection from very strong sunshine. Water moderately and discard the plant when it has finished flowering. Propagate by seed in spring, keeping seed trays at a minimum temperature of 18°C (65°F). When the seedlings are large enough to handle, prick out and pot in a peat-based compost. Make a first potting in 3 inch (8 cm) pots, then into larger ones for flowering. Feed weekly with liquid fertilizer when the young flowers just begin to show.

Celsia arcturus
CRETAN BEAR'S TAIL

©○

A native of Crete, this shrub is usually grown as an annual but can be kept for longer and may reach 60–90 cm (2–4 ft). It has lobed basal leaves and 30–45 cm (12–18 in) spikes of yellow flowers, with purple, bearded stamens, which open from July to September. This plant likes plenty of fresh air in warm weather. Keep soil moist at all times but never allow it to get waterlogged. Feed weekly from July to September. After flowering, discard the plant. Propagate by seeds in March or April and plant seedlings in any good proprietary potting compost.

Cephalocereus senilis
OLD MAN CACTUS

☆

In its natural habitat this pillar cactus can grow to 12 m (40 ft). When they appear, its flowers are nocturnal and summer-opening. Position in a dry and sunny, draught-free location whose winter temperature is no lower than 4°C (40°F). Keep soil moist in summer and dry from November to February. Do not wet its long, silky white hairs too often. Apply a liquid fertilizer monthly from May to August. Repot every two years in spring in potting compost mixed with equal parts of limestone grit. Propagate by cuttings or seed in spring.

Chamaecereus silvestrii
GHERKIN CACTUS, PEANUT CACTUS

In summer the finger-length and cylindrical branched stems of this low-growing Argentinian cactus bear several handsome scarlet flowers. Plenty of light in winter is essential and the temperature should not fall below 4°C (40°F) or rise above 16°C (60°F). Water regularly in summer but allow soil to dry out between waterings. At other times water very sparingly to prevent shrivelling. Use a liquid fertilizer monthly from April to August. Repot carefully, preferably in a compost containing extra gritty sand. Propagate by using separate stems as cuttings.

Chamaecyparis lawsoniana 'Ellwoodii'
LAWSON CYPRESS

The North American species plant of this hardy conifer grows to a height of over 45 m (150 ft) and eventually this dwarf variety will reach 3 m (10 ft). It can spend its first years in a window box and then be transferred to a tub and positioned next to the front door. Its neat, classical shape gives style to an entrance and it thrives in both sunny situations and light shade. In October, plant in a window box or tub containing reliable potting compost. Propagate by heel cuttings of one-year-old stems in late summer. Replant every three or four years.

Chamaedorea elegans
DWARF MOUNTAIN PALM

This graceful, slow-growing Mexican palm rarely grows more than 120 cm (4 ft) in a pot. Each of its green leaves has an arching stalk from which many narrow leaflets grow. In winter the temperature should not be allowed to fall below 10-13°C (50-55°F) and soil should be kept just moist. Spray and water freely in summer. Feed monthly from April to September. Repot annually in spring for three years and then every two years in an all-peat compost. Propagate by seed sown in spring and maintain a temperature of 24°C (75°F).

Chamaerops humilis
'Elegans'
EUROPEAN FAN PALM

The only palm that grows wild in
Europe, notably in Spain, Sicily
and southern Italy, this plant has
grey-green, fan-shaped leaves
split into narrow segments which
grow at the top of 60–120 cm
(2–4 ft) spiny stems. In a pot, these
stems rarely attain half this size.
Tolerant of the cold, it can survive
a winter temperature as low as
4–7°C (40–45°F). Keep soil moist
all year and feed fortnightly from
March to October. Repot every
other March. Remove any dead
leaves. Propagate in spring by
removing any suckers and
replanting these separately then.

Chlorophytum elatum
'Variegatum'
SPIDER PLANT

This fast-growing plant from South
Africa has long, arching green-
and-white striped leaves and looks
best in a hanging basket. In spring
and summer white starry flowers
and small plantlets develop on
distinctive long and wiry stems.
From February to September
water freely and feed once a week.
Water sparingly from October
until the end of January and keep
at a temperature no lower than
7°C (45°F). Repot in spring in
potting compost. Propagate by
division or by pegging down well-
grown plantlets into pots to take
root.

Chrysanthemum
CHRYSANTHEMUM

While there are two hundred
known species of this native of
China and Japan, it is the short-
day treated types that are the most
popular as indoor flowering plants
since they need little attention.
Keep cool, water well and do not
feed. Discard these plants when
flowering ceases. Other types
should also be kept cool and well
watered, especially in hot weather
and fed weekly from April until
flowering begins. To encourage
bushiness, pinch out the main
shoot tips in March. Propagate by
basal cuttings the following spring.
Discard the old plant.

Cissus antarctica
KANGAROO VINE

This Australian climber is very easy to grow and can reach well over 2 m (6 ft) in a large pot. By pinching out growing tips, it can be kept to half this height in a smaller pot. Its leathery green leaves have a metallic sheen when the vine is young and it requires a winter temperature of about 10–13°C (50–55°F). Water moderately in summer, sparingly in winter and feed fortnightly between March and September. Repot every other year. In spring pinch out main growing shoots to encourage bushiness. Propagate by cuttings in April and May.

Cissus discolor
REX BEGONIA VINE

This native of the East Indies is a semi-evergreen so in winter loses some of its richly coloured leaves. These are a bright metallic green marbled with purple and white with a hint of crimson and peach. Their undersides are deep crimson. The temperature should not fall below 13°C (55°F) in winter when its soil should be kept just moist. Water liberally in spring and summer. Feed fortnightly from May to September. Prune in February. Repot in March or April, preferably in all-peat compost. Propagate by cuttings of lateral shoots in June or July.

Cissus striata
MINIATURE GRAPE IVY

This delicate South American plant looks particularly graceful if allowed to trail and its leaves, which are pink when young and later dark green, comprise five leaflets, each barely 2 cm (1 in) long. It needs a well-lit position but should be shaded from direct sun. In winter the temperature should not fall below 7°C (45°F). Water liberally in spring and summer, less freely in winter. When new shoots begin to grow, feed monthly until September. Repot in March. Pinch out new shoots occasionally. Propagate by cuttings of stem pieces in summer.

Citrus limon
LEMON

This plant has pointed, glossy green leaves and is easy to grow from a pip. It grows slowly but may eventually reach a height of 120 cm (4 ft). Sweet-smelling white flowers and the familiar fruit appear only on large, mature plants and rarely indoors. Plant the pip in March in an 8 cm (3 in) pot and germinate at 16°C (60°F). Water freely in spring and summer and spray in hot weather. Water sparingly in winter and maintain a temperature of 10°C (50°F). Keep in a well-lit situation. Cut back hard every other March. Repot or pot on every other winter.

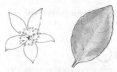

Citrus mitis
CALAMONDIN ORANGE

A slow-growing dwarf from the Philippines, this bushy plant has small, scented, waxy flowers which appear intermittently throughout the year. It requires plenty of sunlight and fresh air and a winter temperature of 13°C (55°F) is ideal. Spray occasionally, when the buds open, to set the fruit. Water moderately all year but more liberally when the fruit begins to swell. Keep drier in June. Feed fortnightly from May to August. If necessary, repot in May and prune back in spring when it should be propagated by seeds or cuttings.

Citrus aurantium, Citrus sinensis
ORANGE TREE

This is the sweet orange as opposed to the sour species used in making marmalade. A pip will germinate easily and produce a rather bushy tree which can grow to 120 cm (4 ft) in a large pot. Fruit and flowers rarely develop indoors. In March plant the pip in an 8 cm (3 in) pot and germinate at 16°C (60°F). Water liberally in spring and summer and spray in hot weather. Water sparingly in winter and keep in a cool but frost-free room. Keep in full light in summer but shade from the hottest sun. Prune in March if necessary. Pot on or repot every other winter.

Clerodendrum speciosissimum
JAVA GLORYBEAN

This Javanese shrub reaches a height of about 90 cm (3 ft) when grown in a pot and in summer tiered clusters of bright scarlet flowers bloom. These are borne on long stems rising above its hairy, heart-shaped leaves. This plant needs plenty of light but should be shaded from very hot sunshine. It will thrive best at a minimum winter temperature of 13°C (55°F). Water sparingly in winter and more liberally in spring and summer. Feed fortnightly from May to September. Repot each April. Prune hard after flowering and propagate by cuttings in summer.

Clerodendrum thomsonae
BLEEDING HEART VINE

This evergreen climber from west Africa has deep green leaves and clusters of blossoms consisting of creamy-white, heart-shaped calyces enclosing bright red, starry flowers. It likes plenty of light but not direct hot sun in summer. From October to February keep in a light position at 10°C (50°F) and water sparingly. In mid-February, move to a warmer room and begin to water. Water well in summer, decreasing gradually from September. In spring, spray regularly and prune old branches right back. Repot in spring and propagate by cuttings then.

Clianthus formosus
(C. dampieri)
GLORY PEA

A native of Australia, this prostrate plant looks best in a hanging basket or pot. Although a short-lived perennial which dies after flowering, it is worth growing for its furry, silver leaves and stems and its claw-shaped flowers. These are bright red with black blotches and open from June to September. Treat the plant like an annual and keep in a fully-lit position in a warm, airy room. Water sparingly from below. Feed fortnightly from May to September. In spring, propagate from seeds using a heated propagator at a temperature of 24°C (75°F).

Clivia miniata
KAFFIR LILY

This attractive house plant has trumpet-shaped orange flowers which usually appear in March. It grows to 45–60 cm (18–24 in). Its winter temperature should not fall below 4°C (40°F) but can rise to 13°C (55°F) or a little higher. There is no need to feed in its first year but afterwards feed with a liquid fertilizer every month from April to August. Water sparingly in summer and otherwise only when the soil dries out completely. Repot only when the pot becomes congested. After flowering, propagate by division or detach offsets with four or five leaves.

Codiaeum variegatum pictum
CROTON, SOUTH SEA LAUREL

The leaves of this Malaysian evergreen come in many shapes and colour combinations including green and pink or scarlet and orange. The plant is fairly demanding and should be placed on an east- or west-facing window-sill to ensure ample light. In winter do not let the temperature fall below 16°C (60°F) and water sparingly. Water liberally and feed fortnightly from April to September. Spray regularly all year. Repot in spring. Pinch out shoot tips to promote bushiness. Propagate by tip cuttings using a heated propagating case.

Coelogyne cristata

This tolerant Nepalese orchid has pendulous clusters of fragrant, yellow-centred, white flowers which open successively from December to March. Grow at a minimum winter temperature of 13°C (55°F). From April to October give plenty of fresh air, spray often and water well, preferably with rain or lime-free water. Use a dilute liquid feed every three weeks from May to September. Repot every two or three years in spring in equal parts of osmunda fibre, sphagnum moss and peat or leaf mould. Propagate by division.

Coffea arabica
COFFEE PLANT

Grown for its glossy, dark green leaves, this native of Africa grows to about 120 cm (4 ft) as a pot plant. Its star-shaped, fragrant, white flowers and red berries which contain the coffee "beans", or seeds, are rarely seen indoors. Provide it with a winter temperature of not less than 7°C (45°F). Water liberally in summer, more sparingly in winter. Spray occasionally. Feed fortnightly from March to October. Repot every other February. Prune back top shoots in March to encourage bushiness. Propagate by lateral stem cuttings in summer.

Coleus blumei
FLAME NETTLE

A native of Java, this foliage plant grows to 30–60 cm (1–2 ft) and has many cultivated varieties with leaves of various colours. They require full sunlight to maintain their bright colours which will, however, lose some intensity in winter. Using soft water, water moderately in summer and slightly less in winter when a minimum temperature of 13°C (55°F) is required. Spray regularly during hot weather. Feed fortnightly from March to September. Cut back in February and repot in lime-free compost. Propagate by cuttings from spring to midsummer.

Columnea microphylla
GOLDFISH VINE

This trailing plant from Costa Rica is ideal for a hanging basket. It has tiny, hairy, dark coppery-green leaves and scarlet and yellow hooded flowers which appear between November and April. A winter temperature no lower than 13–16°C (55–60°F) should be provided and the soil kept moist. Spray and water moderately in summer. Feed every ten days from May to September. Repot every other June in an all-peat compost. Remove dead or bare stems. In spring, propagate by potting 8 cm (3 in) stem sections as cuttings after flowering.

46

Convallaria majalis
LILY OF THE VALLEY

This sweet-smelling plant has small, white, waxy textured, bell-shaped flowers and slender green leaves. It grows about 20 cm (8 in) tall and is a short-term pot plant. In October or November plant a dozen single crowns in a 15 cm (6 inch) pot containing any good-quality proprietary potting compost. The tops of the crowns should be just visible. Place in an unheated but frost-free room. Keep soil moist. In January bring the plant into a warmer room where the temperature is about 13–18°C (55–65°F). Water freely. Discard the plant after flowering.

Cordyline terminalis
CABBAGE PALM

In its natural habitat this tropical Asian shrub will reach 3 m (10 ft) but in a 15 cm (6 in) pot will seldom exceed 60 or 90 cm. Its sword-shaped green leaves grow about 45 cm (18 in) long and are flushed with red or red and cream patterns. Keep at a minimum winter temperature of 16°C (60°F). Water liberally in summer and moderately in winter. Feed fortnightly from April to October. Repot every second spring, preferably in an all-peat mixture. Propagate by sucker shoots from the base of the plant or use the tops of old leggy stems.

Crassula argentea
JADE PLANT, SILVERY SUCCULENT, MONEY TREE

This small, tree-like succulent from South Africa is prized chiefly for its thick, bright green, oval leaves which have an almost metallic gloss. Indoors it rarely produces its white flowers. A dry atmosphere and a winter temperature that does not fall below 4°C (40°F) is best. In summer water sparingly; keep soil dry during the rest of the year. From April to July use a dilute liquid feed monthly. Spray only if the leaves are dusty. Repot every second April in any good potting compost. Propagate by cuttings from leaves or shoot tips in spring and summer.

Crocus vernus
CROCUS

Of the many cultivated varieties developed from this plant, the pale blue and silver-grey 'Vanguard', the pure white 'Joan of Arc' and the deep purple 'Purpureus Grandiflorus' are ones most suitable for indoor cultivation. The flowers open in February and are 10–13 cm (4–5 in) high. Plant corms in a shallow pan in October. Water once, then place in a cool, dark cupboard. When shoots appear in mid-January, move to a well-lit, cool position and water moderately. After flowering, discard old corms or plant outdoors. Buy new corms annually.

Crossandra undulifolia (infundibuliformis)

This plant from India and Sri Lanka grows naturally to 90 cm (3 ft) but seldom exceeds half this size in a pot. It has vivid orange-red flowers which appear from spring until autumn. Shade from the hottest summer sun but provide plenty of direct light in winter. Maintain a permanently humid atmosphere by standing on a tray of wet pebbles. Water liberally from March to September, moderately at other times. From April to August feed fortnightly with liquid fertilizer. Repot in spring. Propagate by cuttings taken in summer.

Cryptanthus acaulis
GREEN EARTH STAR

Although only 8 cm (3 in) tall, this native of Brazil will enhance any arrangement of small indoor plants. It has a compact rosette of broad, prickle-toothed leaves that are mid-green above and white and scaly beneath. It needs plenty of light but no direct sun. Humidity and a winter temperature of 13–16°C (55–60°F) are also necessary. Keep the soil moist in summer, almost dry in winter. Feeding is not essential. Repot in April and May using a proprietary all-peat compost and a small or shallow pot. Propagate by offsets in April.

Easy care plants

Most plants will thrive where conditions of light, temperature and humidity approximate those of their natural habitat. There are some plants, however, which are particularly hardy and are capable of flourishing indoors, despite fluctuating temperatures and a certain amount of neglect.

Busy Lizzie/*Impatiens wallerana*

Kentia Palm/*Howea forsteriana*

Shrimp Plant/*Beloperone guttata*

Rubber Plant/*Ficus elastica decora*

(Left) Spider Plant/ *Chlorophytum elatum*

(Below) False Castor-oil Plant/*Fatsia japonica*

Flowering plants

Massed flowering plants create a transient but exciting blaze of colour in the living-room. They are most effective in a group, where they can stand out while doing their star turn and retire into the background when flowering finishes. While some short-term pot plants, such as the *Convallaria majalis* have to be discarded after flowering, perennial house plants such as *Impatiens wallerana* produce a profusion of flowers throughout the year. Others, like the *Gardenia jasminoides* have beautiful foliage all year round, with the bonus of glorious flowers in summer. Flowering bulbs will provide some colour at almost any time in the year.

Slipper Orchid/
Paphiopedilum insigne

Common *or* Blue Passion
Flower/*Passiflora caerulea*

Lace Flower/*Episcia dianthiflora*

African Violet/
Saintpaulia ionantha

Geranium/*Pelargonium*

Plants with patterned leaves

Flowers are transient, but variegated leaves give more permanent colour and can effectively complement the colour scheme of a room. Variegation, however, can fade or even disappear if the plant is not given adequate light. Plants with patterned leaves will therefore need more light than the corresponding green varieties. It is often difficult to keep them healthy in a living-room if they are those needing a moist atmosphere. *Rhoeo spathacea*, one of the most striking of variegated plants, gives little trouble. The excitingly marked *Maranta leuconeura* is a great favourite, while a flamboyant *Begonia rex* enlivens any room.

Zebra Plant/*Aphelandra squarrosa*

Caladium x hortulanum

Prayer Plant/*Maranta leuconeura*

Silver Net Leaf/*Fittonia argyroneura*

Mixed planting

There are several ways of arranging plants in groups. A plant which has brilliantly coloured flowers or foliage such as *Pelargonium* or *Coleus* can be used in considerable numbers to achieve an eye-catching effect. Another approach is to group plants with a common characteristic such as variegation of leaves or to juxtapose plants with contrasting colours and shapes. It is important that the plants included should have similar light, warmth and water requirements. Bottle gardens are excellent for grouping plants which need a humid atmosphere, and an indoor window box in a well-lit room can provide a useful herb-garden.

A hanging basket with *Fittonia argyroneura* and *Tradescantia fluminensis*

An aerial view of an attractive bottle garden

A mixed arrangement of flowers and foliage plants

An unusual combination of *Dracaena*, *Anthurium* and *Pellaea rotundifolia*

Bulbs

Bulbs need little attention once they have been planted and their colourful flowers give a great deal of pleasure. The usual spring varieties, such as Narcissus, Hyacinth and Tulip, provide a wonderful short-term show but exhaust themselves with a single flowering. Fortunately, however, there is also a wide range of gorgeous, easy-to-grow flowering bulbs for other seasons, such as the *Gloriosa rothschildiana*, *Amaryllis belladonna* and many of the other lilies. These exotic looking and relatively untemperamental bulbs flower in summer and autumn and should continue to do so for many years to come.

Kaffir Lily/*Clivia miniata*

Easter Lily/*Lilium longiflorum*

Glory Lily/*Gloriosa rothschildiana*

Crocus/*Crocus vernus*

Snowdrop/*Galanthus nivalis*

Cacti and succulents

Cacti are succulents but not all succulents belong to the cactus family. All of them can store water but a true cactus can be identified by the little cushion-like tufts called areoles from which spines and barbed hairs sometimes grow. Success with cacti, especially if they are to flower well, depends on providing them with cool and dry conditions during their seasonal resting period but generally they will thrive with little attention. Shapes are often weird or comic but by contrast, their beauty when in flower is all the more staggering. For pretty, odd or interesting shapes, choose from the great variety of cacti available.

Jade Plant/*Crassula argentea*

Tom Thumb/*Kalanchoe blossfeldiana*

One of the *Rebutia* species
Rat's-tail Cactus/*Aporocactus flagelliformis*

Bromeliads

The flamboyant bromeliads, natives of the New World, are grown both for the beauty of their foliage and for their delicate flowers. They can be either epiphytic (living on a tree branch) or terrestrial. The stiff, spiny leaves of many species form a rosette around a central watertight "cup" at the base which, in its natural jungle habitat, collects rainwater. After flowering, the rosette dies, and the offsets it has put out are nourished by the decaying leaves of the parent. When in flower, the flower head or bract provides a splash of colour in its nest at the centre. In spite of their exotic appearance, bromeliads are fairly easy to grow in the home.

Urn Plant/*Aechmea fasciata*

Scarlet Star/*Guzmania lingulata*
Flaming Sword/*Vriesea splendens*

Bonsai

True Japanese bonsai are hardy trees that are trained to stay small as perfect miniatures of majestic trees growing in the wild. They should be kept outdoors, although in the West the art of bonsai is now being extended to include tropical plants that can be grown indoors.

Japanese Maple/*Acer palmatum* in autumn colours

Grey-bark Elm/*Zelkova serrata*

Cryptanthus bromelioides 'Tricolor'
RAINBOW STAR

Prominent cream-and-white-striped leaves with pink-tinged margins characterize this stemless plant from Brazil. Although its flowers are insignificant, it produces handsome offsets. Keep at a winter temperature of 16°C (60°F) in a humid, well-lit situation out of direct sunlight. In summer water moderately and keep leaf rosette filled with tepid water. Very little water is required in winter. Feed monthly from April to September. Repot in April and May using an all-peat compost. Propagate by offsets in late spring.

Cryptomeria japonica
JAPANESE CEDAR

This bonsai is an elegant conifer with small, leathery leaves. In its natural state it grows to 15 m (50 ft). Keep outdoors in a well-lit or partially shaded position. In summer it may be brought indoors for a few days. Keep compost always moist. If possible, plunge pot into peat or sand in winter to protect the roots from frost. Prune the roots every autumn or winter and repot in loam-based compost. In summer trim side shoots and pinch out growing point. Propagate by seed in spring or by heel cuttings in late summer.

Ctenanthe oppenheimiana 'Variegata'
NEVER–NEVER PLANT

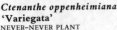

This Brazilian foliage plant bears fan-shaped sprays of oblong to oval leaves. The upper surface of each leaf is boldly splashed with white and has silver-grey bands; the lower surface is purple-red. This species benefits from a humid environment in summer and should be shaded from direct sunlight. Keep soil always just moist but water even less in winter at a minimum temperature of 13°C (55°F). Feed fortnightly from spring to autumn. Repot in any good proprietary potting compost, preferably all peat. Propagate by division in late spring.

Cupressus cashmeriana
KASHMIR CYPRESS

This graceful, pyramid-shaped tree from Tibet grows 120–180 cm (4–6 ft) tall when planted indoors. Placed in a street-facing bay window, its pendant, blue-green, frond-like branchlets will ensure considerable privacy. Provide a winter temperature of not less than 7°C (45°F) and keep soil just moist. Water more liberally in spring and summer. Feed monthly from March to September. Prune top shoots in February. Repot every other spring in any reliable potting compost. Propagate by heel cuttings taken between June and August, or by seed in spring.

Cyanotis kewensis
TEDDY-BEAR VINE

This trailing plant from India suits a hanging basket and has fleshy leaves with green tops and purple undersides. These leaves and their stems are covered with rust-coloured "fur". Small, purplish-red flowers open in winter and spring. A cool position is preferable but the temperature should never fall below 7°C (45°F). Water freely in spring and summer but let soil dry out between waterings. Water sparingly in winter. Feed fortnightly from May to September. Repot every other April. Propagate by cuttings in spring or summer.

Cyclamen persicum
CYCLAMEN

This native of the Middle East has many cultivated varieties whose flowers range through shades of white to deep crimson. In winter keep at a temperature of 13–16°C (55–60°F). From autumn to late winter, when in full growth, keep compost just moist, then gradually water less and allow to dry out. Carefully remove dead and yellowing leaves and flowers from the corm. Keep dry from May to June, then gradually water again. Feed fortnightly when flower buds begin to show. Repot every August. It is only possible to propagate from seed.

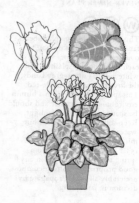

Cymbidium x Rosanna
'PINKIE'

This orchid hybrid has erect 45–60 cm (18–45 in) spikes of white, pink-flushed flowers which open in spring. Keep in a cool, airy room at a minimum winter temperature of 7–13°C (45–55°F). Protect from strong summer sun but expose to autumn and winter sunshine. Water freely in summer but sparingly in winter. Spray regularly and feed fortnightly with half-strength liquid fertilizer from April to August. Repot every three years after flowering in equal parts of fibrous loam or peat, osmunda fibre and sphagnum moss. Propagate by division.

Cyperus alternifolius
UMBRELLA GRASS

Slender, arching, leaf-like, green bracts at the end of long stems give this African plant the appearance of a bunch of umbrella frames. In summer small, yellowish-brown or green flowers appear at the base of the bracts. In a pot, this plant rarely exceeds a height of 60 cm (2 ft). Provide a winter temperature of 10–13°C (50–55°F) and keep the pot standing in a water-filled saucer. Feed fortnightly from April to September. Repot in April and again in autumn if many new stems appear. Cut off old stems. Propagate by division when repotting.

Cyrtomium falcatum
HOLLY FERN, FISH-TAIL FERN

A native of the Far East, this long-living fern is a very tolerant house plant. Its arching fronds are about 45 cm (18 in) long and its dark green, glossy pinnules (the leaflets forming the fronds) are about 8 cm (3 in) long. Protect this fern from sunlight at all times and provide a winter temperature of 7–10°C (45–50°F). During the April to August growing period feed fortnightly and water liberally. Spray in hot weather. Water sparingly from October to February. Repot every other March. Propagate by division when repotting.

Daucus carota
CARROT

Carrots make interesting plants and can be grown in several ways. After cutting the top off a carrot, remove all but the youngest central leaves and plant in a 10 cm (4 in) pot of moist peat, sand or potting compost. Alternatively, stand it on a spiked flower holder in a saucer of water. Kept on a partially shaded window-sill in a cool room, feathery leaves will soon appear. A further method is to cut 8 cm (3 in) from a large carrot top and after digging out the core, make two holes near the top of this shell and hang up with string. Keep almost full of water.

Dendrobium nobile

This Asian orchid blooms in winter and each of its blossoms consists of white petals shaded with pink or lilac, a rounded white or yellow lip with a deep purple blotch in the throat and pink to purple margins. Provide direct light in winter but shade at other times. In winter maintain a minimum temperature of 7–16°C (45–60°F) and provide fresh air. From April to October water liberally and feed every three weeks. Repot every three years after flowering with equal parts of sphagnum moss and osmunda fibre. Propagate by division.

Dianthus chinensis
CHINESE or INDIAN PINK

Several cultivated varieties have been developed from this clove-scented plant from eastern Asia. An annual, it has narrow green leaves and 23 cm (9 in) stems bearing single or double flat-petalled flowers in white and varying shades of pink and red. It blooms from summer to autumn. In mid-April sow the seeds in any good-quality potting compost. When seedlings are large enough to handle, thin them out to 15 cm (6 in) apart. Water well in dry weather. Cut off dead flower heads. Discard the plants after flowering.

Dichorisandra thyrsiflora
BLUE GINGER

This exotic plant from Brazil will usually grow to about 60 cm (2 ft) in a pot. It has shiny, lance-shaped green leaves with purplish undersides and clusters of blue and yellow flowers which bloom in summer. Keep compost almost dry at a minimum winter temperature of 16°C (60°F). From spring to autumn, water liberally, feed fortnightly and stand the pot on a tray of wet pebbles to provide a moist, humid atmosphere. Repot every spring in any good proprietary compost and propagate by division when repotting, or by cuttings in summer.

Dieffenbachia picta
DUMB CANE

Large, creamy-white blotches spatter the green leaves of this highly poisonous plant from Brazil. There are several cultivated varieties which have different leaf markings. It grows to 60–120 cm (2–3 ft) tall and is highly poisonous. It needs a minimum winter temperature of 16°C (60°F) for healthy growth. Always keep the soil moist, spray regularly and feed weekly from March to August. Repot every spring in good-quality potting compost. Propagate by tip or stem-section cuttings if you have a heated propagator.

Dionaea muscipula
VENUS' FLY TRAP

When an insect lands on this macabre plant from Carolina, the leaf promptly folds to trap its prey. Special glands secrete a substance that digests the insect. Spikes of pretty white flowers appear in summer. The plant should always stand in a shallow tray filled with water. It needs a minimum winter temperature of 7°C (40°F). Small, newly swatted flies may be dropped on to the leaves occasionally. Repot every second or third spring in equal quantities of peat and sphagnum moss. Propagate by division when repotting.

Dipladenia splendens
PINK ALLAMANDA

This glossy-leaved climbing plant from Brazil may grow more than 4 m (13 ft) tall. When it is only about 30 cm (1 ft) tall, large heads of trumpet-shaped, pink flowers appear from June to September. Keep soil moist at a minimum winter temperature of 13°C (55°F), increasing to 16°C (60°F) in March when the new growth begins. Water liberally and spray often. Feed weekly during flowering season. Repot every March in any good proprietary potting compost. Cut the stems back after flowering. Propagate by cuttings in summer.

Dizygotheca elegantissima
FALSE ARALIA, FINGER ARALIA

When young, this elegant plant from the New Hebrides has coppery-red leaves of several 8 cm (3 in) long, narrow, tooth-edged leaflets. As the plant grows – often up to 150 cm (5 ft) – its leaves become coarse and dark green. Water sparingly in winter and provide a minimum temperature of 10°C (50°F). Water moderately in summer. Spray all year round and feed fortnightly from May to August. Repot every other May in any good proprietary potting compost. Old plants may be pruned hard in March. Propagate by seed in spring.

Dracaena deremensis
DRAGON PLANT

This palm-like East African plant has glossy, dark green leaves which can grow to 45 cm (18 in) long and have two silver stripes running from base to tip. The plant can reach a height of 120 cm (4 ft) or more. 'Bausei' and 'Warneckii' are popular cultivated varieties. Water sparingly in winter and do not allow the temperature to fall below 13°C (55°F). Water liberally in spring and summer. Feed fortnightly from May to September. Repot every other April. Propagate by tip or stem-section cuttings in summer, preferably in a heated propagator.

Dracaena godseffiana
GOLD–DUST DRACAENA

This central African shrub has wiry, branching stems with 8 cm (3 in) long leaves which are dark green with creamy-yellow spots. Small, pale yellow flowers may appear in spring, followed by red berries. The plant grows to a height of about 60 cm (2 ft). Provide a winter temperature no lower than 7°C (45°F). Keep soil just moist from spring to autumn and water even less in winter. Feed fortnightly from June to September. Pinch out top shoots in spring. Repot every other April. Propagate by cuttings in summer in a heated propagator.

Dracaena marginata 'Variegata'
MADAGASCAR DRAGON TREE

This is a tree-like species but it grows very slowly and takes some years to reach even a height of 120 cm (4 ft). Its hard, narrow leaves grow up to 45 cm (18 in) and are dark green with pink-tinted, cream stripes. It will tolerate a winter temperature of 10°C (50°F) but prefers one of 13–16°C (55–60°F). Water sparingly in winter, more liberally in spring and summer and feed fortnightly from June to September. Repot every other April. Propagate by tip or stem-section cuttings in March or April, preferably in a heated propagator.

Duchesnea indica (Fragaria indica)
INDIAN STRAWBERRY

Brought to Europe from India in the seventeenth century, this creeping plant is ideal for a hanging basket. It has wiry stems, green leaves and small, bright yellow flowers which open in succession from spring to autumn. These are followed by glossy, red, strawberry-like but tasteless fruit. In winter keep in a frost-free, unheated room and keep soil just moist. In spring and summer water more liberally. From April to September feed fortnightly. Repot in winter or early spring. Propagate by division then or by detaching plantlets in late summer.

Echeveria gibbiflora 'Carunculata'

From Mexico, this plant has a rosette of fleshy, blue-mauve leaves, each branded with wart-like blisters. Occasional sprays of bell-shaped scarlet and yellow flowers are borne on long arching stems from autumn to winter. Stand in a position affording full sunlight all year round and allow a minimum temperature of 4°C (40°F) in winter. Water sparingly in winter and keep moisture away from leaf rosette. Apply a monthly liquid feed from April to August. Repot each (or every other) April. Propagate in summer by leaf or stem cuttings.

Echinocactus grusonii
GOLDEN BALL, GOLDEN BARREL, MOTHER-IN-LAW'S CHAIR

This pale green, globular cactus has a covering of golden-yellow spines. A slow developer, it rarely produces its small, yellow flowers when grown indoors. To ensure good spine colour, place in a location receiving strong light and good ventilation. Do not allow winter temperature to fall below 4°C (40°F). Keep moist in summer but dry from October to March. Apply liquid fertilizer monthly from March to mid-August. Repot every two to three years in a reliable potting compost mixed with extra coarse sand. To propagate, sow seeds in spring.

Echinocereus pectinatus

This fast growing central Mexican cactus grows to 20 cm (8 in) and has oval stems set with star-like patterns of white spines. In summer, long funnel-shaped flowers open widely to reveal their bright pink interiors. A winter temperature of about 4°C (40°F) and a location offering maximum sunlight are advisable. Water well in summer but keep absolutely dry from October to March. Repot in a wide shallow pan with a reliable compost mixed with grit or coarse sand. Propagate in early spring by seed or by stem cuttings from April to August.

Echinopsis rhodotricha

A native of Argentina and
Paraguay, this cactus has oval or
cylindrical stems whose ribs bear
yellowish, black-tipped spines.
Funnel-shaped white flowers, 15
cm (6 in) long, open in summer.
The plant will thrive in full light
but some shade from the hottest
sun is advisable. To ensure it
flowers successfully, provide a
winter temperature of about 4°C
(40°F), keeping compost moist in
summer and almost dry in winter.
Apply a liquid fertilizer fortnightly
from April to August. Repot in
alternate Aprils. Propagate by
offsets in summer or seed in spring.

Epidendrum prismatocarpum
RAINBOW ORCHID

This epiphyte from Central
America bears mid-green leaves
and 40 cm (16 in) spikes of 10–20
waxy flowers from May to
August. Their petals are yellowish-
green with maroon spots; their
pointed lips are rosy-purple with
yellow tips and white margins.
Shade from summer sun and keep
at a minimum winter temperature
of 13°C (55°F). Keep compost
moist from April to September,
otherwise water sparingly. Repot
in spring in a mixture of two parts
osmunda fibre and one of
sphagnum moss. Propagate by
division when repotting.

Epiphyllum × ackermannii
ORCHID CACTUS

These hybrids bear fragrant,
scarlet flowers which open in
daylight in May and June. The
related white and yellow forms
flower in the evening. They
require well-lit, airy positions with
shelter from direct sunlight and
winter temperatures of 7–10°C
(45–50°F). Water liberally in
summer, more moderately in
winter. When flower buds begin
to form, give a high-potassium
fertilizer every two weeks. Repot
annually after spring flowering in
a loam, sphagnum moss, peat and
sand mixture. Propagate by seed
in spring or cuttings in summer.

Episcia cupreata
FLAME VIOLET

Only when placed in a hanging basket can the magnificent foliage of this plant be fully appreciated. Its downy leaves have a red and silver band down their centres. Bright red flowers appear from June to September. Supply a minimum winter temperature of 13°C (55°F). Stand plant on a tray of wet pebbles or moist peat. Spray hanging basket and leaf undersides regularly. Always keep soil moist but water less in winter. Apply a dilute fertilizer fortnightly in summer. Repot in April in an all-peat compost. Propagate by runners in summer.

Episcia dianthiflora
LACE FLOWER

This Mexican evergreen has dark green leaves and its beauty is enhanced by the summertime blooms of delicately-fringed white flowers which give it its name. Highly suitable for a hanging basket, both basket and the undersides of the leaves should be sprayed regularly if grown in this way; otherwise stand on a tray of wet pebbles or moist peat. Water regularly but less in winter. Give a fortnightly feed of liquid fertilizer from April to August. Repot in April in a pan or basket with all-peat compost. Propagate by runners in spring or summer.

Erica carnea
HEATH, HEATHER

This compact, low-growing, winter-flowering shrub from the European Alps is easily grown in a south-, east- or west-facing window box. Its 15 cm (6 in) branches are covered with needle-like green leaves and, from November to May, it bears a profusion of pink or white, tiny, bell-shaped flowers. In spring or summer set out several plants 30 cm (12 in) apart. Water liberally in dry weather. Prune after flowering. From July to September propagate by heel cuttings of one-year-old shoots. Replant every few years. Discard straggly plants.

Erica gracilis
CHRISTMAS HEATHER, ROSE HEATH

A native of southern Africa, this small bushy shrub has pale green leaves and small, bell-shaped, pink and purple flowers. In a pot, it rarely exceeds 45 cm (18 in) and flowers from October to January. Provide a continually well-lit position and a winter temperature around 10°C (50°F). In spring and summer spray weekly with soft water, always keeping soil moist. Feed fortnightly from May to July. In spring, after flowering, repot in a lime-free, soilless compost. In April pinch out new shoot tips to encourage bushiness. Propagate by cuttings in March.

Eucalyptus globulus
BLUE GUM TREE

☆ ©️ ◯

This native of Australia has a distinctively astringent scent. Its young leaves are blue-grey and oval but after two to four years, long, narrow, dark adult leaves are formed. The fluffy white flowers it bears in the bush seldom appear. It can reach heights of 45 m (150 ft) but pinching out its top shoots will forestall this. Water well in spring and summer. In winter give less water but do not allow soil to dry out completely and keep cool at 4–7°C (40–45°F). Feed fortnightly from April to October. Repot young plants each spring in a good potting compost.

Euonymus japonicus
JAPANESE SPINDLE TREE

☆ ©️ ⊘

In its native Japan, this shrub can reach 4 m (13 ft) or more but when grown indoors as a pot plant rarely exceeds a height of 180 cm (6 ft). It requires a light, airy position but tolerates considerable shade. Water liberally in summer but from August onwards gradually reduce and keep soil just moist in winter when it should be kept in an unheated but frost-free room. Feed fortnightly from April to August. Repot annually for two years, then every alternate March. Pinch out shoot tips in spring or summer. Propagate by cuttings in summer.

Euonymus japonicus 'Microphyllus Variegatus'
JAPANESE SPINDLE TREE

This bushy shrub has serrated, tough, green leaves with white margins. Clusters of greenish-white flowers open in May and June and, on mature plants, are sometimes followed by orange and pink fruit. In spring or autumn, a young plant can be started in a window box containing potting compost. When it reaches 60–90 cm (2–3 ft) it should be transferred to a tub and kept in a sheltered position. Water liberally in dry weather. Pinch out top shoots to encourage bushiness. Replant every few years.
Propagate in August from cuttings of lateral shoots.

Euphorbia fulgens
SCARLET PLUME

Scarlet, petal-shaped bracts surround the insignificant orange flowers covering the slender, arching stems of this 120 cm (4 ft) Mexican shrub from November to February. Maintain a winter temperature of 13–16°C (55–60°F) and water sparingly. A month after flowering ceases, gradually dry plant off and move to a warmer room at about 18°C (65°F). Moisten soil and increase humidity. Feed fortnightly from June to September. Repot every other March. Prune during the dry dormant period. Propagate from young shoots after pruning.

Euphorbia milii (E. splendens)
CROWN OF THORNS

This Malagasy shrub has angular branches covered with sharp thorns and clusters of green-yellow flowers borne on long, scarlet stems in spring. Blood-red bracts surround these blooms. The plant enjoys hot sun, dry air and good ventilation. In winter the temperature should not fall below 13°C (55°F). Water moderately from May to August but otherwise keep barely moist. Use a fortnightly liquid fertilizer from June to August. Repot every second spring in compost mixed with extra sand. Propagate by cuttings in spring or summer.

Euphorbia obesa
TURKISH TEMPLE

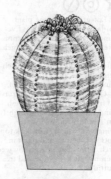

This 15 cm (6 in) tall, globular succulent from South Africa resembles a spineless sea urchin. Its grey-green, leafless stem has eight broad ribs covered with brown-purple bands. Minute, sweet-scented, bell-shaped flowers appear in summer. It likes dry air and a very sunny situation as well as a winter temperature of about 7°C (45°F). Keep just moist from April to early autumn but let compost dry out from autumn to spring. Use a dilute fertilizer every three weeks from May to August. Repot every second or third year in May in sandy compost.

Euphorbia pulcherrima
POINSETTIA

This plant has insignificant flowers surrounded by red, pink or white leaf-like bracts. The normal flowering season is winter but flowers can be produced at other times by keeping in the dark for 14 hours a day for 8 weeks. In winter the temperature must not fall below 13–16°C (55–60°F). After flowering keep almost dry until May. Spray in hot weather. Feed weekly from June to October. Prune back top shoots in May and repot in a good potting compost. Propagate by cutting off shoots in early summer and plant in a mixture of sand and peat.

x Fatshedera lizei
FAT-HEADED LIZZIE, IVY TREE

A semi-climbing hybrid, in a large pot or tub this plant reaches 180 cm (6 ft) with support but can be kept small and bushy by judicious pruning in spring. It has glossy, dark green leaves and greenish flowers which appear in October and November. In winter, rest at a temperature no lower than 2°C (35°F) and water sparingly. From April to August feed fortnightly and keep soil moist. Do not overwater. Pinch out top shoots to encourage bushiness. Repot in March in potting compost. Propagate by cuttings in late summer or autumn.

77

Fatsia japonica
FALSE CASTOR-OIL PLANT,
FIG-LEAF PALM

This fast-growing house plant
from Japan and Taiwan has five-
to nine-lobed leaves and greenish-
white, round flower heads which
only appear in autumn on large
plants. In a large pot, it can reach
a height of 90 cm (3 ft). It can
endure a winter temperature of
4–7°C (40–45°F) and even survive
mild frosts. Give plenty of fresh
air and water and feed fortnightly
from April to August. Water
sparingly in winter. Cut back top
shoots in February and repot in
March. Propagate in April by seed
or remove sucker shoots and treat
as cuttings.

Faucaria tigrina
TIGER'S JAWS, CAT'S JAWS

This South African succulent is
5 cm (2 in) high and has a criss-
cross arrangement of fleshy, thick,
grey-green leaves with a covering
of white dots and sharply toothed
margins. In autumn large, bright
yellow, daisy-like flowers appear.
It likes full sunlight but needs a
winter temperature no less than
4°C (40°F). Keep compost moist
during late summer and autumn
growing season. Let it dry out in
winter. Repot every third year in
April in potting compost mixed
with equal parts of sharp sand.
Propagate by seed in spring or by
cuttings from June to August.

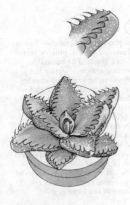

Ficus benjamina
WEEPING FIG

A graceful plant with arching or
pendulous side branches, this has
slender, pointed leaves which are
grass green and darker later. In the
Indian jungle it grows up to 12 m
(40 ft) in height; grown as a house
plant in a large pot it is unlikely to
exceed 180 cm (6 ft). Provide a
continually humid atmosphere.
Do not let the temperature fall
below 10°C (50°F) in winter when
soil should be kept just damp.
Water liberally in spring and
summer. Feed fortnightly from
May to September. Repot every
other April. Propagate by cuttings
in summer.

Ficus elastica decora
RUBBER PLANT

This cultivated variety of a plant much loved by the Victorians has become very popular in both office and home. In tropical Asia it may reach 30 m (100 ft) but in a large pot indoors 180 cm (6 ft) is its usual upper limit. Supply a winter temperature not less than 16°C (60°F) and keep soil just moist. In spring and summer water liberally. Feed fortnightly from May to September. Sponge the glossy, dark green leaves regularly. Repot every other April in potting compost. Propagate by leaf-bud or stem-tip cuttings in summer, using a heated propagator.

Fittonia argyroneura
SILVER NET LEAF

A delicate network of white veins covers the bright green leaves of this low-growing plant from Peru. Occasional, inconspicuous flowers develop but are best pinched out before they open. Eminently suitable for centrally-heated homes, it needs a temperature not lower than 16°C (60°F) in winter when it should be watered sparingly. In spring and summer water freely and spray regularly. Feed fortnightly from June to September. Cut back in March. Repot in April, in an all-peat compost. Propagate by cuttings or by division in spring or summer.

Fittonia verschaffeltii
PAINTED NET LEAF

A network of red veins spreading across its dark green leaves gives this Peruvian creeping plant a purple appearance from a distance. Its winter temperature should not fall below 13°C (55°F) and it should be watered sparingly then, to keep the soil just moist. Water liberally and spray often in spring and summer. Feed fortnightly from June to September. Prune lightly in spring. Repot in April, using a good-quality proprietary potting compost, preferably of an all-peat composition. Propagate by cuttings or by division in late spring or summer.

Fortunella margarita
KUMQUAT

This small tree grows to an average height of 90 cm (3 ft) when kept in a pot. It produces clusters of small, white, scented flowers in spring and summer and small, orange fruit which ripens in autumn and in winter when it should be kept at a minimum temperature of 10°C (50°F). Place by a sunny, open window in summer. This plant requires plenty of water except in winter when it should be kept considerably drier but always moist. Feed fortnightly from April to October. Repot in February using a loamless mixture. Propagate by cuttings.

Freesia x kewensis
(Freesia x hybrida)
FREESIA

These scented hybrids have narrow, sword-shaped leaves and funnel-shaped flowers in a wide variety of colours, opening in early spring. In October plant a dozen corms in a 13 cm (5 in) pot. Keep in a sunny position and water moderately. When each corm has 3 or 4 leaves, and until flower buds appear, apply a liquid feed fortnightly. The temperature should be kept between 7–18°C (45–65°F). When the leaves become yellow, dry off and store the corms in a cool, dry place. Repot largest corms in autumn. Propagate by offsets.

Fuchsia magellanica
FUCHSIA

This species has clusters of delicate, half-red and half-purple flowers. Numerous hybrid cultivated varieties exist in different colour combinations – the most common are pink and white, purple and red, and pink and red. Provide a minimum winter temperature of 7°C (45°F) and water sparingly then. In summer water moderately and spray often. Feed weekly from April to September. Fresh air is appreciated on warm days but shield from direct sunlight. Prune lightly in February, then repot in good-quality potting compost. Propagate by cuttings in March.

Fuchsia triphylla
FUCHSIA

(T) (N)

Growing to a height of 60 cm
(2 ft), this species has lance-shaped
leaves which are green on top and
purple underneath. Its orange-
scarlet flowers grow in pendant
clusters and open from July to
October. In winter the
temperature should not fall below
10°C (50°F) when the soil should
be kept just damp. Spray regularly
and water freely in spring and
summer. Feed weekly from April
to September. Supply plenty of
fresh air on warm days. Cut out
dead stems and prune leggy plants
in February before repotting.
Propagate by cuttings in March.

Galanthus nivalis
SNOWDROP

This European woodlander has
slender leaves, erect 15 cm (6 in)
stems and solitary white and green
pendant flowers which open in
January and February. In
September, place 6–10 bulbs in
pans with potting compost. Water
once, then place in the coolest part
of the house, ideally in the dark.
When shoots appear in late
November bring into moderate
light but still keep as cool as
possible. An unheated room is best.
Keep moist but not wet. After
flowering, plant out in the garden
or discard. It is best to plant
newly-purchased bulbs each year.

Gardenia jasminoides
GARDENIA, CAPE JASMINE

(T) (N)

A native of China, this plant has
glossy leaves and white, waxy,
double flowers which open in
summer and are heavily scented.
Growing to 60–120 cm (2–4 ft), it
requires a winter temperature of
13–16°C (55–60°F). Water
sparingly in winter, more freely in
summer. Falling buds indicate
over- or under-watering. Feed
fortnightly and spray often from
May to October. Repot every
other April in a good-quality
potting compost. Prune after
flowering. Propagate by cuttings
taken in spring or summer,
preferably in a heated propagator.

Gasteria verrucosa

This South African succulent has dark green, fleshy leaves marked with pearly-white warts and with grooved upper surfaces. Orange-red, tubular flowers open in spring and summer. It thrives in a sunny, airy position. In winter the temperature must not fall below 4°C (40°F). Keep moist from March to September but almost dry in winter. Feed every three weeks from April to August. Repot every second or third year in spring, or after flowering, in compost mixed with extra sand. Propagate by seed, leaf cuttings or division in summer.

Geogenanthus undatus
SEERSUCKER PLANT

Mid-green with dark green stripes on top and brownish-red undersides, the uneven texture of this Peruvian plant's leaves is perfectly described by its common name. It grows to a height of 30 cm (12 in). In winter a minimum temperature of 13°C (55°F) should be maintained. Water liberally in spring and summer and sparingly in winter. Spray often with tepid water throughout the year. Feed fortnightly from March to August. Repot each April in any good-quality proprietary potting compost. Propagate by cuttings or by division in late spring.

Gloriosa rothschildiana
GLORY LILY

A native of tropical Africa, this climbing lily grows to a height of 120 cm (4 ft) or more. It has lance-shaped leaves and crimson and yellow flowers which open from June to August. Plant the tuber in a 15 cm (6 in) pot in spring. Keep humid in a temperature not lower than 16°C (60°F) and water sparingly. Support stems with canes. Water freely and feed fortnightly. After flowering, reduce watering. When leaves turn yellow, dry off. Store the tuber in its pot at a temperature of about 10°C (50°F). Propagate from offsets removed when repotting.

Godetia grandiflora
(G. amoena whitneyi)

Producing a dense mass of showy, fragrant, flowers, this Californian annual has 38 cm (15 in) stems bearing pointed leaves and, from June to August, spikes of rose-purple, poppy-like flowers. Several dwarf varieties have flowers of white, lilac and shades of pink and red. In March sow the seed in a south-, east- or west-facing window box. In April or May thin seedlings 10–15 cm (4–6 in) apart. Keep soil moist at all times. Unless the compost has been used before, do not feed since fertilizer encourages too much leaf growth.

Graptophyllum pictum
CARICATURE PLANT

This interesting East Indian shrub has hard, green leaves with white markings which sometimes resemble human faces. It grows to a height of 60 cm (2 ft) or more and bears small clusters of bright crimson flowers which open in summer. In winter provide a temperature of 13°C (55°F) and as much light as possible. Water freely in spring and summer and keep soil just moist in winter. Spray in warm weather and shade from hot sun. Feed fortnightly from April to September. Repot every April. Propagate by cuttings from April to June.

Grevillea robusta
SILK BARK OAK

In Western Australia this tree grows to a height of 48 m (160 ft) and kept as a pot plant will reach the ceiling within 3 or 4 years when it should be transferred to a conservatory. Its evergreen fern-like leaves make it a useful foliage plant but indoors it will never produce its yellow flowers. Water moderately and regularly. Feed fortnightly in summer and always maintain an even temperature. Extremes of heat and moisture cause leaf-fall and can kill the plant. Pot in an all-peat compost. Propagate by seed or by cuttings taken in spring or late summer.

83

Guzmania lingulata
SCARLET STAR

This plant from the South American rain forests has hard, spear-shaped, 45 cm (18 in) leaves growing in a rosette to form a funnel. A cluster of yellow-white flowers surrounded by crimson bracts appears in winter. Keep at a winter temperature no lower than 16°C (60°F). Water liberally in summer, sparingly in winter, preferably using tepid, soft water. Keep the rosette filled with water except in winter. Feed monthly with dilute liquid fertilizer. Repot every second or third spring. Propagate by planting offsets in compost and sphagnum moss.

Gynura aurantiaca
VELVET PLANT

Violet hairs cover the stems and velvet-textured leaves of this Javanese shrub which grows to 90 cm (3 ft). Its clusters of small orange flowers, which appear on erect stems in February, have such a pungent scent that they are often removed before they open. In winter the temperature should not fall below 13°C (55°F). Keep in a well-lit position and water sparingly then. Water liberally in summer. Feed fortnightly from June to September. Repot in April in potting compost. Prune hard in March. Propagate by cuttings in summer.

Habranthus robustus

A native of Argentina, this plant grows from a bulb to a height of about 60 cm (2 ft). Narrow, strap-shaped leaves appear first, followed by long-stemmed, trumpet-shaped flowers which are purplish-pink fading to white. Its flowers open in June and July. Bring the bulb into growth in spring by watering moderately. Keep in good light but protect from strong sun. From March to May feed fortnightly. When flowering ends, stop watering and move to a cool but frost-free position. Repot every other spring. Propagate by removing offsets when repotting.

Haemanthus multiflorus
SALMON BLOOD LILY

This central African plant grows
to about 60–90 cm (2–3 ft) in
height. It has lance-shaped leaves
and large, round flower heads
which are pink or red and open in
spring. In March provide a
temperature of 13–16 °C (55–60°F)
and a moderate amount of water.
From May to August feed
fortnightly. After flowering,
gradually reduce the water,
position in a minimum winter
temperature of 10–13°C (50–55°F)
and keep almost dry. Repot every
third March in a 15 cm (6 in) pot
with potting compost. Propagate
by offsets when repotting.

Haworthia margaritifera
PEARL PLANT

This South African succulent has
rosettes of tapering leaves
thickly covered with large, white nodules.
The flowers are insignificant. It
favours full light but can tolerate
some shade. Supply a minimum
winter temperature of 4°C (40°F).
In spring and summer keep the
compost moist but almost dry the
rest of the year. Give a dilute
liquid fertilizer fortnightly from
April to August. Repot annually
in spring in pans or half pots using
equal parts of loam-based compost
and sharp sand. Propagate by
removing offsets in summer or
from seed in spring.

Hebe rakiensis

This bushy shrub from New
Zealand is extremely hardy and
can survive at temperatures below
freezing. It has oval, glossy
evergreen leaves and clusters of
pure white flowers which open
from late spring to early summer
but only appear on unpruned
plants. It is capable of reaching a
height of 45 cm (18 in) but can be
pruned back regularly to 30 cm
(12 in). Plant in an east- or west-
facing window box kept moist at
all times. Feed monthly from
April to September. Replant every
other spring. Propagate by cuttings
in late summer.

Hedera canariensis
CANARY ISLAND IVY

This species has larger leaves and grows more slowly than the Common Ivy. The leaves of the most attractive cultivated variety, 'Gloire de Marengo', have dark green centres paling through silver-grey to a white border. From April to August keep the soil moist but never overwater. Feed fortnightly and spray in dry weather. Keep in an unheated, frost-free place and water sparingly from October to February. Do not repot until three years old, then do so in alternate springs. Pinch out shoots in March. Propagate by cuttings in summer.

Hedera helix
COMMON IVY, ENGLISH IVY

Of widespread origin, this adaptable evergreen attaches itself by aerial roots to any available support. It will trail decoratively from a hanging basket. Cultivated varieties are numerous and the size and shape of their leaves vary enormously; some are variegated. The plant thrives in cold but frost-free rooms. Keep soil moist and the leaves regularly sponged. Feed fortnightly from April to September. Repot every other February in potting compost and cut the plant back to half its size in March or April. Propagate by cuttings taken in autumn.

Heliotropium x *hybridum*
HELIOTROPE, CHERRY PIE

This evergreen shrub from Peru produces masses of small, delicately perfumed flowers from May to October. These range in colour from deep purple through lavender to white. In winter maintain a temperature of 4–7°C (40–45°F). This plant enjoys a bright window but must be shaded from scorching sun. Water well, keeping moist at all times. Spray occasionally in hot weather. Feed fortnightly from May to August. Repot each March in a loamless mixture and pinch out top shoots to encourage flowering. Propagate by stem cuttings in late summer.

Hemigraphis colorata
RED IVY

A native of Malaysia, this plant is seen at its best in a hanging basket. Its leaves are metallic violet-purple on top and reddish-purple underneath. Small white flowers open in summer. As it is a tropical plant, it likes both warmth and a humid atmosphere all year. Keep the temperature above 13°C (55°F) and spray regularly. Water liberally in spring and summer. In winter keep soil just damp. Feed fortnightly from May to September. Cut back any straggling stems in late winter. Repot every March or April. Propagate by cuttings.

Heuchera sanguinea
CORAL BELLS

Spikes of pink, bell-shaped flowers, which open from June to September, grow in loose clusters on the 30–45 cm (12–18 in) stems of this Mexican perennial. Round or heart-shaped evergreen leaves grow at the base of the plant. Several hybrids and cultivated varieties have pink, red or white flowers, some of which grow on slightly longer stems. Plant in a sunny or partially shaded window box. Water freely in dry weather. Replant every other year between autumn and spring. Propagate by division when replanting or by seed in spring.

Hibiscus rosa-sinensis
ROSE OF CHINA

This evergreen shrub is a native of China. It has toothed leaves and large flowers in several colours including red, pink, white and yellow. It can grow to 180 cm (6 ft) in a tub but may be pruned back hard. It needs light throughout the year, preferably from an east- or west-facing window. In winter the temperature should not fall below 13°C (55°F). Water liberally and spray in summer. Water less in winter. Feed weekly from February to August. Prune in February and repot in loamless mixture. Propagate by cuttings.

Hippeastrum
AMARYLLIS

The trumpet-shaped flowers of these hybrids are available in a wide variety of colours – pure white, white with orange streaks, pure pink, pink with orange veins, pure red and orange-red – and open from December to May. Start its bulb into growth in October at 13–16°C (55–60°F), place in a well-lit position and water sparingly. Water more liberally and feed weekly when the first foliage appears; stop when the leaves turn yellow. Repot every other October leaving the top half of the bulb uncovered. Propagate by removing offsets.

Howea forsteriana
KENTIA PALM, PARADISE PALM

The traditional foliage of the palm court orchestra, this native of the Pacific grows long and graceful, dark green leaves which are divided into numerous slender leaflets. In a tub it grows up to 3 m (10 ft) tall. Provide a winter temperature of 13°C (55°F) and keep soil just moist. Water liberally from April to July, then moderately until October. Feed fortnightly from April to September. Remove dead leaves. Repot every other April. Propagate by seed in spring; for the best results use a heated propagating case with a temperature of 24–27°C (75–80°F).

Hoya bella
MINIATURE WAX PLANT

This sweet-scented Indian plant looks best in a hanging basket. Its arching branches bear oval, green leaves occasionally spotted with silver. Clusters of small, waxy flowers with red-purple centres open from May to September. In spring and summer spray regularly and do not let the temperature fall below 16°C (60°F). A winter temperature of about 13°C (55°F) is ideal. Water liberally in summer, sparingly in winter. Feed fortnightly from March to September. Pinch out new shoot tips. Repot every other April. Propagate by cuttings in summer.

Hoya carnosa
WAX PLANT

This vigorous climber from Queensland clings on to bark or a moss-covered stick by means of aerial roots. It can grow to 6 m (20 ft) tall. Umbels of pinkish-white, fragrant star-shaped flowers open from May to September. Keep at a minimum temperature of 16°C (60°F) in spring and summer in a humid atmosphere and 10°C (50°F) in winter. Water liberally in summer, sparingly in winter. Feed fortnightly when in flower from May to September. Repot in April in good-quality potting compost. Propagate by cuttings in summer.

Hyacinthus orientalis
HYACINTH

The cultivated varieties known as Dutch Hyacinths have dense spikes of fragrant, bell-shaped flowers, generally blue, pink or white. Those known as Roman Hyacinths have looser, blue or white flower spikes, several to each bulb. In September or October plant bulbs in moist potting compost or bulb fibre. Leave tops uncovered. Keep in a cool, dark place until shoots appear, then move to a well-lit, cool room. Water sparingly. When leaves develop, temperature may be increased to about 18°C (65°F). Discard the bulbs after flowering.

Hydrangea macrophylla
HYDRANGEA

This plant has white, pink, red, purple or blue flowers (blue occurring when the soil is acid and makes the aluminium in it available). Feed weekly and water freely from February to August, twice a day if necessary for a well-rooted plant. Reduce the amount of water gradually from August. Water sparingly in winter and keep the plant in an unheated but frost-free place. Cut back stems after flowering and repot in an all-peat mixture. Use a proprietary blueing compound for blue flowers. Propagate by cuttings in spring.

Hymenocallis calathina
(*H. narcissiflora*)
SPIDER LILY

From Peru, this fragrant, deciduous
lily grows over 60 cm (2 ft) tall. It
has arching green leaves and large
white flowers with slender, pointed
petals which open in spring or
summer. Plant from November
to January in moist potting
compost. Leave top of bulb
uncovered. Temperature should
not be below 13°C (55°F). When
shoots appear, water moderately
and feed fortnightly. Shade from
the sun. After flowering, stop
feeding and keep soil just moist.
Repot every second April and
propagate by removing offsets
from the bulb.

Hypocyrta nummularia
MINIATURE POUCH FLOWER

This creeping or hanging plant
from Central America has red,
hairy stems and fleshy, glossy
green leaves. Its red flowers have a
tubular base, expand into a broad
pouch with five yellow petals at
the mouth and bloom in summer.
Water sparingly at a minimum
winter temperature of 13°C (55°F).
In spring and summer keep the
soil just moist and spray regularly.
Feed monthly from April to
September. Repot every second
spring preferably in a peat compost
or in a good-quality potting
mixture. Propagate by shoot-tip
cuttings in spring or summer.

Hypoestes sanguinolenta
FRECKLE-FACE

In comparison to its downy, dark
leaves with pink spots and red
veins, the pale lilac, white and
purple summer flowers of this
plant from Madagascar are
insignificant. It grows 50 cm (20 in)
tall. Water sparingly in winter to
keep soil just moist at a minimum
temperature of 13°C (55°F). Water
liberally in spring and summer.
Spray regularly. Feed weekly from
June to September. In spring cut
back leggy stems and pinch out
top shoots to encourage bushiness.
Repot in April in any good
compost. Propagate by cuttings
in summer.

Hypoestes taeniata

Indigenous to Madagascar, this species has purple flowers which are protected by pink bracts and grow on long stems. These flowers open in autumn and early winter. The temperature in winter should not fall below 13°C (55°F) and the plant should be watered sparingly. In spring and summer water liberally. Spray regularly or stand on wet pebbles or moist peat. Feed weekly from June to October. To keep bushy, pinch out top shoots in spring. Repot every April in any good-quality potting compost or propagate annually by cuttings taken in spring.

Impatiens wallerana 'Holstii'
BUSY LIZZIE

This popular house plant produces a profusion of red, pink or white flowers throughout the year and grows to a height of 30–60 cm (1–2 ft). In spring and summer shade from the hottest sun and water well, sometimes more than once on the hottest days. In autumn and winter place in full light, in a temperature as low as 10°C (50°F), watering sparingly. From February to September feed weekly. Repot in a loamless mixture in spring and prune back top shoots to encourage bushiness. To propagate, put top shoots in water or potting compost to root.

Ipomoea batatas
SWEET-POTATO VINE

Grown from a tuber which produces twining stems with heart-shaped, sometimes lobed leaves, this plant grows quickly to about 180 cm (6 ft). If the sprouted end of the tuber is placed in good-quality compost, shoots will appear, provided the 15 cm (6 in) pot is kept in a temperature which never falls below 16°C (60°F). Water freely in spring and summer, more sparingly at other times. Supply a minimum winter temperature of 13°C (55°F). Repot in spring. Propagate by cuttings or by detaching and replanting any new tubers.

Iresine herbstii
BEEFSTEAK PLANT

The beauty of this South American plant lies in its veined, heart-shaped, dark red leaves; its flowers are small and insignificant. It grows to 50 cm (20 in) in height and requires sunlight to intensify its leaf colour. Although an annual it may be kept for more than one year but its winter temperature must not fall below 16°C (60°F). Water and spray liberally with tepid water in summer. Feed fortnightly from March to September. Repot in March in a loam-based compost. Propagate from stem cuttings in March or September.

Iresine lindenii
BLOODLEAF

This species requires sunlight to bring out the colour of its pointed leaves which are dark red with a paler central vein. One variation has yellow leaves with pale green veins and red stems. Although usually grown as an annual it may be kept for two or three years. Provide a winter temperature above 16°C (60°F). In summer, water and spray liberally but keep soil dry in winter. Feed fortnightly from March to September. In March nip out growing shoots and repot in loam-based compost. Propagate from stem cuttings in March or September.

Iris pumila
BEARDED DWARF IRIS

From southern Europe, this dwarf Iris grows from a rhizome to a height of some 10 cm (4 in). It is a sun-loving hardy perennial and has sword-shaped leaves and white, yellow or purple flowers with hairy patches on the arched, outer petals. These open from early April to May. After flowering, or in autumn, plant the rhizomes about 25 cm (10 in) apart in a south-facing window box. Leave the top of each rhizome partially uncovered. Water freely in dry weather. Remove dead leaves regularly. Replant every third autumn. Propagate by division.

Jacaranda mimosifolia
JACARANDA

Ⓣ Ⓞ

Only young specimens of this Brazilian flowering tree can be grown as house plants so it is for its beautiful fern-like foliage rather than its blue-mauve flowers that it is cultivated indoors. Light but not too much direct sun, especially in summer, is ideal and a humid atmosphere should be maintained as well as a minimum winter temperature of 13°C (55°F). Use only tepid, soft water. From April to September feed fortnightly. Repot in spring when the plant puts out new shoots. Propagate by cuttings in summer or by seed in spring.

Jacobinia carnea
JACOBINIA

Ⓣ Ⓞ Ⓗ

This tropical, evergreen shrub from Brazil has dark green, pointed leaves and dense terminal heads of pink flowers which open during August and September. During the hottest months the plant will appreciate shade from direct sun. An ideal winter temperature is 10–13°C (50–55°F). Water well at all times of year except after it has been cut back in March to promote bushiness. Spray in hot weather. Feed weekly from March to August. Repot in February. Propagate from cuttings taken from shoots that grow after the plant has been cut back.

Jacobinia pauciflora
JACOBINIA

Ⓣ Ⓞ

This native of Brazil grows to 60 cm (2 ft) and flowers from October to May. Its long flowers are scarlet, tipped with yellow. Provide sun and fresh air in summer and a minimum winter temperature of 10–13°C (50–55°F). From June to September water sufficiently to keep soil moist; from September until May water liberally and feed fortnightly. Repot annually in a loam-based compost when flowering ceases. Cut shoots back two weeks after repotting and again when side shoots are 5–8 cm (2–3 in) long. Propagate by cuttings in spring.

Jacobinia suberecta

This evergreen plant from
Uruguay has downy, grey-green
stems and leaves and clusters of
bright, or orange-scarlet flowers
which open from July to
September. It can be grown in a
hanging basket. It should be kept
at a temperature no lower than
13°C (55°F) during winter when
soil should be just moist. Shade
from very hot sun from April to
September. During this time
water liberally and weekly.
The plant can be pruned back
rigorously each spring and then
repotted. Propagate by cuttings in
spring or summer.

Jasminum mesnyi
PRIMROSE JASMINE

Ⓒ ◯

This rambling evergreen from
China has pretty, yellow, semi-
double flowers which have no
fragrance. They open from March
to May. To enjoy its full beauty it
can be trained to grow up a trellis
or around a window embrasure.
This plant requires plenty of
light but not direct sunlight.
In winter, place in a cool
but frost-free room. Water
regularly throughout the year,
decreasing the quantity slightly in
winter. Spray in spring. Feed
weekly from March to September.
Repot in February. Propagate by
cuttings in late summer.

Jasminum polyanthum
JASMINE

☆ Ⓒ ◯

A native of China, this is a
vigorous climber with white,
pink-flushed, fragrant flowers that
bloom in spring. A wire hoop is
often inserted into the pot so the
leading shoot can be trained round
it. In winter, position in a cool,
frost-free room, moving to a
warmer position in January.
Water sparingly until the end of
December and increase slightly
then and when the buds begin to
swell. Do not overwater. Feed
weekly from February to July.
Discard or repot in a loamless
mixture in March. Cut back in
February. Propagate by cuttings.

Juniperus chinensis
CHINESE JUNIPER

This columnar evergreen, a native of China, Japan and Mongolia, has blue-green leaves when young which later turn grey-green. In the wild it grows to 6 m (20 ft). It thrives best if kept in partial shade outdoors but may be brought inside for short periods in summer after new growth has appeared. Always keep compost moist. In winter the pot should be plunged in sand or peat to protect its roots from frost and be repotted every autumn or winter. Prune roots then. Pinch out growing point, trim side shoots in summer and propagate by cuttings.

Juniperus communis 'Compressa'
JUNIPER

This is a slow-growing, columnar, dwarf conifer developed from the species plant. It only reaches a height of about 60 cm (2 ft) after many years. Its close-growing branches are covered with grey-blue, awl-shaped foliage. In April, plant in a sunny or partially shaded window box which contains good-quality potting compost. Water liberally in dry weather. No pruning is necessary. Replant every few years or when it gets too large for the window box. In autumn propagate by heel cuttings. In winter, the cuttings should be placed in a cool room.

Kalanchoe blossfeldiana
TOM THUMB

If short-day treatment is applied, this leaf succulent from the Malagasy highlands can be made to produce clusters of orange-red flowers nearly all year round. Several plants are needed for an all-year succession. Its dark green, notched leaves are edged with red. Place in full light. Supply a winter temperature of at least 4°C (40°F) and water freely in summer and sparingly in winter. Feed fortnightly from May until August. Pinch out shoot tips when young. Repot each spring, and propagate by seed then or by stem cuttings in summer.

95

Kohleria eriantha

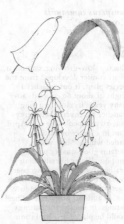

The stems and leaf margins of this 30–90 cm (1–3 ft) plant are covered with purplish-red hairs. Spotted, scarlet flowers appear from June to September. In February or March, plant a rhizome in shallow peat at a temperature of 21°C (70°F). When shoots grow, plant in potting compost, water moderately and keep at about 16°C (60°F). Feed every fortnight and spray until flowering ends. Stop watering when leaves turn yellow. Cut back stems and store rhizome at a temperature of 13°C (55°F). Propagate by division in spring.

Lachenalia aloides
CAPE COWSLIP

About 30 cm (12 in) tall, this plant has strap-shaped leaves, sometimes flecked purple, and loose spikes of pendant, tubular, yellow flowers with red and green markings which open between December and March. In late August plant six bulbs in a 15 cm (6 in) pan with potting compost. Water well once. Keep in good light at a temperature of 10–13°C (50–55°F). When shoots appear, water moderately and feed fortnightly. Gradually stop watering after flowering ends. Keep soil dry until repotting in August. Propagate by detaching bulblets or offsets.

Laelia pumila

This autumn-flowering orchid from Guyana is ideal for the novice. Its 15 cm (6 in) spikes bear one or two rose-purple flowers, whose lips are crimson-purple with raised yellow stripes. Protect it from hot sun but ensure ample sunlight. Provide a minimum winter temperature of 13°C (55°F) and ventilate freely during warm weather. Water liberally during growing season from April to September, sparingly from November to March. Repot in a small, perforated pot with equal parts osmunda fibre and sphagnum moss. Propagate by division.

Lilium longiflorum
EASTER LILY

Despite its common name, this
Japanese lily bears heavily-scented,
trumpet-shaped white flowers in
July and August. They are borne
on 90 cm (3 ft) stems, covered
with narrow, pointed leaves. In
autumn plant each bulb in a 15 cm
(6 in) pot with potting compost.
Put in a cool, dark place and keep
soil moist. When shoots appear,
move to a well-lit position. Water
liberally and feed fortnightly.
Shade from direct sun. After
flowering, keep soil just moist
until repotting in autumn. Then
propagate by offsets or by seeds in
autumn or spring.

Linaria maroccana
TOADFLAX

This slender annual comes from
Morocco. In June and July
flowers blotched white or yellow
develop at the top of leafy stems,
which grow 20–38 cm (8–15 in)
tall. Colours range from yellow to
various shades of blue and pink.
In March or April sow seeds in
a fairly sunny window box filled
with any good-quality proprietary
potting compost. When seedlings
can be handled easily, thin them
out to 15 cm (6 in) apart. Water
liberally in dry weather. There is
no need to feed the plants at all.
Discard them when flowering
finishes.

Liriope muscari
BLUE LILY TURF

Known and admired in the United
States as the Big Blue Lily Turf,
this plant from China and Japan
is quite easy to grow indoors and
has broad, grass-like leaves. Spikes
of violet-mauve, bell-shaped
flowers are borne on 30 cm (12 in)
stems. They open from August to
November. Provide a winter
temperature of 7–10°C (45–50°F).
Water liberally in spring and
summer, sparingly in winter. Feed
once a fortnight from June to
October. Repot every April in
good-quality proprietary potting
compost. To propagate, divide the
roots of the plant when repotting.

Litchi chinensis
LYCHEE

From southern China, this tree has
glossy, lance-shaped leaves and
inconspicuous flowers. Grown in
the tropics for its delicious fruit,
it will never flower or fruit
indoors. It grows to 90 cm (3 ft).
Plant the stone in March in an
8 cm (3 in) pot with potting
compost. It will germinate slowly
at a temperature of 18°C (65°F).
In spring and summer water
liberally. Keep at a minimum
winter temperature of 16°C (60°F)
and water sparingly. Feed monthly
from March to September. Keep
in good light. Prune every other
March. Repot every spring.

Lithops lesliei
LIVING STONES, PEBBLE PLANT

This succulent from the deserts of
South Africa resembles a pebble
in colour and shape. Its reddish-
brown upper surface is marked
with green-brown grooves and its
pair of thick leaves is joined
together to form a single body
with a slit across the top. Place in
sunlight at a minimum winter
temperature of 4°C (40°F).
Withhold water from October to
April. When old leaves die and
new ones appear, keep soil just
moist. Repot every third April in
a pan with equal parts of potting
compost and coarse sand. Propagate
by seed in spring.

Lycaste deppei

This Mexican orchid produces
winter and spring flowers on 15
cm (6 in) stems. The yellow-
crested flowers have white petals
and jade sepals mottled with
crimson. Keep in partial shade
from April to September, then in
the sun. Provide a minimum
winter temperature of 13°C (55°F).
In warm weather give plenty of
fresh air. Keep compost moist
from May to September, otherwise
barely moist. In spring repot in
two parts loam, one part osmunda
fibre, one part sphagnum moss and
one part peat or leaf mould and
propagate by division.

Lycopersicon esculentum
TOMATO

Although the tomato plant will tolerate a temperature as low as 10°C (50°F), it thrives better in warmth. Give it plenty of sunshine and fresh air. Support the plant with canes. Water every day in hot weather. Tap flower clusters daily to help pollination. When fruiting, feed weekly with liquid tomato fertilizer. Cut off any yellow leaves and remove side shoots unless lush cultivated varieties are grown. Propagate by seed at a temperature of 18°C (65°F). Pot seedlings singly into 8 cm (3 in) pots, then pot on into 15–18 cm (6–7 in) pots.

Lycoris aurea
GOLDEN SPIDER LILY

This lily from China grows to 30 cm (12 in). It has strap-shaped leaves which die before the yellow, funnel-shaped flowers open in August and September. Keep in good light at a minimum temperature of 16°C (60°F). Bring bulb into growth by watering moderately after flowering. Once plant is in full leaf, spray regularly and feed fortnightly. When leaves turn yellow, keep dry until flowering ends. Repot every other summer in any good-quality potting compost. Propagate by removing offsets from the bulbs when repotting.

Malcolmia maritima
VIRGINIA STOCK

Although this plant comes from the southern Mediterranean area and thrives in a sunny situation, it is a good-natured, hardy annual which will tolerate a certain amount of shade. The tiny, white, pink, red or lilac, sweet-scented, long-lasting flowers open about six weeks after sowing and are borne on delicate, leafy, 20 cm (8 in) stems. From March to July, sow the seed thinly in a window box containing any good-quality potting compost. Water freely in dry weather. There is no need to feed the plants. Discard when flowering finishes.

Mammillaria bocasana
POWDER PUFF

This undemanding cactus has silvery-white spines and hairs covering its blue-green globular body. In June small, cream flowers encircle the crown; these are later followed by purple berries. Maximum sunlight is essential and the plant must be turned occasionally to prevent lopsided growth. Keep compost dry at a minimum winter temperature of 4°C (40°F). In summer water liberally and use a liquid fertilizer monthly. Repot annually in April in finely sieved potting compost. Propagate by seed in April or by offsets in summer.

Manettia bicolor
FIRECRACKER PLANT

With a profusion of fleshy-textured, tubular, half-red, half-yellow flowers, borne on twining stems like the lights on a Christmas tree, this Brazilian plant will both trail and climb. It flowers from early spring to late autumn. Its resting period begins after flowering ends, when it should be moved to a room temperature of 10°C (50°F). Water liberally in spring and summer and sparingly in winter. Feed weekly from April to October. Repot every March in any good-quality potting compost. Propagate by cuttings of young shoots in summer.

Mangifera indica

Mangoes are in season in May. To produce attractive little trees with lance-shaped green leaves, plant the stone in a 10 cm (4 in) pot with potting compost. Germinate at a temperature of 21–24°C (70–75°F), keeping soil moist. When the seedling is 30 cm (12 in) tall, pinch out growing tip to encourage bushiness and pot on into a 15 cm (6 in) pot. Keep on a partially shaded window-sill. Water liberally and spray regularly from spring to autumn. Provide a minimum winter temperature of 16°C (60°F) and keep the soil barely moist.

Maranta leuconeura 'Erythrophylla'

PRAYER PLANT, RED HERRING–BONE PLANT

Sometimes sold as *M. Leuconeura* 'Tricolor', this plant has dark green leaves with yellowish-green margins and crimson veins. It is only about 20 cm (8 in) tall. Provide a winter temperature of 13°C (55°F) and water sparingly without letting the soil dry out completely. In spring and summer spray and water liberally with tepid, soft water. Feed every fortnight from April to August. No pruning is necessary. Repot every other spring in any good-quality proprietary potting compost. Propagate by dividing the rhizome when repotting.

Maranta leuconeura 'Kerchoveana'

PRAYER PLANT, RABBIT'S TRACKS

By day the leaves of this fascinating plant lie horizontally, but at night they become upright like folded hands. It has a strange colour scheme; the leaves are greyish-green with lighter veins and big brown blotches which in time turn dark green. It grows to a height of 20 cm (8 in). In winter the most suitable temperature is between 13–16°C (55–60°F). In spring and summer, spray regularly and water freely with tepid, soft water. Feed fortnightly from April to August. Repot every other spring in good-quality potting compost. Propagate by division when repotting.

Medinilla magnifica

ROSE GRAPE

From the Philippines and Java, this plant has boldly-veined, leathery leaves and rose-pink and purple flower clusters, on long pendulous stems. They open from April to August. It can grow to 120–150 cm (4–5 ft). The winter temperature should not fall below 16°C (60°F). Water liberally in spring and summer and more sparingly in winter. Spray often. Feed fortnightly from April to September. If the plant becomes straggly, cut back after flowering. Repot every other April in all-peat compost. Propagate by cuttings in late spring in a heated propagator.

Mentha spicata
MINT, SPEARMINT

Since the third century this hardy
perennial has been used in cooking.
It grows 60 cm (2 ft) tall and bears
spikes of small, purple flowers in
summer which should be pinched
out. In March or April plant the
root in a 15 cm (6 in) pot with
potting compost. Keep on an
outdoor window-sill and shade
from direct sun. Allow stems to
grow to at least 8 cm (3 in) before
cutting. Water liberally from
spring to autumn but sparingly in
winter. Repot every spring.
Propagate by cuttings in spring
or summer or by root division
when repotting.

Microcoelum martianum
(Syagrus or Cocos weddelliana)
DWARF COCONUT PALM, TERRARIUM
PALM

The ideal palm for a small room,
this plant takes about twenty
years to reach its full height of
180 cm (6 ft). It has elegant,
arching stems bearing long,
narrow, green leaflets. Keep at a
minimum winter temperature of
16°C (60°F). Spray often during
the year. From May to September
feed fortnightly and water
liberally, otherwise keep soil just
moist or the leaves will turn
brown if it dries out. Repot every
other April in a reliable proprietary
potting compost. Propagate in
spring by seed, using a heated
propagator.

Miltonia vexillaria
PANSY ORCHID

In May and June, the slender,
arching spikes of this Colombian
orchid bear fragrant, flat, pansy-
like, rose-mauve blooms with
yellow veining on the lips. Shade
from bright summer sun but
expose to full light from
November to February. Keep at a
winter temperature of 13°C (55°F).
Spray plant often in summer and
give it fresh air. Keep compost
always just moist. Repot after
flowering every July in a mixture
of two parts osmunda fibre and
one part sphagnum moss.
Propagate by division every two
years in spring or late summer.

Mimosa pudica
SENSITIVE PLANT, HUMBLE PLANT

From Brazil, here is the performing plant! When its feathery leaves are touched, they fold and droop. After about thirty minutes they rise and spread again. An annual, this intriguing plant grows about 60 cm (2 ft) tall and bears small, ball-like pink flower clusters in summer. Spray regularly from June to September and feed fortnightly with liquid fertilizer. Always keep the soil moist. Discard the plant in late autumn. Propagate by seed in spring at a temperature of 18–21°C (65–70°F). Seedlings should be planted in any good-quality potting compost.

Monstera deliciosa
SWISS CHEESE PLANT

Large holes occur naturally in this popular Mexican plant's deeply slashed, shield-shaped leaves. It may reach 6 m (20 ft). The mature plant has arum-like, creamy-white flowering spathes, followed by edible pineapple-flavoured fruit. Grow it up a moss-covered stick for support. Keep soil just moist at a minimum winter temperature of 13°C (55°F). In spring and summer water liberally, spray often and feed fortnightly with dilute fertilizer. Repot every second or third April in an all-peat compost. Propagate by stem-tip or leaf-bud cuttings in summer.

Musa velutina

This plant from Assam grows 120 cm (4 ft) tall and 150 cm (5 ft) wide. Its leaves, either pure green or blotched with maroon, grow in clumps on pink stems. Clusters of yellow flowers with red bracts open from June to August, followed by enticing but inedible red fruit. Keep soil barely moist in winter at a minimum temperature of 16°C (60°F). Water liberally in spring and summer, and feed fortnightly with dilute fertilizer. Cut out dead flower stems. Before repotting in any good-quality potting compost every other March, propagate by division.

Myrtus communis 'Microphylla'
SMALL-LEAVED MYRTLE

A native of the Mediterranean, this aromatic evergreen bush has small oval leaves and white flowers and grows 30–60 cm (1–2 ft) tall. It likes a winter temperature of 4°C (40°F) in a light, well-ventilated room. It dislikes too much direct sun. Turn the plant regularly so that it grows straight. Always water with rain or lime-free water, liberally in summer and sparingly in winter. From March to July feed once a week using a lime-free fertilizer. Repot in spring in any good proprietary compost. Propagate by cuttings in summer.

Nandina domestica
CHINESE SACRED BAMBOO

The long stems and narrow leaflets of this evergreen Chinese shrub turn red in autumn. Since it can reach 180 cm (6 ft), only the young plant is suitable for indoor cultivation. White flowers may appear in July. It likes a light, well-ventilated position, cold but frost-free in winter. Water liberally during summer. Keep the plant drier in winter. Feed fortnightly from April to August. Repot in late March in potting compost. Prune out dead wood after flowering ends. Propagate by division in April or by stem cuttings in August.

Narcissus

The *Narcissus* genus, including the Daffodil, embraces many species and hybrids with strap-shaped leaves and yellow, red or white flowers, each with a central cup or trumpet borne on stiff stems. They grow to 38–45 cm (15–18 in). In early autumn plant bulbs close together in moist potting compost or bulb fibre, leaving tops bare. Keep in a cool, dark place. When shoots appear, move to a well-lit position in a cool room. Water moderately. When flower buds are well developed, move to a warmer room – about 16°C (60°F). Discard after flowering or plant outdoors.

Neoregelia carolinae

☆ Ⓣ ⊘

This Brazilian plant has a rosette of
sword-shaped leaves. Insignificant
flowers may emerge at any time
from the rosette centre, while the
surrounding leaves open out and
turn red or purple. It grows to
30 cm (12 in). Keep at a minimum
winter temperature of 13°C (55°F).
Water compost and spray
moderately in summer. Water less
in winter. Keep the rosette full of
water from spring to autumn but
allow to dry out in winter. Feed
fortnightly from April to August.
Repot every other April in potting
compost. Propagate by rooted
offsets in June.

Nephrolepis exaltata
SWORD FERN, LADDER FERN

☆ Ⓣ ⊘

If protected from draughts, this
fern will live up to twelve years
indoors. It is ideal for a hanging
basket. The species plant has stiff
green fronds which grow to
60 cm (2 ft). There are several
cultivated varieties with feathery,
arching or spiralling fronds which
vary in colour from pale to bright
green. Provide a minimum water
temperature of 10°C (50°F).
Water freely in summer, and keep
soil just moist in winter. Feed
fortnightly from March to August.
Repot every other year in April in
potting compost. Propagate by
division.

Nerine flexuosa

☆

From September to November
this South African bulb produces
large, pink flower heads with up
to twelve frilly-petalled blooms,
on 60–90 cm (2–3 ft) stems. The
arching, strap-shaped leaves also
develop then. In August plant
each bulb, with the tops bare, in
an 8–10 cm (3–4 in) pot with
potting compost. Water
moderately when leaves appear
and feed fortnightly. Keep in a
well-lit position at a winter
temperature of 10–13°C (50–55°F).
When leaves turn yellow stop
watering and feeding. Repot every
three years. Propagate by offsets.

Nerium oleander
OLEANDER

© ○

This poisonous evergreen shrub is
tall, with narrow, grey-green
leaves and scented white, pink, red
or yellow flowers. One variety has
variegated leaves. From early
April to September water freely
with tepid water. The rest of the
year water only enough to keep
the soil from drying out. Provide
light in winter and keep at 4°C
(40°F). Feed weekly from April to
August. Repot in February in
loam-based compost with bone-
meal. In February or March cut
back young stems by half.
Propagate by cuttings in May or
September.

Nertera depressa (granadensis)
BEAD PLANT

© ⊘ Ⓗ

This hummock-forming perennial
is a native of New Zealand and
South America. The tiny, whitish
flowers, which appear in late April
or early May, by August become
glassy, orange berries lasting all
winter. Provide ample fresh air and
shade from direct light. Keep soil
quite moist in winter but in
summer allow it to dry a little.
Spray often before and after
flowering. Feed monthly from
April to September with weak
liquid fertilizer. Repot in all-peat
compost. Propagate from seed in
February or March, or by division
when the pot gets congested.

Nidularium innocentii
BIRD'S NEST

Ⓣ ⊘

In autumn this Brazilian plant
puts forth from its 45 cm (18 in)
rosette of strap-like, purple-flecked
leaves a cluster of small white
flowers. The undersides of the
leaves are deep red. Provide a
minimum winter temperature of
10°C (50°F). From April to
September spray often, keep soil
moist and feed weekly. In autumn
and winter the soil should be just
moist. Keep the centre of the
rosette filled with water from
spring to autumn but dry in
winter. Repot every other April in
compost. Propagate from basal
offsets in spring or summer.

Ochna serrulata

This shrub from Nepal grows to about 120 cm (4 ft) but can be kept smaller in a pot. It has glossy leaves with serrated edges and the flowers, which open in summer, are yellow and green. Shiny black berries develop several weeks after flowering, borne on the red and swollen flower centres. Keep in light shade and spray occasionally during the hottest months. In winter keep cool and water sparingly. Feed fortnightly from April to September. Repot every other spring in potting compost. Propagate by seed in spring or by cuttings in winter.

Ocimum basilicum
SWEET BASIL

Basil bears shiny leaves on four-sided stems. Tiny white flowers open in August – remove these to promote leaf growth. Treat as an annual and keep on a south-facing window-sill. The plant can grow to 60 cm (2 ft). To keep smaller, regularly pinch out the top shoots. In March sow seeds in moist seed compost. Germinate at 13°C (55°F). Plant each seedling in potting compost in an 8 cm (3 in) pot. Water freely. Pot on later into a 13 cm (5 in) container. Pinch out top shoots to encourage bushiness. Pick the leaves from July onwards.

Odontoglossum grande
CLOWN ORCHID, TIGER ORCHID

Between August and November, this Guatemalan plant usually bears up to seven large, cinnamon-barred, bright yellow flowers on each of its 30 cm (12 in) spikes. In winter provide ample light and a minimum temperature of 7°C (45°F). In summer keep in the shade with plenty of air. Keep the compost moist but after flowering withhold water until new bulb growth starts to develop. Spray often in summer. Repot every two or three years in a mixture of two parts osmunda fibre to one part sphagnum moss. Propagate by division when repotting.

Oncidium varicosum

This orchid can grow to 90 cm (3 ft). Blooms appear in autumn on a many-branched stem. Each flower has greenish-yellow and brown petals and sepals, and a large, yellow and red lip. Keep in a humid place in summer away from hot sun. Feed monthly from May to September with dilute fertilizer. Provide a winter temperature of 7–10°C (45–50°F). Always keep soil just moist. Repot every second or third spring, when new shoots appear, in one part sphagnum moss to two parts osmunda fibre with a little sand. Propagate by division.

Ophiopogon jaburan
WHITE LILY TURF

This Japanese evergreen has leathery but grass-like, dark leaves, 60–90 cm (2–3 ft) long, which grow in dense clumps. Drooping clusters of white or pale purple flowers grow on stalks in July. The cream-striped cultivated variety 'Variegatus' is recommended for growing in a pot. In winter keep in an unheated but frost-free room. Always keep soil just moist. From May to August provide ample fresh air and feed fortnightly. Repot in good proprietary potting compost every other March or April. Propagate by division when repotting.

Ophiopogon planiscapus
LILY TURF

The species plant is seldom seen today but the cultivated variety 'Nigrescens' is widely available. The interesting purplish-black, arching leaves grow in small clumps. Clusters of tiny white or pale purple flowers are borne on short stems in June. Keep in an unheated but frost-free room in winter. Always ensure that the soil is just moist and do not let the soil ball dry out. From May to July feed fortnightly and provide ample fresh air. Repot every March or April in good proprietary potting compost. Propagate by division when repotting.

Oplismenus hirtellus 'Variegatus'
BASKET GRASS

This creeping plant from the West Indies trails nicely from a hanging basket or wall pot. The slender stems root easily at the joints where the white-and-pink-striped, narrow, lance-shaped leaves appear. It will tolerate a temperature of 7°C (45°F) but keep at 13°C (55°F) in winter to ensure good growth. Water freely in spring and summer. Keep soil just moist in winter. Feed fortnightly from May to September. Repot in April in potting compost. Propagate by division when repotting or by removing rooted shoots in spring or summer.

Opuntia microdasys
BUNNY EARS, INDIAN FIG,
PRICKLY PEAR

This succulent, found throughout the Americas, has jointed, flattened stems. Handle with care, as its yellow areoles are covered with numerous glochids, or barbed bristles, which can easily break off and painfully penetrate the skin. Keep in a light, airy position. Provide a minimum winter temperature of 7°C (45°F). Keep the compost moist in summer but water sparingly in winter. From spring until August use a liquid fertilizer fortnightly. Repot every other spring in potting compost with added sand. Propagate by cuttings in summer.

Origanum majorana
SWEET MARJORAM

The hairy, greyish-green leaves are borne on reddish stems which can grow to 30–60 cm (1–2 ft). It will thrive on a sunny outdoor window-sill in spring and summer. Pink or white flowers appear in summer and may be used to provide a sweet yet spicy flavouring. In March sow seeds in moist seed compost. When seedlings are large enough to handle, plant in potting compost in an 8 cm (3 in) pot. Water freely. Later transfer to a 13–15 cm (5–6 in) container. Start cutting when stems are about 10–15 cm (4–6 in). Discard in late autumn.

Ornithogalum thyrsoides
CHINCHERINCHEE

This bulb, from South Africa, has 30–45 cm (12–18 in) stems, each of which bears twenty to thirty star-like, white, cream or yellow flowers from May to July. The leaves are strap-shaped and fleshy. In October plant four to six bulbs in potting compost in a 15 cm (6 in) pot. Keep at a minimum temperature of 7°C (45°F) in a well-lit place. Make sure that the soil is kept moist and feed fortnightly. After flowering finishes in July, stop feeding and gradually cease watering. Repot every autumn. Propagate by removing offsets when repotting.

Oxalis deppei
LUCKY CLOVER

This plant, thought to be lucky because the leaves are like a four-leafed clover, is often given as a New Year present in Europe. The small red flowers have yellow hearts and each of the four mid-green leaflets bears a red-brown, curved marking. The plant can easily be grown indoors and will do well on a west-facing window-sill. Always keep in cool conditions. Water freely and feed fortnightly from March to August. In winter water sparingly. Repot in March in a loamless mixture. Propagate by detaching side tubers when repotting.

Pachystachys lutea
LOLLIPOP PLANT

This plant fell from favour at the beginning of the 20th century but has recently become available again. It grows to about 45 cm (18 in) and bears bright green, oval leaves and yellow, erect, cone-shaped clusters of bracts from which little tongue-like, white flowers emerge. It needs a minimum winter temperature of 13°C (55°F) and should be watered very sparingly. In spring and summer shade from hot sun, water liberally and feed once a week. Repot every spring in loam-based compost. Prune in early spring. Propagate from new shoots.

Pandanus veitchii
SCREW PINE

This plant from Polynesia has narrow, evergreen leaves forming a large rosette. The leaves are spiny margined, strikingly tipped and bordered with creamy-white bands. They grow to a length of 60–90 cm (2–3 in) in a pot. Provide a minimum winter temperature of 18°C (65°F). Use tepid water liberally in spring and summer, but moderately in winter. Feed fortnightly from March to October and spray in summer. Repot in potting compost in March. To propagate, remove suckers when they have about six leaves and treat as cuttings.

Paphiopedilum insigne
SLIPPER ORCHID, LADY'S SLIPPER

This Himalayan plant bears single flowers on 30 cm (12 in) stems from November to March. They have yellow-green dorsal petals with purple-brown veins and a slipper-shaped lip flecked with brown. It needs a minimum winter temperature of 4°C (40°F). Provide fresh air and shade from direct sun from March to October. Keep compost moist all year. Use a dilute liquid feed fortnightly from May to September. Repot in equal parts of osmunda fibre, sphagnum moss and loam every second or third spring and propagate by division.

Paphiopedilum venustum
SLIPPER ORCHID, LADY'S SLIPPER

This Nepalese orchid bears single flowers on 25 cm (10 in) stems from October to January. Each blossom consists of white sepals and petals striped with green and flushed palest purple around a shiny yellow-green lip. It needs a minimum winter temperature of 7°C (45°F). Shade from hot sun and keep in fresh air. Always keep compost just moist. Use a dilute liquid feed monthly from May to September. Every second or third spring repot in equal parts of osmunda fibre, sphagnum moss and fibrous loam and propagate by division.

Passiflora caerulea
COMMON or BLUE PASSION FLOWER

This climbing plant from South
America has long been associated
with the story of the Passion of
Christ. It flowers from July to
September, each of the white and
blue flowers lasting for only a few
days. Feed every week from April
to September and water well.
Water less in winter but do not
allow the soil to dry out. The
winter temperature should be
about 4°C (40°F). Repot in early
spring using any good potting
compost. Every spring cut back
the flowering shoots of the previous
year 15–23 cm (6–9 in). Propagate
by cuttings, layers or seeds.

Pastinaca sativa
PARSNIP

Parsnips have long-stemmed, pale
leaves, divided into oval leaflets
which are further divided into
toothed lobes. To grow in a pot,
cut off the top of the parsnip,
remove all but the central leaves
and plant in a 10 cm (4 in) pot in
peat, sand or potting compost.
Water moderately, keeping soil
moist and place on a partially
shaded window-sill. Leaves will
develop within a month. The
plant can also be grown on a
spiked flower holder in a saucer of
water or it can be hollowed out
like a carrot. Discard when
leaves turn yellow.

Pedilanthus tithymaloides
'Variegata'
RIBBON CACTUS, DEVIL'S BACKBONE,
REDBIRD CACTUS

Despite two of its common names,
this fleshy, bushy plant is not a
cactus. It grows about 60 cm (2 ft)
tall, and has branched, greyish-
green, zig-zag stems, and reddish-
green leaves with white margins.
Bright scarlet flowers appear in
summer. In winter it needs a
minimum temperature of 10°C
(50°F) and should be watered very
sparingly. In spring and summer
water moderately, keeping soil
just moist. Feed monthly from
May to September. Repot every
spring in any reliable potting
compost. Propagate by cuttings in
summer.

Pelargonium crispum
SCENTED–LEAVED GERANIUM

The fan-shaped leaves of this
South African shrub have a
pleasant lemon scent. It grows
about 60 cm (2 ft) tall, and has
pink or pale violet flowers which
open from May to October. Lots
of summer sunshine and fresh air
are essential. From March to
August water freely and feed once
a week. In winter water sparingly
and keep at a minimum
temperature of 4°C (40°F). Repot
in February in a good proprietary
potting compost. Prune and take
cuttings from the plant in spring,
but discard after flowering in the
third year.

Pelargonium x domesticum
REGAL PELARGONIUM

This plant has large, often frilled,
pink, red or white flowers marked
with a deeper colour. They are
open all summer. The leaves are
downy and pointed. Good
cultivated varieties are Aztec,
Grand Slam and Kingston Beauty.
Provide plenty of fresh air and a
winter temperature of 4°C (40°F).
Always keep the soil just moist
and water even more sparingly in
winter. Feed every week from
April to August. Prune in August
after flowering. Repot in
February in potting compost.
Propagate by cuttings in spring
or late summer.

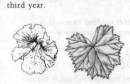

Pelargonium x hortorum
GERANIUM

The leaves of the common
Pelargonium may have brown ring
markings. The flowers, which are
pink, red, mauve or white, single
or double, open from April to
October. Good cultivated varieties
are Henry Cox, Mrs Pollock,
Sprite, Red Black Vesuvius and
Irene. Water liberally from spring
to autumn but do not waterlog
roots. Keep soil just moist in
winter at a temperature even as
low as 4°C (40°F). Feed weekly
from March to August. Repot
annually in late February. Prune in
early spring. Take stem-tip
cuttings in spring or summer.

Pelargonium peltatum

The large dark-centred, white, pink, red or purple flowers of this plant grow on trailing stems of up to 90 cm (3 ft), making it ideal for hanging baskets. It has leaves like Ivy. Recommended varieties are l'Elegante, Sussex Lace and Madame Crousse. It likes fresh air and plenty of sunshine. Water regularly in summer but keep fairly dry at a minimum winter temperature of 10°C (50°F). Feed weekly from April to September. Repot in a loamless mixture to which sand or gravel may be added each spring and propagate by cuttings in late summer.

Pelargonium tomentosum
PEPPERMINT GERANIUM

This low South African climber has grey-green, mint-scented leaves and white flowers, open from early summer to late autumn. It can grow to 60 cm (2 ft) in a 15 cm (6 in) pot and even taller if potted on. Although it likes plenty of sunshine, shade from hot sun. Water well in spring and summer and feed weekly. Keep at a winter temperature of 7°C (45°F) and water less, keeping soil just moist. Repot in February in any good proprietary potting compost. In spring prune back the stems by about half. Propagate by cuttings in spring or late summer.

Pellaea rotundifolia
BUTTON FERN, CLIFF BRAKE FERN

This fern has dark brown, arching stalks, 30 cm (12 in) long, on which waxy, green leaflets grow. These are round on young plants, but oval to oblong on mature ones. It tolerates quite heavy shade but can be kept in a well-lit position if shaded from direct sunshine. Keep at a minimum winter temperature of 10°C (50°F). Ventilate and water freely in summer. In winter water sparingly, but do not let the soil dry out. Feed once a fortnight from March to August. Repot every other April in potting compost and propagate by division at the same time.

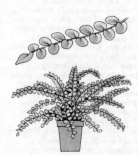

Pellionia pulchra
DARK NETTING

This creeper from the Far East has purplish, succulent stems and small, silvery-green leaves with red, turning to dark green, markings on the veins. Always keep in a draught-free place. From October to January provide a temperature of 10–13°C (50–55°F) and water sparingly, but do not let the soil dry out. In spring and summer water freely. Feed fortnightly from April to September. Repot every March or April in potting compost. Propagate by division when repotting or by cuttings in spring or summer.

Pentas lanceolata
EGYPTIAN STAR CLUSTER

This native of tropical Africa has hairy leaves and terminal clusters of starry flowers, pink to red, which appear at intervals during the year. It may become leggy, so prune hard each year to keep height under 60 cm (2 ft). It needs a minimum winter temperature of 13°C (55°F). In summer water liberally, otherwise keep soil just moist. From April to November feed fortnightly. In March prune hard and pinch out young shoots, then repot in any good-quality potting compost. Propagate from young shoots that arise after cutting back.

Peperomia argyreia
WATERMELON PEPEROMIA

This red-stemmed Brazilian plant has dark green leaves with curved, silver-grey, feather-edged bands – from a distance the leaves look like strange round fruit. It grows about 23 cm (9 in) tall. In winter it needs a minimum temperature of 13°C (55°F), and should be watered sparingly. Water moderately in spring and summer but always let the soil dry out between watering. From May to September feed monthly. Spray in hot weather. In April repot in any good-quality potting compost. Propagate by leaf cuttings in summer.

The heart-shaped, deeply corrugated leaves of this plant, which are dark with a silvery-grey sheen, grow in a dense clump on pinkish stems up to 8 cm (3 in) long. The 15 cm (6 in) long white flower spikes appear from April to December. It needs a minimum winter temperature of 10°C (50°F). Water moderately in spring and summer, sparingly in winter, letting the soil dry out between watering. Spray on hot days. Feed monthly from May to September. In April repot in potting compost. Propagate by leaf cuttings from April to August.

Peperomia hederifolia
IVY-LEAVED PEPEROMIA

This little plant from Brazil grows to about 15 cm (6 in). Borne on pink stems, the heart-shaped, quilted-looking leaves are silver-grey with dark green veins. In winter provide a well-lit position at a temperature of about 10°C (50°F) and water sparingly, keeping almost dry. In spring and summer water moderately, letting the compost dry out between watering. Provide a humid atmosphere. From April to September feed fortnightly. Repot annually or biennially in April in potting compost. Propagate by leaf cuttings in summer.

Peperomia magnoliifolia
DESERT PRIVET

Although the species plant, with glossy green leaves on purplish stems, is rare, there are two cultivated varieties, 'Variegata' and 'Green Gold', with green-and-cream leaves. They grow to 15 cm (6 in). Keep at a minimum winter temperature of 10°C (50°F) in barely moist soil. Water moderately in spring and summer. Stand on a tray of wet pebbles or moist peat. Spray in hot weather. From March to September feed fortnightly. Repot in compost every April. Pinch out new shoots in summer. Propagate by stem cuttings from April to August.

Persea gratissima
AVOCADO PEAR

A home-grown tree will not bear
fruit. As the tree matures the stem
develops into a woody trunk and
bears large, dark green leaves. It
can grow to 120 cm (4 ft). In
spring plant the stone, pointed end
up, in a 15 cm (6 in) pot of potting
compost, leaving the top half of
the stone uncovered. Keep in good
light at 18°C (65°F). In spring and
summer water liberally. Provide a
minimum winter temperature of
10°C (50°F) and water sparingly.
Feed monthly from March to
September. Pinch out the growing
tip to encourage bushiness. Pot on
regularly in spring.

Petroselinum crispum
PARSLEY

These flat or curly leaves grow
from ribbed stems. Treated either
as an annual or biennial, parsley
may be grown in a pot on a sunny
or partially shaded window-sill.
However, it thrives best outside in
a window box or pot. From April
to June sow the seeds in seed
compost and keep moist.
Transplant seedlings singly into
8 cm (3 in) pots containing any
reliable potting compost. Keep the
soil moist. When well grown, pot
on into a 13 cm (5 in) pot. Pick the
parsley regularly to promote
growth. Discard the plant when it
loses its vigour.

Phaseolus aureus
MUNG BEAN (BEAN SPROUTS)

These beans from India can be
grown quite easily and at little
cost to produce Bean Sprouts. To
sprout the beans, soak them
overnight in cold water, then put
a single layer in a shallow container
and keep them in a completely
dark place, such as a cupboard. A
temperature of 21°C (70°F) is
essential. Sprinkle with water
several times a day to keep
constantly moist. In about seven
days they will be 5 cm (2 in) long
and ready to use. A word of
caution: do not overgrow them or
the flavour will be ruined. They
are excellent in salads.

Philodendron andreanum (*P. melanochryson*)
VELOUR PHILODENDRON

This climber from Colombia grows to 120–180 cm (4–6 ft). The heart-shaped, white-veined, velvety green leaves have purplish undersides. Grow in a large pot and support well. Provide a minimum winter temperature of 13°C (55°F). From April to October water liberally. At other times keep the soil just moist. From May to September feed fortnightly. Stand the plant on a tray of wet pebbles or moist peat. Spray in hot weather. Repot every second April in all-peat compost. Propagate by stem-tip or leaf-bud cuttings in summer.

Philodendron oxycardium (*P. scandens*)
PARLOUR IVY, HEART-LEAF PHILODENDRON

This climber from Panama with its heart-shaped green leaves is very tolerant of deep shade and polluted air. It will grow 180 cm (6 ft). Provide a minimum winter temperature of 13–16°C (55–60°F). From November to March keep soil just moist. Otherwise water liberally. Stand the plant on a tray of wet pebbles or moist peat to provide humidity. From May to September feed every fortnight. Pinch out new shoots occasionally to encourage bushiness. Repot every second April in all-peat compost. Propagate by stem-tip cuttings in summer.

Philodendron selloum
LACY TREE PHILODENDRON

This species from Brazil gradually develops a trunk which can reach 150 cm (5 ft). The deeply lobed, dark leaves can grow up to 90 cm (3 ft). Do not let the winter temperature drop below 13°C (55°F). From April to October water liberally. At other times keep the soil just moist. From May to September feed fortnightly. Stand the plant on a tray of wet pebbles or moist peat. Spray in hot weather. Repot every other April, in an all-peat compost. Propagate by stem-tip or leaf-bud cuttings in May or June, using old leggy plants.

Phlox drummondii
DWARF ANNUAL PHLOX

This annual from Texas is the most suitable, of the many varieties of *Phlox*, for a window box. Its leafy 38 cm (15 in) stems bear dense clusters of flowers which open from July to September. The flowers may be purple, red, pink, white and lavender. In March sow the seed and keep at about 16°C (60°F). In late April harden off the seedlings in a cool but frost-free room. In May plant them in a south- or west-facing window box containing potting compost. In dry weather water liberally. Cut off dead flower heads.

Phoenix dactylifera
DATE PALM

This palm from northern Africa can be grown, with patience, from a date stone. It has stiff leaves, composed of narrow, pleated leaflets. It can grow to 180 cm (6 ft). Sandpaper the stone and plant it in spring in a 15 cm (6 in) pot containing potting compost. Germination in a warm room, about 18°C (65°F), may take three months. In spring and summer water freely. In winter keep at 10–13°C (50–55°F) and water sparingly. From May to September feed fortnightly. Pot on every spring until about 60 cm (2 ft) tall, then repot every few years.

Phoenix roebelenii
PYGMY DATE PALM

This subtropical palm is slow-growing and undemanding. After 15–20 years it may need moving to a conservatory. It requires plenty of light, but keep out of direct sunlight in summer. In winter the temperature should not fall below 10°C (50°F). Water liberally in summer, and sparingly in winter, using soft, tepid water. Never let the soil dry out. From March to October feed weekly after watering. Spray all year. Repot in loamless potting compost every March for the first three years, then every two to three years. Propagate by seed.

Pilea cadierei
ALUMINIUM PLANT

From Indo-China, the species plant has dark green, quilted leaves with shining silvery patches. It grows to 30 cm (12 in) and tends to become leggy, while the cultivated variety 'Nana' is more compact but has similarly marked leaves. Water moderately in winter at a minimum temperature of 10°C (50°F). Water freely in spring and summer. Feed fortnightly from March to September. Spray occasionally. Cut back leggy stems and pinch out new shoots in spring. Repot in April in good proprietary potting compost. Propagate by cuttings in late spring or summer.

Pilea muscosa (microphylla)
GUNPOWDER PLANT,
ARTILLERY PLANT

From May to September this plant produces tiny greenish-yellow flowers which puff out tiny clouds of pollen when touched. The small leaves grow profusely on many-branched stems, giving a mossy appearance. It comes from tropical America and grows to 15–23 cm (6–9 in). Provide a minimum winter temperature of 10°C (50°F). Water freely in spring and summer. moderately in winter – do not let the soil dry out. Feed fortnightly from March to September. Spray occasionally. Repot every other April in potting compost. Propagate by cuttings in summer.

Piper ornatum
ORNAMENTAL PEPPER

Not used for seasoning at all, this purely ornamental plant from Sulawesi (Celebes) has heart-shaped leaves, with pale pink dots along the main veins, and it will either trail or climb. It prefers a winter temperature of not less than 16°C (60°F), but it will survive in slightly cooler conditions, although some leaves may fall. Water moderately all year round and spray regularly. Feed fortnightly from March to August. Repot every other April in good-quality potting compost. Propagate by cuttings in summer, using a propagating case.

Pitcairnia xanthocalyx

This native of Mexico and the
West Indies grows to 45 cm (18 in).
Its arching leaves are green on top
and white below. Tall spikes of
yellow flowers open in summer.
It tolerates both light and partial
shade but not direct sunlight. It
survives a winter temperature of
10°C (50°F) but prefers 13–16°C
(55–60°F). Water moderately in
spring and summer, sparingly in
winter. Spray on hot days. Feed
monthly from April to September.
Repot every second spring in
equal parts of compost and moss.
Propagate in summer by offset
cuttings.

Platycerium bifurcatum
STAG'S-HORN FERN

This humorous plant has antler-
shaped fronds which grow up to
75 cm (30 in) long, and smaller
supporting fronds. In the wild in
Australia it grows in trees, but can
be grown indoors in a hanging
basket. Provide a minimum winter
temperature of 13°C (55°F). Water
freely in spring and summer,
sparingly in winter. Spray
regularly in hot weather. Feed
fortnightly from April to August.
Repot every second or third
spring in an equal mixture of peat
and sphagnum moss. In spring or
summer propagate by detaching
the plantlets on the roots.

Plectranthus coleoides 'Marginatus'
CANDLE PLANT

This low, bushy plant from India
has oval, rich green leaves with
irregular white margins. The
white and purple flowers are
insignificant. Shade from fierce
summer sun during the hottest
part of the day. The ideal winter
temperature for this plant is
between 13–16°C (55–60°F).
Water well in summer, but in
winter the soil should be kept
barely moist. In March prune
vigorously to improve the shape
of the plant. Repot in April using
potting compost. Propagate in
spring, either by stem-tip cuttings
or by division.

Plectranthus oertendahlii
PROSTRATE COLEUS, SWEDISH IVY

This creeping plant from South Africa will trail from a hanging basket. It has dark, rounded leaves with silvery-white veins on top and purple below. Loose clusters of pale violet flowers on erect stems appear from late winter to early summer. The plant tolerates a winter temperature of 7°C (45°F) but prefers to be slightly warmer. Water freely from spring to autumn, but keep soil just moist in winter. Feed fortnightly from March to September. Repot every April in potting compost. Propagate by division in spring or by cuttings in spring or summer.

Pleione formosana
INDIAN CROCUS

This small orchid, from the high altitudes from Tibet to Formosa, flowers from January to May. Its petals range from white to deep mauve-pink; the paler lip has red, magenta or yellow flecks. It tolerates a winter temperature of 4°C (40°F). It needs protection from direct sun in summer and plenty of fresh air. Use a dilute liquid fertilizer monthly from May to September and keep moist. Stop watering when leaves turn yellow. Repot every two years after flowering, in two parts potting compost and one sphagnum moss. Propagate by offsets or bulbils.

Polyscias balfouriana
DINNER PLATE ARALIA

In the wild in Africa, this plant can reach 7.5 m (25 ft), but in a pot it rarely grows taller than 120 cm (4 ft). It has round leaves with serrated edges. It will survive at a winter temperature of 13°C (55°F), but thrives better at 16°C (60°F) or higher. In spring and summer water moderately. At other times keep the soil just moist. From April to September feed fortnightly and spray regularly. Repot every other spring in an all-peat potting compost. Propagate by stem-tip, leaf-bud or root cuttings in early summer, using a heated propagating case.

Polystichum acrostichioides
CHRISTMAS FERN, SHIELD FERN

A native of North America, where it decorates homes at Christmas, this plant has glossy, dark green feathery fronds which grow in a dense clump and keep their colour all year. In the wild they can grow up to 90 cm (3 ft) long, but in pots they rarely exceed 30–60 cm (1–2 ft). Provide a minimum winter temperature of 10°C (50°F). Water freely from spring to autumn, and keep the soil just moist in winter. Feed once a month from April to September. Repot every second or third April in potting compost. Propagate by division in spring.

Primula auricula
PRIMULA

The species plant is a hardy perennial from the European Alps. It has rosettes of grey-green leaves on short, erect rhizomes. Umbels of purple or yellow flowers are borne on 10–15 cm (4–6 in) stems from March to May. Numerous cultivated varieties exist in various colours. In autumn, winter or spring plant in a sunny or partially shaded window box containing a good-quality potting compost. Water liberally in dry weather. Replant every other year after flowering. Propagate by division when replanting or by seed from May to September.

Primula malacoides
FAIRY PRIMROSE, BABY PRIMROSE

From December to April this native of China, with its rosettes of pale leaves, is a mass of scented, star-like flowers, ranging from carmine to dark purple to white. It requires a winter temperature of 7–13°C (45–55°F). It prospers in half shade, but needs more light in winter to stop the colour of the flowers fading. Always keep the soil moist. Provide a humid atmosphere by standing the plant on a tray of wet pebbles. Feed fortnightly with liquid fertilizer. Discard the plant once flowering has ended. Propagate by seed in late June or early July.

Primula obconica
PRIMULA

This plant has umbels of up to fifteen flowers, ranging from pale pink to blue-purple, which open from December to May. The leaves are covered with short glandular hairs. This perennial should be kept at a temperature of 10–13°C (50–55°F). It likes to be in half shade in summer, but needs more light in winter. Keep the air humid, and the soil damp, but do not spray. Feed with dilute liquid fertilizer fortnightly from August to March. Repot in May after it has flowered, using a light, loamless mixture. Propagate by seed at the end of May.

Pseuderanthemum kewense (*Eranthemum atropurpureum*)

This Pacific island shrub has 10–15 cm (4–6 in) black-purple leaves. In spring the red-spotted white flowers appear. The winter temperature must not fall below 16°C (60°F). A north-facing window-sill is ideal. In summer keep the air humid and the soil moist. Water moderately from October to February. Feed every three weeks from April to August with a liquid fertilizer. Repot in early spring in potting compost. To encourage bushiness pinch out leading growths. Propagate in spring or summer by cuttings of lateral shoots.

Pteris cretica
RIBBON FERN

The graceful fronds of this fern can grow as long as 30 cm (12 in). It is a tough plant which makes few demands. It needs a minimum winter temperature of 10°C (50°F). To maintain a moist atmosphere spray daily, or stand on a tray of wet pebbles. Water liberally from March to July, moderately in winter. From March to October feed every two to three weeks with liquid fertilizer. Repot in potting compost in spring. Rapid growth may necessitate a second repotting later in the year. Propagation is usually by division in spring.

Pteris ensiformis 'Victoriae'
VARIEGATED SWORD BRAKE

☆ Ⓣ 🚫

This is a cultivated variety that has
arisen from the species plant
which is found in India, Sri Lanka
and Australia. It is an unusual fern
because it has green and white
variegated leaflets. The slender
stems, some arched, others erect,
grow to about 45 cm (18 in). In
winter the temperature must not
fall below 13°C (55°F) and the soil
should be just moist. In spring and
summer water freely. From April
to September feed monthly. Cut
out dead leaves. Repot every other
April in any good-quality potting
compost and propagate by division
at this time.

Punica granatum
POMEGRANATE

This tree has red-stemmed, shiny
green leaves which fall in winter
but provide pleasing foliage the
rest of the year. It will not flower
or fruit in a pot, and grows to
180 cm (6 ft) unless pruned
annually. Plant some seeds in an
8 cm (3 in) pot with potting
compost and place on a south-
facing window-sill. Repot the
strongest seedling. From late
spring to early autumn water
freely. Spray in hot weather. In
winter move to a cool frost-free
room and water sparingly. From
May to September feed fortnightly.
Repot every other April.

Punica granatum 'Nana'
POMEGRANATE

☆ Ⓒ ○ Ⓗ

This miniature Pomegranate grows
to 60 cm (2 ft) and may be
cultivated as a standard. It has
scarlet flowers and bright orange-
red fruit. From mid-May until the
end of summer place on a sunny
window-sill. In winter keep at a
temperature of about 7°C (45°F).
Water liberally and spray in
summer; keep it drier in winter,
but never let the soil dry out. Feed
fortnightly from March to late
August. Repot, if necessary, in
February in potting compost.
A fortnight after repotting cut
back straggly stems. Propagate by
cuttings.

This South American plant has
30–60 cm (1–2 ft) tubular rosettes
of tough, slightly serrated leaves,
green on top and greyish-green
below. Spikes of red and blue
flowers open in winter. Provide a
minimum winter temperature of
10°C (50°F). Always water
moderately, keeping soil just moist.
Spray regularly in summer to
provide a humid atmosphere.
Feed monthly from May to
September. Repot every second
spring in equal parts of good-
quality potting compost and moss.
Propagate in summer by detaching
offsets.

Rebutia kupperiana
RED CROWN

From May to July brilliant red,
trumpet-shaped flowers emerge
from areoles at the base of this
Bolivian cactus with its spherical
red-green stems. In bloom for only
a week, they open each morning
and close each evening. Provide a
well-ventilated, sunny location
and a minimum winter temperature
of 4°C (40°F). While the buds are
developing keep compost moist
but in winter provide just enough
moisture to prevent plant from
shrivelling. Repot in potting
compost mixed with extra sand.
Propagate by seed in spring or
offsets in summer.

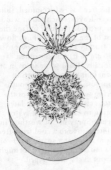

Rechsteineria cardinalis
CARDINAL FLOWER

This plant has tube-shaped flowers
as scarlet as a cardinal's cassock
from May to September, and
downy emerald-green leaves. It
grows about 45 cm (18 in) high.
Water well in spring and summer
and feed weekly. After flowering,
water sparingly until the leaves and
stems have withered. Leave at a
minimum winter temperature of
13°C (55°F) without water. In
February repot in any good
proprietary potting mixture and
begin watering. Start feeding six
weeks later. To propagate, divide
the tuber as soon as shoots show,
or take cuttings of young shoots.

Rechsteineria leucotricha
BRAZILIAN EDELWEISS

This Brazilian plant grows to about 45 cm (18 in). It has soft bright silver-grey leaves which are covered with fine, white hairs. Clusters of coral tube-shaped flowers open from August until October. Water well in spring and summer and feed weekly. After flowering, water sparingly until the leaves and stems have withered. Leave tuber at a minimum winter temperature of 13°C (55°F) in the pot and do not water. In February repot in good proprietary compost. To propagate, divide the tuber as soon as shoots show or take cuttings.

Rhipsalidopsis gaertneri
EASTER CACTUS

In spring this Brazilian cactus bears a profusion of scarlet tubular flowers, which emerge from the areoles on top of its jointed stems. It grows 45 cm (18 in) tall. A humid, warm environment is needed, with partial shade in summer and light in winter. It requires a minimum winter temperature of 13°C (55°F). Feed monthly and water liberally from August to December. Then water sparingly. Spray often in spring and summer. Repot after flowering in potting compost and an equal part of sphagnum moss. Propagate by cuttings in summer.

Rhododendron simsii
INDIAN AZALEA

This compact little bush from China has pointed evergreen leaves and clusters of single or double pink, white, crimson or red flowers which open in May. Forced plants will flower in winter or early spring. Water well with soft water, not hard, always keeping the soil moist but never water-logged. The leaves will fall if the soil becomes dry. Feed weekly from March to August. Repot after flowering in an all-peat mixture. It can be propagated by cuttings, but these are slow and difficult to root without a propagating case with bottom heat.

127

Rhododendron simsii 'Satsuki'
SATSUKI AZALEA

This exquisite cultivated variety has been developed from the Chinese species plant *R. simsii*. It has small, glossy, dark green leaves and deep pink flowers which open in May. Keep outdoors in partial shade. It may be kept indoors while flowering. In winter plunge the pot into sand or peat to protect roots from frost. Always keep compost moist. Prune roots in autumn or winter and repot in bonsai or loam-based compost. Trim side shoots in summer and pinch out growing point to keep a good shape. Propagate by cuttings in summer.

Rhoeo spathacea
BOAT LILY

This Mexican plant has clusters of tiny, white flowers enclosed by purple, boat-shaped bracts. Flowers open from May to July. Its lance-shaped leaves are green or green with yellow and white stripes on top and reddish-purple below. Spray regularly and water well in spring and summer, less in August and September and very little in winter. Keep at a minimum winter temperature of 10°C (50°F). Feed fortnightly from March to September. Repot in spring in an all-peat compost and propagate by basal shoots or from seeds at the same time.

Rhoicissus rhomboidea
GRAPE IVY, NATAL IVY

This attractive climbing plant from Natal grows to 120–180 cm (4–6 ft). The toothed trifoliate leaves of the mature plant are green and shiny but covered with hairs when young. Ideally, place on a north-facing window-sill at a minimum temperature of 7°C (45°F). Ensure fresh air in summer and water moderately all year. Use a liquid fertilizer fortnightly from April to September. Spray leaves regularly and sponge occasionally. Repot in loam-based compost in April. Pinch out young shoots to encourage growth. Propagate by lateral cuttings in spring.

Rondeletia roezlii

(T) (○) (H)

This evergreen shrub from
Guatemala has oval, glossy leaves
and clusters of pinkish-purple
flowers with yellow centres which
bloom in summer and autumn.
It grows to about 120 cm (4 ft).
A winter temperature of 13–16°C
(55–60°F) is required. Stand the
plant on a tray of wet pebbles or
moist peat to provide humidity.
Water liberally in spring and
summer and sparingly in winter.
Feed fortnightly from April to
October. Repot every April in
potting compost. Propagation by
cuttings in spring is not easy
without a heated propagating case.

Ruellia macrantha
CHRISTMAS PRIDE

(W) (○) (H)

The large, trumpet-shaped, purple
flowers of this perennial appear in
clusters from late autumn to
spring. It grows to about 90 cm
(3 ft). A winter temperature of
13–16°C (55–60°F) encourages
flowering. In summer shade lightly
from direct sun. Water regularly
all year. After one year feed
fortnightly with weak liquid
fertilizer from October to June.
Repot in potting compost in
September. After flowering, cut
shoots back to within 8 cm (3 in)
of the base. Propagate in spring by
using shoots which grow after
pruning as cuttings.

Saintpaulia ionantha
AFRICAN VIOLET

  (H)

This native of eastern Africa
produces long-lasting, violet-like,
deep purple, pink or white flowers
and has velvety heart-shaped
leaves. Plenty of light but no direct
sun, a temperature of 16–21°C
(60–70°F) all year and high
humidity are essential. Keep soil
moist by standing pot in a base
dish of tepid water for half an hour.
Avoid wetting leaves or heart. Use
a liquid fertilizer every 3–4 weeks
from April to September. Repot
every other April in shallow pots,
preferably in an all-peat compost.
Propagate by seed or leaf cuttings
in March or April.

Salpiglossis sinuata
PAINTED TONGUE

This Chilean annual is grown for its eye-catching, funnel-shaped flowers, borne on delicate leafy stems. They open from July to September and are pale purple, red, orange or yellow with contrasting veins and different coloured centres. The plant grows to 60 cm (2 ft) and likes a south-, east- or west-facing window-sill. Always keep soil moist and feed fortnightly from May to September. Support stems with sticks or canes. Propagate by seed in spring. Plant seedlings in compost in 13 cm (5 in) pots. Discard plants after flowering.

Salvia officinalis
SAGE

This hardy evergreen shrub grows to 60 cm (2 ft). It has soft, grey-green leaves and attractive tubular purple flowers which open in summer. In March sow seeds in moist seed compost. Germinate in a cool but frost-free room. Plant seedlings when large enough to handle in an 8 cm (3 in) pot containing potting compost and keep on a sunny outdoor window-sill. Later pot on into a 13–15 cm (5–6 in) pot. Keep soil moist at all times. Start cutting when stems are at least 15 cm (6 in) tall. Repot every spring. Propagate by cuttings in summer or autumn.

Sanchezia nobilis

Bold yellow veins pattern the long, oval leaves of this South American shrub, and clusters of pretty yellow flowers emerge from bright red bracts in late autumn. Ensure a minimum winter temperature of 10°C (50°F) and shade from hottest sun. Spray daily with tepid water or stand on a tray of moist peat or pebbles. Always keep soil moist but less so in winter. Feed every two or three weeks with dilute liquid fertilizer. Prune adult plants heavily in early spring and repot in good compost. Propagate by stem cuttings in winter.

Sansevieria hahnii
DWARF MOTHER-IN-LAW'S TONGUE,
BIRD'S NEST, BOWSTRING HEMP

A rosette is formed by the 10 cm
(4 in) dark green leaves,
decoratively marked with wavy
grey and yellow bands of this
plant from western Africa. Leaves
of the cultivated 'Golden Hahnii'
have yellow margins. This good-
natured plant tolerates both sun
and shade. Keep at a minimum
winter temperature of 10°C (50°F)
and water sparingly, but more
liberally in summer. Feed monthly
from May to September with liquid
fertilizer. Repot in spring in an
all-peat potting compost, but only
when the pot is congested or roots
need to be divided.

Sansevieria trifasciata
'Laurentii'
MOTHER-IN-LAW'S TONGUE, SNAKE
PLANT

Creamy-yellow margins and
greyish green or yellow cross-
bandings characterize the fleshy,
green sword-shaped leaves of this
plant from western Africa. It
rarely exceeds a height of 45 cm
(18 in) in a pot. It tolerates sun or
shade and dry air, but needs a
minimum winter temperature of
10°C (50°F). Water moderately in
summer, but only monthly in
winter. Repotting is seldom
required, but when it is necessary,
do so in spring in any good
potting compost. Propagate by
division of the roots.

Saxifraga sarmentosa
MOTHER OF THOUSANDS,
STRAWBERRY GERANIUM

This tufted plant from the Far
East has dark green leaves with
white veins on top and red veins
underneath. Its long, trailing
runners have small plantlets at
their ends. Clusters of small,
crimson-spotted, white flowers
appear in late spring and summer.
A minimum winter temperature
of 4°C (40°F) is required. Keep
compost always just moist. Feed
fortnightly from April to
September. Repot in any good
proprietary compost in early
spring. Propagate by taking
plantlets from runners and potting
separately.

Schefflera actinophylla
(Brassaia actinophylla)
QUEENSLAND UMBRELLA TREE

The elegant, glossy, mid-green leaves of this Australian and Polynesian native divide into long, oval, pointed leaflets, varying up to sixteen in number. This slow-growing plant reaches 240 cm (8 ft). Its foliage needs a minimum temperature of 13°C (55°F). It likes light but not direct sunlight. Always keep the air moderately humid and the soil moist. Use a dilute liquid fertilizer monthly from March to September. Repot in any good proprietary potting compost every alternate April. Propagate by seed in February or March.

Schlumbergera truncata
CHRISTMAS CACTUS, CRAB CACTUS

The red, trumpet-shaped flowers of this plant emerge at the tips of its bright green, flat, leaf-like branches from November to January. It needs a light position shaded from the summer sun, and a minimum winter temperature of 13°C (55°F). When buds form, water well and feed weekly with dilute liquid fertilizer. Keep soil almost dry in summer when plant is resting. Spray often during growing season. Repot in a compost containing equal parts of loam, peat, moss and sand. Propagate by cuttings during the summer.

Scindapsus aureus
DEVIL'S IVY, GOLDEN POTHOS

This plant from the Solomon Islands has bright green oval leaves splashed with yellow when young. As the vine matures, they become heart-shaped. It reaches 180 cm (6 ft) and should be supported with canes or a trellis. Keep soil barely moist at a minimum winter temperature of 10°C (50°F). Water moderately at other times. Feed monthly from May to September with liquid fertilizer. Repot every second April in potting compost. Remove stem tips in summer to promote branching and use the pruned shoots for propagation.

Scirpus cernuus
(Isolepis gracilis)
SLENDER CLUB RUSH

 ☆ Ⓣ 🚫

This small marsh plant from
western and southern Europe and
northern Africa is an ideal hanging
plant for as it grows, its dark,
shiny, threadlike blades curve over
the edge of the pot. It requires
partial shade in summer. Spray
daily and keep the air moist in
spring and summer. It needs full
light in winter and a minimum
temperature of 4°C (40°F). The
base dish should always contain
soft water. Feed fortnightly from
March to September. Repot in
February in any good-quality
potting compost and propagate
by division.

Selaginella kraussiana
SPREADING CLUB MOSS,
CREEPING CLUB MOSS

Ⓣ 🚫

With its branching filigree of
yellow-green, prostrate stems,
this South African plant appears
both fern-like and mossy. It is
ideal for a hanging basket. It can
survive a winter temperature of
4°C (40°F) but will thrive at a
minimum temperature of 10–13°C
(50–55°F). Spray often and water
moderately in spring and summer,
sparingly in winter. Feed once a
month from April to October.
Repot every April in good-quality
potting compost. Discard plant
when it becomes thin and straggly.
Propagate by cuttings in spring or
summer.

Senecio cruentus (Cineraria)
CINERARIA

☆ Ⓒ 🚫

The original species of Cineraria
is native to the Canary Islands,
but since the eighteenth century
it has been cultivated in Europe
and many different strains are now
available. They vary from dwarf,
large-flowered, cultivated varieties
to tall, smaller-flowered ones and
range through the spectrum from
red to blue. As a house plant it
flowers from winter to early
summer and will remain in flower
for up to six weeks. Water
liberally without feeding. Cineraria has a
limited life and is never kept after
it has ceased flowering but always
discarded.

Senecio rowleyanus
STRING OF BEADS

A hanging basket is ideal for this South West African succulent, with its creeping stems and globular leaves. Sweet-scented, daisy-like heads of white florets with deep purple stigmas appear from September to November. 5 cm (2 in) tall, this plant has a spread of 60–90 cm (2–3 ft). It requires plenty of sunlight and a minimum winter temperature of 10°C (50°F). From March to September water liberally. Keep compost just moist at other times. Repot in March in potting compost with extra sand. Propagate by stem cuttings from spring to autumn.

Setcreasea purpurea
PURPLE HEART

This is not a plant for the tidy-minded. Its leafy stems will sprawl in all directions unless supported, yet its all-over purple colour looks superb among a group of green plants. Brought from Mexico as recently as 1955, it has small, deep pink flowers from May to December. Good light is essential or its intense purple colouring will become green. Water well in summer and feed weekly. Keep soil just moist at a minimum winter temperature of 7°C (45°F). Repot every April in potting compost but preferably grow annually from summer cuttings.

Siderasis fuscata
BROWN SPIDERWORT

This low-growing South African plant has oval, light-green leaves thickly covered with reddish-brown hairs. They grow in rosettes and have a buff-coloured central stripe. Small, pinkish-purple flowers may open in summer. Provide a minimum winter temperature of 13°C (55°F). Keep soil moist in spring and summer, otherwise water sparingly. Stand plant on a tray of wet pebbles for humidity. Feed monthly from April to September. Repot every spring in good-quality potting compost. Propagate by division when repotting.

Sinningia speciosa
GLOXINIA

The large, velvety, bell-shaped
Gloxinia flowers, varying in colour
from crimson to violet and white,
open from May to October. Keep
soil moist during flowering, then
reduce water, stopping as plant
dies down. Leave at a winter
temperature of 10°C (50°F). Repot
in February, in an all-peat compost
at a temperature of 18°C (65°F).
As the plant begins to grow, water
sparingly, increasing the amount
with growth. When the plant is
established, feed weekly with
liquid fertilizer until it flowers.
Propagate by seed or leaf and stem
cuttings.

Smithiantha zebrina
TEMPLE BELLS

Indigenous to Mexico, this plant
has velvety, heart-shaped, reddish
mottled leaves and bell-shaped,
scarlet flowers with yellow throats
which open from June to
September. Use liquid fertilizer
fortnightly from March until
flowers open. Water liberally in
summer, then reduce and stop a
month or two after flowering
ceases. Remove dead foliage and
leave tubers in pot at a winter
temperature of 10–13°C (50–55°F).
In February repot several tubers
in a 13–15 cm (5–6 in) pot using
all-peat potting compost. Propagate
by division of rhizomes in spring.

Solanum capsicastrum
WINTER CHERRY, CHRISTMAS CHERRY

This native of Brazil has dark
green, lance-like leaves and small
white, star-shaped flowers which
bloom in May. In late summer,
round, dark green fruit, turning to
yellow and then orange-red
appear. A little direct sunlight in
late autumn will help to ripen the
fruit. Keep at a minimum winter
temperature of 7°C (45°F) and
water sparingly. In summer water
liberally and feed fortnightly from
April to August. Plants can be
pruned back in February and
repotted in a loamless compost in
March but preferably raise
annually from seeds.

Solanum melongena ovigerum
AUBERGINE, EGGPLANT

Depending on the cultivated type, this southern Asian vegetable fruit may be round, oval or oblong with smooth, purple or white skin. Keep in full light but shade from hot sun, and provide a minimum winter temperature of 16°C (60°F). Water liberally in summer and use liquid fertilizer fortnightly. Pinch out growing tip when plant is 15 cm (6 in) and only allow up to three shoots to develop. When they bear a young fruit, pinch out tip and any side shoots. Discard plant after fruit has matured. Propagate by seed in February or March.

Sonerila margaritacea 'Argentea'
PEARLY SONERILA

Heavily speckled with silver-white spots, the 10 cm (4 in) dark green, oval leaves of this low-growing, Javanese plant have purple undersides and red stems. Purplish-pink flowers open from May to September. Keep at a minimum winter temperature of 16°C (60°F) to avoid leaf fall. Always keep soil just moist but water less in winter. From May to September feed fortnightly. Stand on a tray of wet pebbles or moist peat for humidity. Repot every other April in potting compost. Propagate by cuttings taken in April, May or June.

Sparaxis tricolor
HARLEQUIN FLOWER, VELVET FLOWER

This native of South Africa grows from a corm to 45 cm (18 in). Sword-shaped leaves form narrow fans from which flat-petalled, multicoloured blooms appear in May and June. The flowers are combinations of red, orange, purple, yellow and white. In September plant six corms in a 15 cm (6 in) pot with potting compost. Water well once and keep at a minimum temperature of 7°C (45°F). When shoots appear, keep soil moist. Dry out when leaves turn yellow. Store corms in a dry frost-free place. Propagate by offsets when repotting.